DEDICATION

For Darien Ford, your love and support make everything possible.
For my Children, you are my everything.

Dear Abbie,

So nice getting
to Know you!
and thank you
for helping us
find our House!
Krystal ford

Dear Abbie,

to know you!
and thank you
for helping us

NOVEMBER HEADLINES

Hate, harassment incidents spike since Trump election
— *CBS News*

Political divide splits family members — and Thanksgiving tables, too
— *The New York Times*

Donald Trump, Groper in Chief
— *The New York Times*

Trump Bulldozes Blue Wall, Wins White House
— *National Review*

Chapter One

❂

ELECTION NIGHT

Megan Thompson stood on stage, silhouetted by a giant American flag, feeling as though she had just run a marathon. Waving to the cheering crowd, she practiced her most congressional smile. The ballroom of the Hilton Hotel in Magnolia Ridge was packed with supporters and buzzing with energy. Conservatives were picking up seats in Florida and across the country, on the verge of realizing a Republican presidency, and the crowd sensed the triumphant swing of the pendulum's return.

Her daydreams were interrupted as Congressman White's victory speech drew to a close. *"We're going to strengthen the military and fight ISIS. We're going to repeal and replace Obamacare. We're going to fight for Social Security…"*

The congressman shook hands with everyone on the stage — his campaign staff plus some of his most valued volunteers — while his wife of fifty years, their two grown children, and five grandchildren waved relentlessly to the crowd. When at last he turned to his campaign manager with a friendly grin, he whispered in her ear, "We need to talk. It's about your next move. Come find me in hotel lobby in thirty minutes." He patted her shoulder and moved on, still shaking hands and smiling.

Half an hour later, still exhausted and exhilarated, Megan flopped onto the nearest couch. Only her hot, swollen feet — and the fear of drawing attention to herself—could stop her from pacing back and forth across the lobby floor. She settled for bouncing her right leg.

Her poor feet had been jammed into heels longer than could be considered humane. She shifted subtly on the couch, trying to remove the underwire of her D-cup bra, which was piercing her flesh. A glimpse came to her of a world with no heels, no Spanx, no push-up bras. Wouldn't it be glorious?

We would all have shapeless calves, muffin tops, and saggy breasts... but we would be comfortable!

Megan sighed at the thought and then tucked it away. She was no feminist. She took pride in her appearance. Her long blond hair was always blown out. She wore mascara and lipstick without fail. Her outfits were conservative yet feminine, like tonight's red silk blouse tucked into a black pencil skirt, accentuating her slender figure. Physical discomfort was a minor annoyance, but well worth it. No one had forced her to wear senselessly high heels, or the Spanx that were cutting off the circulation at her torso. She had chosen this profession, and to experience the thrill of inhabiting the world of politics, she would happily put up with a lot more.

If I wanted to be comfortable, she reminded herself, *I would have been a gym teacher.*

Even more nagging than her uncomfortable attire was her sense of foreboding. Why did Congressman White want to talk about her next career move? Hadn't she already agreed to join the legislative team in his Ocala district office? She would have preferred D.C., but she'd graciously accepted a position working locally, knowing it was a good next step for her. Here in Florida, she could start laying the groundwork for her run in four years, or whenever White finally retired. It was no secret that she'd had her eye on his seat since the moment she agreed to manage his campaign.

Lost in thought, and still high on caffeine and adrenaline, Megan startled when Congressman White and his wife entered the hotel lobby, holding hands and looking like any other couple out on the town. They had spotted her and were walking toward the couch. She wondered whether gray-haired Mrs. White, in her canary yellow pantsuit, white blouse, and big strand of pearls, ever wished she were wearing sweatpants instead. The thought made her laugh. Mrs. White probably didn't even own a pair of sweatpants, or jeans for that matter. The congressman's wife was a true lady to the core.

The Whites sat across from her on the couch, still holding hands. Megan admired the affection they had for each other, so obvious and enduring. Congressman White unbuttoned his suit jacket and loosened his tie. Dark circles drooped under his eyes, and what little of his white hair remained was combed over his sun-freckled scalp.

"Well, Megan, we did it! By god, I don't think I've worked so hard to win an election since the first time I ran for the House." He sighed.

Megan tried to count backward. How many election cycles had he seen in those forty-four years?

"You worked your ass off for me," White continued. "And it wasn't an easy campaign. Hell, I've never had anyone challenge me in the primaries before! Goddamned Tea Partiers. No government experience. No interest in actually working in government. Just want to throw a wrench into the system."

She had to agree. In the race to represent his conservative Florida district, the biggest obstacle by far had been the runoff against four other Republican candidates.

"What a mistake to let those jokers in! I have another word I'd use, but there are ladies present." He winked at Megan, inviting her into conspiracy. "Anyways, thank you, Miss Thompson. Thank you for everything. We couldn't have done it without you."

Megan's facial expression remained passive. "Of course, sir. That was my job. To make sure you won."

He chuckled. "I guess I didn't help myself any with that comment back in February."

Megan knew right away the one he meant—about how choosing between Ted Cruz and Donald Trump was like deciding between death by poison or by shot gun. The RNC had not been pleased. She had been forced to do damage control for a good week. But now Congressman White had won, and she could loosen up a bit. She flashed the briefest of smiles before her face snapped back to its default position, her mouth turned slightly downward as though she were perpetually pissed off.

"Lighten up, darlin'," chuckled Congressman White. "And smile a little. You just got someone elected to the House of Representatives!"

Megan tried, but her great, big, toothy grin felt unnatural, like opening your mouth too wide at the dentist's office.

White nodded in approval and then turned serious. "Megan. I know we talked about you working in the district office starting in January."

That sense of alarm rose to her throat. *I need that job,* she thought.

"Well, I've got some good news. A legislative aide position just opened up, in the energy area. How would you like to come to D.C. with me?"

Megan exhaled relief and unclenched a fist, leaving five little half-moons in her palm. "Yes. I'd love that. Thank you, sir."

He gave her a thoughtful look. "Were you still thinking of running for office someday?"

"Yes, sir, I am." Megan gave a shrug, unwilling to give her timeline away. "One day."

Congressman White leaned in closer and lowered his voice. "This is just between us, OK?"

She nodded again, intrigued. *Why the secretive demeanor?* she wondered.

"This is my last term. I'm not going to run in 2018."

"Oh no, sir! Why?" Megan's concern was genuine.

White shook his head. "This election took a lot out of me. I just don't have the energy or the passion anymore. I'm an old man, Megan. I'll be seventy-seven this year. It's time for me to retire." He sat back and winked at Mrs. White. "Maybe get to know my wife again and see if she still likes me."

Megan felt a tug of sympathy for Jean White. It couldn't be easy, being the wife of a congressman. No one realized all the behind-the-scenes sacrifices a spouse has to make. All the birthday parties and anniversary celebrations were really just fundraisers in disguise — and those were the only ones she could be sure her husband would show up at. What about the many dinners eaten alone? Not to mention the constant scrutiny and nonstop campaigning. And of course, for all the support Mrs. White gives, she gets none of the glory.

"Plus, the Republican Party is going to need young blood," the congressman continued. "I just heard the latest numbers, and it looks like Clinton really might lose this thing. If Trump wins, who the hell knows what's going to happen — to our country, to our party…" White shook his head in disbelief. "We'll need more good legislators, folks who will fight for our core values and stop putting politics over people. I can see you have the drive, the passion. And we share the same values."

Megan agreed wholeheartedly. She knew all too well the average age of a Republican congressman: fifty-eight. And she saw little reason for confidence in the president-elect's values as a conservative.

"That's what we're missing in this party," White was saying. "Youth, optimism, a fresh outlook."

And diversity, Megan thought. Women made up only 17 percent of the Republican Party, and people of color a measly 5 percent. The party of the *male, pale, and frail,* indeed.

Congressman White pointed a finger at her. "And that's why I am going to groom you to take over my seat."

She heard the words but couldn't quite believe them.

"My endorsement will go a long way with voters, you know. We can promise them continuity, a smooth transition. But also, a new vision for the future."

Megan finally found her tongue. "Really? I am flattered you think so highly of me, sir, and that you would help me run for office. But I don't know if I'm ready. There's so much to think about, and…" *And I wasn't ready for this to happen now!* She didn't want to say it aloud, but she knew it was true.

Congressman White interrupted her with a sober look. "Oh, I am well aware this is an uphill battle. You're young. You have no money, and no connections. Most PACs will ignore you. And no offense, hon, but"—he ticked the last point on his pinkie finger—"you're a woman."

"And you're not even married, dear," Mrs. White added, shaking her head. "It's just a shame about your Jason. A real shame."

Megan bristled. *Marriage* and *Jason*: two words she'd rather not hear again. Besides, she didn't need to be convinced of the marks against her as a candidate. But did the Whites really think she needed a man to advance her career?

"Well, I think you'll find people care less about marital status these days. The youngest woman ever elected to a national office was thirty years old and unmarried—"

"That might work in New York, honey, but not in Florida," Mrs. White interjected. "We're pretty traditional here, as you well know. And again, no offense, but you can be a little uptight... bossy... How do I say this politely?" She struggled for the right word, but then patted Megan's leg in a grandmotherly way. "You come off as a bitch, dear."

Congressman White nodded his agreement. "It's emasculating. You don't want voters to think you're a man-hater."

"Or a lesbian," his wife chimed in.

This was possibly the most ridiculous conversation Megan had ever had with the Whites, her trusted mentors. But she had to admit, she hadn't considered what would happen if she ran as a single woman. That had never been part of her plan.

Would the conservative people in her district elect a strong, single woman? Especially one who was as introverted by nature as she was? Megan knew herself well enough to consider that having a husband could help soften her image. To get where she was, she'd been focused on giving off a vibe of strength more than warmth, and that made a lot of people uncomfortable. Maybe Congressman White was right. Maybe being a Mrs. would make her seem not only strong and capable, but also loving and approachable.

Still, she was unconvinced. "Sir, I would love nothing more than to run for office. That is my end goal. But as you've just pointed out — and as much as I hate to admit this — I may be rather unappealing to voters. Perhaps even unelectable at the moment." She sighed. "I have enough experience to know an unwinnable race when I see one. Out of all those issues, the only one I could fix is my marital status. And I most certainly have no interest in falling in love anytime soon." The back of her throat began to sting. The mere mention of love made her want to throw up.

Congressman White waved her concerns away as though he were shooing a pesky fly. "No one said anything about falling in love. No, I'm talking about a strategic power match."

Megan couldn't hide her confusion. But White seemed to be enjoying his little fantasy.

"Young, attractive, connected, intelligent, preferably wealthy… You could be the Republican version of the Obamas. Irresistible to voters! And I'm going to help you find your Mr. Right."

Full-blown dread washed over Megan. "Oh no, sir. Thank you, that's very kind. But you don't need to do that."

White made it clear she wasn't going to get off the hook so easily. "It will be my pleasure!" He turned to his wife. "You know, I kind of think this will be fun. I'll start making a list of eligible candidates."

"Oh, darling, remember that young lobbyist we met at the fundraiser a couple months ago? From Exxon Mobil? He was so handsome, and polite!" Mrs. White clapped her hands together.

Megan groaned inwardly. Blind dates were beneath her, reserved for the desperate and lonely. She was neither. Her clock was not ticking in the least, and her single status didn't keep her up at night. It was more of a relief — one less thing on her to-do list.

"OK, then. Should three weeks be enough time for you to get moved to D.C.?" Before Megan could reply, Congressman White pushed himself from the couch with a quiet groan, as his wife grasped his arm to assist in the effort. "Alright, great talking with you. Let me know the moment you're settled in D.C. And I'll start setting up some dates!"

Megan, still in shock, watched them exit the lobby together. What had she just agreed to? A job promotion? A move to D.C.? And a *husband*?

Chapter Two

————— ✪ —————

TO-DO LIST

It felt weird to be back in her dad's house, in her old childhood bedroom—a place that was both foreign and familiar, like a reoccurring dream. Forever associated with grief and turmoil, it was a room Megan would much rather not sleep in again. Yet here she sat, a few hours after leaving the Hilton lobby, her back up against the white puffy headboard as though she were thirteen again. What an awful thought!

When she called off her wedding, right in the middle of White's congressional campaign, she didn't have the time or money to find a new place of her own. She had sucked it up and asked to stay temporarily with her father, who lived a convenient hour's drive from campaign headquarters in Magnolia Ridge, just outside Orlando. The only way she could tolerate living at home again, though, was spending the bare minimum of hours there, preferably sleeping. She practically lived at the campaign headquarters anyway—first one in, last one out—making on average of three hundred phone calls a day. The long hours and daily exhaustion, plus a touch of wine, were the perfect sleep aids. That way she rarely fell asleep thinking of her failed relationship or the fact that she'd moved back into her childhood bedroom.

Sitting cross-legged on her twin bed, Megan laughed quietly to herself now. How ironic! Working on the campaign had ended her engagement, yet the campaign had turned out to be the perfect balm for forgetting all about her doomed relationship in the first place. That is, until every time she'd looked down at her call list and picked up the phone to ring someone named Jason. She could barely restrain herself from screaming into the mouthpiece, "Jason! How dare you do that to me, and so close to our wedding date!"

Instead, when those other Jasons had answered, she had pulled herself together and earnestly asked for their vote, reminding them politely about Election Day—yes, it was on Tuesday, and yes, they would be voting for president, too—all while good-naturedly rolling her eyes or miming a gunshot to the head for the benefit of the other campaign workers.

Coming home was worse, depressing—a reminder that everything she was running away from still existed. Work was safety, but even that feeling was an illusion. At any moment, fate could reach out its bony hand and drag her back down the few rungs of the ladder she'd managed to climb. For Megan, at least, there was an upward trajectory. For her father, it was a flatline. Life would continue on as it had for twenty years and would stay that way until the day he died.

She knew she should try to sleep, but her muscles were unwilling to relax and her mind was still jumping, replaying the day's surreal events and her conversation with Congressman White. Was a door finally opening for her? Were her patience and perseverance paying off at last?

She reached for her cell phone and dialed the one person who could possibly understand right now: Mike.

The phone rang just once before he picked up. *Always on duty,* she thought. Loud music, singing, and shouting blasted in her ear.

"Hey! Just a second!" came Mike's yell. Then all went quiet. "Is that you, Meg?"

"Yes, and I want to kick your ass."

He chuckled. "Congrats! You did it!"

She had to smile. "You, too. I guess you guys are still celebrating the senator's victory?"

"Heck, yeah! You may not know this, newbie, but getting a freshman senator elected is kind of a big deal."

"Yes, I know," Megan teased. "That's why I worked for you. You may not know this, but you're kind of a big deal yourself."

"At least you recognize talent when you see it." Mike's booming laugh comforted her.

She stifled a snort. "It's a good thing I paid attention! After you bailed on me to go work on Senator Kelley's campaign, this so-called slam dunk reelection you promised me turned into *Game of Thrones*."

She was hardly exaggerating, and he knew it. Of those four primary challengers the White campaign had faced, two were no more articulate than an army of the dead, but their lack of intelligence was no deterrent to some extremists in this Republican stronghold. And that was before Congressman White had gone up against a Bernie Sanders–endorsed Democrat. The past eight months had been nothing short of insanity.

"And you survived, didn't you?" Mike replied, his voice tinged with pride. "The throne was saved, and you got the credit. So I guess you should be thanking me."

"Oh, trust me, I am thankful now. And I deserve the credit—I certainly worked hard enough for it. But that doesn't mean I ever stopped wanting to kick your ass." Megan leaned back against her headboard, absentmindedly played with a childhood stuffed animal. She was beginning to relax at last. "Can I tell you something, Mike? In complete confidence?"

"You know you can always trust me," he said, all seriousness now.

"White's retiring. He wants me to run for his seat next election."

Mike went quiet for a moment. "He's going to endorse you?"

"Yes. And I'm going to D.C. to work in his office."

"Meg, this is a big fucking deal. Are you ready for it? I mean, I know we talked about me running your campaign someday. But are you sure you're ready for someday... now?"

This time, Megan didn't hesitate. "Hell. Yes."

Of course she was nervous. She had pangs of self-doubt like anyone else—maybe more so. But hadn't she been hoping and planning and plotting to run for office for the past twenty years? She had been the youngest member of the zoning board, served on the board of education, and helped half the city council get elected. Her name was out there, and she had just run a winning national campaign. If not now, when?

Mike interrupted her inner pep talk. "You still living with… ?"

"My dad. Yes."

"Well, you need to buy a place in district, ASAP. Doesn't matter if it's a piece-of-shit trailer home. Do it. You need to keep your residency. You don't want anyone questioning your legitimacy when you move to Washington."

"Right." Megan grabbed the note pad from her nightstand and started a new list.

"You writing this down? Make a list of all the friends and family who will donate two thousand dollars to your campaign."

"Well, including my brother and you, that's a list of two," she joked.

"Not good enough," Mike replied. "Take the budget you had for White, and double it. We're talking open-seat race in what has just become a very crazy time. This is going to be a race with no incumbent, so you can expect the money to pour in. Especially now," he added. "When the world wakes up tomorrow to a Trump presidency, I guarantee you this: There's gonna be backlash, and it's gonna be big."

Megan knew he was right. The next elections might be two years down the road, but it was a safe bet that Democrats would go out hard for any seat they thought they had a shot at. Plus, she was a moderate conservative, and if tonight's presidential election was any indication, the base was moving more and more to the right.

"You should beware of challenges from within the party as well," Mike warned her.

Megan hesitated to tell Mike about what else she and White had discussed—she would be up against enough without this extra problem—but she needed to confide in someone. "White wants to play matchmaker with me in D.C. He wants to find me a rich, connected husband."

"Hmm, that's actually a good strategy. Being single is a liability. A rich Republican husband will be a huge asset. Plus, money tends to attract more money. The law of attraction, you know."

Megan was quiet for a moment. "You don't think that's a bit... outdated?"

"Meh."

"Come on, Mike. It's deceitful!"

"Get with the program, Meg. People marry for security and money *all the time*. Even with that, you'll be the most honest candidate I know. Hands down."

She knew that was supposed to be reassuring.

"Meg, you need to find a consultant as soon as you get to D.C., and start planning out your strategy. I can give you some names. I wish I could help you full-time, but you know I'm already committed to a big House race in Georgia... But you know you can always call me for advice. Anytime. I mean that."

"Thanks, Mike."

"And work on your 'why.' Why do you want to run for office? Think about it. Then commit it to memory—you'll be saying it a lot. To your staff, donors, voters... and especially to yourself, when you're banging your head against the wall, screaming, 'Why? Why am I doing this?'"

Megan laughed. It felt good.

"Alright, Meg, I gotta get back inside to the party. All these tequila shots ain't gonna drink themselves. But seriously, I'm happy for you. Now get a good night's sleep—it may be your last for the next two years."

"Thanks, Mike, you're the best. Try not to take home of one of the underage volunteers, OK?" she teased. "At least ask for her ID first."

"Ha, ha. That happened only one time. And she was nineteen!"

"Whatever you say. 'Night, Mike."

It was too bad Mike Horowitz wasn't her type. He was a great friend: loud, high-energy, and a tad on the juvenile side, but big-hearted—like a giant teddy bear. Mike was the one person she could call up after a really hard day campaigning. He always knew just what to say to cheer her up or, at the very least, convince her not to quit.

Megan scribbled another task on her to-do list: *Find a place in D.C.* Stretching her legs and leaning back against her pillow, she thought for a moment. Did she know anyone in D.C. who could help her find an apartment on such short notice? It had been over a decade since she had lived there while attending American University. What about her college roommate's friend, Emily?

Grabbing her phone, Megan logged on to her LinkedIn account and found Emily's profile. Yes, Emily was still living in D.C.

Why wait? Megan thought, and shot off a brief, too-the-point message:

> *Hi, Emily.*
>
> *I hope everything is going well with you. Just found out I'm moving to D.C. in three weeks. Any chance you know of someone looking for a roommate? Thanks in advance—and I hope we can catch up when I arrive.*
>
> *Sincerely,*
> *Megan*

She put her phone away and collapsed into her pillow, feeling like she'd just stepped out of a hot bath. Her limbs were maple syrup. She nestled into her time capsule and began fading into sleep. *I'm on the cusp of change,* was the last thing she remembered thinking. Something big is about to happen.

DECEMBER HEADLINES

Putin offers cooperation with Trump in Christmas letter
— *Washington Times*

Even in great despair, there is hope
— *Esquire*

Radio City Rockette speaks out on Trump inauguration controversy
— *People*

Trump: We're going to start saying 'Merry Christmas' again
— *Fox News*

Chapter Three

———————— ✪ ————————

MEET THE ROOMMATE

On the morning of her move to Washington, Megan surveyed what had to be packed into her modest Ford sedan. After thirty-five years of life on this earth, her sum existence could be packed up in six boxes. Was that admirable, or just pathetic? She wasn't sure.

Some people need books to tell them how to rid themselves of clutter. Not Megan. Instead of old clothes and useless tchotchkes, her boxes were filled with practical things: books, office files, her carefully selected wardrobe, bedding, towels, dishes, all neatly packed in boxes, uniformly labeled. She could write the book on decluttering.

Today, though, she felt strangely nomadic. She told herself it wasn't that she disliked having nice things; she just didn't like to get too attached. The life she had built with Jason, she'd left behind as easily as one closes the door.

"Don't you want to split up the furniture at least?" he had asked.

But she had refused it, and everything else they had accumulated over the years. She wasn't interested in living in the past.

He'd offered—out of guilt, of course—to cut her a check instead, which she happily took. It was generous enough that she could start her life over from scratch, and that suited her just fine. As it turned out, he had every right to feel guilty: Connie, her best friend from high school and the woman he had cheated on her with, had moved in the week after Megan had moved out, seamlessly replacing her. Maybe it wasn't a replacement so much as an upgrade—from his perspective, at least—because this model cooked and cleaned and was actually home to spend time with him. But Megan knew that was only because Connie didn't have grand ambitions—or any ambitions, really. They'd probably be married with kids by this time next year: happy wife, happy children, happy family, happy life. The suburban dream!

Megan scoffed at the mediocrity of it all.

Her little vacation from White's campaign had flown by. She had found a modest three-bedroom ranch in Gatorville, close to her father so he could keep an eye on it, and was already under contract. She had met her younger brother, Gabe, for lunch. And of course, in politics there never really was such thing as a vacation. She'd dined with members of the city council and joined Mrs. White's Bunco hour so she could connect with politically active Republican seniors.

She'd also spent several days corresponding with her new roommate, Andrew Croswell, thanks to a D.C. acquaintance who put them in contact—his sister, Emily Croswell. Over email, they had negotiated the rent and the terms of her sublease.

Megan was fine with that. She was certain he would like having her as a roommate—all her former roommates did. What wasn't to like? She was neat and quiet, she worked long hours, and she mostly kept to herself. She never even considered the idea that she wouldn't like Andrew. Emily was her friend, and he was Emily's brother. How bad could he be?

Andrew unlocked the door, balancing a box in one hand and rebuffing his mother's halfhearted offers to hold the box for him. "I've got it, Mom, thanks." Stepping inside, he set the box down and surveyed his new apartment.

"Sweetie, this place is filthy!" his mother exclaimed, aghast, as she pushed by him to begin her inspection. Jacqueline Croswell made no attempt to hide her disgust, and Andrew felt a little badly for her. In the empty, dust-filled living room, her Céline handbag looked completely out of place.

Why did I let her drive me here? thought Andrew.

"Mom, it just needs a good cleaning," he insisted. "Did you see the kitchen, though? It's pretty big."

Jacqueline turned as sharply as her skirt suit would allow and squinted at the kitchen: pale gray ceramic tile floor, granite counters that doubled as prep and dining space, a decent amount of cupboard storage. "Yeah. It looks OK." Her expression said otherwise.

Andrew could barely keep the exasperation from his voice. "Mom, do you know how hard it is to find a kitchen this size?"

She gave him a look. "I'm surprised you still cook, seeing as how Naomi never ate anything. Paleo, juice cleanse, gluten-free—was there any diet she didn't try?"

Andrew sighed. "We're not together anymore, Mom, so it doesn't matter, does it? But good to know what you really thought about her."

"It's not my place to say anything, dear…"

But you will, he thought.

"… but no, I didn't like her. There was something fake about her. She wasn't right for you."

"Mom, if you don't stop wrinkling your nose, you're going to need another shot of Botox," Andrew teased.

"That's very unkind, Andrew." She lifted her chin, insulted. "You know I don't use Botox."

"Sorry." *A five-hundred-dollar facial, then*, he thought. "Admit it. Mother. You hate my place."

"The neighborhood looks seedy, Andrew. Did you see that guy rolling a joint on the steps of his apartment? On a Sunday at eleven a.m.? Some of these buildings, all the windows are broken and boarded up! And the lawn, if you can call it that, is three feet tall!"

"It's safe here, Mom. I did my research. And I can bike to work, or take the Metro…"

"And you don't have a doorman, and it's small and noisy…" she retorted. A police siren filled the room on cue, and then grew faint. Jacqueline pointed at the window dramatically. "I don't know how you'll sleep with all that traffic outside your window. How much are you paying for this?"

"Twenty-seven hundred."

His mother frowned. "If that's all you can afford, Andrew, clearly your new job is not paying you what you deserve. I'm still not sure why you accepted the position." She paused. "Will you need help, sweetie?"

"Mom, I don't want help. I'm a grown man!" It was true that his latest move had been more lateral than upward. Given his age and experience, his parents were baffled that he was still in a midlevel position rather than an executive director by now. But he didn't want to be in upper management. He didn't want to worry about fundraising and day-to-day operations. He liked being on the ground floor, where things were more exciting. "You know I chose a career in environmental science to make a difference, not to make money. And if you recall, you were the one who encouraged me to pursue my dreams."

"Yes, sweetie, that's true. But that was fifteen years ago! I figured eventually you'd work your way up. I know you don't care about money, but there is something to be said about being financially secure." She patted his cheek. "I love that you're saving the world. Really, I do. But as your mother, I will never stop worrying about you." Jacqueline sighed dramatically "I suppose I should be thankful you're no longer protesting the Dakota Access Pipeline. I kept waiting for a call saying you'd been arrested. Or worse, shot."

Andrew reached out and hugged his lively, easily ruffled mother. "Way to look on the bright side, Mom. I'm proud of you." She stiffened slightly, and he pulled back. Then he spun around toward the apartment door. "I'm going down to the car to bring more boxes up."

"Sweetie, let me call the driver. He can bring them up for you." She reached for her cell phone.

"It's OK, Mom, really. I don't mind getting them."

A look of concern flashed across her face.

"Will you be fine for five minutes alone in my seedy apartment?"

He raised an eyebrow.

"Of course I'll be fine," she replied haughtily.

Andrew shot her one last glance before leaving. His mother looked anything but fine. She looked like she was afraid to touch anything in the apartment. He was willing to bet that she wouldn't move from that spot.

On his way to the car, he thought about how his beautiful mother had slipped so easily into a life of comfort. Growing up in a solidly middle-class neighborhood in a modest three-bedroom house outside of Boston, her family had all the necessities in life but none of the luxuries. Her father had been a salesman who budgeted carefully for expenses. Clothes were passed down from sister to sister to sister. Vacations had meant driving to Florida or camping out closer to home. But with luck and brains, Jacqueline had married up. She had a brilliant mind and went to Yale to study law, where she met and married Christopher Croswell. Now her law degree was framed and tucked away in the study on the Upper West Side, alongside the oil paintings of schooners and the rare maps, religiously dusted by the help.

Andrew's father, on the other hand came from money and carried on the family tradition of making even more money. His influence on his wife must have been powerful, because in many ways, Andrew's mother was now indistinguishable from any other person born into money—except she had maintained a strong sense of social justice. She was ever rooting for the underdog, was incredibly generous to social causes of all sorts, and had encouraged her son to follow his dreams in spite of her husband's demands that Andrew find a real job.

Andrew gave a gloomy chuckle. Right about now, his mother was probably regretting that choice.

Back in the elevator, Andrew placed two boxes on the floor and pressed the button for the fourth floor. The doors were almost closed when a voice called out, "Hold the elevator!"

Andrew stuck out his arm at the last minute. Through the widening gap, he spotted a tall, slender blonde dragging two large suitcases behind her, tiling at an angle as though she were walking against a blizzard. He held the doors for her as she struggled to get the suitcases in. The heel of her boot caught on the rug, and she stumbled into the elevator. Andrew threw out his arms, and she clutched at him. When he helped right her, she smiled at him shyly.

"Thank you!" she said, out of breath, tucking stray hairs from a messy bun behind her ears.

Andrew smiled and said nothing. Normally outgoing, he found himself a little tongue-tied as he tried not to look at her sizeable chest.

"Uh, what floor are you going to?" she asked, at least once or possibly twice.

Lost in thought, Andrew was suddenly hyperaware of how close she was. Her suitcases and his boxes took up most of the space, pressing the elevator's two occupants closer. He hadn't been zapped by that sort of instant attraction in a long time. But wait: her suitcases... his boxes...

He glanced at the buttons. She had pressed 4.

"Same as you." Andrew looked at her directly now, and the cogwheels in his head started turning again. Was this his new roommate?

She stared straight ahead, observing proper elevator protocol.

"Are you, by chance, Megan?" he asked.

"Yes," she replied, drawing it out somewhat cautiously as she turned to look at him. "Are you... Andrew?"

He noticed her pale blue eyes and caught a hint of a smile in them. "Yes! I didn't think you'd be in until late tonight." He reached out a hand.

Megan fumbled with her suitcase handles and managed to shake hands.

The doors opened onto the fourth floor, and the two roommates navigated the many obstacles en route to the apartment door, making brief eye contact now and again. Andrew set his boxes on the floor in the entryway and saw that his mother indeed had not moved from her spot.

"Sweetie, I found you a cleaning lady," she smiled proudly, holding up her cell phone like a trophy. "She said she couldn't come today, but she'll be here tomorrow morning at nine."

"Oh. You didn't have to do that." Andrew's voice went up an octave.

Jacqueline waved her hand at him and slipped the phone back into her handbag. "Think of it as a housewarming gift." When she looked up, Andrew saw the confusion on her face.

"Mom, this is Megan," he said quickly, gesturing to the woman standing behind him. "My new roommate."

The two women shook hands. His mother's hand seemed tiny and fragile in the taller woman's grasp, like she was shaking the wing of a bird. "It's a pleasure to meet you, Megan," Jacqueline said sweetly. "Andrew tells me you used to be roommates with my Emily?"

"Nice to meet you, Mrs. Croswell. Actually, Emily's friend Heather was my roommate, but we hung out a little bit. It was so nice of Emily to put me in contact with Andrew."

"Please, call me Jacqueline."

So far, so good, thought Andrew. His usual friendliness seemed to be returning at last. "Megan, I still can't believe how lucky I am I found you," he called out from the kitchen, unloading two paper bags from Whole Foods. "I was counting on splitting the rent with... someone else. That is, until... well, something came up last minute."

"His girlfriend dumped him. She was a fake vegan," his mother whispered, loud enough that he had no trouble hearing. "They were supposed to move here together. She wanted him to propose, but Andrew wouldn't do it." Jacqueline swept her eyes over the apartment once more. "And for some reason, he insists on being 'independent' and paying his own way. I guess until he lands a more lucrative position, or a wife, he'll be stuck sharing apartments for the rest of his life."

"Mother, please!" Andrew yelled, ducking his head into the fridge.

"Oh. I see," Megan mumbled.

Andrew focused all his attention on placing the fresh fruits and vegetables in their respective plastic drawers. "At least the fridge was cleaned out," he muttered before rejoining his mom and his new roommate in the living room.

"I'm happy you needed a roommate," Megan said kindly. "It worked out for both of us. I've got a mortgage to cover back in Florida."

Jacqueline looked from her son to Megan and back again. "Well, looks like you two are going to get along just wonderfully."

Andrew had no trouble recognizing the sarcasm in his mother's tone, but he could tell she was impressed and relieved nonetheless.

"I'm so happy for both of you," she continued. "I'm guessing you're single, Megan?"

Andrew's eyes flew wide. "Mother!"

Megan blushed three shades of red. "Um, yes."

"Well, then you both have something in common. Are the movers coming with your furniture, dear? Or were you in a rush to leave your partner behind like Andrew was?"

Megan hesitated. "This is pretty much all I have, but for a few boxes still in the car."

Jacqueline nodded. "Ah, so you are both starting over fresh." She nodded, smiling. "Well, I'm sure you've left some man broken-hearted somewhere. And don't worry about being single, dear. I'm sure that won't last long."

Andrew shot his mother a warning look and continued aggressively folding up his grocery bags into nice little brown paper squares, making as much noise as possible. *I love my mother. I love my mother,* he repeated, reminding himself that in just a few minutes, she would be on her way back to New York.

Jacqueline pretended not to notice. Instead she looked down at her rose gold, diamond-encrusted watch. "Oh, shoot. Andrew, I have to get back to New York. I'm so sorry I won't be able to have lunch with you or take you shopping! But I really have to be at a gala tonight. And you know Eduardo is such a slow driver..."

"You mean he drives the speed limit," Andrew joked. "Don't worry, Mom, I can order stuff online. I'll just sleep on my air mattress until then. Thanks for the lift."

His mother regarded him skeptically.

"I'm a grown man, Mother," he reminded her for the second time that hour. He kissed her cheek, which was smooth and tight for a sixty-four-year-old's, and caught a hint of her perfume, a floral, citrus, soapy smell, like a dried flower arrangement stored in a closet for years.

She straightened and smiled at him. "I'm glad I could see your place and catch up a little with you, sweetie." Then she turned to Megan, placing a hand on her shoulder. "And I'm sure I'll be seeing plenty of you. Next time I'll take you both out to lunch."

Chapter Four

————— ✪ —————

LINE IN THE SAND

Alone with Megan again, Andrew felt the awkwardness return. "Your mother drove you here from New York," she said. It wasn't a question, but somehow it required an answer.

Andrew squirmed a little. "Uh, yeah. I haven't seen her in a while, so she offered to drive me so we could catch up on the way."

Megan raised her eyebrows. "That's sweet."

Looking to shift the conversation away from the topic of his mother, Andrew motioned to the pile of his stuff on the living room floor: a TV, a modern turntable with speakers, two milk crates filled with records, a guitar, a yoga mat, an antique table lamp, and a rolled-up Persian rug his mother insisted he take with him. She had wanted to give him more furniture, but there was no room in her Lexus even if Andrew had wanted to accept it. Which he didn't. Expensive antiques in his modest apartment—it wasn't quite the vibe he was going for. And out of guilt he let his ex-girlfriend keep everything in their apartment.

"Guess I'm a light packer. You, too, huh?" Andrew asked.

"Yes," she replied, matter-of-factly. "You don't even own a couch, or chairs?" One perfectly shaped eyebrow lifted in a question, as if she were still trying to wrap her head around why a person so clearly privileged was living like a vagabond.

"Or a bed... or a dresser..." He laughed a little self-consciously. She must have taken pity on him because she gave him a tiny smile, for a brief moment he glimpsed her playful side but it quickly disappeared behind her no-nonsense pursed lips. Andrew was able to breathe again. "I feel like I'm back in college. What a weird feeling, to be starting over again at my age."

Megan nodded and looked a little relieved. "Well, looks like we're in the same boat. If you want, we can unpack what we brought and make a list of everything we need. Then we can go shopping for it together, if you'd like. I have a car."

"Sure, that sounds great," Andrew said, grinning as he pulled out his phone, ready to search for directions. "Where would you like to go shopping?" He hoped she wasn't going to suggest Target.

Megan chewed her lip while she weighed her options—a tic Andrew found kind of endearing. She was so serious and composed, clearly used to taking control, yet this tiny gesture made her seem innocent and vulnerable.

"You know, why don't we just find an IKEA" she replied finally. "I don't know how long I'll be in D.C. I don't want to jinx myself. Plus, it kind of fits with the whole college feel we've got going on." She smiled slyly.

★ ★ ★

Megan drove, content to let Andrew do most of the talking. He seemed to be forever grinning at her. Was he waiting for something, or just perpetually amused? Well, she'd be amused, too, if she had that kind of money.

"Just so you know," she warned him, pulling into the parking lot, "I'm kind of obsessed with decorating."

Andrew shot her a worried look. "Like, how obsessed?"

"One year I asked for a subscription to *Country Home* for my birthday. I was eleven."

"Can I ask why?"

She shrugged. "I liked looking at pictures of warm, inviting rooms—kitchens and living rooms and bedrooms—that evoke all the feelings of home." She said it quietly, almost to herself.

Andrew didn't follow up with any questions, but seemed eager to lighten the mood, joking, "Well, that seems completely normal to me. You don't exactly seem like you were a *Teen Beat* girl."

"What does that mean?"

"Nothing, nothing. I don't mean to insult you. You just seem... serious, like you're above frivolous things like ogling cute boys."

"You're right. I've always been pretty serious." Ever the taskmaster, she pulled out a notepad from her purse. "Anyway, I hope you're a patient person, because this may take a while."

"I've got all day." He grinned at her.

Megan and Andrew entered the maze that was IKEA. If Megan had been knuckle-cracking person, that's exactly what she would've done. Instead she grabbed a giant blue bag for Andrew and one for herself, and inhaled deeply. The smell of MDF, meatballs, and cinnamon buns is intoxicating.

To Megan, the meaning of retail therapy was clear. The more stressed she was at work and in her personal life, the more she would rearrange and redecorate it all away, reinventing her life as she reinvented her living space. About some things—food, for example, or beauty products—she was indifferent and frugal. Get her into a Pottery Barn, though, and she could do some real damage. She had gone through all the fads: contemporary, modern, cottage chic, French country, Spanish hacienda. She had once spent an entire day hunting for antique glass handles in the middle of a hurricane. It drove Jason crazy. No detail was too small, no expense too great, to achieve at least this one aspect of perfect order in her life. Megan knew all too well the difference between a house and a home.

As she walked around IKEA, trying on all the possibilities in her mind, Megan spotted couple after couple, some strolling leisurely, hand in hand, and others arguing the way couples do. Meanwhile, she wasn't shopping with her fiancé, but here with her new roommate— someone she'd known only a few hours. She wasn't shopping at her favorite stores, either, but at a warehouse full of throwaway furniture. She hadn't been entirely truthful with Andrew and his mother. Did she miss the trappings of her old house—the gas fireplace, the Carrera marble console table, the expensive white leather sectional, the black wool egg chair, the royal blue rug from ABC Carpet? Of course. But all that was gone now—as far behind her as her life with Jason.

Her mood dropped from high on retail excitement to that low point reserved for life's disappointments. She was playing a high-stakes game of Chutes and Ladders—and she had just slid down a big chute and landed at the beginning all over again.

Better not to dwell too much on the ground you've lost, she reminded herself. *You're on the cusp of something bigger and better.* All of this—the rented apartment with a stranger, the twentysomething furniture— was temporary, a skin to be shed.

Back in the apartment, they got to work, bringing up the boxes and sorting things into their proper rooms. An hour later, Andrew gave a triumphant shout from the living room. "Bookshelf is done!"

Megan came out of her bedroom to find Andrew's back turned to her as he finished bolting the bookshelf to the wall. Waiting for him to step back, she was distracted by the way his back moved under his tight blue T-shirt.

He was just a little taller than her, six foot one to her five foot eleven, and not overly muscular, although she could tell he was physically active. His jeans fit just snug enough to outline his bottom. Megan found herself thinking about how, in spite of the full beard and his hipster attire, he was actually quite attractive. His dark hair was slicked back, his blue eyes were expressive, his eyelashes were longer than any she'd ever seen. He seemed sweet and genuine, too—in other words, not at all her type.

She broke off that train of thought. "I'm impressed! You're a regular ol' handy man." She pushed her box of books over to the bookshelf. "Which rows can I have?"

Andrew shrugged. "Doesn't matter to me. Choose what you like. I'm just psyched that you like books too. Reading is a dying art, isn't it? You know, most people never read a book again after high school. It's crazy!" Then he went over to his record player, put on a classic rock album, and headed for the kitchen. "I can't possibly put the rest of this crap together on an empty stomach," he said motioning to the piles of IKEA boxes that still surrounded them.

Opening the kitchen cupboards, he pulled out extra-virgin olive oil, Arborio rice, some dehydrated wild mushrooms, thyme, and organic chicken stock. Then he cracked open a bottle of chilled white wine and added a generous splash to the rice sizzling in the pan.

Maybe it was the music or the aroma coming from the kitchen, but she felt herself starting to relax in his presence. "I follow directions very well, but in my limited experience assembling IKEA furniture, it always helps to be a little drunk."

Andrew took two wine glasses from the cupboard and poured out the remaining wine. "In that case, here. If I drink too much and start assembling upside down, you can help me." He laughed, holding a glass out to her.

She sipped at it. "I didn't say I'd be any help. It's just that when I'm relaxed, I'm less likely to lose my cool if I'm missing that one nut or washer, or if they forgot to put in the Allen key, or whatever."

"Ahh. So you have a bit of temper?"

"I try very hard to restrain myself." She looked at him without a trace of smile. "But when I blow up, watch out."

Andrew raised an eyebrow. "OK. I'll consider myself warned."

Thirty minutes later, as Megan screwed in the last leg of their new coffee table, Andrew entered the living room with a glass of wine and a bowl of risotto garnished generously with freshly shaved Parmesan.

Megan took a bite of her risotto. "Wow. This is so good." She took another bite. "You can really cook! I think I'm going to enjoy being your roommate." She looked him right in the eyes. "As long as you don't piss me off." He held her gaze for a beat too long and then abruptly looked away.

Andrew met her eyes for a moment, then took a sip of his wine and looked away.

Megan laughed, self-conscious all of a sudden. "Sorry. I'm terrible at sarcasm."

"No, no. Your voice said 'joke.' But your eyes said, 'But really, don't mess with me.'"

They ate in silence for a while.

Megan decided to try again. "You know what's great about IKEA? Since we have to put it together ourselves, it's technically *made* in America."

Andrew laughed. "See, you can make jokes. Are you happy to be back in D.C.?"

"Yeah, it's been thirteen, fourteen years now. I always knew I'd be back someday, though."

"Why didn't you just stay after college?"

She shrugged. "Lots of reasons. My brother was starting a business and needed help. I wanted to get involved with the community at home. Plus, I wanted to keep an eye on my father." She mumbled the last part.

Thankfully, Andrew remained quiet.

But by then, the wine had loosened Megan up a little bit. "When I was in high school, we took a class trip to D.C., and I toured the Capitol and the White House, and I remember being blown away. Not just by the beautiful architecture, but by what it symbolized, by everything America was built on. I was in the presence of greatness, and I wanted to live surrounded by it, if you know what I mean."

Andrew shook his head slowly. "D.C. is cool, and the buildings are beautiful. But to me it's a symbol of everything gone wrong in this country—how far we've come from our ideals, from what the Founding Fathers intended. Our government doesn't work for us. It's not *for* the people, *by* the people. These days it's for the corporations."

Megan was a little confused. *Is it just me, or is his mood turning a bit dark?*

He gulped back the last of his wine, got up from the floor, and brought the bowls to the kitchen. "You know what's funny?" he called out. "We spent the whole afternoon together, and I still don't even know what you do for work."

"You're right." Megan laughed. "That's usually one of the first things I ask people. I'm going to be working at the Capitol, as a legislative aide. What about you?"

"Cool," Andrew replied. "I'm starting work for an environmental nonprofit, as the legislative director."

Wait, that can't be right, thought Megan.

She turned away, trying to regroup, and her gaze landed on the bookshelf. She scanned his row: Titles by Elizabeth Warren, Noam Chomsky, and Barack Obama lined up alongside Al Gore's *An Inconvenient Truth* and, Rachel Carson's *Silent Spring*. Megan's hopes fell. Until that moment, she didn't even know she had any.

"You're a... Democrat?"

Andrew looked taken aback. "Yeah, of course I'm a Democrat." He scoffed. "I'm a decent, rational person, aren't I? I mean, look what the Republican Party has just given us: an internet troll for president! If that doesn't turn the entire country Democrat, I don't know what..."

He trailed off and glanced at her row of books: Bill O'Reilly, Sean Hannity, the George Bushes, Senator Goldwater's *The Conscience of a Conservative,* all organized alphabetically. "Who did you say you'll be working for?"

Megan's voice was flat. "I just finished as campaign manager for Congressman White, from Florida. I'm here now as his legislative aide."

"Oh, crap," Andrew stammered. "OK, OK, it's fine. You can't be a Republican if you're not used to people talking shit about you, right?" He attempted a friendly chuckle.

"You know, it's getting late. I'm going to call it a night," Megan said icily, "before you say anything you might regret." She was pretty sure he got the sarcasm that time.

Chapter Five

———————— ✪ ————————

FIRST DAY ON THE HILL

M egan's jumbled dreams were interrupted by the jarring sound of the alarm clock. It had always been a source of contention with her ex. *Can't you find a gentler way to wake up?* Jason would plead. But she stubbornly insisted, using her retro alarm clock that went *enh-enh-enh-enh-enh*, and leaving it on the bureau on the other side of the room. She would stumble over clothes in the dark, eyes blurry, searching out the offending object and slamming a fist on every button. A creature of habit, she was sure this was the only way she could get up in the morning: with a sense of urgency and purpose, propelled out the door for her predawn run.

In her new apartment, the alarm clock was placed as far away from her bed as possible to remove the snooze button temptation. It vibrated angrily and urgently on the parquet floor. That first morning, though, getting out of bed proved slightly more difficult than usual. She had slept on her air mattress, which partially deflated overnight. At 5:45 a.m., she resorted to rolling off it and onto the floor, and crawling toward the sound, her mind awake but her body still tired.

Tugging at her suitcase and pulling out her running gear, she said a little prayer that bed and dresser would be delivered by tomorrow as promised. She had been in D.C. only one day, and already the disorder and chaos of her room were stressing her out.

Thirty minutes later, after her quick run, Megan showered,

changed, and decided to grab breakfast from On Rye, the trendy Jewish deli two streets over. Reminding herself that running in the cold burns more calories, she treated herself to a coffee with half-and-half and a slice of chocolate babka, a whopping 400 non-nutritious, insulin-inducing calories.

The morning was cool and the streets were empty. Megan sipped her coffee as she walked down 7th Street toward the Gallery Place–Chinatown Station. It had been forever since she'd been on the Metro or traveled anywhere in D.C., and she felt like a tourist all over again. She made her way to the transit map and stood there, deciding which train to take. She faced the dilemma common to all urban commuters: Switch trains to get closer to her destination? Or take one train and walk farther? For Megan, that choice was strictly weather dependent: Too cold, raining, or oppressively humid, and she'd make the switch. Otherwise she preferred to walk. Both got you there at about the same time, but taking one train left less up to fate. Will the train be on time? Will the train be too full? Will the train break down? Too many variables that could interfere and take things out of her control.

Andrew's got the right idea, biking to work, she allowed. But she would never be caught dead riding a bicycle to her job.

Standing on the platform, she noticed how clean the Metro station was, how the tiles reminded her of a burnt umber honeycomb, how the domed concrete roof had captured the sole piece of litter in the station—a helium Happy Birthday balloon. Megan wondered about the story behind the balloon. She imagined an estranged father realizing too late that it was his child's birthday… searching through the closest grocery store for the most kid-appropriate gift… finding a bag of discount Halloween candy and this balloon… the string slipping out of his hands and floating to the ceiling… the balloon bobbing and sparkling from way up high, taunting him, *You're a shitty father…*

To Megan, birthdays were nothing but annual disappointments anyway. The memory of her thirteenth birthday replayed itself, when her father had brought home a cake that said *Happy Retirement, Rick!* She had blown out the single candle and wished she could trade places with Rick, wherever he was.

Megan snapped out of her reminiscence. Why was she digging up old memories? *This is a happy day!* she insisted. *It's a birthday balloon that a happy kid accidentally lost. Just let it go.*

After a short ride, the train pulled into Judiciary Square. Exiting the station, Megan walked briskly toward her office. Once she caught sight of the Capitol Building, she felt the excitement rising. Here she was, finally returning to D.C. For a split second, she imagined what life would have been like if she had never left the capital, had never answered the call of family duty.

For some, the highlight of their formative years is winning a sports championship or dating their first real boyfriend. For Megan, that life-changing moment was her visit to D.C. Simply put, she had fallen in love. For over two hundred years this building had housed Congress. Here, the laws of this great nation discussed and debated. Here, presidents had been inaugurated and the State of the Union had been pronounced. The halls and even the domed ceiling were lined with statues and paintings representing great events and greater people.

She bounded up the steps of Longworth House Office Building, entered the hallowed building, and flashed her security card. The lobby was quiet enough now but would soon be filled with lobbyists and representatives from special interest groups, each vying for their fifteen allotted minutes. Union reps, big oil and big pharma lawyers, NRA members, Americans with disabilities, climate activists, Farm Bureau agents, Garden Clubbers of America—they would all spread throughout the hallways and take over the cafeterias, strategizing over coffee and donuts, asserting their right to be heard.

Standing in front of Congressman White's office, she hesitated for only a moment, to prompt herself with her special brand of pep talk. She repeated her mantra: *Once you set your sights on something, you don't back down.*

She opened the door to the office to find it completely empty. She stepped in and wandered around the office. Finally locating the conference room, she found a woman standing with her back to the door, pouring a cup of coffee. The woman wore a navy wool-cashmere blend skirt suit, which on anyone else might seem boring and sexless. But not on her.

Megan's eyes traveled from the three-inch black heels to the perfectly tanned and sculpted calf muscles and up the length of the woman's leg, a view that terminated at the hem of the skirt, which strained against a sizable bootie and quickly tapered to a tiny waist. Megan recognized that ass. It was a three-dimensional wonder from all angles. The woman turned around slowly. Carmela Lopez, Congressman White's chief of staff.

A gorgeous Latina, Carmela was not only perfectly formed, tanned, and coiffed, but also smart as a vixen and more precise than a calculator. They'd met a dozen times when Megan was running White's campaign. If there was an opposite of instant chemistry, Megan and Carmela had it. Their relationship was based on instantaneous, inescapable hatred. Megan knew why: They were two alphas who recognized in each other the same ambition and competitiveness, and who knew there would likely be room for just one.

Megan and Carmela stared at each other, their eyes and facial expression giving nothing away. Carmela cocked her head to one side. "Have we met before?" she drawled.

Megan snorted. "Yes, many times. Your memory must be going. I helped get your boss reelected, remember?"

Carmela paused. "Oh, yes. Now I recall. It's... Melissa, right?"

"Megan."

"Well, you got a pretty lucky break... *Megan*. If I recall, Mike Horowitz was running the campaign from the start? And then, lucky you!" Carmela smirked. "You got to swoop in and claim the victory."

Megan cleared her throat. "Actually, my good friend Mike left very early in the campaign. I have no qualms about accepting the praise I deserve."

"Well, we'll see how you manage working in the office with no one to hold your hand." Carmela took a long sip of coffee, holding her left hand aloft.

Megan noticed the four-carat solitaire diamond being held purposefully at her eye level. *That's new,* she thought. "I'll be just fine. Thanks for your concern. Can you show me where my desk is?"

Carmela beckoned for her to follow. "And just so you know, you're early. Everyone else will get here at eight forty-five. And I don't like to be disturbed before then. I have a lot of *important* work to do," she emphasized.

The morning wore on, and still no one had arrived with instructions for Megan. She sat in her tiny, cramped office with nothing to do. There was nothing she hated more than being idle! Reaching for her cell phone, she shot Mike a text.

> **Megan:** Hey, so guess what? My roommate is a Democrat!
>
> **Mike:** Ha! Great, you get a chance to "sleep with the enemy" and learn his weakness. That's a good thing.
>
> **Megan:** Hmm, good point. Might as well learn how liberals think so I can use it against them.
>
> **Mike:** Just don't actually sleep with him!
>
> **Megan:** Not likely! I have standards, you know.
>
> **Mike:** Oh, I forgot. You have no problem marrying a guy for money, but you draw the line at snowflakes.

Megan was chuckling quietly when several people walked past her office, headed for the conference room. She wondered if she should follow, when at last someone popped her head into the office.

"Hi! I'm Katie. The congressman's executive assistant. You must be Megan, right?" She didn't wait for an answer. "We're having our weekly staff meeting in the conference room. Why don't you join?"

Megan leaped up from her desk and followed Katie to the conference room. Twelve people crowded around the conference table, eying the box of donuts and platter of fresh fruit in the center. Megan thought how easy it was to sort out the staff by age and status, according to their food choices.

The fresh, young staff in their late twenties to mid-thirties, picking at the fruit and drinking from oversized coffee mugs, were the backbone of the office: aides, schedulers, correspondents. They were chronically overworked and underpaid, trying to climb the government ladder.

The even fresher, younger staff diving for the donuts were in their late teens and early twenties—the interns, squeezing in their hours between classes.

The staff members chatted until Carmela appeared, and then silence smothered the room. Carmela stood in front of the conference table, glaring at the rest of the staff, who took their seats without delay.

"Are we connected to the Florida office yet, Brian?" Carmela asked one of the legislative correspondents, who ranked just above intern in the office pecking order. Brian checked the Skype connection to the other district offices, and when they were all onscreen, he turned the laptop to face Carmela and the rest of the team.

"OK. Before we go over this week's agenda, I want quick updates from scheduling, communications, legislation, and press." Carmela said, pointing in turn to each culprit.

The D.C. office and the district offices provided their updates. Then Carmela handed an intern a stack of handouts to pass around. "These are our policy priorities and the legislation the congressman wants us to work on."

Megan perused the handout and quickly raised her hand. "There's no assignment here for the energy aide. What would you like me to work on?"

"Oh, well," Carmela jeered, her voice cool. "Maybe you can sit with the interns and answer the phones this week. You know, get to know the constituents. That should be useful."

It occurred to Megan that Carmela was even more spiteful than she remembered. She wondered how much White had told his chief of staff about his plans to groom Megan for his seat. She hoped he wouldn't tell Carmela a damn thing. If he did, it would only make Megan's time working in this office all the more difficult.

★ ★ ★

T he day passed quickly, with Megan answering phone call after phone call while she waited to speak with Congressman White. He was in and out of the office all day, she was told, moving from one meeting to the next, and when he wasn't in a meeting, he was on some important phone call or other. Finally, in the late afternoon, his assistant Katie stopped by Megan's desk again. "The boss is free to see you now," she chirped.

"Thanks, Katie."

When Megan entered White's office, he motioned toward a chair. "Come in, Miss Thompson! Sit, sit. How's your first day going, darlin'? Are you all settled in now?" His face was friendly and open.

Megan breathed a sigh of relief. "Yes, sir. I'm all settled in, and looking forward to getting started on some policy research, so — "

"I hope you don't mind that I put you in charge of energy and environment legislation," White interrupted. His words implied concern, but his demeanor said, *If you don't like it, tough.* Beneath his gentlemanly appearance, Megan knew, was a serious man who ran a tight ship. Hierarchy mattered.

"Not at all!" Megan replied. "I'm thrilled. Whatever you need. I'm really looking forward to getting started. I spent today on the phone recording constituents' complaints."

"Ah, yes. Not the most enjoyable task, that's for sure." He nodded sympathetically and then quickly added, "But necessary all the same. Don't worry. I'm sure Carmela will give you a larger task soon. She knows what she's doing. I trust her completely."

Well, everyone has his weak spot, thought Megan.

"Oh, and I hope you don't take this the wrong way, hon," White added, "but I think you need to join the local Toastmasters."

Megan was taken aback. That club still existed? She had to ask. "Why?"

White practically rolled his eyes. "Honey, most politicians aren't born — they're made." He beckoned, and she leaned in toward the desk. "I've been watching you over the past year or so, and it's clear you're more comfortable being a wallflower than the belle of the ball. You need to break out of your comfort zone, Megan!" He leaned back into his revolving, reclining leather chair and squinted at her. "You'll need the confidence to speak in front of large crowds. To take criticism. To keep your cool in a debate, or when constituents are shouting at you. You need to come out of your shell more, darlin'. You've got to learn how to work a crowd. And a donor."

Megan frowned.

White gave her a small acknowledgment of commiseration. "Go to the Toastmasters club, and you'll see everyone in the room has the same goals as you. Think of it as just another skill to be mastered."

"Of course. You're right, sir."

"Did you line up a political consultant yet?" he asked.

"My friend gave me a few names. I plan to give them a call this week."

"When your campaign is up and running, I'll give you the leftover seventy-five hundred from my campaign. You can use my donor database to build yours."

"Thank you so much, sir. I really appreciate this." And she did. But it was just a sad little drop in the bucket. *Only $492,500 more to raise*, she thought, suppressing a moan.

"It's my pleasure, Miss Thompson. Oh, and wait just a minute." White searched through a pile of papers and found a neon pink Post-it note. "Ah, here it is. Your first date. Set for next Friday. He'll pick you up at your place, eight p.m."

"Oh. Wow. That was fast." Megan laughed a little nervously.

"Well, we don't have time to waste." White smiled and looked up at his assistant hovering in the doorway. He signaled for her to come in.

"Sorry to interrupt, sir," Katie said. "I have some things for you to sign… ?"

The congressman took the stack of greeting cards—sympathy, birthday, congratulations on your wedding/baby/anniversary—and put them to the side of his desk so he could personally write a note in each. "Oh, did you mail out the baby blanket that Mrs. White knitted yet?"

"Yes, sir, it went out yesterday."

White nodded his appreciation. Katie quietly left the room, knowing when she'd been dismissed.

"Now, where were we? Oh, yes. Give Carmela your address so she can give it to your date."

Megan had a sinking feeling. "Carmela is helping you?" Blind dates were one thing. She wondered uneasily how much "help" Carmela would be providing.

White slid his glasses off their perch on his forehead and down to the tip of his ball-shaped nose. Instead of answering, he began poking at his computer. Megan wondered if he'd forgotten she was still in the room, until he murmured, "Anything else you'd like to discuss?"

Megan fidgeted with the pen in her hand. "Can I ask you something, sir?"

White looked up from his messy desk.

"Why me? Why not Carmela?" Megan realized she was whispering. "She's more than capable. She's been your chief of staff for three years. And I notice that she's engaged."

"Yes." White paused and then lowered his voice too, even though Katie had shut the door behind her. "She got engaged last month. Some hotshot lawyer." He sighed. "Carmela is a very competent chief of staff. A hard worker. Driven. But… Megan, honey, she would sell her grandmama if she thought she could get ahead. She'd make a great politician, yes. But in the very worst way."

Megan could see no reason to contradict him.

"I know it may seem selfish, but I want to preserve my legacy. I think you and I share more of the same values."

"But sir, does she know?"

The congressman gave her a blank look.

"Does Carmela know you're grooming me to run for your seat in 2018?"

White sighed again. "No. I haven't told her. She'll probably quit when she finds out, and I need her. I'll have to wait until the last minute. In the meantime, be careful around her. Keep your head down. Be polite and do your job. Understand?"

Megan nodded. She understood perfectly what her boss was saying: She was going to have to suck it up and play by someone else's rules.

Chapter Six

———————— ✪ ————————

DIVIDED WE FALL

Andrew spent the day mulling the odd, unsettling turn of events. His roommate was a Republican. A Republican! He didn't know how to separate how he felt about her from his feelings about her political party. The party of faux fiscal conservatives. The party of "responsible" gun owners. The party of corporate greed run amok. The party of small government except when it came to meddling in the bedroom and interfering in women's health.

Is there such a thing as a good Republican? he wondered. No, of course there wasn't. Even at their best, conservatives were constantly pulling the wool over the eyes of the middle class and decimating safety nets for the poor. And that was *before* Trump.

The night Hillary Clinton lost the election, Andrew—like so much of the country—had been in a state of shock and disbelief. Watching the election results with family and friends in the Croswell penthouse overlooking Central Park, and seeing the numbers come in, he had felt a cocktail of fear and anger burning his throat and unsettling his stomach. The Champagne, protruding from silver ice buckets, had sat uncorked until it turned lukewarm. There was nothing to celebrate now.

In the dead of night, when the election was called for Trump, a small wail had escaped from his mother's mouth. Jacqueline who had worked tirelessly for the Clinton campaign, hosting fundraisers and donating money, then took to her bedroom and didn't reemerge for two days. Emily had tended to their mother like one would treat a wounded soldier, while his father rolled his eyes and poured another scotch. The whole family had been paralyzed by his mother's grief.

Andrew had been rooting for Bernie Sanders throughout the early days of the campaign, and he felt a twinge of schadenfreude even though he suffered Hillary's devastation alongside his family. *If I were her, I'd be smashing everything in sight,* he had thought. *To lose to* him, *of all people?* It was the highest insult possible.

The days following Trump's election were surreal. November had been a funeral. People were crying in each other's arms in the breakroom at work, in the parking lots of shops and their children's schools, in the grocery store aisles. Everywhere Andrew looked, Americans were mourning the loss of civility, of human decency. All the progress made, all the sacrifices and gains hard-won by activists over the past decade and more, erased in one night.

And the rage! Andrew had never felt that way before. *How the fuck did we end up here? Is the whole fucking country stupid?* When he complained to his parents, his father would shrug his usual indifference. His mother would break down and cry.

Nothing had been the same since the election. Facebook friends were defriended, relatives said "no, thanks" to Thanksgiving dinner, family members were uninvited to weddings, spouses threatened divorce. The line in the sand was distinct: those who voted for Trump, and those who didn't.

He spent the day distracted, unpacking and tidying up the apartment, and texting his sister as though he were going through the five stages of grief.

> **8:30 a.m.:** You didn't tell me Megan is a Republican!
>
> **10:00 a.m.:** How can Megan be a Republican? She seemed so nice and smart.
>
> **11:30 a.m.:** I can't believe you didn't tell me she is a Republican. I am literally sleeping next door to the enemy.
>
> **12:00 p.m.:** Maybe she's not that bad. Maybe she

couldn't bring herself to vote for Trump.

12:30 p.m.: Of course she voted for Trump! This is terrible. I'm so depressed, I am eating ice cream at noon. How am I supposed to watch John Oliver with her in the room? Or Rachel Maddow?

1:15 p.m.: Well, I guess I get to observe first-hand how they plan to destroy our country.

He tried to put Megan out of his mind. It wasn't working. Something had wrapped its arms around him and squeezed the air from his lungs. Yoga. He needed to do some yoga.

★ ★ ★

His phone rang just as he opened the glass door and peered up the steps leading to the yoga studio. He glanced down at the name. *Finally!* he thought.

"Hey. Are you all settled in?" Emily sounded far away, and Andrew could hear the banging of drawers.

"Am I on speakerphone? Are you unloading the dishwasher or something?" His tone, he knew, was a tad accusatory.

"Sorry, just finished. You now have my undivided attention." Emily's voice was clearer and louder now. "I wish I could have been there yesterday. I would have loved to have gone out to dinner with you two! But my flight got in late."

Andrew relaxed a little. He would have to forgive his sister for the omission about Megan. He never could hold a grudge against her for very long. "The place is nice. Mom left right away. She had some event to go to." He began stomping up the second flight of stairs.

"When *doesn't* she have an event to go to, right?"

Andrew saw what his sister was doing here. "Emily, back to the reason I texted," he demanded. "Why didn't you tell me Megan's a Republican?"

"Andrew, it's not like I forgot to mention she murdered her past two roommates. She's a good person."

Andrew pictured her rolling her eyes, a tic she reserved just for family members. He gave a sardonic snort. There was no such thing as a good Republican.

In a gentler tone, Emily added, "It's been a long time since I've seen her. And it's not exactly like we hung out a lot. She was my best friend's roommate, but she practically lived in the library. And in her running gear. Sometimes she'd take a break and watch chick flicks with us. She was always very nice. We most *certainly* didn't talk politics. And honestly, who cares if she's Republican?"

Who cares? Andrew couldn't believe his ears. Was she serious?

"You guys will probably be so busy with your jobs, you won't even see each other."

Andrew stopped in the hallway for a moment, absentmindedly stroking his beard. "Em, I don't even know how to act around her now. We were having such a great time yesterday. I can't handle it." A sigh escaped him. "Every time I hear the word 'Republican,' I feel like I've woken up from a bad nightmare. And then I realize that no, the nightmare hasn't even begun yet."

Emily gave a cheerful scoff. "You don't even know her, Andrew. So she thinks differently from you! It doesn't make her a bad person."

"White nationalists and misogynists think differently! Are *they* good people?" Andrew was yelling now, oblivious to the other yogis who squeezed by him with their yoga mats, throwing him dirty looks. He and his rage took up all the space in the narrow hallway.

"What I'm saying is, you don't know her. So just give her a chance. And don't write the whole party off as white nationalists! That's inaccurate." Her gentle tone had taken an edge a preschool teacher might employ: soothing, but firm with authority.

Stepping into the studio, Andrew felt a tap on his shoulder and turned to face an older man with his lips pressed together in disapproval. The white-haired yogi pointed dramatically to a sign on the wall, setting off a clatter as his wooden and gem prayer bead necklaces collided. Andrew read the sign: *Silence, please. Namaste.*

He rolled his eyes; class didn't start for another ten minutes. He loved yoga, but these people took themselves too seriously.

"Why don't all three of us have dinner together?" Emily offered. "I haven't seen Megan in years. We can properly celebrate your new job. And maybe you can get to know her better."

"I guess we could do that." Rolling out his mat, Andrew lowered his voice. "But she's single. What if she brings home a gun-toting neo-Nazi?"

"I'd say be polite and offer him a beverage."

Megan sat alone at a square table toward the back of a chic taco dive bar on 1st and D Streets. The place was filled with the happy hour crowd: suits and skirts drinking high-end tequila. It was called *happy hour* not because the drinks were cheap—the drinks were never cheap there, or anywhere in D.C., for that matter—but because the patrons were happy their eighty-hour workweek was over. Theoretically, at least. Megan knew you were never off-duty in this city. And she wasn't out to celebrate with coworkers or friends. She was there to plot her rise to the top.

Too self-conscious to drink just water, and never a big fan of soda, she took tiny sips from the long straw in her giant frozen margarita and waited for the political consultant.

A slender man with a shaved head approached her table. His suit fit him perfectly. Based on his height and the quality of the tailoring, she had no doubt it was custom made. "Megan?" the man asked.

"Yes. Are you Hakeem?" She stood to shake hands.

His grip was firm but not overpowering, and she had to crane her neck to look him in the eye. He had the build of an athlete. *Probably played basketball,* she thought. Had he parlayed his skills into a scholarship, as she had? Megan tried to shake the thought loose. Just because he was tall and black didn't mean he was an athlete! She of all people should know better than to make assumptions.

When he smiled, a dimple appeared on his cheek. It made him seem boyish, but when the smile receded, he was all no-nonsense. He motioned for Megan to take her seat, and waited for her to sit before joining her.

"Thank you for taking the time to meet with me. I've heard you have a great track record of getting people elected." She didn't wait for a response, but instead began ticking her fingers. "As you know, we have four factors to juggle: time, information, money, and people. I need to file my petition by May to get my name on the ballot. And I need forty-seven hundred signatures, but really, we should triple that number in case some are thrown out or contested. We have some time on our hands, so at least we've got that going for us. There's over a year to work on building the team, making connections, gathering information. I also have the congressman's endorsement, and that will go a long way toward—"

Hakeem held up his hands and leaned back as if to stop an oncoming truck from running him over. "Easy, tiger," he chuckled. "I don't mean to cut you off, but this is just a preliminary meeting. I know you can run a campaign, OK? But you're going to have to switch roles now, from getting a candidate elected to *being* the candidate."

Megan nodded reluctantly. "Right. You're right. Can I just add that Congressman White has pledged the remaining money in his campaign fund? About seventy-five hundred. And my brother will chip in ten thousand."

"Great. That's a good start." The dimple reappeared on his cheek. "White will be able to introduce you to donors as well. Is he willing to do that?"

"Yes," she replied, hoping she sounded confident. "He's committed to helping me win in any way he can."

"Good. You have a real advantage here, Megan." Hakeem leaned toward her, pushing aside the complimentary basket of tortilla chips. "I was a little hesitant to meet with you at first. I mean, no offense, but you're not exactly the ideal candidate. At least on paper." It was his turn to tick his fingers one by one. "Young. Single. No money. No family connections. No widespread name recognition. And frankly, a woman."

How many times had her age, gender, and marital status been flung at her like this? It irked her. As if all these characteristics meant she had a Sisyphean task ahead of her! Shouldn't being smart and qualified be enough? She had paid her dues. She had gotten other people elected and worked in public service at the local level.

"What I want to do right now is get to know you, Megan the Candidate. Tell me about yourself. Where did you go to college? Where have you worked? When did you get started in politics?"

Megan could barely hide a nostalgic grin as she described her road to politics. "In high school I knocked on doors, getting out the vote for Bush. I went to American University, studied political science, ran track on a scholarship. I interned for a Senator for a semester and I was offered a position after graduation, but I turned it down and returned to Florida."

She hesitated to reveal more, but supposed she would have to get used to it. Taking a breath, she plunged ahead. "My father had lost his job again, and my brother dropped out of college to start his own business as a real estate developer. I needed to be there for them..." She turned up her palms in a *hey, that's life* gesture. "I used this tiny setback to gain local political experience. Joined the town planning board. Served as chair of the Gatorville Chamber of Commerce for a year. I started volunteering on campaigns four years ago while working full-time, and then decided to go all in and work on White's Florida campaign. I brought on more young volunteers to the campaign than he's ever had before. And now I work as his legislative aide."

Hakeem gave a curt nod, which seemed to indicate he was satisfied with her answer. "And you have a house in the district?" He glanced at the approaching waitress and waved a hand to fend her off.

"Yes. It's modest, but it's in my hometown."

"That's fine. Shows you have humble roots. A lot of voters can relate to that. When you go back to Florida over the Christmas break... I assume you will be?"

She nodded. Of course she would be heading home. She couldn't imagine leaving her father and brother alone at Christmastime — especially not alone *together*.

"Well, I want you to set up a bunch of meetings with local businesses and elected officials. Do you still have contacts on the city council?"

"Yes. I've already set up some meetings while I'm home. I know a lot of small business owners and everyone on the city council. There is very little turnover there."

"Good. Talk with them. Right now, it's just information gathering. Don't let on that you're planning on running," he warned. "Do you have any idea who you'll bring on to your campaign team?"

"I have a few people in mind," she replied, as if she hadn't already made a list of people from White's campaign whom she would tap when the time came.

"Great. We're off to a really good start so far." He paused, looking her dead in the eye. "Now, one final question: Is there anything in your past I need to know about?"

Megan shifted in her seat. "My past?" The volume in the room had gotten louder as the evening wore on, and she almost had to yell. "Does that include my family? Because I don't really feel comfortable talking about them." She spoke quickly while stabbing her straw into the bright orange slush of her melting margarita.

"I need to know everything, family included," Hakeem answered gently. "If there is anything lurking in your closet, Megan, I need to know about it so we can prepare. Nothing worse than being caught off guard—except being caught trying to cover something up. People can find anything on the internet these days. Think of me as your priest. My lips are sealed. Nothing leaves this room."

She took another long sip of her drink, grabbed a tortilla chip from the basket, dipped it into the salsa, and folded it into her mouth. She chewed very slowly.

"Start with your family. Any skeletons? Any arrests? Did anyone ever make the newspaper?"

Megan groaned and closed her eyes briefly. "My father. He was arrested, three years ago."

"For what?" Hakeem prompted.

"Propositioning a police officer."

Hakeem waited, eyebrows raised.

"He offered her three dollars and a steak dinner. For sex."

Hakeem tried to stifle a laugh, covering it with a fake cough before apologizing. "I'm sorry. That was so unprofessional of me. It's just... the first time I've heard something like that."

Megan shrugged it off, but her face had betrayed her by turning red. "Well, in his defense, he was really drunk at the time. And it was a female investigator, an undercover cop posing as a prostitute."

Just his luck, she thought humorlessly.

"I don't think he actually would have gone through with it," she quickly added. "He's been... a bit unstable since my mother died."

"That's good information. I need to know it all. Anything else in the family?"

Megan thought for a moment. "My aunt was fired from her job as a nurse for stealing oxycodone. She did a bit of time for selling it."

"OK. Anyone else?"

Megan said nothing, but pursed her lips.

Hakeem's eyes narrowed. "What about you? Any drug use? Affairs? Convictions? Et cetera?"

Megan squirmed a little. "No drugs. No arrests. I'm very straight. But..." She couldn't look at him. She lowered her voice. "I sent some... pictures to Jason. Jason Bates, my ex-fiancé. They were..."

He had to lean forward. "What? I'm sorry, I couldn't hear you."

A large group of people were just streaming into the bar. Had someone cranked the music volume since she'd come in? Megan closed her eyes again.

"I SENT NAKED PICTURES TO MY EX!"

A few people milling near the bar turned their heads to look at Megan, who buried her head behind a menu. *Shit! This is mortifying*, she thought.

Hakeem didn't bat an eyelash. "How long ago was that?"

Megan lowered the menu. "Nine months."

"And how did things end with you two? Is he bitter? Do you think he would try to extort you, or release them for revenge?"

"No. He's not like that. I broke up with him because he was cheating on me. He lives with… with that hussy now. So no, I don't see why he would use them against me." She made a point of looking Hakeem in the eye. How could she make him understand? This sort of thing wasn't her. It was completely out of character, a moment of weakness. She'd been working long hours on the White campaign and feared she was losing him. Her fears had been confirmed.

"Hakeem, that's the only time I've allowed myself to do something so stupid. I will never make that mistake again."

"I believe you," he replied, with a smile designed to signal compassion. "And on the grand scheme of things, it's not that bad. Trust me, I've heard much, much worse." He glanced down at his wristwatch and stood up from the table. "Sorry, time's up. Let's touch base in a few weeks." He pulled a card from his wallet and handed it to Megan. "I recommend giving her a call."

Megan took the card and read it: SYLVIA RICARDO, STYLIST. Her eyebrows furrowed. "What's this for?"

Towering over her, Hakeem raised an eyebrow and waved a hand along the length of her body, from her cream silk blouse down to her knee-high leather boots. "You want to be taken seriously? Start channeling Senator Murkowski, not Sarah Palin." He winked. "Oh, and a word of advice. Make sure your family is on board. No more soliciting police officers for sex."

As he turned to go, Megan picked up the business card. It felt heavy with its own importance. She slowly traced the gold cursive letters. Then, with a flick of the wrist, she tossed the card onto the table next to her crumpled, salsa-soiled napkin. She knew how this worked. A little change here, a little change there, and if she wasn't careful, her essence would be stripped away. She would be unrecognizable, even to herself—just a shell to hold everyone else's agenda.

Anyway, she liked wearing silk blouses. They felt luxurious, and they sent a particular message: that she could afford dry cleaning. Plus, she didn't need to be told how to dress or reminded not to do anything risqué. One thing was for sure: Never again was she going to risk her career for love.

Chapter Seven

———————— ✪ ————————

GUESS WHO'S COMING TO SUPPER

It was Saturday night, and Megan was hiding in her bedroom. She wished, not for the first time since she'd returned to D.C., that she was more outgoing and social. Why did she have to be so serious? Last weekend, some of the staff had invited her to come out for drinks, and her automatic reaction had been to politely decline. They hadn't asked again, and Megan was kicking herself now.

She couldn't avoid Andrew the whole weekend long, but she couldn't exactly be around him either. Ever since he'd found out she was a Republican, things had gotten awkward. Even a little hostile.

For one thing, he was obsessed with watching the news. He turned it on first thing when he got home and didn't turn it off until bedtime. Whether he was always like this or just since the election, she couldn't say for sure. But there was only so much MSNBC-hyped liberal hysteria she could handle, and she had reached that threshold.

Even in her bedroom she couldn't escape him. A few days earlier, as she'd been arranging her new bedroom set, she had heard him through the uninsulated wall separating their rooms, talking on the phone, cataloguing a litany of so-called offenses committed by the Republican Party over the years. She didn't know whom to feel sorry for: herself or the person he was boring on the other end of the phone. She tried to tune it out, but his anger reverberated right through the darn wall.

We're not in Kansas anymore, Megan thought glumly. It used to be you could at least have a conversation with someone who didn't share the same beliefs, and you would agree to disagree. Then again, she'd been living in Florida for the past ten years. Maybe she was a little too used to having conversations with people who were just varying shades of Republican.

The upside to having no social life and hating your roommate was that there was nothing to distract her from her planning her campaign. She might not be the wealthiest candidate, but she would be the most prepared. Mike had once called her a Republican Leslie Knope. Megan had watched *Parks and Recreation* a few times and was inclined to agree. *Finally!* she had thought. *Someone who understands the joy of binders and public service!*

Megan reached for the binder on her desk labeled *Take-Out Menus.* She flipped through the plastic sheets containing various menus, arranged alphabetically and by continent. A picture of spring rolls, pad Thai, and green curry caught her eye, and her salivary glands watered on cue. *Bingo.* She was just about to dial the number for Bangkok Express when she heard a knock at the door.

Hmm. What does he want? She opened the bedroom door to find Andrew wearing a grave expression, as though he'd come to confess that he ran over her dog. As she looked into his blue eyes, her heart started pounding in her chest. A familiar rush of adrenaline flooded her limbs as though she were approaching the final sprint. Was it fight, flight, or something else?

"Yes?" She fought the urge to close the door in his face. Instead she stepped out into the hall and closed it behind her. Her bedroom was *her* sanctuary, and he most certainly was not welcome. And (if she were being honest) the thought of him in her bedroom unnerved her. She didn't need reminding that it had been a while. Her body would probably respond to any man wearing cologne, or at least not stinking of body odor. Standing in her doorway, they were nearly the same height; their eyes and lips matched up almost perfectly. The things they could do, alone in the dark… She shivered. That she could be so primal repulsed her.

"Do you want to eat supper with Emily and me?" he asked, not meeting her eyes.

Emily was coming over. She'd forgotten. Would it be rude not to join them? Megan hesitated. It would be nice to see her old acquaintance, though she wished Emily had mentioned her brother was a hardcore liberal. Then again, it had been a while. Emily must have forgotten Megan was a Republican.

"If you think we can maintain a civil conversation for more than two minutes, then yes, I would be glad to join you guys."

He placed one hand mockingly over his heart and held the other high. "No politics at the dinner table. I promise."

For an instant, seeing that mischievous grin on his face, Megan could picture him swearing a Cub Scout oath. He was probably the type of kid she'd always hated: smart and charming, a troublemaker who knew when to push the envelope and when to back off. The kid who, of course, was never held accountable for his actions.

"Fine. I'll do it for your sister." Then she indulged herself by closing the door in his face after all.

Changing from her sweatpants into a pair of skinny jeans and a collarless striped oxford, partially tucked in, Megan reflected on the great myth that women dress for men. The reality was, women dressed for women. If women did dress exclusively for men, they'd all be wearing red evening gowns with their cleavage spilling out. The image made her laugh: women shopping or going to tailgating parties in long, sequined dresses. Who said she didn't have a sense of humor? *Well, most people,* she thought. *But screw them.*

Just for fun, she decided to leave the top three buttons of her shirt undone. Maybe it would distract Andrew from his liberal ranting and raving. *Just for fun,* she reassured herself. Then she ran a brush through her hair and put on some lip gloss just in time. The doorbell was ringing.

In the living room, Emily bypassed Andrew's outstretched arms and headed straight for Megan. After they embraced, Megan stepped back to admire her friend's appearance. Emily's long, straight chestnut hair was now shoulder-length, with a sprinkling of silver highlights. But it didn't make her look old. Megan recalled that she was in the presence of wealth and felt a familiar pang of envy. Of course Emily would age stylishly.

At the thought, guilt overtook her. Emily was always so nice and so... real. With Emily, what you saw was what you got.

"You look great, Megan!" she said now. "Haven't changed a bit."

"And you look amazing, as always," Megan replied, reaching out a hand to touch the white cashmere. How could anything be that soft? "I love your sweater."

Emily laughed. "I should give it to you! I still owe you one. Remember when I borrowed that sweater dress of yours for some big date?"

Megan remembered. Emily had tried to return the dress in the middle of the night, when Heather was staying at her boyfriend's place. "And I didn't hear you throwing rocks at the window—"

"Because you always wore ear plugs! Then I climbed up the tree and banged on the window—"

"And scared the living shit out of me!"

Emily chuckled. "I still feel bad about it."

Megan shook her head. "The things you did for love. I never could get the sap off that sweater."

"What can I say? Some girls spend their college years drunk on cheap wine. I was always drunk on love." Emily flashed a grin that made the sibling resemblance suddenly quite obvious.

Andrew cleared his throat loudly.

Emily gave her brother a big smacking kiss on the cheek. "I brought some microbrews and a bottle of wine. What are you in the mood for?"

"I'll take a beer," Andrew and Megan said in unison.

Emily smiled, showing her perfect white teeth. "I'm glad to see you two getting along so well!" She returned to the front hall, picked up a six-pack and a bottle of wine off the floor, and carried them into the kitchen.

Megan and Andrew shot each other an incredulous look.

If you only knew how much of a jerk he is to me, Megan thought.

"I'm going to check on supper," Andrew scowled, his facial expression reminding Megan of a toddler on the verge of tears or a tantrum.

Emily reemerged from the kitchen and handed Megan a beer. They looped arms.

"Let me give you a tour first." Megan grinned. "It should take a whole minute." Her eyes widened at the sight of Emily's ring finger: a bright sapphire-and-diamond engagement ring sitting snug against a platinum wedding band. "You're married? Congratulations!"

"Yes." Emily beamed "His name is David. We met in grad school."

"Any kids?"

Emily's face fell momentarily, and Megan realized her mistake. But her old acquaintance quickly recovered. "No, not yet."

When they came back to the living room, Andrew had already set the coffee table for supper. "Sorry, Em, but we don't have enough chairs to eat at the island." He motioned to the cushions on the floor.

"I don't mind at all. The apartment looks amazing. I didn't know what to expect. You should have heard how Mom described the place."

"Let me guess. One step up from a homeless shelter?" he offered with a satisfied grin.

"Close. More like you'd moved into a housing project."

Andrew shook his head. "God, she can be such a snob. That's why I didn't want her to come along. But you know how she is! Once she gets an idea in her head, there's no stopping her."

Emily nodded sympathetically.

"Actually, I can't take any credit for how the apartment looks. It was all Megan. She did a great job."

Megan was in mild shock. For a brief second, Andrew made eye contact with her. Did he just say something nice? And completely true, she might add.

On a modest budget she had managed to make the place feel not only put together but inviting — somewhere you'd want to hang out with friends or spend a quiet evening reading. The living room had become soothing and cozy, thanks to a dark gray couch, a birch chair with deep blue fabric, matching nesting tables and bookcase, a Persian rug (a gift from Andrew's mother), floor-length ice blue drapes, and a couple of accent lights.

Megan was pleasantly surprised by how well the evening was going so far. Andrew had prepared a large, steaming bowl of thick noodles covered in a thick, hearty ragu, and they ate family style, sitting on the floor, passing dishes back and forth, tearing hunks of good Italian bread, and drinking earthy Italian red wine. Once, as Megan and Andrew reached for the salad at the same time, their hands touched briefly. They exchanged timid smiles and then quickly looked away. Their conversation was light and superficial, but enjoyable. Like butterflies, they fluttered from topic to topic — books, travel, the latest Smithsonian exhibit — in no hurry to get anywhere. *Wow, we actually managed to have a civilized supper!* Megan thought when it was over. *Maybe this will be our chance to start over.*

Her hopes were quickly dashed when Andrew made a wisecrack about working in government, and then things started to unravel. Emily had simply asked how working in Congressman White's office was going, and Andrew couldn't seem to help himself from interrupting.

"Why would anyone want to work in the political system? It's ineffective. Broken. Corrupt. Megan, can you shed some light on this for me?" Andrew sneered.

She stared at him, defiant. Why did he have to be so rude? All the comfort of those delicious carbs suddenly settled heavy and dense in her stomach. "Maybe some people want to make the world a better place. Maybe some people think that to be involved in a democracy, you need to do more than just share a post on Facebook. Or smoke pot and give long-winded soliloquies. You actually need to get up off your duff and *do* something."

Andrew snorted. "Oh, I don't deny that you are 'doing something.' The world is a much better place now, for billionaires and corporations at least. Thank you *so much* for looking out for them." He clapped his hands.

Emily glanced from Megan to Andrew like a referee ready to make a call. "I think we need both, don't you agree? We need good people working in government and good people working as activists from the outside."

"That might be true. But in my experience, there's no such thing as a good Republican."

Megan knew he was baiting her. Her cheeks flushed red, but she didn't bite. "I'm going to clean up and turn in for the night," she said, standing to collect the empty plates. Her heart was racing, but she'd be damned if she was going to let him know he'd gotten under her skin.

Emily narrowed her eyes at Andrew and begged Megan to stay.

Megan leaned down and hugged Emily. "I have an early morning tomorrow. So nice seeing you again."

"But tomorrow's Sunday," Emily protested.

"And I have research to do. But this was nice, Emily. Let's go out for drinks sometime." Megan moved toward the kitchen.

"It's just a discussion, Megan!" Andrew yelled after her. "You don't need to be offended every time someone voices their opinion!"

She hurried away, hoping the faucet running over the dishes would drown out the sound of his voice, and willed her heart to stop racing.

Andrew stared after Megan as she left the room. What on earth had possessed him to act like he was in junior high? It was sixth-grade math class all over again, and he was tugging the pigtails of Lisa Gibson, seated in front of him. Any second, Megan would whip around and tell him to drop dead, just as Lisa had done, and Andrew's heart would flutter simply because she acknowledged him!

Without even turning his head, he could tell his sister was frowning. He braced himself for what was coming next.

"What was that all about?" she hissed. "I'm guessing you're still not getting along, then?"

Andrew sighed. "Things are little tense, I'll admit. But look, it's not my fault she doesn't want to have a conversation. What did I say that was so offensive anyway?"

"Andrew—"

He held up a hand to stop her with her mouth frozen half open. "Emily, I'm sorry, but I don't want to talk about Megan." Just saying her name aloud made his stomach hollow out with... something. Was it guilt? All he knew was, when he was in the same room with her, he felt a mix of repulsion and attraction. But then he remembered that she, and people like her, had helped usher in the president-elect and this horrible new era in American history.

"OK, fine," his sister replied. "What about we talk about Naomi instead."

"Can we not talk about women at all?" he pleaded.

"Andrew, something's obviously going on with you. Are you on edge because of the election? Or is it because you and Naomi broke up?" She said it gently, but still. "I can't help you if I don't know what's wrong."

Andrew's patience was slipping away. "Maybe I don't want your analysis. Not everything needs to be broken down and rehashed a thousand times! Besides, Naomi is in the past."

"But you must want some sort of closure! It was your longest relationship, and then it just suddenly... wasn't. You must want to talk about it?"

Andrew sucked in a breath. If he didn't tell her, she would keep hounding him about it. And she definitely had the stamina to wait it out. With Emily, it was never of matter of *if*, but of *when*.

"Fine," he said, resigned. "But let's get dessert first." He went into the kitchen and returned with a warm-from-the-oven pecan pie and two forks. He handed one to Emily.

She accepted the fork suspiciously.

"It's just the two of us. No need to be proper here." He began digging into the pie and carefully chewed a mouthful, savoring it. "When I got this job offer, I didn't so much *ask* Naomi what she thought about me taking the job. I kind of just *told* her I was taking the job." His face looked pained. "This whole thing makes me sound like a total jerk."

His sister looked him straight in the eye. "You are not a jerk, OK? You are the most generous, caring person I know."

Andrew looked at her, unconvinced. "She started making arrangements to come here with me, but then she kept dropping hints about marriage or engagements into our conversations. I think she thought she was being casual about it."

"What do you mean?"

"Well, she would criticize other people's wedding venues or colors or gowns. Say how tacky and over-the-top they were, or how lame and outdated, and how when *she* gets married, it will be classy and tasteful and modern and —"

"Andrew, that doesn't sound so —"

"Then I started finding bridal magazines around the house. Believe me, Em. I got the message loud and clear. She wanted to get engaged."

Emily cocked her head to one side. "And you didn't propose?"

He should have felt bad about hurting Naomi — leading her on, he supposed. But at the time, all he kept hearing a tiny voice in his head: *Don't do it.*

"No. I couldn't do it. Finally, a few weeks before we were supposed to move, she just walked into the living room and said she couldn't wait any longer. Said I either had to propose or we would break up. We broke up."

"Sounds like you didn't really want her to come with you."

"It's not that I didn't want her to come with me. I just didn't want to marry her. We were comfortable. I liked talking to her and cooking for her. But to be honest, I'd been having some doubts about us for a long time. She just wasn't... you know. The One."

Emily frowned and put her fork down. "Really? Last time I saw you together, you guys seemed so happy."

"The last time you saw us was over six months ago. We were

happy. But then I found out... well, something that kind of changed how I saw her."

"Like... ?"

How does she do it? he wondered, taking another bit of pie. How did Emily always coax the information out of him, like feeding a baby, one spoonful at a time? He sighed. "She's a fake and a liar."

"In what way?"

"OK, so get this. We were sitting in a bar in SoHo, and this super buff CrossFit guy comes up and gives her a great, big hug. Then he says, 'Where have you been? Haven't seen you at the club in forever. And we miss your homemade beef jerky! It was the best.' She turned beet red. I asked her what it was about, considering she's supposedly a hardcore vegan and always made fun of CrossFit people. She used to say they were a cult of meatheads."

"I can see how that must have seemed a little weird. So you confronted her? What did she say?"

"She said something about dating a CrossFit guy a long time ago. Which she'd never happened to mention before. And get this — she used to do CrossFit, too. And eat meat!"

Emily nodded sympathetically. She lifted the bottle of wine off the table and offered Andrew a refill, pouring it before he could respond.

"But then we met, and a few months later she quit her corporate job. Said it was soul sucking, and she wanted to be an urban gardener. Wanted to live a life with purpose and connection. So we did yoga together, and joined the Park Slope co-op. And she had *me* eating vegan. Even though I love meat!"

"Sounds like she just wanted to impress you." Emily offered.

"It was worse than that. She didn't just want to impress me. She wanted to change herself to be someone I'd like." He shook his head. "And I did like her! But it was all bullshit! It was all manufactured and tailored to my tastes, based off what I told her about myself. And then I find out she's done it with all the guys she's dated. I kept asking myself, who is she really?"

"It sounds like you feel deceived." Emily empathized.

"That's it exactly. I mean, if she can't be herself with me, what kind of foundation is that for a relationship?"

"Did you love her?"

He shrugged. "I really liked her, you know? I thought I loved her. But after I found out all that stuff, it totally changed how I felt. I should have broken up with her right then, instead of dragging it on."

"That's too bad. I'm sorry."

"Yeah. I just want to find someone to honest and real with me. But not only that. I want her to be passionate about something. I don't want someone who fakes it because she thinks that's what I want."

"You just want someone who will save the world with you," Emily teased.

Andrew had to laugh a little. "Maybe I've set the bar a little high"

"You probably don't want to hear this right now, little brother, but no one's perfect. Take you, for example. You have many good qualities, but forgiveness is not one of them." She playfully nudged him.

But Andrew didn't smile. "Why should I forgive her? Why should I put up with being lied to?" He muttered into his wine glass and then took a big sip. "Is it too much to expect honesty these days?"

The truth was, Andrew didn't feel at all sad about his relationship with Naomi. Indeed, he couldn't help feeling that he had dodged a bullet. That maybe the universe had other plans for him.

Chapter Eight

✪

THE WIDOWER

Checking out her reflection in the mirror, Megan saw excitement and nausea arguing for supremacy. *I look good enough for a blind date. Don't I?*

She hadn't been sure what to wear. Was this a date, or an interview? Both, she decided in the end. She chose her A-line black dress, which hit right above the knee and struck the right note: It didn't scream *desperate*, and the cleavage was safely hidden away, but it also gave the impression that she had made an effort.

She had still been planning to get out of these embarrassing blind dates somehow, until she'd noticed Carmela was engaged. Something about that big, sparkly ring and the smug grin on Carmela's face had prompted her to reevaluate. Maybe it wasn't such a bad idea to find a partner, someone who would support her career ambitions. And to help her decide on a suitable suitor, she would rate her date based on four criteria: personality, compatibility, connections and wealth, and presentation. After all, she wasn't looking for love. Not that she had anything against love, per se. It was the after part, the loss of love — the pain, the rejection — that she couldn't handle. But she was going to be pragmatic this time.

When the doorbell rang, Megan put the cover on her lipstick and strode with purpose through the living room, eager for a first glimpse of her prospective trophy husband. But Andrew stood blocking the door, and seemed to be chatting politely with her date. When she cleared her throat, he turned to her with a smirk pasted on his face. He stepped aside, and in the doorway stood Megan's date, whose shock-white hair and thick black-rimmed glasses clearly qualified him for AARP.

Oh, hell no! Megan couldn't help but cringe at the thought of sitting across a table from a man who could be her grandfather. Nothing screamed desperation like a young woman dating an old guy. This was who Congressman White had in mind for her?

The older man smiled pleasantly and looked around the room. "Howdy! I'm Bob," he said in a Texan drawl. "Nice place you got here. I've never been to this part of town."

Megan took a deep breath and stuck her hand out, hoping it would answer any question in his mind. *Definitely not a date.*

Fake smile firmly in place, she chirped, "Pleasure to meet you, Bob. I'm Megan. This is my roommate, Andrew. Shall we go?"

When she passed Andrew in the doorway, he whispered, "Want me to pick up some Viagra for you? In case the date goes well?" He was standing too close. It made her jittery.

"I'm sure he's got some on him already," she retorted through closed teeth.

"Pardon?" Bob turned around slowly. "You'll have to speak up, my dear. The hearing's no good in my right ear."

At the restaurant, a slightly upscale version of Olive Garden, the waiter plopped down two menus and glasses of water. Without even waiting for them to open their menus, he asked for their drink order. Megan wondered why he was rushing them. The restaurant was practically empty! Then she heard cheers coming from the kitchen. Was there a game on TV? Whatever the case, it was clearly more exciting than waiting on customers.

"Nothing for me, thanks," Bob replied with a wave of his wrinkled hand. "I'm on too many medications."

"Dark and Stormy, please," Megan implored with a serious look. When the waiter turned to leave, she snaked out a hand and grabbed his arm. Pulling him to her, she whispered solemnly, "Make it *very* strong. And if you see my glass is empty, get me another one."

Over the course of a mediocre dinner, Bob recounted his life story.

"My wife, Marian, passed away two years ago, God rest her soul. We were together for fifty-five years. Three children, nine beautiful grandkids. Want to see them?" He didn't wait for Megan's reply before rummaging through his wallet, but pulled out a stack of photos and handed them to her one at a time.

Megan politely scrutinized the family portraits and awkward school photos. She empathized with his grandkids, in the throes of their most awkward years: teeth too big for their face, ears too big for their head. Not to mention the acne, the braces, the haircuts!

"Very nice," she said.

"You know, I worked in the House of Representatives for forty-two years. I retired after Marian passed. Just couldn't get myself motivated, you know? But boy, oh boy, did we have some good times. Did I tell you I was good friends with Reagan? Went to his Christmas parties and all that. Marian would make her famous Texas chili and cornbread, and we would wear matching Christmas sweaters... So much fun..." Bob's eyes misted, and he looked off into the distance. "What were we talking about again?"

"President Reagan? Congressman White?"

"Oh, yes, that's right. Clayton tells me you want to make a run for his seat?" He lowered his voice and leaned closer. "Are you sure a young, pretty lady like you wants to get into the snake pit? Them boys can be pretty mean. It might get rough."

Megan stiffened. "Yes, I know what I am getting myself into." Then she remembered to soften her tone and let him down gently. "But I just want to be upfront with you, Bob. There is no way I am going to marry you."

Bob guffawed, nearly tipping over his glass of water. "What in heaven's name are you talking about? Honey, I'm not looking to marry you."

Now it was Megan's turn to be confused. "Didn't the congressman tell you about our plan? He's trying to find me a Republican husband."

"Nobody told me anything about that!" He shook his head and chuckled as if had Megan made the most hilarious joke in the world. "Every now and then I like to take a lady out to dinner. It gets me out of the house and helps me take my mind off my Marian. Now, I can tell by the way you're looking at me, you're asking why on earth a young woman would go out with an old fart like me? I suppose some of them want to be introduced to donors or politicians. But mostly they come for the free dinner." He winked.

"Oh. Well." Megan's cheeks flushed. "I'm sorry, Bob. I don't know what to say."

The elderly gentleman reached out and placed a hand on top of hers. "You're a beauty, Megan. Trust me, you'll have no trouble bagging a nice, handsome, rich Republican, if that's what you want. But this ol' man said good-bye to the love of his life already, and he's not looking to ever replace her memory."

At another point in her life, Megan might have found this story more endearing, but right now it was more annoying than anything. What a waste of her time! She started involuntarily running down the list of work she still had to do to get ready for her campaign. She didn't have time to be dating old lonely widowers! She lifted the napkin from her lap and started fumbling for an excuse to leave.

"How about we order some dessert? They have the most delicious cheesecake here." Bob smiled at her—a peace offering. "C'mon, honey, there's nothing a little sugar can't fix. If you'd like, I can give you a little history lesson about the Republican Party. Might be important for you to understand how we got to where we are today."

Megan hesitated. She did have a sweet tooth. And there was no point in skipping dessert. Bob had said it himself: A free meal was a free meal.

He was right about the cheesecake, too. While Megan savored each creamy, tangy morsel, her "date" transformed into a history professor. "It comes as no shock to you that many older Republicans have happily remained the Party of Reagan, our hero who was elected thirty-seven years ago. Long before you were born, I expect."

Megan lifted her chin in defiance. "I was two."

Bob chuckled again. "Same thing. No one under the age of fifty-five was old enough to vote for Ronald Reagan that first time. We know how to appeal to older voters now. But on the whole, we are very out of touch with younger voters like yourself. Part of the problem is that the party's not good enough in connecting the dots to show how our policies are the best ones to improve the lives of American people. That's why I'm glad White is grooming you to replace him. This sort of thing will be good for the party."

Megan's couldn't contain her grin. The former congressman had just confirmed her instincts. "Want to know a secret? I've already thought of my campaign slogan."

"Is that right? Please, share it."

"New Leadership, Old Values."

He nodded in approval. "I like it. Actually, I love it. Very clever."

"I know it's a risk in this political climate, but I'm a moderate Republican. I think we need to take the best parts of conservatism and blend them with a new vision for the future. We need to stop being the party that alienates gays and minorities. We are losing the millennial votes and showing how out of touch we are with the population." Megan could feel her enthusiasm shining through her words. "I'll be honest with you. My brother is gay, and my first instinct as a politician is hide him in the closet. But that's ridiculous! I love him. I have nothing to be ashamed of, and he has nothing to be ashamed of. And I don't want to dance around the subject and pivot anytime someone asks me about gay rights."

Bob scooped up the last bite of cheesecake from his plate and wiped his mouth with the cloth napkin. "I agree. But you have to tread a fine line. I consider myself a church-going, God-fearing man, and to me, when it comes to what people do in their bedrooms, I honestly don't care. But the people who *do* care are very politically active. They are a force to be reckoned with."

He sighed and put the napkin on the table. "I commend you for taking on this challenge, though. I've been around a long time now, and I've watched with my own eyes as the parties have become increasingly polarized. We've lost regular order. There's no more deliberation in the law-making process. Instead what we have is extreme partisanship, the culture of corruption. And what I find most concerning is the loss of patriotism—I mean *true* patriotism. We can't say that only half the country is patriotic and the other half is the enemy. That's downright wrong, and it's dangerous."

Megan nodded sympathetically. "What was it like working in Congress under Obama?"

"One word: ugly. We weren't governing. It was nothing but strategy—a strategy of opposing every one of Obama's initiatives. And don't get me started on the debt ceiling crisis. A few years after I finished up in the House, they threatened a government shutdown and public default. Remember? The country's credit was downgraded. Appalling, the lengths they went to! I almost came out of retirement, I was so mad at those people. How dare they call themselves public servants! The public stopped trusting the government to work for them, to solve the serious problems facing the country. People were pessimistic about the future, and one of the few issues voters were united on was the belief that politics and governance were utterly dysfunctional. We got what we got now because we haven't been doing our job." He shook his head and dropped his voice to a whisper. It was dangerous now for Republicans to be vocal in their unflattering opinions of their leader. "Trump is on us."

In front of her apartment building two hours later, Megan thanked Bob for the date. In spite of the awkward situation, she had enjoyed spending time with him. It was refreshing to talk with someone who felt the same way she did about the state of politics. He reminded her of Congressman White, with whom she had spent many hours while on the campaign trail, mulling over many of the same things.

"Thank you for indulging an old man," Bob said with a slow smile as he escorted her to the front doors. "Let me know if you need any help with your campaign. I'll gladly introduce you to some wealthy donors."

"I won't say no to that, Bob. And thank you again for a lovely evening." Megan returned the smile. "Let me know if you change your mind about remarrying."

"You'll be the first lady I call," he replied, with a slight bow.

ndrew stretched out on the couch with a pint of Cherry Garcia, trying to lose himself in an episode of SNL. Alec Baldwin was doing his comical, all-too-real bit as Trump again, but all Andrew could think about was Megan on a date with an older man. No, not an older man. An *old* man. What the hell was that all about? He found it disturbing, but couldn't quite say why.

It's none of my business who she dates, he reminded himself. She was a Republican, no different from anyone on *Fox and Friends*. A hot young blonde paired up with a wrinkled white dude. He kept checking his phone, unconsciously tracking the time. How long was this date going to last anyway?

When she finally got home, he had to stop himself from jumping off the couch. Without meaning to, he had waited up for her, and now he was about to interrogate her like an anxious father or a spurned lover.

Without saying anything, Megan walked straight into the kitchen and grabbed a glass from the cupboard.

"How was your date?" Andrew called out from the living room. He tried to sound casual, but his tone had a sarcastic edge.

She turned her back to him and put the glass under the ice dispenser. He heard the clang of ice hitting her glass, then the gurgling of water.

He lay motionless on the couch. Was she ignoring him now? She hadn't forgiven him for the way he behaved when Emily came for supper. In fact, she'd done her best to avoid him over the past few weeks, and when they did cross paths, she gave him nothing but one-word responses, like she just couldn't wait to get away.

She brushed past the couch and stopped, looking him right in the eye without a hint of expression. "Great." She took a sip of her ice water and held his gaze.

A cold chill ran down the length of his spine. How had they gotten to this point? Ever since she'd found out he was a Democrat, she had all but ignored him. He kept wishing they could go back to the first day they'd met. But their relationship had taken a different trajectory, and it seemed he was helpless to stop it.

★ ★ ★

It was the Friday before Christmas—time to head home for the holidays.

Andrew grabbed his overnight bag off his bed and headed for the living room. The apartment had been particularly quiet since Megan had left for Florida that morning. Not that she ever made much noise, but he noticed her absence. No annoying alarm clock at 5 a.m. No Fox News rousing him from sleep. No signature Herbal Essence shampoo smell in the shower.

There was no denying that things had become tense in the apartment. The whole situation most certainly hadn't turned out the way he'd imagined. Why the hell had he agreed to have a roommate in the first place? He was too old for this shit.

He hadn't even intended to look for someone after Naomi left, but his sister had reached out with the news about an old friend in need, and he had agreed. *Maybe I'm afraid to be alone?* Andrew wondered, before shaking the thought from his head. In the past ten years, he'd been single for a combined total of less than twelve months. Being a player, picking up random girls at the bar—it had never appealed to him. He couldn't help it. He was just a hopeless romantic.

He set his bag down in the living room and glanced at the clock in the kitchen. Emily would be arriving soon, and he had to pack the refrigerated lunch he'd prepared for them the night before. As he walked toward the kitchen, he noticed something odd on the counter: a small red box wrapped in shiny paper, with a silver bow on top. Curious, he flipped open the card:

Andrew,
A signed piece of history for you. Merry Christmas.
Megan

For a moment, he felt guilty. Why hadn't he bought her a gift? But then again, if she hated him so much, why had she bought him one in the first place? He was baffled—and just a tad hopeful.

He unwrapped the present and opened the box. Removing the white tissue paper, he discovered a red baseball cap embroidered with the words MAKE AMERICA GREAT AGAIN. On the back of the hat, under the buckle, was Trump's signature.

Cute. What was she trying to do? Pour salt on his wounds? He opened the foyer closet and shoved the hat to the back of the top shelf.

History, she'd written. Well, there was no doubt in his mind that history would not be kind to this president. He thought of a joke he'd once heard: that George W. Bush was counting down the days until he was no longer the worst American president of all time. Oh, how the tides had turned! Every Democrat Andrew knew was thinking wistfully of President Bush now.

Andrew chuckled softly. Laughter was keeping him afloat these days, the only thing that made him feel normal or sane anymore. If he couldn't laugh, he would cry. Or resort to angry outbursts. It was all so tiring.

When a soft knock came from the front door, he checked the clock again: 8 a.m. on the dot. *Right on time, as usual.* Punctuality was one of the many traits he admired in his sister. If Emily said she would do something, she kept her word. She was trustworthy, steady as a rock. Her role as family peacemaker had prepared her well for a career as a corporate mediator. She had honed her skills in effective listening, negotiating, and human psychology at their family dinner table.

Because the Croswell family excelled in WASP-speak, a language Andrew still didn't understand, Emily would translate for him. According to her, when their dad said, "You should find a real career," what he really meant was "I love you, and I just want you to be secure." But Andrew still couldn't grasp how she interpreted "3.8 GPA? Hope McDonald's is hiring" to mean "Good job! I'm proud of you."

He swung the picnic basket from the countertop, grabbed his bag from the floor, and followed his sister out of the apartment.

"What's in the basket this time?" Emily asked as he tossed his bag in the trunk.

Andrew cleared his throat and recited the menu like a trained waiter. "Today, we have a special treat: the chef's famous homemade pesto, roasted vegetable and goat cheese wraps, crudités, and for dessert, the chef decided to go retro and make chocolate oatmeal no-bake cookies." Andrew listed off the menu as they stepped into the elevator.

"Food snob." Emily sneered, although she rubbed her hands gleefully. "I do love our road trip meals!"

"I am not a food snob!" he said indignantly. "I have a legitimate allergy to mediocre food. It gives me indigestion. And road rage." He smiled, placing the basket in the backseat, within reach. "Where's the hubby?"

"David had to fly to Atlanta yesterday for work. He'll be coming in later tonight."

They walked toward Emily's powder blue BMW illegally parked with her hazard lights on. Once settled into the front seat, Emily turned to her brother, her expression grave. "We have a decision to make. What are we listening to?"

Andrew held up his iPhone. "I made us a road trip playlist. A little seventies rock, a little nineties alternative. It'll be like old times, when we drove around just the two of us, looking at colleges."

Emily grinned and started the car. "Those were the days."

"I'm glad someone was willing to do it. Mom was only interested in touring the Ivy Leagues. And Dad couldn't be bothered."

She rolled her eyes. "Dad was busy with work, Andrew. You should cut him some slack. And Mom meant well. She just wanted us to get the quality education she got. And to her, that meant Ivy League."

"It's not like she ever used her degree," he muttered.

Emily shot him a disapproving look. "She's used it in plenty of ways. She just never gets paid for what she does."

Andrew didn't respond right away. "And I had to go and piss everyone off by going to a SUNY school instead of Yale. And Dad threatened not to pay for it! Even though it was so much cheaper." He shook his head, still in disbelief all those years later.

"Well, I'm glad you went to the school that was right for you. But sometimes I wonder… Seems almost like you chose SUNY not because you wanted to go there, but because our parents *didn't* want you to."

He turned his head and looked out the window, just in time to see them pass underneath the ornate Chinatown arches. It was the age-old argument, with them but with himself, too. He'd never asked to be born wealthy. Was he grateful for his pampered upbringing? Sure. Did he feel the urge to please his parents? Of course. But his conscience wouldn't allow it. He was going to earn his wealth—either honorably, or not at all.

Chapter Nine

✪

CHRISTMAS IN NEW YORK

The Croswells were firm adherents to tradition. Christmas always took place at their country home "upstate," in Bedford. And dinner was always preceded by a few rounds of cocktails in the sitting room. His mother, Jacqueline, played bartender. She happily stood by the drink cart, crystal martini glasses lined up in a row, shaker in hand, wearing a vintage apron over her designer dress. It reminded Andrew of a little girl playing house—a rare glimpse at his mother's playful side. His father, Christopher, in the meantime, was lecturing Emily on which stocks she should be investing in, while Andrew and David had spent the past half hour talking about the best national parks for climbing.

Two of Jacqueline's famous dirty martinis later, and "the boys" (as Christopher called them) were rolling up pants legs and pulling back shirtsleeves to compare their outdoor adventure scars. Andrew had just begun unbuttoning his shirt, ready to show David a doozy of a scar that ran along his collarbone—"Got it falling off my mountain bike in Sedona!"—when Jacqueline loudly cleared her throat and shot him a warning look. In his mother's eyes, things were getting a bit rowdy, and she always stopped serving the drinks once she was satisfied everyone was sufficiently tipsy.

Her duty fulfilled, she sat down next Andrew on the couch. Her posture was perfectly erect as usual, as though she were afraid to touch the back of her $10,000 sofa. As she surveyed her audience, Andrew silently counted down: *three, two, one...*

Jacqueline commenced her monologue. "You know, the goddamn Republicans have had it out for Hillary and the Clintons for the past twenty years. I mean, how many investigations were there into Benghazi?"

Another Christmas tradition, Andrew thought with a private smile. *The skewering of the Republican Party.* The rest of the family typically sat silent, a captive audience forced to watch the same one-woman play unfold year after year. Andrew knew he should resist, but this year it was too tempting. He had to join in.

"Five," he mumbled. "I think there were five investigations."

"Seven! They spent twenty million dollars and found no goddamn evidence that Secretary Clinton did anything wrong!" Jaqueline threw her hands up in the air, spilling some of her martini on the rug, and continued with her rant. "And then that Republican congressman, I forget his name, but he has the gall to admit on Fox so-called News that the purpose of the whole Benghazi special committee was to drop Hillary's numbers in the polls!"

"McCarthy," David said helpfully, draping his arm around Emily's shoulder.

Andrew turned to stare at his sister's husband. *Guess he never got the memo either:* No audience participation.

Jacqueline stared at him, too. "What?"

"The congressman's name. He's from California. Representative McCarthy."

"Oh, right," Jacqueline grudgingly admitted, thrown off-kilter by actual dialogue. "Well, the fact that they gave any airtime to Donald Trump in the first place! I mean, he never, ever changed his position on the whole ridiculous question of whether President Obama was born in the U.S." She downed the rest of her cocktail and went to the drink cart for another.

Andrew's fists were clenched as tight as his teeth. Cocktails were the fuel to his rage, making it white hot. "It would have been political suicide for anyone else! Calling Mexicans 'rapists'? Proposing to ban Muslims? Being caught on tape saying he likes to grab women by the pussy? And it actually made him more popular! So totally messed up."

"Andrew!" his mother admonished. "The word 'pussy' does not belong in my house. Civilized people don't talk like that!"

"Oh, but it's perfectly OK to talk about politics?" muttered Christopher. Given his slumped position, it was easy to forget a person was sitting there. He looked as though someone had thrown an Italian suit over the leather wingback chair, and it had slid down along the contours of the seat. And indeed, Jacqueline did ignore his comment. But the suit moved, downing the contents of an old-fashioned scotch glass and slamming it on the black walnut side table, purposefully eschewing the coaster.

"I hate to say this, but it's clear to me now that half our country is filled with racist, bigoted, uneducated losers," Andrew declared with disgust. "And Republican politicians are so corrupt, they're willing to say whatever the poor and the middle class want to hear, even though they have nothing in common with these people or their struggles. The Republican Party is for the rich. Yet somehow these people keep voting for Republicans, even when it goes against their own best interests!"

He joined his mother in silence for a moment, allowing Emily, David, and Christopher an intermission during which to talk business, investments, foreign policy—topics completely alien to the majority of their fellow citizens—while fixing another round of drinks.

And then Act Two began. Andrew noticed that the louder he and his mother got, the quieter his father became. This continued even when they moved to the dining room for supper, and it didn't let up during dessert. Jacqueline fetched her beloved apple pie—the only time she had stepped into the kitchen throughout the entire Christmas feast—and served Christopher a slice on the Royal Crown Derby china. "Would you like some ice cream too, dear?" she asked.

"No, thank you." He sounded sullen.

"Is everything alright, dear?" Jacqueline's voice turned saccharine.

"Is there something else you'd like?"

"I'll tell you what I would like." Christopher looked at his wife, his eyes watery from who-knew-how-many glasses of aged scotch, his jaw muscles tight. "I'd like one bloody meal—just one!—without hearing about Trump this, and Trump that. The guy hasn't even taken office yet, and you all are acting like we've entered World War Three."

Jacqueline took a step back, bringing a hand to her cheek as though she'd been slapped. "I'm sorry if talking politics is not considered proper, Christopher, but it's just us. We're family, and we are all deeply affected by this. What else can we possibly talk about at a time like this?"

"We are not ALL deeply affected," he growled, hanging his head again.

Jacqueline's eyes narrowed. "Christopher, what on earth do you mean?" The silence grew louder as the seconds ticked by. "Tell me you didn't vote for that man."

Christopher didn't respond.

"Tell me you didn't vote for Trump!" she yelled.

Christopher lifted his head and looked her right in the eye. "I did." Andrew heard the hint of rebellion in his voice.

Jacqueline dropped the silver serving utensil on the snow-white tablecloth. It hit a dessert plate with a loud clang, clearing the air for the deafening silence that followed. When at last she spoke, her voice was hard. "Of all the things you could do to hurt me, you chose this! I'd rather find out you've been sleeping with your secretary then find out you voted for that megalomaniac. He is a sexual predator. He is a racist. And above all else, he is stupid!"

Christopher took a sip of his wine. "Not everything is about you, Jacqueline. I didn't do it to hurt you. To hurt any of you." He crossed his arms, giving the impression of a petulant child. "I have my reasons."

"Well, you did hurt us! And unless someone was pointing a gun to your head, I can't possibly understand why you would have voted for that man!" She reached for the closest wine bottle, a hundred-dollar Burgundy, and stepped away from the table. "Merry Christmas, everyone. I'm going to bed." She stabbed a manicured finger in her husband's direction. "And you can sleep in the spare bedroom tonight, until I decide whether I'm going to divorce you."

"You missed your calling as an actress, dear," Christopher said flatly.

The silence at the table was beyond awkward. Emily dabbed at her mouth with her linen napkin. David stared at his half-eaten pie, watching the ice cream melt into a sticky puddle. Andrew just glared at his father.

Emily got up from the table. "I'm going to check on Mom." David quickly followed, claiming he forgot to call his parents and wish them Merry Christmas.

Only father and son remained. Andrew was psyching himself up, ready to give his father a piece of his mind. But when he glanced over at Christopher, he couldn't do it. His father suddenly looked tired and much older. He was still an attractive man for his age, with a body trim from daily jogs and weekend golf outings, but Andrew could see there was a permanent sag now to his shoulders, as though he'd been carrying some burden for far too long.

Why hadn't he retired yet? Andrew thought he knew the answer. It wasn't as though the Croswell family needed more money. But his father wouldn't know what to do with himself, wouldn't know who he was supposed to be without his title or his power or his routine.

Andrew gave up on confronting his father and started to clear the table instead.

"Do you know why I voted for Trump?" came his father's weary voice.

Andrew refused to look at him. Did his father feel the need to explain, to justify himself to someone? Well, good luck with that. Andrew couldn't imagine any explanation that would be justifiable.

Christopher continued, "I was afraid Hillary would have been forced to take on Bernie Sanders–type policies. That seems to be the direction the Democrats are heading, and I don't believe in socialism. I've always been for entrepreneurship." He pushed his chair back and started collecting utensils, plates, dirty napkins.

Andrew was nearly sure it was the first time his father had ever helped clear the table. "Dad, I know you've always been an independent. But this is different. That man is truly a danger to this country. Couldn't you have just sucked it up for four years?"

His father gave a sad little chuckle. "Can't you guys just suck it up for four years? Yes, he's a little vulgar. And he's by far the least articulate president we will probably ever have. But I really don't think he'll make good on any of his crazy promises. I mean, come on, son. Building a wall along the Mexican border? Banning Muslim immigrants? Last time I heard, we still had a checks-and-balances system." He sighed. "I didn't think your mom would be so mad."

Andrew looked at him in disbelief. "Yes, you did. That's why you never told her in the first place."

"You're right," Christopher conceded. "I may be the king on Wall Street, but she's queen of the house, of the family." He tried to smile, but his facial muscles snapped back to a frown. "I knew she wasn't going to be happy, and that's why I wasn't planning on telling her. But I don't think I can handle four years of her bitching about Trump nonstop. I had to say something."

Andrew hated seeing his father this way: vulnerable, beaten, unsure. Instead of being mad, he felt an unusual rush of sympathy. In the kitchen, he turned to Christopher. "Dad, I have something to tell you that might make you feel a little better," he blurted. "My roommate is a Republican, and I think I had a crush on her... for about thirty seconds," he added quickly. It felt good to say it, to share this small, shameful secret he'd been carrying around. The enemy should never be sympathized with. No, they should be kept at a distance. Otherwise it was too dangerous.

Christopher chuckled softly again, but genuinely smiling this time. He put the plates down in the kitchen sink and placed a hand on his son's shoulder. "Andrew, I know we don't see eye to eye on a lot of things, but if I can give you one piece of advice... Listen, your mother loves you so much. More than she loves me, I sometimes think. So do yourself a favor. *Do not date a Republican.*"

The idea was repulsive. Not only that, but it was impossible. But Andrew said nothing. His father's expression was deadly serious.

"I don't care how hot she is, or how great the sex is. You and I, we can't afford to both be in the doghouse. It might literally kill your mother."

Andrew nodded solemnly. A father–son bonding moment had just taken place — one of their very few.

"I think everything will just be fine," Christopher continued quietly. "You'll see. It'll still be the same old politics. Nothing is going to change too much."

Was he talking about the Croswell family or the entire country? Andrew wasn't quite sure.

He stayed in the kitchen while his father retreated to his study. The housekeeper had Christmas off to be with her own family, and he didn't want her to return to a load of dishes. Besides, he had read somewhere that doing the dishes could be very meditative. And what Andrew needed more than anything right now was a clear head. He was still trying to process the events of this year's Christmas dinner and desperately trying not to think of his attractive Republican roommate — her sneaky smile, the one she used when she let her guard down, or when she thought no one was watching — when his father made an announcement: He had voted for Trump.

Just as he placed the last pan in the dish rack, Emily walked in with the look of a triumphant teenager. "Come with me. Take a well-earned break with us." She was holding a bottle of twenty-year-old scotch, pilfered from her father's stash.

Andrew dried his hands and followed her into the living room. He sat across from Emily and her husband with his scotch in hand and took small, half-hearted sips. For some reason, partaking in their dad's reserve cellar didn't have the same appeal as when they were younger. Maybe it was because they could legally drink, or because they had the money to buy their own bottle. Or maybe he just wanted to give his father a break this one time. After all, Christopher was a person with feelings, like anyone else. And he'd had a rough day.

Andrew stared at the fire. The only sounds in the house were the hiss and pop of burning logs, the occasional clink of ice striking the tumblers, and all the unvoiced thoughts hovering above them.

"Do you think mom will be all right? Will she forgive him?" he asked, desperate to get out of his head.

Emily's legs were draped lazily across her husband's lap. She was quiet for a moment, and Andrew knew she was looking for a way to reassure him. "I want to say yes. But honestly? I don't know."

"Well, your mediation skills are definitely going to be put to the test this time."

"Yeah." She let out a heavy sigh. "I kind of would prefer to stick with divvying up assets rather than the fate of the nation."

"Your sister is one amazing woman. I've never met a more patient, genuine, caring person." David squeezed Emily's knee with affection. "But personally, Andrew, I think this is between your parents. Let them handle it on their own."

Andrew snorted a little. On their own? Fat chance. His sister loved this — being right in the middle of the action, taking credit for the outcomes. "David, you're a great guy, but you clearly don't know my sister." He raised his glass in salute. "To Emily!"

Their glasses were nearly finished. Emily shook the bottle, gauging who was ready for a refill. David shook his head. "I don't know how you guys can drink like this," he groaned. "I'm about ready to pass out."

"Well, you have been up since five a.m., sweetie," Emily replied.

"And don't forget our Mayflower genes," Andrew inserted. "Our ancestors drank beer instead of water. We Croswells process alcohol at a superior rate."

"Well, Croswells, I can't keep my eyes open anymore." David kissed his wife goodnight and headed for the guest bedroom.

Emily started to rise from the couch.

"You're not leaving me, too, are you?" Andrew protested. His eyelids must have weighed five pounds each, but he wasn't ready to call it a night.

"No, of course not. I'm going to the kitchen to get some snacks." Emily returned balancing a plate in one hand, loaded with artisanal cheeses, olives, charcuterie, and crackers, and her laptop tucked under the other arm.

Andrew looked at her with curiosity. "What's the laptop for?"

"You." Emily had a mischievous grin on her face.

"Wait, what?"

"We're setting up your online dating profile."

"No. Please, no." Andrew's instinct was to put up a fight, but he was surprised to discover he'd reached the drunk state of happy complacency. Plus, once his sister got an idea in her head, it was impossible to talk her out of it. So why not humor her?

Emily placed her computer on her lap, flipped it open, and extended her feet onto the ottoman. Andrew, resigned to his fate, stretched out on the couch, one arm flung over his eyes like a fainting debutante. Maybe he could fall asleep right here and she'd forget this silly idea.

No such luck.

"When I found David, I used Match.com. We can start there. Unless you're done with America and want to marry a Canadian? I could set up your profile on MapleMatch.com instead..."

"No, thanks. I don't need to run away. Not yet, anyway. Why don't you choose, and you can make up a profile for me?" He knew it sounded arrogant, but wasn't online dating for the desperate? And, maybe it was corny, but he wanted to meet The One serendipitously, not algorithmically.

"It doesn't work like that, Andrew. I know you pretty well, but I don't know what you like in a woman."

He arched an eyebrow. "I like what all men like."

She looked up from the screen. "First, gross. Second, you're not a player, so don't pretend to be one. You've never — how do I put this? — you've never been a 'casual' dater."

He sighed. "That's true. I'm pretty bad at one-night stands. But it's not for lack of trying! It's just that my one-night stands usually turn into long-term relationships."

"So, what do you want in a woman?"

"I don't know. I mean, she has to be a nonsmoker. And a liberal, of course. Red hats need not apply."

"Really? You're just going to write off half the female population? Over who they voted for?"

He couldn't tell if she was serious. "Um, yes, Emily! Of course I am! How can she be The One if we don't share the same core values? No Nazi lovers for me, thanks." He laughed. "Maybe you should be setting up a profile for Dad instead of me. Maybe look up Trump Love? Or wait, I got one: Troll Mate."

Emily shot him a dirty look. "It's not a good sign when you're the only who laughs at your jokes." She typed *dating websites for liberals* into her search engine and clicked on the website LiberalHearts.com. The tagline read:

*Uniting single Democrats, progressives, and
environmental and animal rights activists who are alike in
mind and liberal in love.*

"And it boasts of being a Trump-free zone. Where liberal singles can unite and multiply." She stifled a giggle.

But Andrew found nothing funny in that. "Yup, that sounds more like it."

"OK, little brother. Let's fill out your profile." She filled in all the answers she knew: white, privileged, college-educated male from New York, seeking woman. Andrew nodded his head in confirmation of each characteristic.

"Religion?"

"None."

"OK. Multiple choice: Your politics are progressive, liberal, or very liberal?"

He thought for a moment. "Liberal."

"You most often agree with Al Franken, Al Sharpton, Bernie Sanders, Hillary Clinton, Elizabeth Warren... ?"

"Bernie Sanders."

"OK. Now list three of each of the following categories. First is personality traits."

"Hm. Easygoing. Sense of humor. Romantic."

"Favorite TV show personality?"

Jon Stewart came to mind, but Andrew thought that might make him seem outdated. "John Oliver."

"Favorite writer or artist?"

Should he go for a classic, like The Beatles or Shakespeare? In the end, he replied, "Led Zeppelin."

"Trusted media source?"

"NPR." No need to linger over that one.

Then Emily cocked her head to one side, as if appraising a piece of art. "Eyes: blue and soulful. Facial hair: manly beard. Most attractive feature: smile."

Andrew rolled his eyes. "Please. Have you seen my ass?"

She ignored him. "Nonsmoker... Light drinker... Right?"

"Light drinker in terms of the Croswells, or the rest of the population?"

"Rest of the population."

"Light to moderate. Ever since Naomi, I barely drink anymore. She kept forcing me to go on those cleanses." Another thing he didn't miss one bit.

"OK, now we have to fill out your match preferences and priorities."

"Can't you just fill that out for me?" he tried again.

She clucked her tongue. "Don't you care about shared hobbies, goals, interests? Or height, weight, hair color, et cetera? Anything besides whether they voted for Trump?"

He shrugged. "Not really."

"Well, kudos for being open-minded, in one respect anyway."

"Actually, I take that back. She has to be idealistic like me. She has to care about the environment and want to make the world a better place. And above all else, she has to be honest. I hate fake."

"Done. And submitted. Who knows? Maybe Santa will help you get laid for Christmas," Emily joked.

Andrew looked at the old mahogany grandfather clock that had been in the family for three generations and whose chimes had long since stopped working. It was just past midnight. "Not Christmas. Maybe in time for New Year's."

Emily put the laptop to the side and pushed Andrew's feet so she could sit next to him on the couch. With great effort, he sat up.

"Em, are we going to be OK?"

"The family?"

"The family? The country? What's going to happen to us?" Andrew leaned his head back, rested it against the arm of the couch, and closed his eyes. Maybe he was too much like his mother. His problem had always been that he felt things too deeply. Everything was personal.

Emily stared into the fire. "I wish I could say yes. But honestly? I just don't know."

Chapter Ten

———————— ✪ ————————

CHRISTMAS IN FLORIDA

Megan's flight landed in Orlando airport late Friday afternoon. She'd been gone for only a short time, but so much had happened in D.C. already. Her schedule had been so hectic over the past year, she'd barely been able to see her younger brother Gabe. It would be good to catch up.

Megan hadn't had anyone to confide in since she'd moved. She could count on one hand the number of people she trusted—her brother, his boyfriend Darren, her father (most of the time), and her friend Mike—and none of them lived in her new city. She felt a twinge of pain, remembering how that list once included two more people: her ex-fiancé and her ex–best friend.

She pulled her rental car into the parking lot of Bistro Jacques, one of Gabe's favorite restaurants. It was their ritual: getting together a day or two before Christmas so they could come up with that year's strategy for dealing with their father. Inside the restaurant, she spotted Gabe and his boyfriend, Darren, seated in a booth, and gave them a quick wave. When she reached the table, they both got up and flung their arms around her.

Megan laughed and hugged them tighter. "I've missed you guys!" She slid onto the bench next to her brother, noticing the new plush, deep red seating. Looking up, she saw other changes: exposed brick columns, a zinc bar, globe-style pendant lighting, modern sconces. "I love what they've done in here!"

Darren's face lit up. "They did an amazing job with the renovations. Who knew those beautiful bricks were hidden under that ugly pink stucco! And did you know they imported the bar and some of the light fixtures from an old bistro in Paris? Très chic!"

Gabe rolled his eyes good-naturedly. "Barely noticed. As long as they serve a good salad niçoise!"

"Yes, we know, honey." Darren patted Gabe's hand. "That's why *you* buy the buildings and *I* make them pretty. We're a great team."

"How convenient for you, Gabe," Megan quipped. "You found a business partner *and* a boyfriend."

"On the same day too. I hired you that morning and took you home that night!" Gabe chuckled.

Once they'd ordered, the waiter reappeared with a chilled white from the Loire Valley and generously filled their wine glasses, leaving the bottle almost empty. The threesome lifted their glasses with a light "Cheers!"

"To Megan!" the couple exclaimed, trying not to spill the contents.

"To my boys!" she responded.

"Speaking of us…" Gabe looked at Darren, eyes twinkling, and they reached across the table for each other's hands. "We have some news. We're getting married!"

It took a moment to process the words, but then Megan threw her arms around Gabe. "Oh my god! I'm so happy for you two. My baby brother is getting married!" Then she froze as a thought flashed in her head. *Shit. The election.*

"What's the matter, Megan?"

"Nothing!" she said quickly. "I'm happy for you." But Gabe had adopted his best wide-eyed, Precious Moments figurine stare. *Damn it, I can't hide anything from him.*

"Any chance you were planning on a 2019 wedding?" She was only half joking.

Gabe's blue eyes flashed to steel. "Why?"

"Um, well, it's very hush-hush, but… I have plans to run for office in 2018," she whispered.

"And what, dear sister, does that have to do with us getting married?"

"You do recall that I'm a Republican, Gabe? Imagine me trying to run for the House of Representatives, from Florida. You know, the state where pastors won't marry you, venues won't host you, and vendors won't serve you, all because you're gay?" Megan sighed. "Look, I know it's bullshit, but if my gay brother gets married, then I'll have to take a public stance on gay marriage."

"So what!" Gabe was practically yelling. "You are *for* gay marriage, aren't you?"

Megan glanced over her shoulder. "Calm down, Gabe. Of course I am, you know that! But I'd rather be evasive with my answer, like Jeb Bush. I'd rather say something like, 'We're a country of laws, and we have to respect the laws,' or some crap like that. But I can't avoid the question if you get married. They'll ask and ask and ask, and I'll have to be honest and say I support gay marriage, and…" She was digging a deeper and deeper hole, but there was no turning back now. "And that is likely to hurt me in the polls."

Darren was no longer trying to hide his annoyance. "You can't be serious, Megan."

"You know when they'll stop being anti-gay! When politicians finally take a stand and speak up!" Gabe looked at Megan pointedly. "I thought you had more of a backbone."

"I'm sorry, Gabe. You know I believe in marriage equality. I will always stand up for you. I'm just stressed. I love you guys, and I want you to be happy."

Her brother continued to glare at her. Megan felt his disapproval like a knife. Politics was a balancing act—she knew that. She would have to juggle her values, the voters' wants and needs, and her donors' priorities. But what if her values were the first ball to fall? She didn't want to dwell on that possibility. "Forgive your sister, please. I have no filter sometimes. This is happy news."

Gabe patted her arm. "You're forgiven."

"Do you have a wedding date?"

"We have a place in Sarasota booked for June," Darren answered. "Invitations are going out in the next few weeks. It will be intimate, maybe two dozen people."

"Have you told Dad yet?' she looked at Gabe with apprehension.

"Dad still isn't talking to me. Not since I told him about Darren."

The waiter arrived, carrying a plate of steak au poivre and two salad niçoises. Megan's mouth began to water. "That was two months ago. Have you called him?" she asked.

Gabe looked down. "No."

She snorted. "Well, what do you expect, then? Dad will never be the first one to call. Dad never calls, period. You know that, so don't take it personally. You need to call him and discuss it."

"What's to discuss? He doesn't like gays, and I'm gay. End of conversation." Gabe sighed, and his look was resigned. "We don't all get to have loving, accepting, non-bigoted parents like Darren's."

Darren shook his head. "I know. It's not fair, babe. But my family's used to not fitting in the neat little box." He looked at Megan. "I keep telling him to give it some time."

Megan had to agree. Her soon-to-be brother-in-law had a biracial mother and grew up in an all-white Connecticut suburb. His family had fought this battle already. "Darren's right about giving Dad a little space. Just a thought, Gabe—do you think he's mad because you're gay? Or because you've been dating Darren for three years, and he just found out?"

Gabe cut though the seared exterior of a strip of tuna, revealing the ruby red interior. "I can't do anything right when it comes to Dad."

"Nobody can. Don't worry, I'll sort this all out over Christmas dinner," Megan said with authority.

"Can't say I'm looking forward to it." Gabe muttered, stabbing his tuna.

"Nobody said it would be fun. But we're family." Megan glanced down at the fries on her plate. Normally she'd polish them off, but today her appetite was shutting down already. Stress brought her digestive system to a halt. "And family sticks together. No matter what."

She waved a thin, crispy frîte in front of her brother's face, trying to lighten the mood, and then popped it in her mouth. "Mmm, so crispy!" She dipped it in mayonnaise and chewed slowly, savoring it. "Oh, this one is even better! It's fat covered in fat."

Gabe gave her shoulder her shoulder a gentle shove. "Stop! The bride-slash-groom needs to look good for his wedding. And seriously, how do you stay so thin? You eat like crap!"

Megan shrugged. "This is the same way I've eaten for years. There's no time to cook when you're working on a campaign."

"But it looks like you've actually *lost* weight." he pouted. "I hate you! I eat healthy. I work out daily. And look at this." He pinched a thin layer of skin. "I'll never be as skinny as you. Tell me your secret!"

"Oh, it's simple. Step one, hate your roommate. Step two, be broke. Step three, run twice a day."

"You're having problems with your roommate?" Gabe asked, looking confused.

Megan immediately regretted bringing it up.

"How can you 'hate' him?" her brother continued, gesturing on the word *hate*. "He's making you look even thinner and more gorgeous."

She frowned. "Why did you just use air quotes? Is it so hard to believe I hate my roommate?"

Gabe shot her a look. "Megan, you worked with that gigantic asshole Frederic on the city council. He publicly demeaned you. Compared you to Reese Witherspoon in *Legally Blonde*. Said when you were tired of playing politics, the big boys could get back to work. And you never once said you hated *him*. So that tells me two things. Either your roommate kills kittens or"—he raised his eyebrows suggestively—"you've got a crush on him."

"What?" Megan flushed. "Absolutely not!"

"You didn't answer the question."

"I don't have a crush. And no, he doesn't kill kittens, exactly. But he's a Democrat! I'll leave it at that."

"Is he cute?" Darren asked, trying to tamp down a smile.

"No. Not my type." Her face flushed hot and red. God, she hated how her body betrayed her! She had to shut this down quickly or there would be no end to the questioning. "He's a wannabe hipster, Ivy League, liberal pain in my ass! Not anyone's type, unless you're into lumberjacks. Which I'm not."

"Ahhh, I see. A liberal libido killer," Gabe said with mock sympathy. "Yes, I can just picture it. You guys are getting it on, and then he says, 'Talk dirty to me.' And you say, 'I love coal. I want to bring back coal jobs, because it's just... so... *dirty.*'"

Megan punched her brother's shoulder. "You damn independents! Too indecisive and cowardly to decide which side you're on."

"Seriously, though. How is it, living with the enemy? I mean, a liberal, of all things?" Her brother's eyes twinkled.

"Pretty awful, actually. It was great for all of one day. Then he found out I was a Republican. Things got frosty between us pretty darn quick. And now we just ignore each other." She explained about extending an olive branch with the Christmas present. "But I haven't heard anything from him. Let's talk about something else. Just thinking about him gets me upset."

Darren perked up. "Next subject. Have you gone on any dates yet?"

Megan mulled the question over. She didn't want to tell her brother about her plan. He would probably disapprove. "Just one. I don't have time to date."

"That's an excuse and you know it. And not a very good one." Gabe's tone softened. "It's been months since you and Jason broke up. I want you to be happy."

Gabe and Darren shared a private look that said, *Like we are.*

Megan rolled her eyes. "Ugh, get a room, you two. It's bad enough you guys look like blond and brunette life-size Ken dolls, but do you also have to be so happily in love?" Her face scrunched, but her smile was still in evidence.

"Now, now. Don't be jealous. It's not like you've got bad luck in the looks department, Megs. You're a smart, less porn-starry version of Barbie."

"That should be your campaign slogan!" Darren exclaimed.

Megan laughed, relieved. "Yes, let me jot that down." She pretended to write on her napkin before crumpling it up and throwing it at his head.

"And you *will* find love again." Gabe looked at her with concern. "I know you hate men right now, and you have every right to. But don't let one heartbreak define the rest of your life."

Megan knew what Gabe was really saying: *Don't end up like Dad.* She cringed at the comparison. Her situation was different. Jason didn't die. He betrayed her.

She had allowed herself to be vulnerable and exposed, like a dog that rolls onto its back expecting a belly rub but ends up getting kicked instead. Maybe most people could make a recovery from that. But not Megan. If you counted her mother's death when she was ten, followed by her father's mental breakdown, she was already on heartbreak number three. And everyone knew the rule: three strikes and you're out.

Every time Megan's heart broke, she pictured a thicker layer of tissue forming over the surface, like a scar. Her heart had become harder to penetrate. She was done with people making her cry.

★ ★ ★

Megan spent all of Sunday preparing for Christmas dinner at her dad's place. She dropped the turkey on the floor, broke a plate, cut her finger. By noon she was so frazzled, she cracked open a bottle of beer.

Get yourself together, Megan! she scolded herself. But she couldn't help it. The thought of her father and Gabe being in the same room put her nerves on edge. Gabe had suggested it be just the three of them, a mini-reunion, to give their father a chance to warm up to the idea of having a gay son.

But Megan had insisted that Darren be there. Her father might as well get used to it now. Better to rip off the Band-Aid all at once. She had faith he would come around. Sure, he could be a miserable son of a bitch sometimes, but family was important to him. And he was never any good at extending the peace offering — only at accepting it.

Megan took a break from cooking, grabbed a pair of scissors, and went out into the yard. She cut a bouquet for the centerpiece: purple coneflowers, bright yellow ox-eye sunflowers, pale pink rain lilies, Egyptian star flowers. *So ironic,* she thought. These plants, her mother's pride and joy, had outlasted her. It wasn't fair.

Megan spotted Gabe and Darren's silver Mercedes turning onto the street. Everything was so familiar here in this indistinguishable lower-middle-class central Florida suburb: concrete block homes, bright painted colors, fertilized lawns, palm trees, orange trees, oleander, magnolia. And of course, the TRUMP/PENCE 2016 signs poking out from freshly mown grass, persistently claiming victory. Her father had chosen to plant a larger, gaudier political sign as a proud lawn statement: TRUMP THAT BITCH. In the driveway, his rusted Ford F-150 was likewise plastered with bumper stickers — not just MAKE AMERICA GREAT AGAIN but also some real classics: HILLARY FOR PRISON. LIAR LIAR PANTSUIT ON FIRE.

Gabe and Darren met Megan on the path, and together they walked toward the front door. "Are you ready?" Her voice sounded steady, but she was nervous for them.

"Yes," Gabe replied. "Is it weird that I feel like a stranger visiting the house I grew up in?"

"It's not weird. I feel the same way. And don't worry." She smiled and squeezed his hand. "Darren and I have your back."

The house was dark, with the curtains drawn, and the A/C in the living room humming loudly. Megan took the bottle of Chardonnay and the key lime pie from Darren's hands and tiptoed into the kitchen. Hesitant to face this homecoming without her as a buffer, the two men trailed her into the living room.

Paul Thompson slumped on the couch in his half-buttoned navy mechanic's shirt, his several Marine Corps tattoos peeking out from the sleeves of both arms. A silver beer can rested within arm's length on the mound that served as his coaster, heaving with every breath. Despite the air-conditioned chill, Megan saw sweat trickling down Gabe's temples.

"Hi, Dad." Gabe's voice croaked a little.

Paul kept his eyes trained on the talking head on TV and didn't move from the couch, but lifted his beer in greeting.

Gabe retreated to the kitchen, followed by Darren and Megan, as though they had poked a beehive with a stick. "What should I do?" Gabe whispered hoarsely.

"Just help me with the table. Things will be better once we're eating," Megan reassured him.

The three of them worked in silence, setting the table with a crisp, white linen tablecloth, Megan's fresh-picked floral centerpiece, and tall red candles. Megan bypassed the good china and chose the heavy brown-and-orange ceramic plates, the ones they'd used when they were kids. The Christmas plates were another painful reminder that Sandra Thompson was gone. It didn't matter that it had happened nearly a quarter-century ago. It never got any easier. Would Megan ever stop being the ten-year-old girl who'd lost her mother? Certainly her father had never recovered, never stopped being the man who lost his wife to cancer. Maybe it was the Thompson curse: You only get one love in your life.

She brushed away the thought and placed the giant, golden-brown turkey on the sideboard. Darren helped her ferry in the dishes of green beans, mashed potatoes, sweet potatoes with marshmallows, and stuffing. Gabe hid in the kitchen with his Chardonnay. Last to arrive was a gravy boat filled to the brim with a congealing beige liquid that looked terrible but tasted delicious. Megan hated cooking, but she made an exception for Christmas.

After her mom passed away and the sympathy casseroles ran out, her father's idea of a meal had been canned beans or a Spam sandwich — or, as six-year-old Gabe had called it, a Spamich. After two weeks Megan had cried uncle and taken on the duties her mother had left behind: cooking, washing, and pretty much everything else. She had learned one lesson quickly: the more elaborate the meal, the more dishes to wash. So, she became an expert in C-food—casseroles, crockpot, and cans. Her favorite dish was tuna casserole: Open up a can of tuna, add Campbell's Cream of Celery soup, toss with a box of cooked pasta, throw it in a casserole dish, top with shredded cheese, and bake. Voilà! Dinner and lunch for two days.

Megan called her father to the table and was relieved when he arrived, though she wished he would at least make eye contact. "Would you like to carve the turkey, Dad?"

Paul shook his head once and sat down, moving the wine glass aside and placing his Budweiser can in its place.

Megan reached for Darren's hand to her right, and for her father's to her left. She motioned with her head, so her dad would take Gabe's hand. Darren, already squeezing Gabe's other hand, seemed to be silently telegraphing to his fiancé: *Breathe.*

Megan led them in a prayer: "Dear heavenly Father, we thank you for your many blessings, for this food, and for family. Amen."

"Amen," echoed around the table.

They ate in silence. Gabe took a long sip of wine. "Delicious as always, Megs."

Her dad spoke at last. "Yes, very good, Megan."

Gabe cleared his throat. "How are things at the garage, Dad?"

"Great," Paul replied with bitter sarcasm. "I love workin' for another man so he can take home all the money."

"Sorry, Dad." Gabe paused. "Why don't you open up your own garage again? We can lend you the money and—"

Paul cut him off. "I don't need no handouts."

"It wouldn't be a handout, Dad. It would be a loan. I've told you that before."

Paul's eye twitched, but his expression remained passive. Megan knew there was more at work here than her father's pride. He was too afraid to go back into business for himself. The fear of bankruptcy, the dread of another failure—it was a hurdle too high for an old man to leap.

"Speaking of handouts," Paul mumbled, "we had a liberal wussy from Connecticut, come in for an oil change. Fancy foreign car. Goin' on and on about how Trump lost the popular vote, how the electoral college shouldn't give him the presidency." For a moment his face lit up. "I told him, 'Hey buddy, take a look around the room and see if anybody cares!' He shut up real quick after that. Guess he never noticed a few of the mechanics wearin' their red caps."

"Well, I don't exactly blame the guy," Megan said, relieved to be talking politics. Safer than traveling down the path of broken dreams. "Trump made a lot of crazy promises on the campaign trail, and I don't think anyone knows what to expect with him. Liberals aren't the only ones worried."

Her dad took a sip of his beer. "You know what's wrong with Republicans today? They're all RINOs. Republican in Name Only." His good humor had disappeared, like a momentary glimpse of blue sky before the clouds rolled back in.

"Are you questioning whether I'm a Republican, Dad?" Megan tried to conceal her flash of anger, but her pursed lips gave her away. "Because I'm far more Republican than Trump. He's an opportunist and a genius marketer, and that's about it."

"People wanted change, Meg," her father muttered. "And now they got it."

"People think they've elected change? They're sick of same old politics as usual? Well, they're in for a very rude wakeup call. This man has no idea how to run a country."

Paul pulled a cigarette from the pack resting in his breast pocket and fumbled for a lighter.

Megan and Gabe shouted at the same time. "Dad!"

"Oh, Jesus. Now I can't even smoke in my own damn house?" He pulled the cigarette from his mouth. "We elected Trump because he's honest. He says what most people think. We elected Trump because he's gonna drain the swamp." Paul poked at the air with his cigarette to emphasize each point. "We elected Trump because he didn't need nobody's money. He told those Koch brothers to go screw themselves. Didn't have to walk on eggshells to protect the fragile egos of half the country. Now he's gonna be president, and I hope everyone in Washington loses their job. Well, except for you honey." He patted Megan's hand. "Because I know you'll teach those boys a thing or two about runnin' the country."

She forced herself not to pursue the conversation any further. It was Christmas, and anyway, she would never dislodge her father from his opinions.

With supper finished, Megan saw the perfect opportunity for Gabe to make amends. "Oh, I almost forgot to give you guys your Christmas present," she bluffed. "Let me run to my room for a second." A look of panic crossed Gabe's face. Megan squeezed his shoulder in reassurance.

But Paul got up from the table, too, saying, "I think I'll take a smoke break."

Damn, thought Megan, *that man is stubborn*.

P oking under her bed for the gift, Megan came across something else: Jason's favorite U of F shirt, a nod to the party-filled days of his youth. Hadn't she gotten rid of all his stuff?

Before she could stop herself, she buried her face in the cotton, inhaling a trace of Old Spice. Then she balled it up and threw it across the room as the throb of anger and hurt returned all over again.

The day her relationship with Jason ended had scarred her memories of him forever. It was just last August. White had won the Republican primary, and she was supposed to be out celebrating. But after just one drink with the campaign staff at a local bar, the jukebox had played a Keith Urban song—her and Jason's song. Suddenly she had wanted to dance with him, to be held by him. Heck, just to cuddle with him on the couch would've been nice. They had barely seen each other in weeks.

When she'd arrived home, his Chevy was parked in the driveway, but all the lights were off in the house. It was only 9 p.m., so she'd found it a little odd. Maybe he was watching TV?

She had opened the front door and called out his name. No answer. An inexplicable dread came over her as she sidled through the hallway that led to their bedroom, listening for danger. Glancing to her right, through the archway in their lavish, spacious kitchen, she saw two half-empty glasses of red wine atop the marble counter. A woman's giggle stopped her in her tracks.

In a burst of rage, she had grabbed a chef's knife from the block and continued down the hall. From the open doorway of their bedroom, she had seen it all: Connie, on the bed and on all fours, taking it like the dog she was.

Megan had cleared her throat loudly and steadied her voice. "Should I wait until you're finished to come back?"

Jason's face had been a caricature of surprise. His foolish instinct must have been to tell a lie, because he sprang off the bed, completely naked, and threw a sheet over Connie's head.

"Are you goddamn kidding me, Jason?" came Megan's voice, unfamiliar to her.

Then she heard a scream, but it wasn't from her. It was Connie, wide-eyed, sitting up in the bed, with the sheet wrapped around her and pointing at the knife in Megan's hand.

Megan hadn't even realized she still held the knife, and she never would have used it. But she did register just a tiny bit of satisfaction in recognizing their fear, the same fear she had felt so often—the fear that seizes you when your world comes crashing down.

She had taken care to keep her face emotionless. She would never give them the satisfaction of seeing how they'd hurt her. The only thing to give her away was the slight tremble of the fingers that gripped the knife. Then she'd turned around and left the room without saying another word.

Jason had followed her to the kitchen, stumbling over himself to pull on his jeans and make some sort of excuse. Megan barely heard him. She was too busy glaring at Connie as she tried to slink invisibly out the door with her blouse partially buttoned and her head down. Then she had returned to their bedroom and stuffed some things in a suitcase. Before she stormed out, Jason had said something that replayed in her mind to this day: "I'm sorry I hurt you. But I want more than just to have a wife. I want to actually *see* my wife. And I want a family. You're not ready for that, Meg. I don't know if you ever will be."

Megan hadn't responded. Instead she carefully removed her engagement ring and threw it at his chest. Then she squealed out of the driveway. She had waited until her car had taken her far away before she'd let the tears run down her face.

Having found the gift, Megan hurried from her bedroom, putting distance between her and the awful memory. Standing in the hallway, she took a few breaths to settle herself, just as her therapist had suggested—the only useful advice she had gotten out of three months of therapy. She forced a smile onto her face and returned to the dining room.

"I'm sorry, Dad," Gabe was saying across the table. "I'm sorry I never told you I was gay. I'm sorry I kept my relationship secret from you all these years."

Megan sat down quietly and observed their father for a moment. He had the look of someone beaten down by life. Poverty showed itself in subtle ways. His teeth—rotten, discolored, missing, and chipped, from smoking, drinking, a poor diet, and infrequent dental visits. The deep lines on his face—like grooves in a stone where water has dripped again and again for centuries—formed by the constant stress of never having enough, of feeling like the deck is stacked against you.

"I knew. I always knew." Paul answered slowly, measuring each word. "I'm not stupid."

Gabe was incredulous. "You knew? Really? Why didn't you say anything?"

Paul took a swig of beer. "Didn't know how. It's just... it's hard for me, OK? Homosexuality's not natural, not what God intended.

He made man and woman for a reason." He gave a ragged sigh. "But I love you. You're my son. I don't know what hurts more—you bein' gay, or you lyin' about bein' gay. And I am sorry for that. For makin' you feel like you couldn't tell me."

Gabe breathed a relieved sigh. "OK, Dad. In the name of the truth, I want you to know that I love Darren, and we are getting married. I hope you will come to the wedding, but we understand if you don't want to."

Paul nodded once. "We're family," he said gruffly. "I'll be there."

JANUARY HEADLINES

Political dating sites are hot—making dating great again
—The Economist

Women's Marches: More than one million protesters
vow to resist President Trump
—The Washington Post

Defiant yet jubilant voices flood U.S. cities as women rally for rights
—The New York Times

Trump targets 11 nations in refugee order: New screening appears
to focus on majority-Muslim nations
—Politico

Chapter Eleven

✪

FEMALE RIVALRY

New Year's Eve had come and gone, and Megan was delighted to be back to work after the holiday recess. She'd been so busy in the past week, she had barely seen Andrew, and that was perfectly fine with her. He hadn't even thanked her for the Christmas present. But the following Tuesday morning, she walked into the kitchen to find a young woman drinking from her favorite REAGAN FOR PRESIDENT! coffee mug. Seated at the kitchen counter with her legs curled beneath her, the girl wore two long, messy braids and seemed to be naked except for a T-shirt that read BLACK LIVES MATTER.

"That's my mug," Megan said, not caring that her tone was nasty. It always surprised her how easy it was to be assertive toward another woman. She had no problem being the alpha dog in an all-female pack. But when it came to men, too often she submitted.

"Oh. I'm, like, so sorry." The girl put the mug down on the counter and unfurled her legs to retrieve another one from the cabinet. "I'm Atticus. I love your mug. It's a joke, right?" She filled the coffee mug and giggled.

Megan stared at her before snatching up her mug. "No, it's not a joke. And just so you know, all lives matter." She brought the mug to the sink and picked up the dish soap just as Andrew entered the living room, fresh from the shower.

He ran a hand through his wet hair, gave the girl a peck on the cheek, and poured himself a cup of coffee. Then he sat next to the girl and watched as Megan rinsed her cup and placed it in the dish rack.

Megan felt a gut-punch of jealousy, but dismissed it as nothing more than the annoyance of having a strange girl in the apartment.

"Uh-oh, did someone use your favorite mug? A Democrat drinking from a Republican mug—I think that's seven years of bad luck." He winked at Megan.

Atticus swung her head back and forth between Andrew and Megan. "Really? Bad luck for who? The Republican or the Democrat?"

Andrew laughed. "Oh, I think the Republicans have it coming to them." He turned to Atticus. "Want me to make you breakfast?"

She smiled. "I wish! But I don't have time. I've got to teach yoga in an hour, and I still need to go home and change." Atticus drained her coffee and headed in the direction of Andrew's room.

Megan avoided looking at him as she put the kettle on to boil and ripped open a package of instant oatmeal. She stared at the morning news on her phone until the kettle popped. Then she poured the hot water into the bowl and slowly stirred the mushy oats.

"You have the worst eating habits," Andrew blurted out.

She glared at him, spoon in hand. What, because she was eating her oatmeal standing up? "We weren't all born with cooks and servants, you know," she retorted.

"How would you know...?" Andrew stopped himself when Atticus reappeared.

"Andrew, you should call me later. Maybe we can hang again. No pressure." She gave a flirty smile and then turned to Megan. "So nice to meet you!"

"Yeah, you too." Megan's voice was uncharacteristically drenched in sarcasm, but it went blissfully unnoticed by Atticus.

She came to the bottom of her oatmeal bowl and rinsed it in the sink. She could wash it later. The less time she spent with Andrew, the better. She could already sense her blood pressure rising.

"I met her online, can you believe it? Thanks for asking. She's super nice. So sweet."

"I didn't ask. And I don't care."

"You should try it. Online dating, I mean. Maybe specify the age range you're going for. Is it sixty that piques your interest, or seventy?" He shrugged. "I guess it doesn't matter, as long as he has money, right? Oh, and you'll be happy to know there's an online dating website just for Trump voters!"

Megan flushed with anger. "And does it say in *your* profile that you're looking to date minors?" She ducked out of the room before he could respond.

"She's twenty-three!" came his voice behind her. As if she cared! And what kind of absurd name was *Atticus* anyway?

A ndrew had awoken that Tuesday morning with a strange sensation in the pit of his stomach, and it wasn't just an ugly hangover. His conscience had been waiting for hours to tell him something. He racked his aching brain for a moment before he noticed an arm draped over him. *Megan?*

It couldn't be. *I wouldn't have,* he thought. *She wouldn't have.*

But his mind was pure fog, and he couldn't see through it to last night's events. He snuck a panicked glance at the rest of the naked body in his bed. A young-looking woman slept in the fetal position, childlike, with her mouth forming a little O. Her long hair painted his crisp white pillow black.

Not Megan. *Phew!* That would have been beyond awkward!

He turned onto his back and relaxed, letting last night's events shine through in tiny rays of clarity.

Let's see...

He had just left the men's changing room at the yoga studio and was picking up his yoga mat when the young woman in black pigtails had jumped off the bench and leaped into his path.

"Hey! We've never met. I'm Atticus, your yoga teacher." She had giggled while extending her hand.

Andrew had thought the formality was sweet, and shook her hand. "I'm Andrew. Nice to meet you."

"I've been watching—well, not 'watching' you, not in a weird way, but... I mean, you're new to the studio, right?"

"Yeah. I just moved from New York." He'd grabbed his mat, fully expecting the conversation to be over. "See you in class." He'd started walking away, but Atticus had trailed after him.

"Wow, you're from New York? I've never been. I just moved here in September. Transferred from my hometown college in Kansas. I'm at Howard, double majoring in gender studies and social justice." Atticus spoke as fast as she moved, following him all the way down the four flights of stairs to the street. "Hey, I have an idea. Why don't we go for a drink, and you can tell me all about New York?"

Andrew had stood on the sidewalk and stared at her. This was not a good idea. Just talking to her made him feel like a predator. What was their age difference anyway, fifteen years?

"Uh, I really wish I could, but I... I'm meeting someone. Maybe another time." He'd smiled at her.

Atticus had smiled brightly in return, but Andrew thought he detected disappointment.

Of course, he didn't really have anyone to meet up with, though the prospect of spending the evening alone in his apartment with the Ice Queen wasn't all that appealing either. So he had wandered around the block and decided to pop into a pub for a pint.

It hadn't taken long to realize he should have drunk water first. Sweating buckets during hot yoga and then drinking alcohol straight after—it was a recipe for instantaneous inebriation. With every sip, he seemed to sink deeper into reflection: on the new year, his new job, his newly single status. He'd skipped the New Year's celebrations this year. Everyone was getting married, having kids, and he was *the single guy*. What was there to be cheerful or optimistic about? What lay ahead for him? No girlfriend, crappy living situation, depressing new job. It was a joke trying to lobby this Congress to act on climate change. He grunted gloomily and took another sip. *Good fucking luck with that!*

For the first time in his life, Andrew felt hopeless. The feeling was so unfamiliar, he didn't know how to cope. To do environmentalist work required a certain amount of determination and a positive attitude that things could improve, that it would work out fine in the end. Now he wasn't so sure. He wished he could stick his head in sand and forget everything—women, politics, the environment... He was losing his purpose.

So, it wasn't his fault, really. His guard had been way down. When Atticus had strolled in the door with a few other young women from the yoga studio, he'd been easy prey.

"Hey, you! What a coincidence! Isn't your friend here yet?" She'd looked around the bar eagerly.

Andrew had hesitated. How far was he willing to go to lie this nice young girl? His hesitation lasted too long. The four girls had claimed the row of barstools next to him, with Atticus right beside him. A few pitchers later, and he was done.

And now he'd woken up with a splitting headache and a stomach filled with regret. Not that he was some moral purist. He didn't look down on one-night stands—it was just that he would much rather be in a relationship. Casual sex was like eating a burger and fries. Sure, it tasted great and was satisfying every now and then. But in the long run, the healthy salad was the better choice. The idea of using someone, or being used, for pleasure didn't sit right with him. It lacked any of the intimacy that he craved. And this... He glanced at Atticus again. This was especially wrong. She was so young, and she seemed so into him. He felt like a total creep.

An alarm beeped on the bedside table. Her phone. She slowly opened her eyes. "Hey, stranger," she said with a slow grin. "I've got to get up now. I'm teaching in a few hours, and then I have class this afternoon."

She threw off the covers and strode buck-naked to his dresser, where she lifted out one of his T-shirts. Then she tugged it over her head and flipped her black hair. "Mind if I get a cup of coffee before I head out?"

Her casualness caught him off guard. He nodded his head. If

Atticus encountered his roommate, he'd just have to blame it all on Match.com. No way was he telling Megan he picked up his yoga teacher at a bar.

"Atticus, ummm, about last night…" He raked his hand through his hair. "I don't think we should do this again. You're beautiful and very sweet, but I'm not looking for any—"

"Hey, don't worry about it!" She grinned and began rebraiding her hair. "I'm not looking either. I'm just experimenting. This year I'm practicing equal opportunity sex. It takes all types, right?"

Andrew's eyebrows knit together in confusion. "What does that make me?"

"You're the old guy."

Megan was in her office long before 9 a.m. as usual, discussing with one of the aides who would attend which Cabinet confirmation hearings. It was difficult to concentrate as she kept replaying the morning's events. How dare Andrew make fun of her for dating an old guy? He had fallen for the same old cliché, only in reverse: dating someone who probably wasn't even old enough to legally drink. And he had brought her back home to their apartment.

Ugh! Megan was about to ask the aide to repeat himself when Carmela strutted in.

"You have a new meeting at ten, with some environmental group. White insisted it be handled by you."

Megan reached for the file, but Carmela dropped it on the desk and awaited her reaction. Megan ignored the discourtesy and picked up the file. "About time," she muttered.

"Excuse me?" Carmela whipped around, eyes narrowed.

"Oh! I was just saying to Aaron, I hope they're on time. Since I have so much work to do. These phones won't answer themselves, you know!" Megan gave her a fake grin and two thumbs up.

"That's right. Enjoy your little reprieve." Carmela spun on her high heels and left the office.

Aaron, who had pushed himself against the wall in Megan's cramped office so Carmela wouldn't notice him, came over to her desk. "Looks like she's gunning for you." He shook his head sympathetically. "What did you do to piss her off?"

Megan shrugged. "We had a few run-ins on the campaign. She gave White advice, and I told him to do the opposite. He sided with me. I was right on all accounts, I might add. But she obviously hasn't gotten over it."

"Well, I'd be careful. The last person who came up against her... Well, it didn't work out so well."

Megan frowned. "She doesn't scare me."

"Well, she should. The woman she had a vendetta against was brilliant. Really sweet, the daughter of a diplomat." Aaron's eyes narrowed as if squinting through a memory. "Nobody knows what really happened, but some think she was getting a little too chummy with White. Rumor has it, she went back to her hometown in Utah and opened up a bakery."

"Good thing I'm not sweet, then." Megan grinned.

Aaron got up to leave her office, giving her one last look as if to say, *You've been warned.*

Megan glanced through the folder Carmela gave her, flipping the pages one by one. She would be meeting with a nonprofit group called EnviroLutions. "'We're building the political will to address climate change, and finding solutions that benefit environment and economy alike,'" she read aloud, following it with a little snort. "Good luck with that."

When the hour arrived, she stepped through the glass conference room door and stopped dead in her tracks. There, sitting at the table, was her roommate.

Chapter Twelve

———— ✪ ————

MEET THE LOBBYIST

ndrew hadn't intended to surprise his roommate with the visit to Congressman White's office. The meeting had been arranged just yesterday, and he had meant to let Megan know. But he had barely exchanged two words with her since she got back from Florida, and this morning she definitely hadn't seemed in the mood to talk.

Part of him enjoyed watching her squirm now. She usually had such a wall built around her, but right now, with her face seized by shock... It was the first time since they'd met that she had dropped her guard for a moment.

Andrew had thought about texting her earlier, as he'd sat in the waiting room with the director of EnviroLutions, Stewart Adams — whose pimply face gave him an unfortunate fresh-out-of-college look — and a team of older volunteers. The cushy seating area surrounding the reception desk had been filled with suit-and-tie representatives from other special interest groups. Irony was alive and well and at work in D.C., with the coal miners lobbying alongside the environmentalists. Everybody was pushing their agenda: pass a bill, repeal a law, add an amendment, fund this, don't fund that...

But Andrew had been distracted by looking around the room at the large map of White's Florida district, the posters of orange trees and golf courses, and the TV screen tuned into the latest Cabinet confirmation hearing. The soon-to-be attorney general was doing his best to say nothing: "I do not recall... I do not remember... not to my knowledge..."

How is it, Andrew wondered, *that so many people working in Washington are in the advanced stages of dementia?*

By the time a staffer came into the reception area, nearly hitting him with the door and a "Ms. Thompson is ready to see you now," it was too late to give Megan fair warning.

Adams was addressing her now. "Thank you so much for taking the time to meet with us today. How much time do you have?"

"Fifteen minutes." Megan said briskly, looking everywhere but at Andrew.

"Great." Adams shifted a pile of papers, looking momentarily lost and not a little bit nervous. "First off, we want to thank Congressmen White for voting to protect five hundred acres of Florida's wetlands and fragile ecosystems, and for supporting the Clean Water Act."

Megan nodded her head in reply.

Adams continued, "We'd like to take a moment to go around the table and introduce ourselves. I'm Stewart Adams, I live in D.C., and I've worked for EnviroLutions for four years, but I'm originally from Orlando. I'm extremely concerned about climate change because of the extreme weather we are already seeing—and will continue to see if climate change is not addressed. Weather events like flooding, droughts, and wildfires will only increase. And it's not just the loss of life and property, which is a tragedy in itself. Climate-related disasters cost the taxpayers billions of dollars and pose a threat to our national security." He turned and signaled the EnviroLutions associate to his right.

Andrew was the last to speak. As his colleagues had addressed the room, he'd been studying Megan's appearance. She seemed to have traded her silk blouses and tight skirts for a plain navy-blue dress with a blazer. *When did that happen?* He had to admit, he had checked her out a few times at the apartment when she wasn't looking. He had even gotten a peek at her chest and the outline of her lacy bra, when she'd dropped her keys once and bent over to pick them up. Then he'd run right into the wall, which served him right for lurking.

"I'm Andrew," he said when the time came, with a gleam in his eye. "I just moved to D.C. and started working at EnviroLutions, as the assistant director of legislative outreach. Climate change can no longer be left for the Democrats to try and fix. There is no denying that climate change is happening right now and in your own backyard. Florida is especially vulnerable, with forty percent of the population at risk from sea-level rise. In South Florida we are already seeing the effects: chronic flooding, threats to freshwater supply, coral bleaching."

He continued, "One of the solutions we are proposing is a bill that would put a fee on fossil carbon-based fuels, such as coal, gas, and oil, and would return all revenue to households. We are calling it 'carbon fee and dividend.' It is not a tax. The fee would be placed on the first point of extraction or import. The dividend that is collected would be returned to households in the form of a monthly check."

When he finished speaking, Megan clasped her hands and said, "Thank you, everyone, for your input. At this point Congressman White is not ready to commit to co-sponsoring any legislation on carbon fee and dividend. We have to carefully consider how it will impact the economy and job creation."

"Well, our carbon fee and dividend would create jobs and help the economy. And we have the data to support that." Andrew wasn't going down that easily. "If I send you the data, will you consider co-sponsoring the legislation?"

"As I said, we can't commit to anything right now. I would also need information on how this will impact the households in his district. Can you send me that, Mr. Adams?" Megan turned toward the director.

But before Adams could reply, Andrew raised his eyebrows. "I'd be happy to provide you with that information, Ms. Thompson." He was practically singing. "We can have a nice, long discussion about it."

That evening Megan delayed her return to the apartment as long as she could. When she entered the apartment, she threw her keys on the kitchen counter so hard, they slid off and hit the floor with a *thunk*. Andrew, lounged lazily on the couch, didn't shift his gaze from *The Daily Show*.

"Hi, roomie," he called out cheerfully.

She felt her anger reaching its boiling point. Megan stormed into the living room and stood in front of the TV, forcing him to look at her. "Thanks for the heads up, *roomie!*" Her voice sounded calm, but her whole body was tense. She stood in front of him silently, cataloging all her complaints: blasting *Rachel Maddow* so loudly she had to wear earplugs, leaving *New York Times* and magazine articles about Trump on the kitchen counter and bathroom floor, hanging the ridiculously large Obama *Hope* poster in the hallway where she had to see it every day.

Just tell him.

Andrew sat on the couch smiling. It was disarming. Her mouth was rough and dry, unable to produce a word. "Why didn't you tell me you were coming to my workplace to lobby?" she said quietly at last.

He sat up, never taking his eyes off her. "And ruin the surprise? It was kind of fun watching the look on your face."

Her confidence wavered. What was going on with her today?

At the office, she'd been flustered as she shook hands with the three men and two women seated around the conference table. "Hi, I'm Megan Thompson," she'd repeated. But it just didn't project the same power and composure she'd practiced so carefully over the years.

It was Andrew. He had unnerved her, looking as handsome as he did in that navy blazer and crisp, white dress shirt, the tan slacks and Italian loafers, the deep blue eyes that gazed right into hers… He had tried to hide his smile, but his cheeks betrayed him.

What the hell is he doing here?

"Hi, Megan. Nice to meet you," he had said, his words dripping with professionalism. She hesitated to shake his hand, but refusing him would appear disrespectful. He had held her hand for a second too long, and she'd felt something akin to a jolt.

Yanking her hand back and smoothing her skirt, she had tried to erase the feeling. "Pleasure to meet you," she'd said coolly, pretending to read the file on the table in front of her as she took a moment to collect herself.

Get a grip, Megan!

It was bad enough at work. Now she was expected to put up with the same aggravation when she came home?

"But you recovered nicely," he was saying, "and I think you handled yourself very well."

"I get it. It's your apartment." She started to pace. She took a deep breath "My work is my sanctuary, so I'm telling you now: Back. Off."

Confidence was growing within her again. *How dare he ambush me!*

"What's next?" she continued. "Are you going to try and convert me? Leave pamphlets and petitions under my door now? Try to drag me to a Save the Polar Bears and Rainforests benefit gala?"

"I'm an environmentalist, not a Jehovah's witness," Andrew drawled.

"Ha! What's the difference? Both aim to convert the 'sinners.' You guys think everyone should live in a yurt, grow their own food, and drive a Prius."

"Communes and off-grid houses are acceptable too," Andrew teased, seeming to enjoy the quarrel.

Sadist!

"You know what my beef with you environmentalists is?" She pointed her finger at him. "You come from money. You don't understand that other people don't have money. You propose all these solutions, and you don't care if costs more money, or hurts the economy, or costs people their jobs. As long as it 'saves the environment.'"

"Well, that's why the carbon fee and dividend is perf—"

"No, no, no! I am not going to let you lobby me at home." Megan waved her hands and stepped back.

Andrew sighed. "Can't we just talk about this, as two rational human beings? I'm not trying to get you to pass legislation right now.

Just trying to have a discussion."

"Yes, because we are *sooo* good at having discussions!"

As usual when she was riled up, Megan felt the urge to run.

White had suggested she join Toastmasters, but that scene belonged to an older generation. Still, she had to fight these fears head on, or she would never make it to Congress. She had known it for a long time, long before Mike had joked that if she really wanted to get out of her comfort zone, she should do slam poetry. He'd bet her twenty bucks she would never do it. After her first session on stage, she had collected her winnings.

Of course, she'd left out the part about her voice alternated between monotone and fast-forward as she read T.S. Eliot's *Burnt Norton*, her body shaking all the while. But everyone had been so nice and friendly, her confidence had improved and she kept going back. Until she realized that standing in front of a nice, friendly audience wasn't quite the type of practice she needed.

Andrew was still looking at her, silently awaiting some response.

"Fine. Let's discuss." She came to stand in front of him, arms crossed. When he patted the seat on the couch next to him, she purposely took the chair furthest away.

"First, let me ask you," Andrew began, "do you believe climate change is real?"

" Megan eyed him warily. "I'll concede there may be some erratic weather patterns, but I don't think it's caused by human activity, and I don't think we can do anything to stop it."

"So, you're not a denier. You're a skeptic."

She shrugged. "Yeah, I guess you can say I'm skeptical."

He pursed his lips, making him look smug. "Have you ever heard of the Koch brothers?"

Megan rolled her eyes. "Gee, let me think about that for a second."

"Sarcasm is beneath you," he replied. "What if I told you the Koch brothers funded a study that proves climate change is real. And that it's caused by human activity." He reached to the floor for his MacBook, then opened it up and started typing. Then he read aloud:

Over the weekend, UC-Berkeley professor Richard Muller outed himself as a "converted" climate "skeptic" in the New York Times *after his Berkeley Earth Surface Temperature project concluded the earth's surface temperature had increased 2.5 degrees Fahrenheit in the past 250 years and one and a half degrees in the past 50 years, likely entirely because of human industrial activity….*

Megan was silent for a moment. "Well, one liberal media article does not a conspiracy make."

Andrew's eyes bulged. "It's from *Business Insider*!"

Megan signed, exasperated. "Even if climate change is real, and even if it's caused by humans, the present policies are counterproductive. I mean, come on! Subsidizing and mandating all those inefficient alternatives? Wind and solar are unreliable, and the costs are enormous. They're making people's lives worse — increasing the cost of energy, corrupting the business community, increasing corporate welfare — "

"OK, do you even hear yourself?" Andrew was shouting now. "You're reciting Koch brothers talking points, verbatim!"

"Oh, so just because I'm a woman, I can't come up with my own intelligent response?"

"Please, don't play the woman card. I know the talking points because I've heard them before, from every other conservative out there! And I googled it. Charles Koch said those exact same things in an interview two years ago!"

Megan stopped to think. She supposed it was possible that she had picked up that particular language somewhere along the line…

"I don't want anyone's talking points," Andrew said, quieter now. "I want your honest opinion."

"OK," Megan sighed, "let's say global warming is happening. And let's say it's caused by human activity. Who says it's going to be catastrophic, or even occur in our lifetime? There's too much uncertainty."

"Lot of people think it *will* be catastrophic and *will* happen in our lifetime! And not just any people, but scientists! The people who dedicate their life's work to researching climate science! I mean, I know you guys hate science, reason, and logic, but what *do* you believe in? What will it take to get it through your heads?"

When Megan didn't answer, he continued shouting. "You Republicans grovel for the chance of getting your hands on some of three-hundred-million-dollar honey pot the Koch brothers offer up every election. But at what point do your morals kick in?"

Megan's cheeks burning as her anger rushed to the surface. "Wow, it must be great always being on the moral high ground! Don't forget, it's the highly educated, wealthy liberals who are the anti-vaxxers, even though the connection between childhood vaccines and autism has been completely debunked. Why aren't *they* listening to the scientists? Why are they ignoring the so-called experts."

She stood up from the chair, signaling the end of the conversation, but then she turned to him instead. "You know what I think? I think it's not about climate change. It's about you, trying to find some meaning in your miserable life." In a moment of honesty, she added, "And I get it, because I want to make a difference, too. But if you're going to be such an ass about it, no one will ever listen to you."

"Thanks for the tip." Andrew's voice was sarcastic. "And I guess we won't have to worry about global warming anyway, because we can probably expect war with North Korea, China, and maybe even Mexico."

Megan walked over to pick up her keys from the floor. "If that's the way you think, then I feel sorry for you. Now, if you'll excuse me, I think I will drive my CO2-producing car around the city, maybe get stuck in a lovely traffic jam somewhere, maybe run over a few endangered species while I clear my head."

H ave a seat, Miss Thompson," said Congressman White the next day. "I called you into my office because I want to hear about your meeting with EnviroLutions."

"Oh, OK." Megan was still fuming over her argument with Andrew. She had come to the conclusion that they simply were not capable of having a civilized conversation. As if she had needed any more proof.

After quickly recapping yesterday's meeting, including the proposed carbon fee and dividend legislation, she concluded, "I told them I didn't think it was something you would be interested in cosponsoring."

Congressman White watched her a moment before responding. "You see, Megan, I've been thinking a lot about my legacy." He leaned back, and his leather chair swayed left and right. "I want to leave office on a high note. Don't get me wrong—I've had a long career, and I'm pretty proud of what I've accomplished. But my grandkids really got me thinking about something."

He picked up a framed photo: the whole White family, taken that last election night. Megan herself had stood on that stage, just outside the reach of the camera lens.

Anyone who'd ever worked for White knew he kept a family photo on display for every election he had won. They hung on the office wall like a visual timeline tracking his career and family life. The first photo, taken in the 1970s, showed a handsome young man with sandy-colored hair and a bushy mustache, with his arm around his beautiful wife, beaming from under her feathered brown hairdo and holding a pink-clad baby girl in her arms. The photos were his pride and joy, and Megan made a show of peering at them now as if for the first time. "I want to make sure I really leave my mark," he was saying.

Megan had her laptop open, fingers hovering over the keyboard, ready to take notes, but she didn't quite follow where he was going with all this. Sometimes he rambled, and it was hard to make out his intentions. Did this have to do with him being chair of the House Energy and Commerce Committee? Or did he want to discuss her upcoming election bid?

117

At last White came to his point. "I'm joining the bipartisan Climate Solutions Caucus, Megan, and I'm signing on to the Republican Climate Change Resolution to put a price on carbon."

Megan wasn't sure she heard him right. "Really, sir?"

"Yes. Some of my colleagues have been trying their damnedest to convince me, and I've come around."

She couldn't believe her ears.

"Unfortunately for you, darlin', it's your generation—and your children's—who are going to be facing the consequences. We need to stop debating whether it's real, and start working on efforts to reduce carbon emissions."

"OK, sir. What would you like me to do?" she asked, her voice flat with acceptance.

White cocked his head to one side. "Megan, you don't seem very enthusiastic about this. I have to say, I am kind of surprised."

Megan nodded slowly. "In all honesty, sir, it's not something I've spent much time thinking about, until this week. It never comes up when I'm running campaigns. Our voters don't prioritize it. Some say they're worried, but it never makes it into the top five or even ten priorities. And I haven't really read up on climate change." Climate change had always been such a taboo for Republicans, she had just stashed it in a box labeled DO NOT OPEN. And until last night, she had managed to avoid being lectured on it.

"Fair enough. But you need to think like a congresswoman now, don't you? We have a responsibility to our constituents and future generations to support market-based solutions—investments and innovations that could help reduce and reverse climate change. What I'm saying, Megan, is that sometimes you listen to what voters want, and sometimes you give voters what they need."

Megan still hesitated. "Sir, won't coming out on the side of climate change cost us donors? Or worse, our seat? It's happened before."

White rubbed his temples and sighed loudly. "It's a delicate balance we must navigate. On the one hand, we're here to serve the constituents, and on the other we're beholden to our donors. But even the military recognizes the climate poses a serious threat, and unless we do something now, we're all screwed. We conservatives can't keep silent any longer. And we also need jobs."

Now he was sounding a little more like the politician she knew and respected.

"We have to be honest with ourselves. Coal has been in decline for a long time. Moving forward, innovation and clean energy will be key. We used to be proud stewards of the environment! Nixon was the one who signed the Clean Air Act. But we've had our head up our own ass for too long, fighting our partisan wars."

Congressman White looked her in the eye, and his sincerity was undeniable. "I understand the reluctance to believe in climate change. Trust me, I do. It's hard to see, and it seems scary but also so far away." He dragged his heavy Rolodex along the desk toward him. "I think you should meet with a friend of mine, a retired Navy commander. He can tell you what he thinks about climate change. Then I want you to do your own research. And we'll set up a time to talk again next week."

Megan finished typing her notes and looked up. "Sounds good, sir."

"And Megan, I'm gonna share one thing that's helped me come around. It's something my pastor told me a long time ago: Sometimes it's the messenger we hate, and not the message. Ask any conservative what they think of Al Gore and that darned movie. We may not like him, but that doesn't mean he's wrong."

As Megan left the congressman's office, she couldn't help but think about how smug Andrew would've been in that meeting, instead of welcoming White into the fold. He was never going to win any political support—much less friends—with an attitude like that.

Andrew's secret appointment at her workplace had stirred up a whole range of Megan's emotions, from surprise to anger to something else she wasn't willing to explore. Even if she did have a change of heart about climate change—and that verdict wasn't in just yet—she would never give him the satisfaction of knowing it. He may have found yet another way to push her buttons, but there was no way she would let him change her mind. About anything.

Chapter Thirteen

─────────── ✪ ───────────

PUSSY HAT PARTY

The extreme heat hit Andrew like opening an oven door. No matter how many times a week he practiced hot yoga, that initial shock of hundred-degree temperatures always evoked panic and a desire to escape. But after an hour of intense discomfort, he invariably felt freer, lighter—as if the weight of the world had dripped off along with his sweat.

Today, though, the longing to flee was stronger than usual. He could still do it. Class wouldn't start for a few moments. The thought of bumping into Atticus again made Andrew's bruised ego throb. He had considered finding a new yoga studio, but why should he? He'd prepaid for twenty classes, and this studio was close to the apartment. Besides, there were lots of class times to choose from. So he'd chosen a new one.

Andrew headed to the back of the room and knelt on a vacant mat. When the teacher twirled around to face the growing class, his mouth fell open. Atticus smiled as if she'd been expecting him.

She skipped toward him. "Hey! Long time no see. You haven't been avoiding me, have you?" She winked and wagged her finger at him.

"No, no—I mean, not all. This class works better for me, timing wise." His face burned. Why was he explaining himself to her? "Where's Zahara?"

Atticus pulled a scrunchy off her wrist and whisked her long hair into a messy bun. "Oh, she called in sick." She pointed to a large blank space facing her yoga mat. "Hey, why don't you move your mat up front? Then I can keep an eye on you." She winked again.

Was she flirting, or making fun of him?

He'd never thought it was possible to feel even more uncomfortable during a hot yoga class, like a trapped animal on display. Moving into downward dog, he spotted her skintight, aqua-colored pants as she circled him like a shark. He still couldn't believe he had slept with her. He couldn't believe he was *that guy.*

He made a speedy exit after class, treading carefully so as not to slip on the puddles of sweat, but Atticus caught up to him in the hall.

"Andrew!" she called loudly.

Sweat dripped off his face and down his arms. What did she want she want from him now? She had already told him he was old and just another notch on her bedpost—how much more could his ego take? He braced himself as she sauntered toward him.

Atticus stopped just shy of him and called out to two onlookers. "Ladies, this is Andrew. The guy I was telling you about."

Andrew shifted his weight from one foot to the other, prepared to take flight if necessary. *Time to cut my losses and find a new studio,* he decided. But that wasn't going to help him right now.

Atticus leaned in, placed a dainty hand on his bicep, and squeezed. "I was telling them how close you live, and how you have a big, open living room."

"I do," he replied cautiously. The two shiny-faced girls eyed him eagerly.

"And I know you totally love women and care about women's rights." She waited for Andrew to confirm.

"Uh, yes. I do care about women's rights." Where was this headed?

"So I was thinking your place would be perfect for our pussy hat party!"

"Your... what?" He stepped backward, right into a rack of yoga mats. Atticus's party sounded like a college orgy. Were vaginas wearing hats now? *Shit, I am getting old.*

"Me and some of the other teachers are making pussy hats for the Women's March." She grinned. "We're gonna sell them here at the studio and give all the profits to Planned Parenthood."

He let out his breath. Not an orgy, then. "Oh, right. I heard something about that. After the inauguration, right?"

"You *are* going to march, aren't you?" Three sets of eyes were staring him down.

"Of course!" he blustered. At least, now he supposed he was.

"Great! The pussy hat party is Thursday night at seven. Thanks for hosting!"

"No prob—wait, hosting?" he said to the back of their heads.

Andrew couldn't help but smile as he tidied the apartment on Thursday evening. There was at least one upside to being held hostage to this knitting party: It was going to piss off Megan.

Atticus arrived just after seven with a half dozen enthusiastic yoga teachers in tow. "Andrew, this is Fatima. My bae." She hooked arms with a yogi in a head scarf, a dark-skinned woman he didn't recognize.

Bae? He pondered the word. "Nice to meet you, Fatima."

Atticus leaned over and kissed Fatima passionately on the lips—a show she put on for Andrew's benefit, no doubt. He should have known. If Atticus was looking to apply affirmative action in her sex life Fatima ticked off all the boxes: woman, black, lesbian, Muslim. He definitely couldn't compete with that. Not that he wanted to be in the running, but her attention had been flattering.

The yoga teachers made themselves right at home, and soon the apartment had been transformed into a mini-Etsy shop. Andrew had never seen so many shades of pink. He felt like an anthropologist studying a rare tribe of late millennials. One college-aged girl's skull-emblazoned sleeve tattoo was in stark contrast to her cherubic face and long braids. Another wore a floral print dress reminiscent of something his mother might wear, except the woman's head was partially shaven and a silver ring pierced one nostril. The women spent half their time knitting and the other half staging pictures for Instagram. They used a language he didn't understand: One knitter's hat was *on fleek*, while another's was *next level*. They playfully placed a hot pink hat on his head and said he was *woke*. Andrew felt himself slipping further and further into irrelevance.

He extricated himself from the tangle of yarn and poured a scotch—exactly, he realized with disdain, what his father would have done in this situation. As the first rush of alcohol hit his bloodstream, all his life decisions seemed to come into sharper focus. He hadn't really thought about it until his Christmas conversation with Emily, but maybe he finally was ready to find The One, to settle down and have a few kids—well, maybe only one, to lessen the environmental impact. It was an urge he had never encountered with Naomi.

But now? Looking around him at the explosion of pink post-pubescence, he was ready to retire from his chain-yourself-to-a-pipeline days. Maybe he'd even apply for a more senior position at work. That's what old people his age were supposed to do, right? Focus on their career and have kids? Because the new generation had already come to replace him. And it might be easier to ignore being pushed aside if he were knee-deep in changing diapers.

Megan's day had started with a mild throbbing at her temples, and now it was ending with a full-on pounding headache. Stuck observing the Cabinet confirmation hearings all day long, she had been forced to skip lunch.

"A good learning opportunity," White had said. Maybe so, yet Megan wondered if maybe it wasn't the lack of food but the three-ring circus on Capitol Hill that was hurting her head. The Democrats, under pressure from their constituents, were contesting the nominees for secretary of education and attorney general. Megan hated to admit it, but she sided with the Democrats on the former. The nominee couldn't answer the most basic questions about the educational system, and her insistence that schools in rural Wyoming needed guns to protect the children from grizzly bears was just too much. After that comment, Megan had kind of checked out and started dreaming of a bubble bath and Chinese takeout.

Her fantasy was deflated three hours later when she opened the apartment door and stumbled into a web of pink yarn.

Is this a full-blown migraine? she wondered. Then her vision expanded to include Andrew, surrounded by a group of crocheting college girls, their faces gleaming as they greeted her.

"Hey, roomie! Want to make some pussy hats with us?" Andrew beamed.

"Hats?" Frozen in place, Megan could only blink.

"For the Women's March. It's to symbolize that our pussies aren't up for grabs. Get it?" The girl who spoke wore big, round old-lady glasses—a trend that baffled Megan. So ugly they're cool? No, she didn't think so. Sometimes ugly is just ugly. "Come sit with us! We have plenty of yarn."

"Uh, no thanks. I'm not much of knitter." Megan could hardly hide her confusion. "Anyway, that's 'domestic work,' isn't it? If you call yourself feminists, shouldn't you be against this? Or at the very least, making *him* knit?" She pointed at Andrew, who sat on the arm of the couch, nursing a scotch.

"No way! We're reclaiming it," said another girl, whose T-shirt read THE FUTURE IS FEMALE. She stepped right up to Megan and settled one of the pink concoctions on her head. "This one fits you perfectly! You can keep it."

Without meaning to, she turned her head and saw her reflection in the TV. The charcoal blazer just didn't have the same impact when paired with the neon pink hat and its little cat ears.

"I'm not wearing a vagina on my head." Her voice was sharper than she intended. The female-future girl looked wounded, and Megan's guilt and compassion kicked in. *This is their Vietnam War,* she realized. Finally, to them, something seemed worth waking up for.

"I mean, thank you, its... uh... very creative. I'm just... I'm not

124

allowed to participate in the Women's March, or in any march. I work for the government."

"The government? Which part?" The girl retrieved the hat and placed it atop a pile before resuming her cross-legged position on the floor and taking up her knitting needles again.

"In Congress. The House of Representatives."

Murmurs of "Wow!" and "Cool!" hummed through the pink room.

Megan straightened up a little taller. *See, Andrew?* she thought. *Not everyone hates the government.*

But Andrew was otherwise engaged. Atticus, her slender arm linked through his, had grabbed a carrot and was dipping it into a bowl of hummus. "Mmmmmmm, amazing! You made it, right?" she purred. Then she called out to Megan, "Tell those old white guys in the government that women are going to keep fighting for access to birth control and abortions. We won't go quietly back to the 1950s!"

The murmurs transformed into a chorus of protest.

"Sure, I'll do that," Megan mumbled.

"Did you hear about that poll?" said the girl with granny glasses. "People ranked lice, Brussels sprouts, colonoscopies, used-car salesmen, traffic jams—all sorts of awful things!—higher than Congress."

Everyone laughed except Megan.

"And you know what ranked lower than Congress?" the girl continued, pushing her glasses back up the bridge of her nose.

Andrew looked intrigued. "What?"

"The Kardashians, lobbyists, and gonorrhea."

"That's unbelievable!" said a young woman (Megan was pretty sure about this) with a shaved head and countless piercings. "I can't believe the *Kardashians* scored lower than *Congress*!"

More laughter ensued.

Megan sensed an opportunity for escape. If she stayed any longer, she might witness a witch burning, and the witch would be her.

She tiptoed away, retreating to the sanctuary of her bedroom and leaving Andrew to his harem of hat-knitting feminazis. This feeling was all too familiar. She'd grown up with a zealot, absorbing her father's ravings against the government: *They're all corrupt! They're evil! The government's out to get your guns and make you go to gay weddings!* He had oscillated between silent, stewing drunk and sober, ranting lunatic. Megan wasn't sure which was worse. Both were embarrassing, especially as she matured from child to teenager.

At first, she could only sense something was off, but as she grew older and saw how other families lived, it confirmed just how abnormal her father's behavior was. She never invited friends to her house. She developed a particular coping mechanism: letting him rant and rave while she nodded her head as if in agreement, never talking back or opposing him. She just waited until he ran out of steam. Then she would run to her room, pick up a book, and escape into another world.

The day her father found out she'd been elected president of her eighth-grade class, he went on an hour-long tirade. "What a waste of time! What does a class president do? Take money from rich kids to buy pizza for poor ones? Let them get a job and stop taking handouts!"

Never mind that the Thompsons were some of the poor ones. One time Megan made muffins for a school bake sale to raise money for the senior class trip to D.C., and her dad charged her for the ingredients, saying the family couldn't afford it. She had dutifully handed over the three dollars, knowing he was really just against her involvement with the class government, and chalking it up to one more disappointment to be endured.

After that incident, Megan had sat in her room and plotted her revenge. She would work in government for the rest of her life. She would prove to him that he was wrong, that government could be good. It was supposed to be her middle finger to him.

As it turned out, she liked being a public servant. She liked knowing that her actions could better people's lives. But then as luck—bad luck—would have it, zealots started to run for office on the platform of shutting the government down. Suddenly, her father was in full support of her government ambitions.

It pissed her off to no end. So the more to the right of the political spectrum he went, the more she was determined to move toward the center. *We are shaped by the events of our lives,* Megan thought. As though she needed more proof of that.

She sat at her desk, gazing at the photo of her mother in its gilded frame, taken when Sarah Thompson was twenty and pregnant. How beautiful she was, with her full cheeks and rounded belly! Megan felt the sharp sting of tears, as she always did when she thought of her mother. What would their life have been like if her mother hadn't died? For one, they would have kept the family business. Her father, buoyed by his work and softened by his wife's influence, would have been less jaded, less mean, and Megan would've had no cause to resent him. Her childhood wouldn't have been ripped away, replaced by the burden of raising her brother, taking care of the house, and trying to make sure her father was eating and not drinking too much. None of that would've fallen on her tiny shoulders.

But if her mother had lived, Megan probably would've stayed far away from politics. She would be married to Jason now, with at least one kid and probably another on the way.

Megan plunked the picture back in its spot and opened her laptop. Time to work on her campaign. *Don't look backward,* she thought. *Only forward.* The what-ifs, the could-have-beens—they could really drag you down.

★ ★ ★

After putting in a few hours at the office Saturday morning, Megan returned to the apartment and a déjà vu moment: Andrew surrounded by eight young women sprawled on the floor amid a rainbow pool of permanent markers and stencils. A song from Pussy Riot blared from the speakers. The furniture was pushed against the wall. Poster boards were spread on the floor and propped against the couch, the chairs, the TV... And the girls were multiplying.

Where is he finding them? Megan wondered. Was he paying college students to come to these knitting parties just to mess with her? Andrew must have understood her expression, because he looked up and gave a resigned shrug as if to say, *I don't know where they came from.*

She didn't want to read the signs, but the temptation proved too much:

THIS PUSSY GRABS BACK

GRAB PATRIARCHY BY THE BALLS

LOVE TRUMPS HATE

BITCHES GET SHIT DONE

TINY HANDS, YUUUUGE ASSHOLE

SUPER CALLOUS FASCIST RACIST EXTRA BRAGGA-DOCIOUS!

WE SHALL OVERCOMB

This last one was in the midst of completion by a practiced hand sketching a well-drawn Trump and his signature combover.

Without meaning to, Megan snorted a little. Eight heads popped up and stared at her. Nobody had noticed her come in to the apartment.

"Don't mind me, I'm just the roommate."

The women said a polite greeting and then turned their attention back to their protest posters. As Megan grabbed items from the fridge to make herself a sandwich for supper, she overheard snippets of their conversation.

"It's the fault of the working class that he got elected. They're stupid, uneducated, unemployed. And mad as hell…"

"Well, it's not *just* their fault. I read that this Steve Bannon had a lot to do with it. He was the mastermind…"

"People are ignorant! They just vote along party lines…"

"Don't forget how much conservatives hate the Clintons. That ridiculous *Clinton Cash* book was released just as Hillary was preparing to launch her candidacy. It did a lot of damage. And Republicans aren't the only ones who see her as corrupt…"

"Yeah, as much as I wanted her to be the first female president, I'll admit, she wasn't exactly likable…" Megan was pretty sure that one came from the young woman wearing an I'M WITH HER T-shirt. *Have these people no loyalty?*

"I was for Bernie the whole time."

A refrain of mournful *Me, too*s followed.

"But seriously, anyone would be fucking better than Trump!"

Overhearing all this from the kitchen, Megan decided to forgo her sandwich for now. She stuffed everything back into the refrigerator and changed into her running gear.

Just as some people were addicted to drugs and alcohol, Megan got high on running. *Although maybe I should switch to alcohol,* she mused. Her clothes were starting to feel a bit too loose. Not that she minded losing weight. Secretly, it thrilled her when her stomach turned concave. But she'd lost so much in the past six weeks, she was starting to look skeletal. People might suspect an eating disorder, and women in particular could be vicious when they sniffed out that most unforgivable of maladies, mocking them ruthlessly and yet simultaneously jealous of anyone who cared too much about her weight. Women were supposed to be naturally fit, not to work for it, and definitely not to starve for it.

Outside the apartment building, a cool breeze hit her face. She popped in her ear buds, took a deep breath, and picked up the pace. As her shoes hit the pavement, she worked to establish her rhythm and get up a sweat. It wasn't enough. She could only run as fast as the streetlights and annoying pedestrians would allow. She needed to vent.

Gabe answered on the second ring. "Hello?"

"I can't deal with this anymore! I need to get out of this lease!"

"Slow down," her brother implored. "Tell me what's going on. And why do you sound out of breath? You're not jogging right now, are you?"

"It's like he's trying to get under my skin! He wants me to feel bad! He wants me to be ashamed of being a Republican. And Gabe, I can't fight back. I need a place to live! And I don't want to give him any dirt—anything he can use on me later, in my campaign. And the lease clause says he can terminate if he's unhappy, but it doesn't let me do the same. But I'm so sick of this guy and his fucking pink pussy hats and pussy posters!"

"Wait, Megan, let me catch up here. You can't break your lease, and you're worried about him leaking stuff to the press when you run. And then you said something about pussy hats?"

"Some silly feminists' march. Oh, and it gets worse. He just strips where he lands! Drops his clothes and shoes all over the place! I trip over it in the morning. Socks next to the couch *all the time*, boxers on the bathroom floor. And get this—he puts dishes in the sink, but not in the dishwasher *which is right next to the goddamn sink*. My life is total chaos right now! screw you, jerk!"

"What?" His voice sharpened.

"Not you. Some driver tried to run me over in a crosswalk."

"Are you sure you should be jogging when you're so upset? Maybe you should call me later. This doesn't seem safe—"

But there was no stopping her now. "I'd be fine, if people knew how to goddamn drive in this city!"

"Megan, have you tried talking to him?"

"Nooo..."

"So just talk to him! You never know." His tone became soothing. "Maybe he doesn't realize he's being a jerk."

Megan was reluctant to give Andrew the benefit of the doubt, but things were getting desperate. "Yeah, I guess you're right."

"And Megan?"

"Yes?"

"Aren't *you* a feminist?"

★ ★ ★

An hour later, Megan opened the door to discover a quiet apartment. Feminist art time was over, and the living room had been put back in order. Her shoulders relaxed, and she headed for the shower. Under the scorching water, her skin tingled from running in the cold. She stayed until steam filled the bathroom and her fingers started to wrinkle. Calm and clearheaded at last, she could see things for what they were. She would just talk to Andrew.

They would have a pleasant, grown-up conversation, with no arguing. How hard could that be?

All afternoon and into the evening, she waited for him to come home. She cleaned. She rearranged the furniture. With nothing left to do, she returned to the kitchen and rummaged around in the refrigerator for leftovers.

But in this apartment, even the fridge was polarized, forced to take sides, split down the middle. Her side had Bud Light, skim milk, sliced and packaged American cheese, eggs, jam, two oranges, butter, and several takeout containers of various shapes and sizes. His side, meanwhile, had micro-brewed beer, organic milk and butter, aged cheddar, crème fraîche, a drawer filled with unnamed yellow and orange vegetables, another drawer of grass-fed beef and pasture-raised hand-fed chicken, artisanal ketchup and truffle mayonnaise, leftover containers of homemade chili, chicken vindaloo, and lasagna. And just in case it wasn't abundantly clear which side belonged to him, a neon yellow Post-it note stuck to the top shelf read THE 99%.

She laughed to herself every time she read it. If only he knew how wrong he was! *Megan Thompson, in the 1%?* She grew up on Wonder Bread and no-name peanut butter and jelly sandwiches! Her clothes had come from Salvation Army and Goodwill, until she'd started working and bought her own clothes. She'd gone to a decent college, but only because she was fast. All that pent-up frustration with poverty and loss — she'd let it loose on the track and won a lot of medals. Being smart had helped, but it hadn't won her a full scholarship. Her brains alone hadn't been enough to break through the meritocracy.

How could Andrew fail to see it? He was the one who was in the 1%! She could just tell that everything had been handed to him. Probably went to Yale or Harvard, just like Mommy and Daddy. Even if she hadn't known Emily in college, she would've recognized that he came from money the moment she met his chic, snooty mother. Yes, he was the 1% all right. He just liked to pretend that he wasn't, that he was above it all. How easy it was for the rich to have sentiments like that! They could certainly afford to.

She stood with the fridge door open, weighing her options: Eat Chinese takeout from last night or the pizza from two days ago? Everything else looked a bit fuzzy, and she could just imagine the microscopic colonies of mold threatening to rise from the decay of her sad, forgotten leftovers. She would have to start cooking. Her strike against the domestic arts had gone on long enough.

Megan looked wistfully at his side of the fridge and thought. She grabbed his leftover chicken vindaloo and ate it with guilty pleasure. Then she washed his container and put it back in the fridge with her own Post-it:

> *Since you're all about redistribution of wealth, I figured you'd have no problem sharing with someone who is actually in the 99%.*

> *Megan*

Chapter Fourteen

———— ✪ ————

THE BILLIONAIRE'S SON

Megan scanned the menu and frowned. She would never get over how expensive everything was in D.C. The cheapest cocktail was the sangria at a whopping $18 a glass. In Florida, she would never have spent $18 on a bottle of wine, let alone a glass with a few ice cubes. But she grudgingly handed her credit card over the marble bar. It was a Thursday night, the eve of the presidential inauguration, and she was right there in the thick of it, at the Trump International Hotel. The place was packed, of course, so at least there was plenty of people watching to do.

With her drink in hand and her date nowhere to be found, she tried to settle in to an ornate blue velvet chair, but she felt like a child in a seat too big, her legs dangling. So now she was getting ripped off *and* mildly humiliated. Still, anything was better than meeting her latest blind date at the apartment—and giving Andrew another opportunity to heap scorn on her.

As discreetly as possible, Megan surveyed the room. Crystal chandeliers loomed overhead, and hanging from the ceiling was the biggest American flag she'd ever seen. The four TVs framing the square bar were tuned to Fox News, which was haranguing the liberals' heroes as usual. She frowned. *Don't they know our side won?* Politics was the new boxing. When had it all become such a bloody, knock-your-opponent-to-the-ground kind of sport?

Megan caught a whiff of bacon, which seemed out of place for 7 p.m. Curious, she peeked around and saw a couple at a nearby table, eating what appeared to be bacon suspended by clothespins. Her stomach grumbled a little—a testament to the power of bacon.

People flowed in and out of the hotel lobby, and Megan found she could place them into three categories: hotel guests, businesspeople, and lurkers. The bacon-loving couple, although dressed in their Midwestern Sunday best, definitely fell into the last category. The one with the bacon remarked to his wife, "You know what's great about this place? People come in for just a bite to eat, or even just a cup of coffee, and they treat us all the same. With respect. He's a real man of the people." The husband shoved a piece of bacon in his mouth and chased it with a swig of his beer.

Megan couldn't avert a sad shake of her head. The only thing that man in the White House respected was money, and she had no doubt he planned to make a lot of it during his presidency.

Glancing at her phone, she realized her date was already fifteen minutes late. How incredibly annoying and rude! She kept picking out potentials as they moved through the room: Was that one him? What about that one? Her breath caught when she glimpsed a man in a blue blazer who looked like Jason from the back, but when he turned around it was clearly someone else. Disappointment flickered in her heart.

With the move, her new job, and her campaign plans, she hadn't thought about her ex in a long time. But now, drinking alone in a bar, her thoughts turned to him. After all, they'd been engaged for two years, and together for five. They had known each other since high school. Jason was handsome and charming—born to be a used car salesman. His smile made you feel special, like he was practically giving the car away, when in truth he had sold you a lemon and made a nice margin on top of it. Part of her had always suspected he had the potential to cheat on her. But she'd overlooked this trait, calling it "charisma" and focusing instead on the others that appealed to her.

He was ambitious and hardworking, and they had shared the same vision: He was going to be rich, and she was going to be powerful. Of course, she was going to use her power to help others, to benefit the powerless. And he was supportive, which was what she'd loved about him most of all. He had encouraged her to follow her dream, and never to stop following it until she became a congresswoman. Then he had realized, rather belatedly, that motherhood and wifely duties might come second to her career.

In high school, she had barely paid him any attention. She had no time to waste on boys. Her only impression of Jason from back then was that he was a smart kid who squeaked by on his good looks and charm whenever he could. Her opinion gradually changed as the years passed. While she was getting her degree in political science, he skipped college and took over his dad's car dealership. He expanded and bought dealerships in two neighboring towns. When Megan came home for the summer her junior year, they ran into each other at the diner and casually dated all summer.

She broke things off before returning for her final year of school, thinking she would have no reason to come back to Florida. Their paths didn't cross again until Megan was almost thirty, when they got into a good-natured argument at a Chamber of Commerce meeting. The exchange continued over dinner, and then overnight. They were inseparable after that. Megan tended to cringe at the word *fate*, yet nothing else could accurately describe how they finally came together. Now she knew just how cruel fate was, leaving her single just when she needed a partner the most.

The only thing in life you can trust is yourself.

Another potential date was approaching—a tall, slender man with dark hair and preppy good looks. In a way he reminded her of Andrew, not necessarily in appearance but in how he carried himself—with all the self-confidence and self-assurance of someone who knows their place in the world is secure.

"Megan?" He flashed her a boyish grin.

She pushed off the blue velvet cushion and started to stand, all set to give him the cold shoulder and point out his tardiness. But when she looked up into his face, a little gasp escaped her. Close up, he was even better-looking, his face a classic mix of jagged edges and boyishness.

"Yes," she breathed, "and you must be Ryan." There was a moment of awkwardness as he tried to kiss her cheek and she tried to shake his hand.

"Sorry I didn't have time for supper. I'm glad you could meet up for drinks instead." His voice was pleasantly deep.

She could have sworn his gaze lingered on her chest before he made eye contact, but she decided to give him the benefit of the doubt. "Well, the good news is, if we don't like each other, we only have to stay for one."

Ryan's eyes swept the length of her body. "I have to say, you're better looking than I thought you'd be."

Did he just lick his lips? Megan grimaced. "Thank you, I guess."

He held his hands up. "No, I don't mean to be rude. It's just that when someone called from Congressman White's office, asking me to go out on a date with you because you're looking for a Republican husband—well, you can imagine what I was picturing." He signaled the waiter with a snap of his fingers. "I'll take a Glenlivet on the rocks."

Megan nodded slowly. "Fair point. So then why did you say yes?"

"My dad has been on my case forever to settle down and get a job, or he's planning to cut me off. I'd rather settle down." He snickered. "Let's just say my father always gets what he wants."

"Wait, you don't have a job? How old are you?" Megan could barely hide her disgust.

"Thirty-seven. And it's not like I've *never* had a job." He shrugged. "I've had several, and they usually end with me being politely told not to come back in on Monday."

Megan was floored. "They let you go? Why?"

"Showing up at noon. Skipping work and not calling in." Ryan grinned. "One time I went on a ski trip to Aspen, and they were all like, 'Where are you? You just started two weeks ago! You can't take vacation yet.' Can you believe them? Do they know who my father is? We're the Rushes! Number ten on the *Forbes* list!"

"Yes," Megan said icily, "when your parents are billionaires, why even bother to get a job?"

"I know, right?" He had missed her tone. "My dad says I'm an embarrassment, but what he doesn't realize is that I'm just networking... with the side benefit of getting drunk on very expensive whiskey. Hey, I like my freedom! I'm not ready to work eighty, a hundred hours a week. That's my father, not me. And that's why you and I would make a great team."

His face was deadpan. Megan searched for a hint of humor and found none. This guy was serious.

"The Rush name will open doors for you. I get to continue living my life, and you get to be a congresswoman."

She was repulsed, but also intrigued. "What kind of doors are we talking about?"

"One phone call by me, and the Congressional Leadership Fund will get out its checkbook. And trust me, it will include a lot of zeros."

Megan tried to imagine how many zeros would make marrying Ryan Rush worth it.

"Of course," he continued, "I'd also want to give input when you're in office. Make sure we're on the same page."

"What sort of input?"

Ryan took a sip of scotch. "Well, we can start by repealing Obamacare. Social programs are immoral. We shouldn't be giving people things they haven't earned. Why should hardworking, moral Americans have to buy health insurance for the lazy and the poor?"

Megan couldn't believe anyone could be so heartless. "So poor people don't deserve health insurance?"

"If you're not disciplined enough to find a job that pays, it's no one's fault but your own. If we're giving them freebies all the time, how will ever learn to pull themselves up by their own bootstraps?"

The hypocrisy was too much to ignore. "But aren't you basically freeloading off of your father's wealth?" she asked.

At least he had the decency to look offended. "I work. I just do it in my own way, behind the scenes. I have dinner and drinks with all the right people, so my dad keeps getting the oil and gas subsidies he likes so much. I lend the Rush name and face to help get candidates elected who share our values. Our family gives millions to PACs every year. You think wining and dining doesn't influence which candidates get that money?"

"I see." It was the only response Megan could come up with.

"I'm tight with some guys in the Freedom Caucus. I could introduce you. It would be great if you could join them in the House."

Thanks, but no thanks, she thought. "Honestly, I'm not interested in accepting money that comes with strings. I don't intend to be anyone's puppet."

Ryan threw his head back and laughed for a long time. "How noble! Don't fool yourself, Megan. All money comes with strings. Keep your principle, then. Just don't be surprised when you lose the election."

Megan stared at him. What was she doing here? Ryan didn't meet any of her criteria, except in the looks department. She began to collect her things.

He placed a hand on her arm. "Hold on. Let's change the subject. How about we drink and share gossip from the Hill?"

"I don't have any gossip," she spat.

"I do. Did you hear about Senator Mack accidentally posting a dick pic on Twitter?"

"What?" She dropped back into the plush chair. "Are you kidding me?"

"I know," he nodded, "that guy is, like, seventy-five years old."

She had to laugh. Senator Mack had never been high on her list. Every woman who had ever worked for him had a story. Word on the Hill was, he preferred his aides young and female. The man was downright creepy. "How can anyone even tell it's *his* dick?"

"Trust me." He gave her a knowing look. "You can tell."

"Who posted it? Must have been an intern or something."

Ryan shook his head. "Nope. The senator was trying to upload another photo, but he didn't have his glasses on. Posted the wrong photo."

Megan shook her head in disbelief. "Who was the picture for?" Surely not Mrs. Mack. She was probably pretty tired of seeing the old snake by now.

"His chief of staff. Rumor has it, they've banged a few times."

Megan shook her head again and blurted out, "Men and their penises." Her hand flew to her mouth. Sangria number two must have been stronger than she thought.

Now that she had eliminated any possibility of marrying Ryan, she was able to relax enough to enjoy his company and even not quite mind his advances. A few sangrias later, he put his hand on her thigh, and she didn't pull away.

"I got a room here. You want to come up?"

Megan deliberated. It had been almost five months. Maybe it was time for a little meaningless sex. If her roommate could do it, why shouldn't she? She debated asking Ryan back to her place, but she would never feel comfortable doing it with Andrew in the next room.

Why am I even thinking about Andrew?

Twenty minutes later, she stepped into Ryan's hotel room. She had just enough time to observe how gaudy the furnishings were, before Ryan hitched up her dress, dropped his pants, and took her on the desk. "Tell me how much you want my dick," he whispered.

What a turnoff, Megan thought, and shook her head.

The sex was about as good as she should've known it would be with a billionaire heir: swift, emotionless, and satisfying for only one of them. At least it had served as a good reminder: Sex wasn't all it's cracked up to be. She could probably survive a sexless marriage, if that's what it came down to.

She fixed her dress and quietly headed for the door. Ryan was reclining on the king-size bed, watching the news. He gave her a half-wave.

On the elevator ride down to the lobby, Megan realized she felt a little sorry for Ryan. How terrible it would be to get everything in life that you've ever wanted! If every day was your birthday, what was there to look forward to? If everything had already been built for you, what was there to strive for? She couldn't imagine a life less purposeful.

And despite what Ryan Rush thought, she refused to believe that every politician could be bought.

Chapter Fifteen

───────── ✪ ─────────

INAUGURATION

Inauguration day had arrived, and Andrew's mood was beyond foul. His morning had started with overhearing Megan on the phone, telling whoever was on the other end of the line about her plans for the inauguration ceremony, and about her date with some hot billionaire. Apparently, it had ended with sex in his hotel room. Andrew sat wallowing in his sweatpants on the couch, trying not to eavesdrop. Why was she so loud? Did she want him to hear all the sordid details?

Ugh.

When she had flounced past him in a poppy-colored dress and flashed a big, fake smile, he'd returned it with a scowl, unable to think of something witty to bring her down off her high horse.

Now he sat at home, alone with his misery, at least until his old college friends arrived later that day from New York. He decided to take a personal day, to bear witness to the downfall of his country.

He took a deep breath and tuned in to watch the coverage on CNN. Ever since the presidential race had heated up the previous summer, he'd turned into a news junkie. He hadn't been sleeping well at night. Since the election, it had only gotten worse. Like all of his friends and colleagues, he'd become addicted to social media, racing to see who could post the most articles and get the scoop on the latest protest.

The day was rainy and gray, which felt appropriate for the general mood of so many Americans. The new president's inauguration address, rather than striving to unite the country, was just a truncated version of his campaign rally speeches: short on actual policy and glowing patriotism, big on outrage and the supremacy of the ruling class. President Trump struck an unusually dark, bleak tone.

The speech wasn't the only thing notable about the event. Sixty-seven Democrats from the House of Representative refused to attend, and the crowd size was noticeably smaller than usual.

It was tempting to join one of the many protests Andrew had heard about, but he yearned to do something more positive, more peaceful. He decided to host a few of his old college friends that night instead, and attend the Women's March the following morning. He didn't know what to expect, but he hoped it would be more along the lines of Woodstock in the summer of '69 and less like the Democratic National Convention in Chicago in '68. These days there was more than enough hate and anger to go around.

★ ★ ★

Megan stood just outside the apartment door, bracing herself for the scene awaiting her inside. Andrew had mentioned a few friends from New York would be spending the night. At least she got a warning this time.

She fiddled with her keys, buying herself time, giving her a chance to process the day's events. The new president's speech had reaffirmed he was breaking away from the conservative philosophy that had governed since Reagan's era. President Trump had given his standard populist cocktail of protectionist economics, isolationist foreign policy, law-and-order bravado, and alarming patriotism. Congressman White, sitting next to her in the crowd, had seemed alert and stoic. Megan wondered if all the other Republican lawmakers were thinking the same thing she was: *We won, but at what cost?*

She straightened her spine and brushed an errant tear away and walked into the apartment. Had she stumbled into a middle-aged sorority house? Sleeping bags were scattered throughout the living room. Women in their mid-thirties were lounging on the couch and floor, cradling glasses of white wine. Aretha Franklin's "R-E-S-P-E-C-T" was blasting through the speakers. The scene was strangely familiar, as though the pussy hat knitters had somehow grown up overnight. "A few friends" had turned out to be four women. And Andrew was nowhere to be seen.

"Hi," one of the women, a brunette, called out. "Are you the roommate? Megan, right?"

There was no backing out now. "Yes."

"Come have some wine with us! I'm Alice."

Megan hesitated, thinking, *Do they know I'm a Republican?* She hated feeling that she needed to hide that piece of information, as though it were a shameful secret. "Ummm… Where's Andrew?"

"He's out getting more wine, and ingredients for supper," Alice explained. "Here, there's a teeny bit left." She poured out the last of the bottle into a fresh glass.

Megan sat on the barstool, putting a bit of distance between herself and the other women. "So, how do you know Andrew?"

Alice waved a bejeweled hand. "We all went to college with him. Environmental studies majors."

"And was he always an asshole?" Megan hadn't meant to say it, but it just slipped out.

The women exchanged quizzical looks, and Alice laughed. "What? Andrew's the nicest guy we know!"

"He was always volunteering for some club or organization. He was president of the Environment Club," a blond woman added. "I'm Claire, by the way."

"He volunteered in Africa one summer, and Honduras another, I think," said another woman, "and he was always organizing group study sessions."

The fourth woman adjusted her position on the couch. "He got the cafeterias to purchase local milk and serve some organic food. And he started a composting program, and campaigned for the school to put in more water fountains to reduce plastic water bottles."

Methinks thou doth protest too much. Megan understood now. "You guys dated him?"

Another round of laughter. "No way! Not that Andrew wasn't cute..."

"He still is!"

"But he had a serious girlfriend at another college. He was always faithful to her. Never even flirted with other girls."

Megan was confused. "We're talking about the same Andrew?"

"He's a serial monogamist," one of the women, as though it were a grave diagnosis.

Alice gave Megan a strange look. "Why on earth do you think he's an asshole?"

"He just seems very rigid with his opinions." Megan took a sip of her wine. "And a little self-righteous."

"Yeah, that can be true," Claire said. "But mostly he's a really nice guy. I mean, look, he let us four come and crash his apartment for the night so we could go to the march..."

"*Our* apartment," Megan muttered.

"And he's said a lot of nice things about you. Said he's never met someone who works as hard at their job, or who is so dedicated."

Megan was speechless. He actually said something nice about her to his friends? It didn't match up with the Andrew she knew.

Alice pulled out her cell phone. "Awww, look at Beatrice. Chris just sent me a picture of her, asleep in her bed with all her stuffed animals." This was met by a chorus of *awww*s.

"My two kids are probably consuming a year's worth of sugar at my parents' place," Claire whined. "God knows when they'll get to sleep tonight! But... not my problem." As if on cue, the women leaned in to clink their wine glasses.

"Do you all have kids?" Megan asked. Yet another thing that set her apart...

All four women nodded.

"My first night away from my kids in four years," proclaimed Claire. "Had to come march for women's rights, didn't I?"

144

Alice grunted. "Can you believe we have to do this? In 2017? It's so fucking wrong. This is the world my daughter's going to grow up in? With the groper-in-chief leading the way?"

The other women nodded emphatically.

"Bye-bye, birth control! Bye-bye, choice!" she continued. "I guess women can look forward to back-alley abortions again, too."

Megan's eyes narrowed. "Don't you think people should take some personal responsibility for themselves, and not get pregnant in the first place?"

Alice cocked her head and smiled. "Sure, personal responsibility is important. I totally agree with you, Megan. So, let's give people the tools to make the right decisions. That means proper sex education in schools, access to birth control, and—if they want to keep the baby— the support they need to live above the poverty line." She reached for a pistachio from the bowl on the table, tossed it up in the air, and caught it her mouth triumphantly. "That abstinence bullshit doesn't work and never did."

Claire put her empty wine glass on the countertop. "That's why so many young girls in our parents' days got married in the first place. They were knocked up! I know it happened to *my* mom. I'm pretty sure she would have preferred to go to law school instead of start raising a baby at age twenty."

Alice was shaking her head. "I'll never understand it. How can they claim to be 'pro-life' when it's a fetus, and then not give a shit what happens to the child after it's born?"

"Anything to keep those 'welfare mothers' from collecting a check. Because, you know, they're all just having babies to scam the system." Claire's tone was thick with sarcasm.

"But you all have children! How can anyone with a child think it's OK to kill a baby?" Megan knew her audience, but she couldn't help herself. "I mean, a baby? It's life! It's just wrong, morally wrong."

All the women's heads turned, and they stared at her as though she were an interloper.

Megan found herself backtracking, trying for some common

ground with these women who, given other circumstances and ideals, might have been her friends. "I agree with you that sexual harassment is unacceptable. I agree that women still aren't paid the same as men for equal work. I agree that women have a tougher road ahead of them to achieve a position of power. But you also have to realize that we've made a lot of progress since the 1950s. Change happens slowly."

Claire popped a pistachio in her mouth and chewed it slowly. "Change would happen a lot faster if the Republicans would stop dragging us back to the fifties. That's why we women have to stick together, right?"

Megan pretended to inspect her nails. She doubted many conservative women would be "sticking together" at the march planned for tomorrow. Megan certainly wasn't going, although she had a lot of respect for these women standing up for themselves. After sitting in the anemic, stifling crowd earlier that day, she was actually enjoying being in the company of these strong-minded women.

The old friends had erupted in long-simmering grievances.

"You know what I hate? Having to pump my breast milk in the bathroom when I go back to work. And after a measly twelve weeks! Do you know in Sweden they get, like, a year?"

"I know! I had six weeks with my baby before I dropped her off at daycare with some stranger. Six weeks! I'd just figured out how to feed her!"

"And just started to feel sort of normal again after what felt like being run over by a truck."

"You know what I hate? Child care is so expensive!"

"So fucking expensive."

"They tell us, 'Go ahead, girls, be whatever you want.' But when it comes time to have babies, they practically kick us out of our careers! They make it so hard to do both."

"The whole system is rigged."

"And of course when the kids get sick, who stays home with them? Not my husband, that's for sure."

The sound of a key in the door mercifully, in Megan's opinion, put an end to all the grumbling about working motherhood. Andrew strolled into the apartment all smiles, holding two canvas bags filled to the brim with groceries and wine. "Want to join us for dinner, Megan? Then you won't have to steal my leftovers in the middle of the night." He winked.

Was he really calling her out in front of his friends? And why did he have to always wink like that? Ignoring him, she got off the floor and bid everyone goodnight.

But she couldn't help mulling over the women's concerns as she sat on her bed, alone and tired. What would *she* do if she and her well-connected, just-for-show conservative husband ever wanted to have kids? Many people, especially among Republicans' constituents, still believed women should stay home with the kids. But it was really only the lucky few who could afford to live off the income of one breadwinner. Women made up a higher percentage of college graduates, she knew, and yet were still expected to put their careers on hold—or forced to terminate them altogether—once it came time to have a family.

Megan had just about resigned herself to never going down that path. She was approaching thirty-five, after all, and still single. And if White did end up finding her a suitable match, she wouldn't want kids right away. She would want to establish herself in her career first. She was sure even Andrew's friends would agree with her on one point: Time was not on a woman's side.

FEBRUARY HEADLINES

Tensions and chaos rattle Trump's National Security Council
—Business Times

Facing scrutiny over Russia call, Flynn steps down
— The Boston Globe

Trump intensifies criticism of F.B.I. and journalists
—The New York Times

When dating in an era of divisive politics,
both sides stick to themselves
—National Public Radio

Chapter Sixteen

✪

THE EAGLE

Megan heard the doorbell from her bedroom and sprinted for the door, hoping Andrew was still at yoga. But he emerged from his room at the same time and raced her to the door, opening it before she could.

A tall, older-looking man with dyed blond hair stood framed by the doorway. His black wide-pinstripe suit jacket struck her as somewhat incongruous with his dark denim jeans, and even more so when paired with blindingly white high-top sneakers. "Uh, hi? I'm looking for... Megan?"

Megan moved to grab her purse and coat from the closet. "I'll be right with you!"

Andrew was still standing in the doorway eyeing the visitor suspiciously, neither moving from his spot nor introducing himself. He had taken on the posture of intimidating father.

Well, Megan already had an intimidating father. "This is my roommate, Andrew." She gently but firmly moved him aside.

"I'm Ted. Ted Eagle." He clamped down on Andrew's hand.

Andrew made no effort to hide his contempt. "Eagle? That's a pretty, uh... all-American name." He arched an eyebrow at Megan as if to say, *Seriously? This guy?*

Ted puffed himself up. "Damn straight it is."

"Andrew's a Democrat," Megan added, stepping into the hall.

"You don't say!" Ted chuckled.

"Don't stay out too late, kids!" Andrew called after them.

Megan smiled to herself as Ted guided her by the elbow to the elevator. At least she had gotten under Andrew's skin.

Thirty minutes later, Megan and her date were seated in a private booth at the Occidental Grill and Seafood, a place where ordinary folk could dine and drink like statesmen. Megan's gaze wandered around the room to the photographs covering the walls, mostly of male politicians and celebrities. Over the past century, the restaurant had seen a lot of power brokering. This was where history had unfolded. Megan liked it already.

She had much more tempered expectations for the man sitting across from her. When the waiter arrived, Ted snapped the menu closed and proceeded to order. "We'll take a bottle of your finest red. I'll have a steak, rare. And she'll have... ?"

Megan rushed to look over the menu. "Ah... I'll have the snapper." The waiter filled their water glasses and whisked the menus away. Ted said nothing, simply staring at her as though she were a butterfly pinned down for his viewing pleasure. She took a sip of her water and tried to make polite conversation. "So, Ted, what do you do?"

"Well, I was formerly a White House communications director. I've also dabbled in lobbying and political consulting. Now I'm the founder and director for TakeOut Strategy, a communications consulting firm. I've written a book exposing the Clintons. And I have a little blog. You may have heard of it? It's called EagleWatch."

"Impressive." Megan nodded her head politely, then froze. "Wait. Isn't EagleWatch a right-wing conspiracy blog?"

Ted grinned, showing teeth as sparkling white as his high-tops. "Why, yes, that's the one."

"With a history of outright lying?"

"Lying, lies, liar..." He chuckled. "It all sounds so harsh. I prefer the term 'alternative facts.'" He seemed rather proud of his own cognitive dissonance.

"Well, *I* prefer to call an ace, an ace." She leveled her gaze at him "Lies are lies, Ted, and people who tell them are liars." She could think of a couple offhand that she'd heard just since the inauguration last week: *Between 3 million and 5 million votes caused me to lose the popular vote. Now, the audience was the biggest ever, but this crowd was massive. Look how far back it goes. This crowd was massive.*

The waiter arrived with the wine, holding the bottle out for Ted and then uncorking it in one swift motion before pouring an inch into the glass.

Ted held it up to the light and, with a showy flick of his wrist, sent the ruby-colored wine swirling like a vortex. He breathed in through his nose, sucked a tiny sip through his teeth, and nodded once to the waiter. Then he held the glass aloft and toasted himself. "I believe in freedom, baby. The freedom for Americans to choose what they believe."

"Well, I miss the good old days, when you could form your own opinion but not your own facts."

He smirked at her from across the table. "You're too young to remember the good old days, Megan. And anyway, those days are long gone thanks to cable television, the internet, social media. Now any conspiracy theorist with a computer can find a community online, willing and eager to reinforce his crazy ideas." His grin stretched wider still. "The good news—for me at least—is that it's extremely profitable."

Megan had to change the subject. The conversation was getting just too depressing. "I have to ask, is your last name really Eagle?"

"Nope. Born Theodore Stein. But I changed it as soon as I legally could."

"And you chose Eagle because… ?"

"What's more American than an eagle? A swift, ruthless predator with sharp claws. Part loner, part badass. Seemed to fit." He laughed a little. Megan couldn't tell whether he was being serious.

Ted downed the last of his wine, poured a second glass from the bottle, and leaned back in his chair, lifting a sneaker to rest on the opposite knee. "So, Megan. Why would a young, attractive woman like you be willing to enter into a marriage of convenience? Which, for the record, is not that uncommon. I just want to know how you justify it."

"Well, I want to run for Congress. And it's been suggested that I might need a little help making myself appealing to fundraisers and the voters, if you know what I mean." She sipped her wine.

"Let me get this straight. This is all about getting you elected?"

She didn't reply.

"Why whore yourself out for a measly hundred and seventy thou a year? Is it the privilege of working long hours, going to endless fundraisers, or dealing with impossible constituent complaints?" Ted paused as if sizing her up. "Or is it about the title? You don't seem like someone who's in it for the money."

"It's not about the title, and no, I don't care about making oodles of money." Here she was, explaining herself again! What was so hard to understand? "I want to help people. I want to make a diff—"

"Why not join the Peace Corps, then?" he smirked. "Or work as a teacher?"

Megan had just about reached the end of her rope. "Look, I don't need to explain my motivations to you. I'm going to be a congresswoman one day. I want a partner who understands the long hours, the sacrifice I'll have to make, and not hold it against me. And it would be nice to find someone I get along with, someone I like, and who—" She stopped herself. Why should she share her feelings with Ted Eagle? She couldn't even bring herself to like him, let alone fall in love with him, and she certainly had no intention of marrying him. Quite the opposite. Her opinion of him was diminishing further and further by the minute. By the end of the dinner, she would probably flat-out hate him.

"And who happens to be handsome, rich, and connected?" He shook out his bleached mane and gave what he probably thought was an impish smile.

Megan shuddered in disgust and stared back at him. "And

preferably not an asshole."

"Afraid I can only help you with the first three things, because I am most definitely an asshole." He laughed like a school boy making a dirty joke.

Megan wished he wasn't enjoying this so much. "Well, what's in for you? Why would you possibly entertain marrying someone you'd just met?"

"Well, for starters, I'm looking to settle down again. Third time's a charm, I hear." He held up his bare ring finger and wiggled it. "And you're hot. A little old for my taste, but I keep getting burned with the young chicks. I'm tired of giving my money away. So I thought, 'Hey, Ted, maybe try a new approach. Maybe date an older, more desperate woman. Someone who's grateful for the opportunity to marry. Maybe even settle down and pop out a kid or two.'"

"I'm thirty-five." Her blue eyes flashed like cold steel. "And I'm not desperate."

Ted ignored her. "Actually, I really like the idea of you running for office. It would be fun to get you elected. Never tried it with a woman before. Truly, that might be the only thing I haven't tried with a woman, if you get my drift." His peroxided eyebrows emphasized the obscenity of the last words.

She suppressed a gag and covered it with a fake cough.

"And we'd be quite the power couple. You in office. Me as the media and political consultant. And who knows," he said, undressing her with his creepy eyes, "maybe one day you'll be our first woman president, and I'll be the first man."

Megan acquired a sudden fascination with her snapper, cutting a tiny piece and dousing it in the fava bean puree. Then she pierced a juicy chanterelle mushroom, imagining for a moment that she was skewering Ted Eagle.

"I've helped out a lot of Republicans with my blog. I mean, I was pretty instrumental in getting Trump elected. Of course, I'll never get credit for it." Ted waved his fork in the air before shoving a large, bloody piece of steak in his mouth. He had only begun chewing when he chased it down with a slosh of wine, nodding all the time. "This has potential."

The waiter presented them with dessert menus. Megan thrust hers back at him. "You know, I've kind of lost my appetite."

Ted didn't seem to get the message. "Glass of Sauternes and the lemon-ginger crème brulée. It's just like me. Crusty on the outside, gooey on the inside."

Dear god, when will this date be over?

When his dessert arrived, Ted shoveled the fancy custard into his mouth. "So you ran White's campaign. How did you take out your opponents?"

"What are you talking about?"

"Did you run negative ads? Bring up dirt during the debates? Or what?"

Megan crossed her arms. "I don't work that way. I run an honest campaign. White has forty-four years of experience His record speaks for itself!"

"Ah, so you're a virgin in the dark arts." He chuckled again. "You know, nice won't get you elected. Not in this world. People vote when you stir up their emotions. And the best emotion is anger."

"I'm getting pretty sick of people telling me that," Megan snapped.

Ted unbuttoned his suit jacket and lifted a navy cashmere sweater to reveal a graphic shirt that looked like a lithograph. It was styled like the Obama *HOPE* posters, but instead it showed the face of Bill Clinton. Megan read the word underneath: *RAPE*.

"Now *this* is how you win elections," he beamed. "Isn't it great? This shirt will forever be a reminder that we took down the Clinton machine…"

Megan sat in stunned silence. Was this jerk seriously the best match Congressman White could find for her?

Ted was still talking. "And you know what I like about us—"

"There is no us," she quickly retorted.

"Not yet." He winked. "Unlike my previous wives, who married me for my money—I married one for her ass and the other for her

154

tits—but this time it would be fun to have a partner in crime. We could work together toward something really great."

Megan took the last sip of her wine, but it didn't rinse the bad taste from her mouth.

Ted squinted at his oversized Rolex. "I've got another meeting in twenty minutes, but I can skip it if you were thinking of inviting me back to your place?" His eyebrows waggled suggestively. "Your liberal wussy roommate can watch a real man in action."

"Ted, let me blunt." Megan pursed her lips, reaching for her wallet. "Never gonna happen."

"The sex? Or the marriage?"

"Thanks for dinner." She stood up to leave, dropping fifty bucks on the table.

Ted reached out with one hand and slid the bills toward himself. "OK, you can think about it."

Megan hurried toward the exit.

"The offer is still on the table," he called after her, "but you better hurry up, Cinderella. Before that ass turns into a pumpkin." His loud guffaw followed her out into the cold.

Outside the restaurant, Megan felt as though she'd stepped out of a bad movie and back into reality. She drew the arctic February air into her lungs. Instead of hailing a cab, she decided to walk a bit to clear her head.

She looked down Pennsylvania Avenue. If she walked one way, she'd reach the White House. The other way took her toward home. Under ordinary circumstances, the beauty of it would buoy her spirits. Here was where the leader of the free world lived! And she wanted him to succeed, because it meant success for the rest of the country. But only a month into this presidency, it was very clear that he had no idea how to govern.

As her feet pounded the frozen sidewalk, she was having second thoughts to White's proposal about making a power match. Valentine's

Day had come and gone three days ago, and she had celebrated her single status by eating a box of chocolates in her room while cleaning up voter lists. Her one consolation was that Andrew had done pretty much the same thing, stuffing his face with chocolates in front of the television. But still, she had felt oddly optimistic about her date with Ted Eagle. Now? She just felt defeated. What were the odds she'd find, in time for her campaign, someone who was decent enough to marry? Removing romance from the equation was supposed to make things easier, but it was turning out to be much harder than she thought.

It wasn't like she was even being very picky. She wasn't rejecting these guys for tiny flaws such as picking food out of one's tooth in full view, or leering at the cocktail waitress, or not-so-discreetly rearranging things "down there," or spending a suspicious amount of time in the restroom. No, Megan liked to believe she could have easily overlooked those totally human foibles. But she drew the line at dating someone whose character was deeply flawed, like Ryan Rush's or Ted Eagle's—much less marrying him. She only had the four criteria, and yet the candidates so far had barely been able to meet two of them. If she was drawing up blank while only looking for a marriage of convenience with someone who wasn't an asshole, what hope did women her age stand of finding love? She had to admit, her motivation to beat Carmela in the fiancée department was fading faster than a sun setting on a flat horizon.

She would have to discuss the whole strategic marriage idea with Congressman White on Monday. Did he really think she could marry one of these men? Did he expect her to overlook their sheer lack of decency and integrity? It occurred to her that maybe a decent man wouldn't want to settle for a loveless power match, and maybe that was why she was having such a hard time.

But what did that make her, then—someone who was indecent? Megan didn't want to dwell on that question. She wanted to hold office ever since she was a young girl, and she still wanted it more than anything. But maybe there were limits to what she was willing to do in order to get there.

A chill ran through her body. Was it from the cold, or was it the sudden tug of loneliness? That was a feeling she couldn't tolerate. Loneliness led to self-pity, which dredged up feelings and memories from the past. Megan didn't operate by looking backward. She only went forward, keeping her eye on the prize, living for the future. *Once you set your sights on something, you don't back down*, she repeated to herself.

Ignoring the awkwardness of her heels on the ice, she sped up until she spotted the Metro entrance beckoning her into its relative warmth. She was eager to get to the apartment, throw on some pajamas, crawl into bed, and forget this date ever happened.

Waiting for the train, she pulled out her phone.

Megan: Had another date tonight. Completely terrible person.

Mike: Do tell!

Megan: Apparently I was too old for him, but he was willing to give me a shot at being wife #3 anyway.

Mike: Lucky you.

Megan: Let me split the check after he ordered the most expensive wine and drank almost the whole bottle.

Mike: How progressive of him!

Megan: Said he knows how "modern women" want to be treated like equals.

Mike: Yes, I seem to recall that's what equal rights is all about. Not equal pay. Equal chance to split the check!

Megan: Worst part is, he'll probably use the whole meal as a tax write-off.

Mike: No nuptials in the future, then?

Megan: Not with this asshole.

Mike: Don't worry, honey. Your shiny white Republican knight is out there!

Megan wasn't so sure. But if he really was out there somewhere, he'd better hurry up and come to her rescue. She was beginning to think she was the last person left with any principles.

★ ★ ★

*S*urely *a few drops could do no harm?* Megan thought optimistically. And even if Andrew did turn out to be angry, she was pretty sure it would be worth it.

It had been a lazy Saturday morning so far. She deserved it, after the fiasco of a date with the Eagle. She had slept in and skipped her run, and now she was filling the bath and preparing for a long soak. She'd found a little aromatherapy bottle lined up along Andrew section of the bathroom counter. *Some hippy-dippy stuff, no doubt.* But when she'd opened the cap and inhaled the lavender scent, it was like the opposite of a shot of espresso—a straight bolt of tranquility flooding her nervous system.

After about ten seconds of debating her conscience, she read the directions and poured several drops under the hot running water. The room seemed to blossom with billowing steam and the smell of Provence. How long had it been since she'd treated herself like this? She made a mental note: *Get massage and facial ASAP.*

Her hour-long spa-like session complete, she wrapped one fluffy white towel around her head and another around her pampered body. Opening the bathroom door, she almost slammed into something: Andrew and… a giant whiteboard?

"What the hell?" So much for her calm, relaxed state of mind.

"Is that lavender I smell?" He peeked at her over the top of the board, one eyebrow arched.

"I might have spilled a little." Embarrassment seeped in, and all that lovely tranquility dissipated.

Andrew was still staring at her, his eyes grazing the point where towel met bare skin. Her skin prickled under his gaze, and she tried to hide an involuntarily shiver, grasping her towel firmly with one hand. The last thing she needed was for the towel to choose this moment to loosen and slide, ensuring her mortification and many more dinners alone in her room.

"What's the whiteboard for?" she asked tersely, rubbing her arms as though to erase an unwanted touch.

"You'll see."

His smile unnerved her.

Andrew waited for Megan to pass by and close her bedroom door behind her. Then he let out his breath and continued toward the front door. His heart was pounding. That brief peek at her nearly naked body had reminded him that she was more than just the enemy. She was a woman, and an attractive one. He was both repulsed and aroused by her at the same time. Andrew shook the thoughts loose. *You're just hungover and lonely. Don't even go there.* He reminded himself of his conversation with his father and his warning about dating a Republican. *Fat chance.*

He screwed the whiteboard to the inside of the door. Then, with a black dry-erase marker, he wrote *Trump Lies*, and beneath it, *Inauguration crowd bigger than Obama's. Bigger than Women's March.*

He stepped back and allowed himself a small, cynical smile. The idea for the board had come to him the previous night at his new home away from home: the dive bar on 7th Street. For the past month, his routine had been work, gym, bar, home. And then repeat. Lifting weights and rock climbing helped release his anger, and beer helped drown his sorrow. Last night, a guy from the gym had suggested recording everything the new administration said and did, as a reminder that none of it was normal. Andrew liked that idea. It would be a good reminder for him. And for his roommate.

Megan came out of her room, slipping her heels on and muttering, "Great, just what I want to read every morning on my way to work."

Andrew was not deterred. "I am simply recording our Dear Leader's wisdom and guidance. As a daily reminder that everything happening in our government right now is *not normal.*"

She let out a sigh. "OK, have fun with that." She brushed past him, reaching into the closet for her coat.

"Where are you going so early on Saturday?"

"Not that you'd care, but I'm meeting with a political consultant."
She lifted her chin defiantly. "Andrew? Can I tell you something?"

He waited.

"You stink. Take a shower."

The door closed behind her with a definitive click.

He brought his nose to his armpit. *Damn, I do need to shower*, he
thought. But it was Saturday morning, so he shrugged his shoulders
and walked to the fridge instead.

Sitting at the couch with a couple of beers and a bag of pretzels, he
changed the channel to MSNBC. Time to play the latest liberal media
drinking game: take a sip every time a talking head threw around the
words *impeachment* or *Russia investigation*—useless life rafts offered to
their drowning viewers.

MARCH HEADLINES

GOP health plan would leave 24 million more uninsured
— The Wall Street Journal

Trump signs rule to block efforts on aiding climate
— The New York Times

Why politics is failing America
—Fortune

Chapter Seventeen

—————— ✪ ——————

ENOUGH IS ENOUGH

T he war of the roommates continued. Megan had gotten accustomed to the ridiculous whiteboard after a few days, and even had to stifle a laugh at some of Andrew's more amusing notations. As the new president's 100-day mark grew nearer, the angry tit-for-tat between the two adversaries was getting old. Megan was even starting to think they had reached some sort of détente. Maybe things were finally going to get better.

Then one Thursday at the end of March, when she was in the bathroom getting ready for work, she opened the medicine cabinet where she stashed her birth control, and found a note attached to her makeup bag:

> Dear Megan,
>
> You might want to stock up on these before you repeal and replace the Affordable Care Act. Also, fun fact: Did you know your friends in Congress think being a woman should be considered a pre-existing condition?
>
> Love,
>
> Andrew

Furious, she crumpled the note and threw it in the little garbage can. *Hell, no.* He had crossed a line.

She grabbed her phone. As usual, Gabe came through, picking up after only one ring. "Hey, I'm driving to work right now, so I may lose you. If I do, just—"

"Gabe, this asshole has gone too far! He's sneaking into my stuff now! He put a note on my birth control!"

"What? Ew. That's creepy, Megan. Are you OK?"

"And he's making donations to all sorts of liberal groups. Planned Parenthood, the ACLU, the NRDC... all in my name! Now I'm on their mailing lists!"

"Very charitable of you."

"It's not funny! He's using me as his punching bag, and I've just about reached my limit."

"I know, I know. I'm sorry. Look, here's my advice. You said his sister was really nice and sane, right? And you two are on friendly terms? So why not reach out to her, see if she can help?"

Megan sighed, considering his suggestion. "Yeah. Maybe."

"Or were you just calling to vent?"

She smiled. Her brother knew her so well. "You know I don't like getting people involved in my problems."

"Then you have no choice but to confront him. I know that's not what you want to hear, but he's all in your business, and that's not right."

Gabe was right, of course. And she wasn't going to back away from conflict this time.

Megan went to the kitchen and dug around under the sink, pulling out a hammer and the largest nail she could find. Gabe was still offering encouragement as she strode into Andrew's room with a renewed sense of purpose.

"Um, Megan? What's that pounding noise?"

Megan threw the phone aside and began hammering. She could hear her brother yelling through the phone as he drove down some Florida highway or other.

"Megan? Megan? What's that noise? Are you still there?"

"Hm? Oh, it's nothing." Megan grabbed one of Andrew's beloved Post-it notes from his desk and scribbled on it. Then she pounded the nail into the wall, stuck the pink note to the end of the nail head, and stepped back to take a look at her handiwork.

That should hammer *home the point*, she thought, giggling. Who knew revenge could be so fun?

"Megan, did you hear me? You have to confront him!"

She lifted the phone from Andrew's bed. "Yes. Confront him. Got it. Love you, little brother." She hung up before he could say anything else.

Megan lingered in his room a little longer than she should, but it was only fair given how Andrew had already violated *her* personal space and privacy. The first thing she noticed was all the beer bottles in the garbage can next to his bed. That was no surprise, given that seeing him passed out on the couch when she left for work in the morning was becoming a common occurrence. Not that it was her problem.

Other than that, it was hard not to notice how tidy he kept his room. His bed was made. No clothes were on the floor or draped over his chair. No dirty dishes were piled under the bed. She had imagined it would be different, considering he'd come from a life of privilege. His walls were decorated with glossy photos of the outdoors: snow-covered mountains, reddish-orange deserts and canyons, giant sequoia trees. Had he clipped these from a magazine, or were they simply shot by an amateur with a good camera?

Maybe he's taken them on his own adventures, she mused. There was so much about him she didn't know. But that was hardly her fault. The only side of himself he ever showed her was that of the asshole making her life more difficult.

A ndrew got home a little after 11 p.m. He dropped his jacket on the floor and braced himself with one hand on the wall in the hallway as he struggled to remove his sneakers. After weaving his way toward his bedroom in darkness, he shed his clothes on the floor and crawled into bed. Just as he was about to doze off, he remembered. *Gotta charge the phone.*

He switched on the light next to his bed—and saw a large nail piercing the wall above his head. Fastened beneath it was a stack of condoms, and above it was a Post-it note.

What the fuck does that mean?

He stumbled back out of bed and down the hallway. Without knocking, he shoved open the door to Megan's bedroom. The door banged against the wall, and she propped herself up on an elbow, rubbing her eyes as if to adjust to the bright hallway light behind him.

Probably just drifting off to sleep. Good.

Andrew spoke quietly from the shadows of the doorway. "Did. You. Nail. My. Condoms. To. The. Wall."

"Yes. Every last one." Her voice was saccharine, and she lifted her head defiantly. "Are you coming to borrow some? Because I don't have any."

"No! I was just about to go to sleep. And you know, what you did—that's pretty messed up." He didn't even know how to respond to the not-so-veiled threat on the Post-it note:

> *I'm a proud member of the NRA. Stay away from my birth control.*

Something occurred suddenly to Andrew: Did she have a gun in there somewhere? Because you just never knew how crazy these conservatives might get. He took a step forward, and she sat up as if on high alert.

"Andrew, don't take another step toward me!" She sounded nervous, and pulled her covers up to her neck as though to hide, even though she was wearing a T-shirt.

He looked at her quizzically. "What's the big d—"

"You're naked!"

"I am?" He looked down and swore under his breath. Flustered, he started searching for a pillow or something to hide behind, at last reaching for a stuffed teddy bear he found on her bureau.

She gasped as he strategically covered himself. "That's it! I can't take this anymore! Get out of my room! NOW!"

He had never seen her so irate. "I—I'm really sorry! It was an accident! I didn't mean—honestly, Megan, I'm sorry!"

"*OUT!*"

Andrew spun around, switching the bear to cover his tush, and hurried back to his room.

Shaking with rage and fear and something else, Megan peeled off her pajamas and hurried downstairs, hopping into her taxi. It was almost midnight when she knocked on the door of her only friend in D.C. "I'm sorry. I just couldn't stay there another night."

Emily took her in without hesitation, settling her on a white leather couch, wrapping her in a crocheted blanket, and making her drink hot chamomile tea. "Do you want me to move Mittens?" Emily asked when she returned to the living room with her own mug of tea and set it down on the coffee table, sinking into the couch next to Megan.

"No, I like cats. My dad would never let me get one." All curled up on Megan's lap, the Maine Coon seemed cozy. The size of a small dog, and extremely fluffy, Mittens reminded her of a miniature bobcat. "Emily, I'm sorry. Thanks again for letting me crash here tonight."

Megan could see Andrew's sister was torn between being a good host who lets her guest relax and being a professional mediator who gets to the bottom of things. The temptation proved too great. "I don't want to intrude," Emily said at last, "but may I ask what's going on between you two?"

Oh, so many things. Megan took a deep breath. Where to begin? "I think he's trying to drive me insane. And it's working."

"What do you mean?"

"He's saving up all his anger about the election, and taking it out on me."

Emily sighed. "Let me guess. Post-it notes? Newspaper clippings? A political sit-in or two at your apartment?"

Megan was stunned. "How did you guess?"

"He did the same thing to my dad, during the financial collapse of 2008. Took all his anger at Wall Street and redirected it. As if Dad were solely responsible!" Emily shook her head. "He's so passive aggressive. Left notes all around the house as reminders of lost retirement savings, houses, jobs. Clipped out articles about housing foreclosure and the employment rate, and put them on the coffee pot and in my dad's briefcase. He hosted Occupy Wall Street in our living room, for god's sake! We looked like a homeless camp for three days. Finally my mother had enough and kicked them all out. And my father just pretended it wasn't happening. It would've gone on forever if I hadn't stepped in."

Megan whistled. "Wow. Your brother has problems."

Emily explained that she had tried for years to get Andrew and their dad to sit down and have an honest, open conversation. And now, with the whole political climate, things were worse than ever.

'He's got a strong sense of justice. He sees things in black and white, so you're either all good or all bad. It's a very unrealistic way to approach the world. But he learned from a young age that strong opinions and feelings should either be redirected, which is what Mom always does, or be ignored, which is what Dad does." She held out both hands as though balancing weights. "So he found another way to communicate how he feels: using in-your-face tactics that you can't ignore."

It made sense to Megan, but she had to draw the line at a naked confrontation in her bedroom.

Emily shook her head. "What was he thinking? Megan, I'm really sorry you're having these problems. I should've seen this coming."

"It's not your fault, Emily! Don't blame yourself. You had no idea."

"Well, let me ask you, did things get worse after Christmas?"

Megan sipped the warm, soothing tea. "Yes. Definitely."

"That's what I thought." Emily nodded. "Look, I'm going to tell you something, but please don't tell Andrew I told you."

No problem, since Megan planned never to speak to him again.

"My father announced to the family over Christmas dinner that he voted for Trump," Emily continued. "My mother is devastated. She kicked him out. He's been staying at the apartment in the city. It's not an excuse for my brother's behavior. He shouldn't be venting his anger on you. But I honestly don't think he realizes what he's doing or how badly it's affecting you."

Megan nodded. Things were starting to make more sense. "Emily, there's something I think you should know." She looked down at her hands, trying to find the right words. "I think your brother is depressed. He's been drinking. A lot."

Emily looked concerned. "What do you mean, drinking a lot?"

"I've been finding him passed out on the couch. And I see all the empty beer bottles..." Megan placed her hand on Emily's. "I know the signs. I've been here before."

Emily shook her head. "I knew he was feeling low, I didn't know it was this bad."

They sat in silence for a long time, and Megan's tears began welling up. It wasn't just Andrew. Half the country was furious with her for voting for Trump—or outright hated her for being a Republican. She turned her head away. "If you don't mind, Emily, I think I'll just go to sleep now. I have an early day tomorrow."

"Sure. Of course." Emily rose, and Mittens leapt up from Megan's lap to follow her. "Let me know if you need any more pillows or blankets."

"No, this is perfect." Megan hated asking for help, let alone imposing. "I'm sorry. I'll find a hotel room tomorrow night, I promise."

"Well, maybe you won't have to." Emily responded. "And thank you for sharing your concern for Andrew."

But Megan tossed and turned on the leather couch, exhausted but still awake, her mind trying to process the events of the day. Everything she was dealing with, and now she could add insomnia to the list! She was desperate for something, anything in her life to be under her control.

As a little girl she had learned to depend on no one but herself, thanks to both minor embarrassments and painful lessons that had left an imprint on her soul. She cringed when remembering how she used to shave her legs dry, with those cheap pink Bic razors—a miracle that she never bled to death!—or how she stole sanitary napkins from her friends' bathrooms and the nurse's office, stuffing her purse any chance she got, like a hotel guest pocketing every toiletry item in the room. Buying them herself was too humiliating for a young girl, and asking her father was worse. As far as he was concerned, she'd never even gotten her period. And Megan was just as ignorant as her father about using tampons.

The last time she'd really reached out for help, she had been only thirteen, calling her Aunt Nancy from the beige rotary phone mounted on the kitchen wall. Stretching the cord away from her father, who sat motionless in the dark living room, she'd whispered, "I'm sorry," over and over into the receiver. Her father had been sitting on the couch for nearly a week, drinking beer and smoking cigarettes. He'd built a fortress of cans around him, impenetrable except for whenever he had to use the bathroom. Then he would stand unsteadily and lurch forward, forgetting about his fortifications, and they would crash to the floor. Megan and Gabe had resorted to mooching food off neighbors and friends, showing up like stray cats at feeding time. Even in the best of times, when their father showed up for work, the Thompson cupboards were sparse. Paul wouldn't go to the food pantry and would rather die than apply for food stamps. This time around, there was neither a morsel in the house nor a dollar bill in his wallet.

The Thompson kids had tried to spread their need over many houses like good strays would—stopping by enough to leave people feeling virtuous and not suspicious or annoyed. But the neighborhood parents were on tight budgets, too, and were starting to lose patience with two extra mouths to feed. And then the school had started to notice. Concerned teachers were pulling Gabe and Megan aside, asking why they had no lunch today. They stopped showing up for class, but Megan knew that wasn't going to work for long. People would start spreading rumors, and that would hurt her father's pride. Plus, Megan couldn't watch her brother go hungry, and she missed going to school.

So Aunt Nancy came over, and in not-so-gentle terms told her father to get off his lazy, miserable ass and provide for his family already, or she would take the kids with her. Megan's dad did get off his ass and go back to work, but he gave Megan the silent treatment for almost two weeks—a time that was among the most excruciating of her childhood memories. He was punishing her for airing their dirty laundry. A man wasn't a man if he couldn't provide for his family.

The consequences of an absent mother, Megan thought now before finally drifting off on Emily's white couch.

Chapter Eighteen

— ✪ —

COMMON GROUND

After work the next evening, Megan timed her arrival at the apartment to coincide with Emily's. Her friend had convinced her not to go to a hotel, but she didn't have the strength or the guts to face Andrew alone.

She had spent all day sitting in on the House Intelligence Committee meeting. White had insisted she take his place and report back about the first public hearing on Russia's meddling in the U.S. election. But instead of paying close attention, her mind kept wandering back to her discussion that morning with Emily, sitting around her modern, glossy white dining table over coffee. Emily's cat had jumped back into Megan's lap and twitched her tail, demanding to be pet. Stroking the cat's smooth fur and long, bushy tail had lulled Megan into a trance.

"You may find hair in your coffee and… well, all over you," Emily had warned with an indulgent smile at Mittens.

"Yeah, it's fine. Really. I'm just sorry I —"

"Megan, if you say sorry one more time! Listen, I don't think you should move out. Andrew called me this morning. He wants to try and work things out."

Megan released a throaty *Ha!*

"Do you want to try?" Emily nudged her gently. "I can come over tonight and help you guys start a conversation."

Megan thought it over. "You mean like… couples therapy?"

Emily chuckled. "Yes, essentially. I'm not going to lie—this sort of mediation makes some people very uncomfortable."

Megan stopped petting Mittens, who arched her back as if to say, *Hello? Over here!*

Maybe it was the thought of having to find a new apartment, especially with her full schedule and her career plans for later that year. Or maybe she kept circling back to the day they first met and how well they had clicked. There had been an instant connection in the elevator, a spark, hadn't there? Until he found out she was a Republican. If she could have *that* Andrew as a roommate, things would be just fine.

Emily's explanation had revealed a whole new layer of Andrew's personality that Megan hadn't known about. *How many layers do we have to penetrate until we get to the real person?* she wondered.

Still a bit on edge, she had decided to give this mediation thing a chance before moving out. Once in the apartment, though, she wasn't so sure.

She didn't look at Andrew, but headed straight to the fridge for a bottle of wine. Maybe if alcohol were permitted during therapy sessions, people would be more inclined to go. It was the liquid courage, the truth serum, the great un-inhibitor. She poured a generous glass.

Emily rearranged the furniture in the living room while Andrew stood by the island, looking like a naughty boy who knows he's about to be punished. She glanced at Megan, who gestured with the bottle of Chardonnay. "None for me, thanks. This is a bit unorthodox, but I will permit you both to have a glass of wine."

Too late, thought Megan, who was on her second glass. She poured out a glass and handed it to Andrew. He gave a half smile and then resumed his awkward stance.

Firmly in charge now, Emily had placed the two barstools a foot's distance apart and an armchair several feet away. "Please, sit." She motioned with an open palm, like a flight attendant—polite but authoritative.

Megan groaned inwardly. Andrew didn't look happy about it either, but Emily's frown was foreboding. Each roommate chose a barstool, and although their bodies faced front, their eyes traveled the room, staring at their hands, the ceiling—anything but each other.

"OK, I know this is going to be hard. But the first thing I want you to do is take thirty seconds and look at each other. Just make eye contact."

Andrew was squirming now, his eyes darting up to Megan's face and back down to his hands. Megan felt no less comfortable, but finally she caught his eye and held his gaze. She had never noticed how deep his blue eyes were, and under such long and thick lashes! The arched eyebrows framing them seemed to magnify their depths. An unfamiliar sensation arose. She broke eye contact.

"Good, that's good," Emily murmured. "We are here today because Megan is having a hard time living with you, Andrew, and she wants to move out. I would like to help you figure out if that is what you both want. We will have a dialogue, not a debate. We will share our feelings, and hopefully we can come to a place of mutual respect and understanding. Agreed?"

Both roommates nodded.

"First, we are going to talk about what's going on. Megan will start by sharing her feelings. Andrew will listen. When she is done, Andrew, you will repeat back to Megan what she has just told you. Then it will be Andrew's turn. And I want you to talk to each other, which means you need to look at each other and not at me."

Megan took a deep breath.

ndrew reached for his wineglass and took a nice, big sip. He shouldn't have ended last night with tequila shots. No good comes from drinking tequila. But embarrassed as he was about walking into her room naked, he was also disturbed by her gunslinger's note and her aggressive condom art. She had warned him that first day about her short fuse, and clearly he had crossed that threshold.

"Andrew," Megan began, her voice quiet and unsteady, crossing her arms in front of her, in a protective gesture, "you've been a jerk to me since the day you found out I was Republican." Her voice grew louder, and she fixed him with a cold stare. "I've been your punching bag for months, and I'm sick of it! Yes, I am a Republican, but I'm not the whole Republican Party. You have no right to attack me every time the president does something you don't like. And he's our President now, so just get over it!"

"OK. Andrew, can you repeat Megan's words so she knows you've heard her?" Emily coaxed, turning toward him.

He resisted rolling his eyes. His sister was really taking her role as mediator to heart. "Megan, you think I've been a jerk to you because you're a Republican. You think I've been treating you unfairly. I don't know what exactly it is I've done to you, but you think I blame you for Trump and I'm punishing you for his actions."

"Do you think he heard you Megan?"

"Yes, except for the part where he doesn't seem to remember how he's made my life hell these past three months." Megan's eyes narrowed. "You know what really gets me about all this? You liberals love to preach tolerance for everyone *except* conservatives. You can't stand anyone who thinks differently from you!"

"Alright, Andrew how would you like to respond?"

"Well," Andrew scoffed, "I would really like Megan to tell me what I supposedly did to make her life such hell?"

Megan was still trying to stare him down. "Let's see... You put up a giant Obama poster to provoke me. You leave magazines on the bathroom floor open to articles about Trump. You host your hat-knitting parties and your poster-making parties here, with no consideration for me. You bring home college girls and have noisy sex with them—"

Andrew's hands flew up in defense. "Whoa!"

"Then there's the giant whiteboard, the Post-it notes... Is that enough, or should I go on?"

He winced. "OK, I'll admit some of that stuff was to piss you off. Like the Post-its. But you weren't exactly innocent either!" He pointed a finger at the TV. "You blast Fox News at six a.m. You eat my leftovers without asking. You use my bathroom products. You gave me a Trump hat for Christmas. And I only brought home one girl! If you recall, you decided that would be a great time to go into the kitchen and unload the dishwasher, drop pans on the floor, slam all the cupboard doors—"

"What about the rest of it?" Megan crossed her arms. "That was all innocent, then?"

"Yes!" Andrew sighed. There was no winning this debate. "The magazines are on the bathroom floor because I like to read when I'm, you know, using the bathroom. The Obama poster is because I need to see something positive, to remind myself that we had a great president once and that there's still hope. The pussy hat parties... well, I kind of got roped into those. But I do genuinely care about women's rights. And if you'll remember, I asked you to join us. I wasn't trying to exclude you. The giant whiteboard is to remind myself that what is going on in this country right now is *not normal*. It's so I don't get complacent and give in to the tide of racism and bigotry all around us. And I admit, the Post-it note on your pills was crossing the line. I shouldn't have done that."

He felt himself coming unglued, but there was no stopping now.

"I wanted to get a reaction out of you. It seems to be the only way to make you acknowledge my presence. And me coming into your room naked..." He could feel the blush rising in his cheeks. "I am very, very sorry about that, and I'm extremely embarrassed. I had a few too many drinks last night, and I forgot I'd already gotten undressed for bed. When I saw the condoms nailed to the wall, I was upset that you invaded my space. I didn't think. I just reacted."

Megan sat very still and straight on her stool, as if letting that sink in for a bit.

Andrew shifted in his seat. Was he supposed to go on? He was beginning to doubt they could repair the damage to their already fragile relationship. Then a little laugh escaped her, and Andrew sensed a thaw in the air. *So she is human after all.*

"OK. Well, I'm sorry about blasting Fox News," she said, tucking a blond strand behind her ear. "I wasn't doing that to annoy you either. I like to listen to the news while I get ready for work. I did use your lavender aromatherapy, which I shouldn't have done. And the Trump hat was meant to be a joke, though it could be valuable someday—"

Andrew raised an eyebrow. *She just had to add that, didn't she?*

"—and I'm sorry about your leftovers. I'm a terrible cook! And you seem to like cooking for people. But it wasn't right, and I should've asked you or at least said thank you, because it's always delicious."

He tried to smother a proud grin.

"And yes, I did purposefully make noise when you had a girl in your room. Her... giggling was keeping me awake." It was Megan's turn to go red. "As you know, I get up very early."

"This is really good, guys," Emily interjected. "You can see a lot of what's been happening here is just miscommunication and wrong assumptions. Megan, would you like to make a request of Andrew?"

The stubborn glint in her pale blue eyes had softened. "Can you admit that you started treating me differently the moment you found out I was a Republican?"

Andrew nodded slowly. "You're right. Things changed after the first night. I was just so mad about the whole thing. I still am. I'm mad that Trump won. I'm mad that Republicans have been preventing government from working and yet both parties got blamed for the dysfunction. I'm mad because this president is completely incompetent and truly a danger to our country in so many ways." His voice was spiraling out of control, but he couldn't hold back. "I'm mad that people bought into the lies about Hillary. I'm mad that people would rather have a sexist, racist misogynist as president instead of a woman. I'm mad that the people who voted for Trump are silent about his attack on the press, about Russian interference in our democracy, about his deranged comments on Twitter and his rambling incoherence and his insults toward foreign heads of state."

Andrew's body, from his tense jaw all the way down his spine, had gone stiff with anger as potent as rigor mortis.

"Where are the people with the backbone, calling him out? Conservatives would be up calling for revolution if President Obama had behaved like this!"

Megan cleared her throat. "May I just say something? Trump won not because of my single vote, but because Hillary lost. Your people did not come out and vote for her. People did not want another Clinton."

"You admit you voted for him!"

"Yes! I had to! Believe me, I wish I could have skipped voting altogether. But it's public record, and not voting would have hurt me politically, maybe jeopardized my future."

"That's the whole problem with your party! You don't care about the good of the American people. You only care about what's good for politics! A year ago, the Republicans mocked Trump, said they would never get behind him. But then he became the presidential nominee, and they all lined up to kiss his ass!"

"Just like you all lined up to back Hillary," she retorted, standing up from her stool. "Look, trust me, I hate Trump as much as you do. He's an embarrassment to the party, and I wish to god he had lost the election. I mean, Christ, he was supposed to lose!" She stormed over to the apartment door.

Andrew held his breath as Emily called after her. Was she going to leave?

Instead of opening the door, Megan snatched a red marker and lifted it to the whiteboard. When she turned around, a new entry was scrawled under *Trump Lies*:

Obama had my "wire tapped." Terrible!

She returned to her barstool feeling a little lighter, with a little more spring in her step. Though she had never been one to thumb her nose at authority, it felt good to call the president out on the lie.

"OK, we're making some progress here. That was really nice sharing." Emily's voice was calm and steady as ever. "Andrew, you've been seeing Megan as a representation of the president and the

Republican Party. You weren't seeing her as an individual who has different motivations, values, and needs. And Megan, you need to be honest and speak up for yourself. Stop letting things fester. And remember, things aren't always what they appear."

Megan nodded, surprised at how much better she felt. Until she cast a glance at Andrew.

His shoulders were slumped and his head hung low, like it was too much effort now to lift. "Megan, I'm truly sorry for causing you pain. I wish we could be friends."

When he looked up, her heart contracted. Those dead eyes, that numb expression, the limp posture—it was all so familiar, the still surface of a lake that roiled beneath with pain and turbulence. In that moment, she saw Andrew, and she saw her father.

Without thinking, she reached out her hand and laid it on his. *He needs connection,* she realized. *He needs to know he's not alone.*

"I accept your apology. I know this election, this result, hasn't been easy on you. It would be nice to see you smiling and laughing." She held his gaze. "And maybe sleeping better... and drinking less."

Andrew didn't respond, but Megan thought he sat up a little straighter.

"Don't let *this* change you. Don't let despair take the place of hope. You'll get through this." She squeezed his hand, and when a strange thought turned up in her mind like an uninvited guest, she tried to squash it.

We'll get through this together.

APRIL HEADLINES

TAXES CHAINSAW MASSACRE, Trump proposes
'biggest cut in history'
—*New York Post*

Trump announces well thought out policy in April Fools Day Prank
—*The Chaser*

White House memo: Trump rejects 100-day test, yet seeks an A
—*The New York Times*

Chapter Nineteen

———————— ✪ ————————

MAKING NICE

It was April Fool's Day, but Andrew was on a serious mission: If Megan woke up as hungover as he had, bacon and eggs should do the trick.

After Emily had left the previous night, the two roommates had continued drinking wine and chatting. Whatever spell Andrew had been under, it was broken. When he looked at Megan now, he no longer saw the Republican Party or a mindless Trump fan. He saw a woman who was passionate about important issues and dedicated to her job.

Megan poked her tousled head through the doorway and squinted into the kitchen, wincing at the light. "I hope you're feeling as shitty as I am."

"Good morning!" he replied brightly. "Yes, but I'm faking it 'til I make it! Extra-greasy bacon, egg, and cheese sandwich, New York–style?"

"And coffee?" she groaned.

"Of course, madame!" He whirled around to grab a mug and poured her a cup. "Milk?"

She nodded but hung back still, eyeing him cautiously. "Ugh. I am such a lightweight. Why does it feel like someone's drilling into my skull?"

He pointed to the three empty bottles lined up on the counter. "Split fifty-fifty, I believe. Very bipartisan of us."

"Please, don't make me laugh." She lifted the coffee mug and offered him a weak smile in salute.

He placed a sandwich in front of her and followed it with a tall glass of water and two aspirin. "Sit," he ordered.

"Thank you," she whispered through a mouthful of egg, alternating between tearing off sloppy bites and staring lovingly at her sandwich. "Did I say anything stupid last night?"

Andrew shrugged. "You mentioned that you couldn't wait for the old geezers in Congress to retire. But for the record, I agree." He sat on the stool next to hers and lifted his own sandwich to his mouth, chewing and swallowing as he worked up his courage to look her in the eye. She had seen him at his lowest — naked, drunk, angry, embarrassed, pathetic — and she didn't berate him or gloat. Instead she had shown him compassion, far more than he deserved. "I want to say again, now that we're sober, that I'm sorry I was such a jerk to you. And that I'm done with drinking that much. You were right. I've been pretty depressed."

In Megan's eyes, he saw genuine concern. "I know it's hard to believe," she said, "but I'm nearly as upset with my party as you are. I still believe in it, or at least in the version that once existed. I know you won't believe me, but there are a lot of good people working really hard in congress."

Queasiness threatened his stomach. "Maybe we shouldn't talk politics at all."

She stopped chewing. "Why can't we just have a discussion?"

Andrew didn't think he wanted to chance it. Plenty of people stayed away from the topics of politics and religion. It was all too personal. People had their beliefs, and they wouldn't be changed. Now that he and Megan seemed to be mending fences, he didn't want his anger to come pouring out again. "Let's not. Maybe someday we can have a real conversation about politics, but right now it's still too raw."

"Someday?" She grinned. "Like, in four years?"

He smiled wide, but inside he was cringing, thinking about the way he'd acted over the past few months. An idea came to him, and he moved toward the front door.

"No, keep it," Megan called out as he brought the eraser to rest on his *Trump Lies* board. "We both agree we're living in Orwellian times. We need to be reminded." She popped the last corner of her breakfast sandwich into her mouth and chewed carefully. "I have an idea. Let's do something fun today."

It sounded good to Andrew—like a second chance, starting all over again. How had he been so quick to dismiss her simply because of her politics? For too long he had lumped all Republicans into one box and avoided them like they were hazardous waste. How had he failed to realize that, like anyone else, she wasn't a black-and-white sketch but a painting composed in many shades?

"Would be nice to finally have someone my age to hang out with," he joked.

Megan shot him a sly look. "We could have been hanging out before, if you were nicer to me."

Touché.

"Would you really have, though?" He cocked his head. "Just an observation, but you seem to prefer being alone. I mean, you could spend time with my sister, but you don't. You're kind of antisocial for a politician." He held his breath, hoping he hadn't taken the banter a step too far.

She didn't seem offended. "Yeah, I guess I'm a bit of a loner. I'm too serious for most people. I want to talk about foreign policy. They want to talk about reality TV…" She trailed off. "What about you? You have lots of friends. All those girls you brought to the apartment before the Women's March? Why don't you go hang out with them and, I don't know, what does Generation Z do? Take selfies or something?"

Time for full disclosure. "They're from the yoga studio. I barely know them."

Megan responded with a friendly but skeptical smirk. "What do you say? Can we have do-over today? I'm willing to give you a chance to prove you can be civilized."

Andrew laughed. "I made you breakfast, didn't I?"

With their reconciliation breakfast over, Megan put her hangover on hold and dressed for a spring Saturday in the city. "OK, where should we go?" she asked.

"Why don't we play tourist?" Andrew suggested. "We can each choose something to visit—one this morning, one this afternoon."

It sounded like a great idea. "There is one museum in particular I've been meaning to go to..."

Andrew took a coin from his pocket. "Heads or tails?"

"How very democratic of you!" she teased. "Heads."

The coin went flying into the air, and he slapped it dramatically on top of his hand. Slowly, he revealed the coin. Heads.

Megan let out a squeal. "OK, let's walk. It's not too far from here."

When she stopped in front of a building ten minutes later, Andrew read the name aloud: "Smithsonian American Art Museum. "OK, cool. You're an art buff?"

She shook her head. "Don't get me wrong. I like art, but that's not where we're going." She pointed across the street, where the sign read *International Spy Museum*.

"Really?"

"I kind of love James Bond," she admitted.

"My opinion of you just went up a notch." He pretended to look her up and down as if seeing her for the first time. "Favorite movie?"

She didn't hesitate. "*GoldenEye*."

"*Skyfall* was better. By a hair." He pressed his thumb and forefinger together, then squinted at her, screwing up his lips. "Let me guess, your favorite Bond is... Hm, I don't peg you as a Craig girl. Definitely Connery."

She laughed. "Straight up Sean Connery, all the way. When I was a kid, I wanted to work for the CIA. I think it's because I was raised on Bond movies and detective shows."

"I wanted to be a superhero," he chuckled. "Of course, that dream was crushed when my dad told me nobody pays Superman to wear tights and save the world, and I should think of what my day job would be."

"Sounds like he's pretty good at crushing dreams." She gave a sympathetic smile. "Like my dad."

Two hours later, carrying gift shop bags with books about real-life spies, they emerged from the subway at the U.S. Botanic Garden.

"You're a plant geek?" Megan asked.

"Had no choice, really. My mother was President of the Spade and Vase Club of America and always hosted meetings at our house."

She had no idea what that was, and it must've showed.

"Think Junior League, but with flower shows, garden tours, garden talks, and even occasionally getting your hands dirty. Well, not *my* mom," he explained. "I would sneak scones from the coffee table and eavesdrop on their conversations. Well, not really sneak. There was one lady who was my co-conspirator. She would always walk by with a goodie wrapped in a napkin and place it near the doorway where I was hiding."

She smiled, thinking about little Andrew amid a bevy of ladies wearing gloves and pearls.

"I loved hearing about all the plants. Their Latin names lent them this air of importance... But even then, I wondered why they knew more about plants than about their own children. These ladies could rattle off soil conditions, light requirements, what to plant next to what, when to dig up a perennial and split it, how to prune, what pollinators were attracted to. But what were their own offspring up to these days? Then it was a shrug, and 'Who knows? Maybe baseball, or was it football?'"

Megan could sympathize. "Flowers are predictable. They do what you ask of them, with minimum care." It was something she'd gathered from her own mother, who had been able to amass a simple treasure in her garden that she could never achieve in everyday life.

Andrew nodded. "Flowers never disappoint you either."

"Or talk back and question your authority."

"Fucking flowers." He laughed.

They walked on through the gardens until Megan stopped and grabbed Andrew's arm, pointing to a tree with green and yellow fruits sprouting along the trunk and branches. "It's an actual chocolate tree!" She peered at the description on the label. "It says here that *Theobroma* means 'food of the gods.' They sure got that right."

"So you have a sweet tooth?"

"I just really, really love chocolate."

"Who doesn't?"

In the exhibit were big, bold purple orchids from Thailand, mixed with tiny pink and chartreuse orchids from Bali. "So beautiful," she murmured.

"My mother's been trying to grow orchids," Andrew mused, "but it requires more work and more patience than she's equipped with."

Megan wrinkled her forehead. "It's hard to picture your mom actually gardening."

Andrew snorted. "You're not wrong about that. So, what do you picture her doing?"

"Uh, I don't feel comfortable—"

His smile was inviting. "I won't be offended, I promise."

She decided to give it a shot. "Well, your mom doesn't work, but she volunteers a lot. She's probably on a board that raises money to fight poverty and hunger, but she can't actually stand to be around poverty." Megan thought for a moment. "She wasn't born into money, but she married it. And now she's indulging you with your environmental 'hobby' because she loves you, but she wishes you were doing something else, something with prestige or status that she could brag to her country club friends about…" She broke off. "Was that too much?"

He was looking at the orchids, nodding along. "OK, now do me."

"I don't think so, Andrew." Her lips pressed tight.

"I'm a big boy. I can handle it."

"Well…" She turned and stopped, and looked him right in his blue eyes. "I think you're embarrassed and ashamed of your wealth. You hide behind Gap clothing, flannel shirts, and your beard. You hide that you went to private school but brag about going to a state university. Though I'm guessing that you got into at least one of the Ivy Leagues."

She waited until he confirmed it. "I got into Yale and Princeton, but I went to SUNY."

"The one piece I don't understand is, why? Why are you embarrassed and ashamed of your wealth? Why hide it? So you're wealthy. It's the American dream!"

He shook his head and looked away. "It's the way we got it that embarrasses me. My grandfather was an executive at GE, and my dad works on Wall Street."

"So?" she demanded. "Did they rob or kill someone to get there?"

He raised an eyebrow at her. "Well, no. Of course not."

"What was their crime? Capitalism?"

"Yes!" Andrew turned away and pretended to examine a cactus. When he finally spoke, it was a whisper, as if he were afraid someone might overhear.

Megan waited for a damning confession to come.

"My grandfather's company helped pollute the Hudson River. My dad's company was part of the reason for the Great Recession. Their capitalist greed has degraded the environment and helped millions of people lose their homes and their savings. That's not the American dream! It's America at its worst."

Megan didn't get it. Why he was so ashamed? "I'll admit that some mechanism on Wall Street went awry, Andrew, but that doesn't mean capitalism can't work. Do you enjoy the life you have?"

"Yeah, of course! But I don't enjoy when it means other people have to suffer."

She wanted to shake him and say, *Wake up! Be grateful!* "Suffering is part of the human experience. And what doesn't kill you makes you stronger." She motioned to the plants surrounding them. "Take all these cactuses, for example. They live in the harshest conditions, extreme heat and drought. And yet they survive. Give them a little water, and they bloom. It's the pampered orchids that can't handle the slightest hiccup."

Andrew looked dubious.

"Guess what?" she blurted out. "I hated my childhood! I hated growing up poor. But I turned that anger into a desire to have a better life. I worked my butt off in school, worked part-time jobs through high school and college, and here I am today, working in a legislative office. Nobody handed me a damn thing in life."

He kicked the stony path. "Are you saying I'm a delicate little orchid with my pampered life? And now I can't handle the real world?"

She bit her lip and proceeded delicately. "You want to be a cactus, but you're still an orchid. You're always going to be an orchid. Embrace it and make the best of it."

They left the cactus exhibit in silence. Megan could've kicked herself. What had possessed her to share her past? She didn't want to be one of those politicians trying to outdo the others by complaining about how poor they were growing up. She still hadn't outgrown the pain and shame. But she had to admit, there was relief in sharing it with him.

When they stopped in front of the miniature log replica of the White House, Andrew turned to her and placed a hand momentarily on her shoulder. "I'm sorry you've had a hard life. You deserve all your success."

"Andrew, you deserve success, too. But you seem to be holding yourself back." She hated to say it, but it had to be said. "You're the same age as me. You're smart. And you're working basically an entry-level position."

It was hard not to notice his agitation at her appraisal. "You think I have no ambition?"

"You don't seem to want anything bad enough."

"I do! I want to make a difference!"

"I believe you. But maybe you've been focusing too much on punishing your father with your righteousness, and not enough on actually using your skills and talents."

He slammed his hands into his pockets. "How would you know if I have any talents!"

"I saw you in action, remember? When you came to lobby me at White's office? You were articulate and knowledgeable. You took charge of the situation. Heck, you're older than your supervisor, that pimple-faced guy wearing the too-big suit!"

Andrew sighed. "I guess you're right. My mom says the same thing—that the job is beneath me. She doesn't want me to 'waste my talents' on the environment at all."

"She's right. You should work in public service." Megan gently nudged his shoulder with hers. "I'm kidding."

They had come full circle. Andrew motioned Megan ahead of him and followed her into the lobby. "You should know Congressman White and I discussed your carbon fee and dividend proposal."

"Really? You did that, even though I was so unforgivably mean to you?"

"Not unforgivably. We're here now, aren't we?"

They stepped out into the warm, sunny afternoon. Even outside the gardens, a whiff of warm dirt and blooming flowers enveloped them.

"I didn't do it for you at all," she continued. "In all honesty, I wanted to put it in the discard pile because of you."

"And then run it over with your car, like you did with those imaginary endangered species after our last talk?" he joked.

But things had changed since they'd last argued about climate change. "Congressman White and his military friends have convinced me that we need to do something about the climate," she confessed. "The congressman is a strategic man, and like you said, Florida is among the most vulnerable states. He really likes the idea of a market-based solution."

"What about all the voters who don't believe climate change is real?"

Megan knew Andrew was right. It would be a tough road. She looked him in the eye. "Sometimes, you just have to do the right thing. Even if it's hard."

Two weeks passed, and to Megan it seemed as though she and Andrew had picked up right where they'd left off that first day in the apartment. No one was more surprised by this, and by how much Andrew's attitude toward her had changed, than Megan. She couldn't help noticing herself smiling—at work, on the subway, during meetings—for no particular reason at all.

One evening after work, as Megan pulled ingredients from the fridge for her typical meal—ham-and-cheese sandwich with a side of Campbell's Tomato Soup—Andrew walked into the kitchen, shaking his head in mock pity.

"Why don't we cook together tonight?" he suggested.

"I already know how to cook," she shot back.

Andrew pulled a frying pan off the rack and placed it on the stove. "Reheating canned soup and slapping deli meat on bread is not what I'd call cooking," he teased.

Megan lifted her chin defiantly. "I can make a casserole, too."

"Ring, ring!" Andrew pretended to answer a phone. "Oh, it's the 1950s! They're calling for you, Megan."

She rolled her eyes and laughed. "OK, maybe my repertoire needs a little updating. What are you making?"

He turned to her, holding out a bag of corn tortillas. "*We* are making tacos." He put her in charge of prepping the toppings, then disappeared into the fridge. When he emerged, his hands were full. "Tomatoes, lettuce, onions, cilantro, avocado, cheese."

She took the ingredients one by one from his hands and set everything in its place on the counter, beside the cutting board. She stared at the food items like they were questions on a pop quiz she hadn't studied for. What was she supposed to do with them? Only pride kept her from asking for direction. She lifted the block of cheese and found a grater. This, she could handle.

The kitchen started to fill with the enticing scent of garlic in the frying pan. "Salsa!" Andrew barked. "Mild, medium, or hot?"

Megan didn't hesitate. "Hot, please."

"That's my girl. Chop some onions."

She flushed with pleasure. Or was it the green chiles he'd just added to the pan? *Jeez, pull yourself together, Megan.*

"What are you doing?" Andrew yelled, stepping up behind her

and cautiously stripping her paring knife from her clenched hand, as though he were talking a suicidal victim off the ledge. "This is not what you chop onions with," he admonished, holding up the ancient paring knife. "It's dull as a butter knife! You'll cut yourself sawing away with it. Now *this*"—he unsheathed a ten-inch Japanese chef knife from its block of wood—"is what you chop onions with."

"I know how to cut onions," she insisted, and started to cut tentatively. Andrew's watchful gaze made her nervous. Her knife movement was clunky and awkward, leaving her with large, uneven hunks of onion.

He smiled indulgently and stepped closer. From behind her came traces of his hippie soap—eucalyptus and mint, she believed—and a pleasant hint of body odor. "May I?" he asked, encircling her arm with his and wrapping his hand around hers, showing the proper way to hold the knife. "Now start with the tip, and then as you push the weight of the blade down, you make a little rocking motion." Her breath went shallow as she allowed him to guide her, to take control.

As they chopped together in culinary intimacy, an unexpected image flashed in her mind, of him fleeing her room with a teddy bear barely covering his muscular butt. And suddenly it sank in—something he'd said during their session with Emily: *I'd already gotten undressed for bed.*

So, she thought, *Andrew sleeps in the buff.*

Her cheeks flushed as he murmured gentle encouragements. When he slowly released his grip and took a step back, disappointment flooded her body.

"There you go! We'll have you cooking in no time." He flashed her a grin.

It took all her concentration to keep holding the knife the way he'd taught her and not chop her fingers off. His scent lingered in her nostrils, mixing with the sharp tang of onion, and she felt the heat of his body long after he'd returned to the stove.

While they cooked, whenever Andrew wasn't barking orders like a happy-go-lucky drill sergeant, they recounted their day. She told him that for the first time, she was starting to enjoy cooking. What she didn't tell him was that for once, she didn't mind someone else being in charge, too.

For too long she'd been a mother to both her brother and her father. Then she was the campaign manager, and again all decisions fell on her shoulders. Here in the kitchen with Andrew, it was a pleasure to have one less thing to decide. He determined the menu. He gave the instructions. And his patient teaching allowed her to hand over the reins. It made her happy to see him in his element: passionate, enthusiastic, at peace.

For long stretches, they stood side by side in companionable silence, accidentally brushing against each other as they chopped and sautéed, and then spooned cheese and tomatoes and the rest of the toppings into the warmed tacos.

Andrew held up a piece of onion for mock inspection. "Beautiful dice, Thompson."

She giggled, turning toward his praise like a flower greeting the afternoon sun.

They carried their plates to the living room. Settling on the floor, his back against the couch, Andrew asked, "What should we watch?"

"Well, you chose last night." She had to admit, *Alpha House* was funny. Too bad there were only two seasons. "How about *Love It or List It*?"

They had settled into a genial TV routine, alternating between his shows (comedy) and hers (HGTV or thrillers). On tonight's episode, the opening scene showed a couple walking hand in hand through New Orleans, searching for their "perfect" house.

"Ever been?" Megan asked.

"Yeah, a few times. First time was after Hurricane Katrina. I volunteered with Habitat for Humanity."

"Me, too! When were you there?"

"Well, it was almost a year later. August."

"I was there for a couple of weeks in June that year."

"I went back five years later, just for a weekend. It still needs a lot of work…"

They bit into their tacos and watched the show, commenting here and there, but just as happy sitting in silence. To Megan the cozy scene felt familiar, like when her own family would pile into the living room for their favorite shows. She and Gabe would lie on the rug or squabble over the single armchair. Her parents would recline on the couch, her mother's legs draped across her father's lap. Dad would crack Mom's toes — Megan always found that gesture simultaneously gross and sweet — and Mom would twirl her long, blond hair absentmindedly. It was a mannerism Megan had noticed in herself as she got older, particularly when she was lost in thought. It reminded her that the Thompsons had been a happy family, once.

Sarah and Paul had married young, at twenty-two, with Megan arriving shortly after. She knew being tied down by domesticity at an age when she yearned to be free must have been hard on her mother, who grew up in a strict Baptist home — like getting released from one prison and landing right in the next, for the simple crime of premarital sex.

Sarah Thompson must have taken pleasure in bucking the system where she could. She didn't cut Gabe's hair until he was five, letting his soft blond curls grow past his shoulder and indulging his interest in dolls and dress-up. She had encouraged Megan to take karate and join the Lego and chess clubs. Megan was grateful to her mom for many things, but she carried one piece of her advice closest to heart: Never give up your dreams for a boy. Her mother loved their father with all her heart, but still she had insisted that her daughter take care of herself first.

Megan wished she had more photos of her mother. The few she had unearthed, hidden in a shoebox on the top shelf in her father's closet, were carefully preserved in a single photo album and the matching frames images she and Gabe kept by their bedsides. As she grew older, Megan was continually surprised at how much she looked like her mother — same smile, same eyes twinkling with rebellion...

Disoriented, Megan blinked her eyes several times. Darkness enveloped her. Where was she? After a moment, her sleepy mind clued in. She was curled up on the couch with a blanket draped over her body.

Must have fallen asleep, she thought, and forced her tired body up from the couch to drag herself to bed.

Passing by Andrew's bedroom, she paused for a moment. Again an image came to her: this time it was of him sleeping in the nude, on his back, with his long limbs taking up the bed, his chest gently rising and falling...

She shook the thoughts loose like an Etch A Sketch, erasing them before they could become permanent. No good could come of them.

MAY HEADLINES

Republican blurts out that sick people don't deserve affordable care
—*New York Magazine*

F.B.I. Director James Comey is fired by Trump
—*New York Times*

Everyone an Enemy
—*National Review*

"

Chapter Twenty

✪

THE NRA SHILL

Drain the swamp indeed.

Megan sat in her office chair, fanning herself with a stack of files after a sweaty morning walk from the Metro. Overnight, the weather had turned muggy and oppressive. She had given up wearing her hair down, instead twisting and binding tight to her head. "Shouldn't you be used to this?" her colleagues had started teasing. "You're from Florida!" Well, there was a reason Floridians traveled from air-conditioning to air-conditioning.

The sticky D.C. air did resemble the sort of habitat where crocodiles and alligators flourished. Never mind that George Washington had carefully selected a dry, sloping riverbank on which to build the nation's capital. Now that Megan lived there, she realized it really was a marshland of those predators known as "establishment politicians." But apparently what President Trump had meant by "draining the swamp" was in fact ridding it of *all* the political species that inhabited it—and replacing them with a much worse species of cronies, opportunists, and incompetents who had nothing in common with real conservative values but the stolen authority of the Republican name.

Megan swabbed her forehead with a baby wipe and prepared to reapply her foundation. Summer had arrived a little early this year, and the building's management still hadn't gotten around to switching on the A/C. She was all for government practicing fiscal responsibility, but this was not exactly what she had in mind.

Congressman White's assistant popped her head in the door. "Hi, Megan!"

Startled, Megan dropped the wipe like it was incriminating evidence.

"You have a second? The boss wants to see you in his office," Katie sang. "It's a hot one out there, isn't it? Good thing you're from Florida!"

Megan suppressed a groan. "Yup, good thing. Thanks, Katie."

When she knocked lightly on White's door, his back was to her, but he craned his neck in her direction and motioned at the empty seat facing his desk. Then he turned back toward the window and continued speaking gruffly into the phone.

Megan crept in and took her seat, trying not to eavesdrop.

"You tell that son-of-a-bitch that I voted on his bill, and now it's his turn to vote on mine... No, I don't care. I got two weeks of angry letters after that one, and I'm counting on him to stay true to his word... Well, you tell that devil of a boss of yours, if he doesn't vote for it, he can kiss my vote on health care reform good-bye."

White slammed the phone down and spun back to face Megan, his tired smile looking plastered on just for her. "Megan! How's the dating going?"

"Umm, a little rough, I would say. Partially my fault, I suppose. I should have specified that I'm more comfortable dating a man under fifty..."

White shrugged by way of apology. "Yes, well, that's understandable. I heard about Carmela setting you up with Bob." He shook his head and chuckled. "I'm sorry about that. I have a confession to make. I asked Carmela to take care of finding the suitors. I gather the others weren't much better than Bob?"

Megan fumed. It all made perfect sense now. Carmela must have been having a great laugh at her expense. The rich, selfish, unemployed playboy. The creepy, cynical, twice-divorced political operative. White would never have seriously believed these men to be her equal.

"Sir, with all due respect, I think I'm done with the blind dates. It was a kind offer, but I really think I have to do this on my own —"

"How about one more date? This one will be great, I promise." He looked up, eyes twinkling with excitement. "I don't know if you remember the guy from the NRA who was in last week? Brock Tolbert's the name. I've met with him a few times. Might be right up your alley."

Brock Tolbert? No, thanks. Sounded like another man who liked to hear himself talk. The revolving door of people coming in and out of the office made it hard to remember names, but Megan was fairly sure that one would have stuck in her mind. Special interests were both a necessity and a nuisance. But she couldn't imagine spending a few hours on a date with one.

Yet she found herself asking politely, "How old?"

"Around your age. And tall, dark, and handsome, or so I'm told. Had the ladies around the office swooning. Guess he looks like some guy from some TV show. Draper something?"

Megan raised an eyebrow. She knew the character he meant, though she never watched *Mad Men*.

"Anyways, he's single. He knows about our plan for you. And he has agreed to take you out." He looked at her like a cat who's placed a dead bird at its owner's feet: *Look what I've brought you!*

Her reaction was a mix of disgust and diplomacy: *What am I supposed to do with this dead bird?* and *Ummm... thanks for thinking of me?* But instead she heard herself say, "Sure. Thanks. That sounds great."

She consoled herself with the knowledge that this would be the last blind date. Congressman White had looked so pleased, she couldn't disappoint him. But she sure as hell wasn't getting her hopes up.

★ ★ ★

T here's something on your mind," Andrew said without looking up from his laptop.

It was Friday night after another long, discouraging week of trying to convince Congress to act on climate change. It was all so frustrating! In private, many Republicans expressed concerns about climate change, but they seemed completely paralyzed when it came to speaking out, let alone taking action. But he'd given up frequenting the dive bars of D.C. in search of solace at the bottom of a bottle. *No, thanks.* He was perfectly content to stay in and read the *New York Times*. Depressing as the news was, it was comfortable sitting there on the couch with Megan, who was reading the *Washington Times* on her laptop.

"No. Why do you say that?" she protested.

"First, you're a terrible liar. And second, you're playing with your hair."

Megan's hand flew to her lap. "I have a blind date tonight." She glanced sideways at him and said, all in one breath, "My-boss-set-me-up-so-please-don't-judge."

"OK…" Andrew didn't know what else to say, but fought to keep his expression neutral. He took a sip of his Holy Basil tea. The bitterness made his eye twitch, but it was supposed to cleanse the liver. He'd heard about it from another yogi and thought, *Why not?* There was something appealing about stripping all the toxins from his body and fortifying his mind. Maybe it would help him swim against the tide of the toxic, topsy-turvy world he inhabited: where liars become president, evil gets rewarded, the wealthy steal from the poor, and hate speech is conflated with free speech. And vile Republican losers win dates with beautiful young women.

Megan looked up from her laptop as if trying to gauge his reaction. What exactly that reaction was supposed to be, Andrew wasn't sure.

So she had a date. Shouldn't he be happy for her? Or at least pleasantly indifferent? But he wanted her here, next to him. If he was going to be honest with himself, she was the first person he'd ever felt so comfortable with. Somehow when they were together, despite their differences, they could both be themselves. And sit in comfortable silence.

Maybe this date would be like the last guy, the "Eagle" with his bleached hair and white tops, trying in vain to recapture his youth."

Andrew chuckled.

Megan shot him a look. "Do you find the thought of me dating amusing?" Her retort came quickly, like the words had been waiting on the tip of her tongue.

He hurried to shake his head. "No. I just hope, for your sake, this guy is younger—I mean better, than the last two guys." Even as he spoke, he couldn't help hoping this date would be *worse*.

Her mouth opened to reply when they were interrupted by a knock at the door. "Jesus, it can't be him already! He's not supposed to be here until eight!"

Andrew glanced at his phone and then held the screen out for her to see: 8 p.m. exactly.

She sprang off the couch, whispering, "Crap! Crap! I haven't... I haven't..." She gestured to her entire body, still sheathed in work clothes: tight black slacks, a creamy silk blouse with a plunging V-neck.

He had lost track of time, too. Their routine—eating dinner and then retiring to the couch to read or watch TV—had grown familiar and comfortable, like slipping into a favorite pair of sweatpants at the end of the workday.

The knock came again, this time with purpose.

Megan froze, suspended between answering the door and disappearing to her bedroom. Panic and humor flickered equally on her face. She turned to him. "You're just going to sit there? Can't you answer the door?"

Andrew shook his head and tried to swallow a smile.

"You're horrible!" she stage-whispered.

But when she finally opened the door, he heard her gasp. Glancing in her direction, he saw that her date was taller than he was, and his shoulders were broader. In fact, his frame almost filled the doorway.

"Hi, Brock," came Megan's voice. It sounded more feeble than usual. "Please, come in."

Brock?

This was worse—much worse—than Andrew had imagined.

B rock Tolbert stepped into the apartment, and Megan understood instantly why they called him "Don" at the office. His confidence and charisma, just like his stature, seemed to fill the room. In one hand, he held a bouquet of tall white lilies.

"These are for you." His voice purred as smooth as an aged scotch.

Mouth agape, she took the flowers. "Um, thank you. They're beautiful." She tucked a loose strand of hair behind her ear. "I... uh... need to... um... get changed. I'm still in my work clothes. I look—"

You look stunning." Brock's dark eyes traveled the length of her body. "Any woman in a cocktail dress would still be jealous."

Megan laughed, a giddy, high-pitched laugh. She felt a little lightheaded. *What the hell is wrong with me?* she scolded herself. "Excuse me a moment. I'll find something to put these in."

She rummaged around in the kitchen cupboards, looking for a vase, wishing Brock had agreed to meet at the restaurant instead. Why had he insisted on picking her up? And why had she been so reluctant to tell Andrew about him?

She knew exactly why. They had just gotten to a place where she considered them friends. She didn't want to open a can of worms over her date with a spokesman for the NRA—not exactly a beloved liberal organization.

While filling the vase with water, Megan peeked over the counter. Brock and Andrew were still sizing each other up from afar. Andrew got off the couch and, in a few confident strides, was at the doorway, shaking Brock's hand.

"Hello." Brock smirked. "Wow, I must ask: What hand lotion do you use?"

"What? I don't use hand lotion." Andrew sounded taken aback.

"Oh, my mistake." Brock's red lips curled into a smile. "It's just... Your hands are so soft. And I smell something... medicinal. Reminds me of my grandmother."

"I guess your grandma smells like my liver-cleansing tea," Andrew retorted.

Brock slapped him on the back, knocking him forward. "Yeah, I guess so! My mistake. No, hard feelings, right?"

Megan was astounded, as always, by the ridiculous behavior of men. What was this, a Wild West showdown?

Returning from the kitchen, she put the flowers in the vase and set it on the bar, taking her time arranging the lilies so she could compose herself, too. "Ready?" she asked at last.

"Ladies first." Brock opened the door for her, turning sideways to give Andrew an insolent wink.

Twenty minutes later, Brock pulled his shiny black Toyota Tundra up to the valet stand. Megan was still amazed at how clean he kept his truck. Some guys were pretty meticulous about their vehicle, but Brock took it to another level.

He came around to Megan's side and opened the door for her, placing a hand on the small of her back. Her spine tingled as anticipation shot through every nerve. A romantic dinner at 1789 with a tall, handsome man... Now *this* felt like a date.

Brock guided her through the gleaming wooden doors of the Federal period house. Once they were seated, he pulled back her chair and pushed it back in, nestling her against the table. He refilled her wine glass again and again. Megan found herself saying *thank you* every few seconds.

"Brock, tell me, how long have you been living in D.C.?"

"Several years." Focused on cutting his lamb sausage, he didn't elaborate. "What about you? Are you enjoying D.C.? Making any friends?"

One friend, she thought, *and you've already met him.*

She nodded. "I love D.C., and I love my job. But sometimes I miss home. My brother. And my dad, of course."

Brock gave her his whole attention as she spoke. "It can be hard to leave loved ones behind," he answered thoughtfully. "I sometimes feel like my body is here, but my mind and heart are somewhere else."

Megan took a bite of burrata, savoring the creaminess. She mulled over Brock's comment while stealing glances of him as he sipped his wine. It seemed he was much deeper than she would have imagined an

NRA spokesman to be. "What about you? Do you miss your family?"

His gaze shifted to something unseen in the distance. "Yes, sometimes I miss being back home." Then his eyes snapped back to Megan, and a slow smile spread across his handsome face. "Now, tell me everything about you. What do you like to eat? What movies do you like? What do you do for fun?"

"Huh. This won't take very long. I'm a bit of a workaholic."

Megan prattled on for a bit, but soon tired of hearing her own voice. "Now it's your turn. Tell me something about you. What did you do before working for the NRA?"

Brock was a suave, captivating orator. He had no problem sharing the details of his professional life, his years in the military, his time at Harvard Business School, his summers spent in South Carolina. He could definitely teach her a few things, Megan realized, when it came to presenting herself. Her political consultant, Hakeem, had joked that she would excel at town hall–style debates. She wasn't in love with the sound of her own voice, so she'd probably be the only candidate actually listening to the constituents.

It was nearing midnight by the time Brock dropped her off in front of the apartment. "Can I see you again?" His voice was thick as warm chocolate.

"Yes, I'd love that." As she nervously fiddled with her keys, her mind raced. Would he kiss her? Did she want him to? Yes. She definitely wanted him to.

"How about next Saturday, then? A day date? Does two p.m. work?"

"Sure, that works for me." She leaned toward him, a little nervous, well aware that the drape of her blouse would afford him a peek at the top of her lacy bra and the soft mounds of flesh beneath. "Would you like to come up for a drink... or something?"

Brock moved closer to her, his warm minty breath next to her ear. "Can't tonight."

She felt a peck on the cheek.

"Plus, I don't think your roommate would be all that happy to see me. Rain check?"

She hoped he couldn't see her blush. "Sure."

"Sweet dreams, Megan." He blew her a kiss.

She watched him walk to his truck, a little disappointed that he had declined her offer, but more relieved than anything. It would have been awkward in the apartment, with Andrew there…

Brock climbed into the truck, brandishing the body of an Adonis with the grace of a ballerina. *Interesting guy*, she thought. Even revealing so much about his life, he had left her with the sense that she hadn't seen anything of the real Brock Tolbert.

Megan decided her new beau could be summed up in three words: *great poker player*. Charismatic and calculating, he'd showed her what he wanted her to see, but kept his cards tight against his chest. Some might find that a turnoff, preferring a partner who would show all his cards, but Megan was intrigued.

She was an excellent poker player.

The week flew by as Megan looked forward to seeing Brock again. Both she and Andrew were occupied with even more work than usual—what with the Trump-Russia collusion and the constant chipping away at environment legislation—and saw each other only in passing. There were no dinners collaborated upon, no TV shows negotiated. More than once, Megan wondered if Andrew was trying to avoid her. Was he worried he might blurt out something negative about Brock and start up their old feud again? If so, she had to admit that was sweet. But the whole thing made her a little sad. She had grown accustomed to their comfortable routine.

For her second date with Brock, Megan hadn't bothered trying to meet up elsewhere. What was the point? Andrew probably would be working out at the gym, and Brock was clearly too much of a gentleman to agree anyway. She didn't even know where they were headed. Brock wanted to surprise her.

She stood in front of her closet. For the first time in as long as she could remember—since she and Jason had just rekindled their relationship—she was excited to go on a date. And this time she would dress up for him. If Brock thought a work outfit was impressive, wait until he saw her in a Saturday ensemble.

She relished the thought of him looking at her, enthralled with her. Running her hands through her outfits, which dangled from hangers like a fabric chandelier, she wondered what would be appropriate. She had no idea where they were going or what they were doing, but midafternoon was hardly the time to wear a cocktail dress. She settled on a black strapless wide-leg jumpsuit, which would've been modest if it weren't for her sizable chest threatening to spill out with any sudden movements. As long as she wasn't bending over, she should be safe from wardrobe malfunctions.

She tinted her lips with gloss and smoothed her hair into a high ponytail, just in time to hear a familiar knock at the door. Opening it, she was dumbstruck once again by how handsome he was, this time in a white T-shirt that stretched across his broad chest and made his biceps bulge, paired with blue jeans, a leather belt, and scuffed cowboy boots.

"You look amazing." He smiled into her eyes, which were level with his thanks to her three-inch heels.

Looking into his baby browns, she thought, *The same goes for you,* and then pulled her gaze away. "Where are we going?"

His smile became coy. "It's a surprise."

At his truck, he opened the door for her once again. Although more than a week had passed, not a speck of dust had landed on the dashboard. Nor had the mats been dirtied, or crumpled receipts or tissues fallen astray. The truck might as well be brand-new, all over again. Megan was about to twist the cap on a bottle of water when Brock shook his head.

"Sorry, no food or beverages in the truck."

"Really?" Megan didn't hide her amazement. "Even water?"

He was gentle, but adamant.

She put the cap back on and slipped the bottle into her purse. "How long have you had this truck?"

"Two years."

"Wow." She made a mental note to never let him step foot in her Ford Focus.

Her own obsession with organization did not extend to her car. It had gone unwashed for months — she just let the rain do it for her. A week-old paper coffee cup was lodged in a holder, its twin encasing an empty plastic water bottle. Paper bits and loose change were scattered everywhere. Sweat-stained running gear spilled from a duffel bag on the backseat, next to an open box of door hangers from White's campaign that she still hadn't gotten around to tossing. And enough dust was caked on her dashboard that you could have mistaken it for gray instead of black. Her car was the only place she, unlike Brock, gave herself a free pass.

But this time Megan was determined to steer the conversation toward him. She had done a little digging on the internet.

"Brock, what was it like for you growing up?" she asked.

His eye twitched. "I had a normal childhood. Church on Sundays, worked the farm weekends and vacations. That sort of thing."

"It wasn't hard having an evangelical pastor for a father? You probably didn't get into too much trouble." She waited for him to reveal something, anything. Most men loved to brag about their wild childhood and teenage years, didn't they?

"Oh, I behaved like any other kid who believes he's got a get-out-of-jail-free card with God. But if I had to guess," he teased, "you've never been naughty in your life."

"That's not true," she protested. "I stole twenty bucks from my dad's wallet once."

"Oh, that *is* naughty. What else?"

"I made my younger brother eat cat food." Her grin was smug.

"Now there's a story I'd like to hear."

How did Brock manage to make her feel like everything she said was fascinating? "One night my brother told me my casseroles tasted like cat food, and he didn't want to eat them anymore. I told him if he didn't like my cooking, then he was more than welcome to take over."

"Naturally he refused?"

"He said it was my job. The next night, I made him a special pot pie, just for him. And he loved it."

Brock looked impressed. "You didn't."

"Oh, yes, I did. Opened a can of cat food and dumped into the pie crust. I told him about it, of course. After he ate it all. He never complained about my cooking again."

Thirty minutes later, they pulled into an unfamiliar parking lot. *Damn, he's good.* She'd spent the whole car ride talking about herself again.

Brock opened the door and held out his hand. "Have you ever shot a gun before?"

Megan glanced up at the sign on the building ahead: NRA RANGE. "Actually, no. My dad never would take me." She allowed Brock to clasp her hand and ease her from the truck's cab. "He never took my brother either. I think he just preferred the time alone. Guns and beer were his therapy after my mom died. With the occasional church service thrown in." Megan blinked, unable to believe the words had escaped her mouth.

Maybe sharing with Andrew lately had opened the floodgates. Or was it a testament to Brock's charms that she felt comfortable enough to reveal things she normally wouldn't dream of sharing so soon? And yet she'd learned nothing about him on the ride over.

"Sorry. I'm rambling. Just a little nervous. About using a gun, I mean." Her heart sank. Now he would think that she was nervous about the date — that he had the upper hand.

Brock chuckled and pulled open the glass door, steering her through the entrance. "You have nothing to apologize for, and nothing to be nervous about. I'll be right there by your side." He leaned over and kissed her cheek.

She could smell his cologne. Brut.

Such a charming gentleman... Megan stifled a nervous giggle. "I am totally not dressed for this. I feel silly wearing this outfit."

"Nonsense. You look fabulous. Don't worry about it. No one will even notice."

Except plenty of people noticed. As they stride down the line of firing booths, men's heads turned one after another, each clinched between by sturdy black earmuffs. Between those and the constant gunfire, at least they couldn't hear the clacking of her pointed heels, announcing her arrival. Some men hugged rifles and shotguns, others held handguns in a loving caress.

After an eternity, they reached the booths Brock had rented: numbers 14 and 15. He handed her the protective eyewear and earmuffs before loading his handgun and firing off a few rounds. When he pressed a button, the target paper came back to them. All perfect shots.

Megan was impressed, but of course she had expected him to be good. He showed her how to hold the gun, encircling her in his arms. The smell of his cologne made it hard for her to concentrate.

"Let me take a picture of you firing off a few rounds." He stepped back, taking his cell phone out of his pocket. "This will look good for your campaign."

She took a breath and squeezed the trigger. She had never been overly interested in guns, although of course she strongly supported ownership as a constitutional right. Right now, though, she couldn't deny the thrill running through her body.

JUNE HEADLINES

NRA video declares war on liberals, critics say
— *USA Today*

Just 17 percent of Americans Approve of Republican
Senate Health Care Bill
— *NPR*

FBI: Gunman had list of six Congress members on him
during baseball shooting
— *Chicago Tribune*

Chapter Twenty-One

✪

WEDDING DATE

At least they were cooking together again.

Ever since Megan had started seeing Brock several times a week, Andrew had put some distance between himself and his roommate. She hadn't seemed to want to see much of him either. They hadn't cooked or eaten dinner together, or watched TV together, in weeks. Andrew had started staying later at work, blaming a huge lobbying push and a conference with powerbrokers and activists from all across the country, who would be meeting their representatives to lobby for carbon pricing. That wasn't entirely true, but it was the best excuse he could come up with.

Then one night the previous week, Andrew had come home from work and stepped into complete darkness. Once his eyes adjusted, he saw an unexpected shape on the couch, a long lumpy ridge. Then he heard it: a sniffle, followed by a loud gulp of air.

"Megan?" he'd called out.

She didn't respond.

He'd bent toward the lamp next to the couch and reached out to flick on the switch.

"Please, don't turn on the lights!" Megan's voice wobbled.

He had blinked once or twice, unsure of how to respond. He wanted to comfort her, but knew she was sensitive about personal space. At last he took a seat on the couch in the dark, leaving a gap between him and the snuffling shape. "Everything OK?"

"Of course." Her voice was tight.

"Then why are you crying?"

"I'm not crying."

"OK," he whispered. "You need a hug?"

She didn't answer.

Andrew had shifted a bit closer and gingerly wrapped his arms around her. She leaned back and rested her weight on his chest. Then she let her head rest on his shoulder. They sat like that for a long time, neither moving nor talking.

A million thoughts had raced through Andrew's head. *Was it that jerk, Brock? Did he hurt her?* He'd known something wasn't right the moment he met that guy. Just wasn't Megan's type—there was something fake about him, like he was used to putting on a show.

Andrew didn't want to admit it, but seeing Megan and Brock together triggered a strange feeling of possessiveness. He'd recognized it after a particularly intense yoga session, likening it to a brotherly feeling. But he certainly didn't *feel* like Megan's brother. Maybe he was just jealous because he and Megan had finally become friends, and he enjoyed her company, and now there was a good chance she'd be too busy with Brock. Or maybe it was just inevitable that living with a female roommate would get awkward sometimes.

He'd decided to avoid her until he could sort it out. But he could see that she needed a friend now, so that's what he'd decided to be.

After a long while, Megan finally spoke, so quietly that Andrew had to lean in. "I'm upset about the health care bill."

At first, he wasn't sure he'd heard right.

She sniffed a few more times. "I can't believe the House actually voted to repeal and replace."

Andrew somehow held back a sarcastic grunt.

"I mean, I knew every single Republican campaigned on repealing and replacing the Affordable Care Act. Even my boss. But I didn't think their proposed bill would be so terrible." Her laugh was stilted. "I thought their constituents, the American people, would object so

210

loudly, they would be forced to listen."

Andrew was confused. They had never discussed health care in particular, but hadn't repeal and replace on every Republican politician's agenda for the past seven years? He decided to proceed cautiously.

"I know," he agreed. "It's terrible. So many people are going to lose their coverage. Just so a bunch of rich people can get a tax cut." He held his breath, hoping he hadn't crossed a line.

She didn't seem to think so. "I didn't like the way the Affordable Care Act was passed, and I think there is a lot of room for improvement. But what they're trying to do is not an improvement. Not in any way." She sighed. "What really kills me is, my boss voted for it. I can't believe it, you know? I thought he was one of the good guys."

Andrew rubbed her back slowly, hoping it was the right thing to do.

"He said he was just making good on his campaign promise. But people in the office are gossiping. His wife just got offered a spot on the board of a pharmaceutical company. She'll get paid a nice salary to do basically nothing."

"It's hard when you learn someone you like and respect is profiting off other people's misery. Trust me, it's worse when your father's doing it. But as Emily likes to remind me, it's not personal."

Megan's voice turned bitter. "This is very personal to me, Andrew. When I was nine, my mother got cancer. We didn't have health insurance. My father owned his own garage, so we made too much to qualify for Medicare. And of course we couldn't get insurance. Cancer was a pre-existing condition." Her voice started to break, making her sound conflicted, like she wanted to cry but was determined to finish her story.

Andrew wasn't sure what to do. Tissues? A glass of water? More back-rubbing? He wanted to help but didn't know how.

Megan had inhaled deeply and pushed on. "My father did what he had to do. Got a second mortgage, extra lines of credit for the business—anything to pay for the medical bills. They just kept coming and coming…"

He'd tried to feel where she was coming from. All his life he'd struggled with his family's wealth, and with people making snap judgements about him because of it. He wanted her to know that despite their different upbringings, he could sympathize with her sorrow. "That's terrible, Megan. It must have been very hard on you. On all of you."

"She died a year later. It was like a sinkhole opened up overnight. We were motherless, widowed, broken, bankrupt, almost homeless. She was gone, and everything was sucked into the void."

Andrew had pulled her tighter to him. "I'm so sorry, Megan. For all that you've lost."

They stayed that way for a while. In Andrew's arms, Megan had felt both strong and soft. Her shampoo and the scent of her skin triggered a cascade of confusion and desire.

Then she had shifted and pulled away from his embrace. "It happened a long time ago. It's in the past." Her voice seemed to firm. "I just wish I could prevent other families from having to go through it. Losing a loved one is tragedy enough. But going bankrupt, too… It's just too much to bear." Then she shook her head sadly, and her tears began to flow again.

Andrew's heart had seized. He hated seeing her in pain. All the more reason to hate Republicans…

Why are you a Republican? he had wanted to shout. But he bit his tongue and instead just kept repeating, "I'm so sorry. I'm so sorry…" until the words had taken on a new meaning of their own.

After that night, Megan had confessed to eating pizza (twice) and Chinese takeout whenever Andrew was "working late." He had immediately marched her into the kitchen to whip up some homemade macaroni and Gruyère.

Megan seemed as happy now as he was to return to their routine, sharing highlights from their day as they prepped the meal, though Andrew secretly wondered if she felt compelled to act cheerful around him after the whole crying-on-the-couch episode.

He supposed it didn't really matter. The slow wheels of Congress were turning, and the nightmare scenario they both feared—millions of Americans losing their health care coverage—was now in the hands of the Republican-controlled Senate. The least they could do while awaiting the outcome was keep themselves well fed.

Tonight they were at it again, with Megan chopping vegetables for a salad to accompany his pasta primavera. Andrew shook the garlic and oil in his heavy skillet once more and stood back from the oven, tossing a tea towel over his shoulder. "Why did you hate cooking so much?"

Megan shrugged without looking up from her cutting board. "It's not that I hated it. I just resented it being forced on me at such a young age, so I stopped doing it when I left home. Working on campaigns, I basically lived on takeout. I was on a first-name basis with *Sal's Pizza* and *Wok This Way*. I kind of feel sorry now that…" She trailed off.

Andrew turned away from the hot skillet, holding a wooden spoon in his hand, waiting for her to continue.

"I… I kind of feel sorry for my wallet. All that wasted money." Her smile wobbled, like the strain of holding it was too great a weight.

Andrew sensed there was more, but he'd grown used to her guardedness. She would reveal things to him when she was ready. "I'd be more worried about your cholesterol level if I was you." He winked, then turned back to the task at hand.

Megan dropped the chopped lettuce and kale into the walnut salad bowl. "Thank you for saving me from a life of clogged arteries."

He turned away from his sautéing vegetables and bowed. "You're welcome."

She grabbed an oven mitt off the counter and playfully swatted him. "I'm looking forward to showing off my new skills when Gabe and Darren visit in July. Speaking of which, I can't believe the wedding is next week." She stopped mid-chop. "I wonder if Brock bought his ticket yet…"

"He's going with you?" Andrew forgot to hide his surprise.

"Of course he's coming." Megan gave him a funny look, snatched the towel from his shoulder, and wiped her hands. "We're dating."

Then she headed to her bedroom.

When she returned to the kitchen five minutes later, her lips were pursed tight, like something foul was lodged in her mouth and yet she didn't want to spit it out. She bumped into him twice while stepping back and forth between refrigerator and counter. When she started slicing the cucumbers with renewed gusto, Andrew knew something was definitely wrong.

"Everything alright?"

After a long pause, she finally replied, "Apparently I don't have a date to the wedding after all."

Andrew almost burned his thumb on the skillet handle. "What? He canceled on you?"

"Yes." Megan didn't elaborate.

"That's a jerk move," Andrew blurted out, trying to concentrate on stirring the vegetables until they were slightly caramelized. "Kind of last minute, isn't it?"

Megan exhaled a frustrated sigh. "One minute, he's hot. The next minute, he's cold. I like him, but I don't know…" She trailed off, casting a forlorn look at her pile of cucumbers. "And why did he wait so long to tell me? I mean, how do I find a date at the last minute?"

"Do you really need one? I know it's a wedding and all, but—"

"It's just… my family. They'll all be saying it should've been me married by now, and that I should've—" Her eyes grew wide.

Andrew frowned. *Should've what?*

"Not that I need a man," she quickly added. "But all my relatives coming up to me, talking about my ticking biological clock… It'll be a distraction from Gabe's happy day."

"I can be your date," he volunteered.

"You?" She clearly hadn't been expecting that. In fact, neither had he. But now that it was out there, a little vacation from work and life didn't sound so bad right now.

He shrugged. "No big deal. I have nothing going on that weekend."

"Are you sure?"

"Yeah. I like a good wedding." He narrowed his eyes. "Wait. Is it safe to assume the food will be excellent?"

"Oh, you bet it will! Gabe and Darren are total foodies."

"Then count me in." He smiled at her and began tossing the pasta with the sautéed vegetables.

"Well then, I insist on paying for your airline ticket." Megan set the salad bowl on the island and chose a stool for herself. "Since you'll be doing me a huge favor."

"No, don't." He scooped out two steaming bowls of pasta and sat down beside her, passing her the freshly grated Parmesan. "I have enough miles. It'll be fun."

She sprinkled the Parmesan and added black pepper, knocking elbows as he reached for the salad tongs. "You have no idea what you're getting yourself into. This is going to be a truly special occasion, Andrew: You're about to witness Trump's America."

"Bring it on," he joked, tossing his gauntlet to the political world. "I'll be sure to wear my MAGA hat."

Tomorrow was the big day. Megan's little brother would be getting married in the gardens of the Hyatt Regency. Andrew and Megan arrived in Sarasota in the early afternoon, with a few hours to kill before the rehearsal dinner. As they checked into the hotel, Megan thought about how much she was looking forward to meeting Darren's parents, both lawyers from Connecticut. From everything Gabe had told her, they were kind and loving people whose only downfall was belonging to the Democratic Party. Thinking about the upcoming evening, she smiled to herself. At least Andrew wouldn't be the only liberal in the house.

When Andrew had wondered why she needed a wedding date so badly, she had made it pretty clear that her family was — well, for lack of a better word, crazy. He had to know that they wouldn't be likely to sympathize much with his grief over the election. But she had left out the part about how she was engaged until a year ago, when her fiancé cheated on her with her best friend, practically at the altar. Half of

Megan's family thought she still should've married Jason! *Men make mistakes,* they said, defending him. She wondered what Andrew might say to that.

They took the elevator to the fourteenth floor and stepped out. The sign informed them that Megan's room was to the left, and Andrew's to the right.

"What are you going to do until six?" he asked, retreating backward down the corridor.

Normally she would be up for a walk or some exploring, but after working long hours over the past few weeks and helping Gabe finalize the wedding, she was exhausted. "All I want to do is sit out by the pool," she confessed.

" Andrew grinned. "I'll join you."

"OK," she called out. "Meet you down there in twenty."

She found him semi-reclined in a lounge chair right next to the waterfall. He was easy to spot from afar: the only guest with pale legs, holding a book about Steve Bannon. "*Devil's Bargain*? Brought some light reading with you, I see."

His laugh was good-natured but sardonic. "It's like a Steven King novel, except this is real life and the bad guys don't get caught. Instead they get promoted to positions of power."

He put the book down next to him, forcing Megan to studiously avoid gawking at his naked chest. *Twice in one day,* she thought ruefully.

Before they had left for the airport early that morning, Megan had been dragging her suitcase down the apartment hallway with one hand while holding her phone in the other, scrolling through email. When Andrew stepped out of the bathroom, fresh from the shower, she had collided with his damp, bare chest.

It was hard to ignore the fact that except for the white towel wrapped around his waist, he was nude. But when her head jerked up, what she saw was even more startling. She had dropped the suitcase handle to the floor with a crash.

"Andrew!"

He stepped back. "Sorry!"

"You shaved your beard off!"

His smile had been bashful as he slid his hand through his wet hair.

Megan thought he looked younger. His face was so naked, it seemed almost indecent to be looking at it. Strong jaw, sturdy chin, full lips... She was tempted to reach out and feel the smoothness of his cheek for herself.

His shy smile had grown. "You want to touch it, don't you?"

"Can I?" She'd reached her hand out tentatively and stroked his cheek with two fingers. *So soft...* Her hand whipped back to her side. She was definitely crossing a line here.

"Why did you... ? Was it for—"

"Uh, it's nothing," he'd shrugged, cutting her off. "Just time for a change. I go through phases, you know? You should have seen my mustache phase." Then he had laughed, spraying Megan with little droplets from his hair.

She'd squinted, trying to picture him with a mustache. From his face, her eyes had involuntarily traveled down to where his body ended and the towel began...

and snapped her head upward and fastened her eyes on his. Terrible. I mean, that probably looked terrible. You with a mustache. Ha!"

Why was she babbling? Her cheeks had started to burn.

Andrew had stood unmoving before her, a puzzled look on his face.

She'd grabbed her suitcase off the floor, now averting her gaze. "Um, so we need to... airport... twenty minutes..."

What was going on? Why had she started acting like a teenager all of sudden? Not enough coffee—surely that was it.

"S-sorry," she had stuttered. "I mean, we need to leave for the airport in twenty minutes."

"OK," he'd nodded, as if everything was normal. "I'll be ready."

By the poolside now, under the protection of her sunglasses, she could spend a little more time examining his body. His shoulders weren't as broad as Brock's, but he was well-defined and compact. His pecs looked solid and his stomach tight, with a healthy sprinkling of dark hair across his chest. This was someone who had functional strength, developed from years of hiking and yoga. *Funny.* she thought to herself, *I've seen more of Andrew's body than of my own boyfriend's.*

Boyfriend. The word was jarring. Was Brock even her boyfriend, really? They'd never talked about their relationship. They had never even progressed past brief kisses yet. And now he had bailed on her at the last minute, leaving her here with her roommate. Her handsome, well-built roommate…

Enough of that nonsense, Megan commanded herself, peeling off her long white tunic to reveal a black one-piece that could have been modest except for the plunging V that emphasized her chest. She returned the floppy white sun hat and black cat-eye sunglasses to their rightful places, stretched out her lean, tanned legs, and let out a soft sigh.

"I could go to sleep right here."

"You can, if you want," came Andrew's gentle voice from beside her. "I'll wake you up in a bit."

She closed her eyes and drifted off for a little siesta in the hot Florida sun. Soon she was dreaming of Brock on the beach, enfolding her in his arms, probing the skin at the edges of her swimsuit. *Megan, Megan,* he whispered again and again in her ear.

She moaned a little, but the voice didn't sound like Brock's. It was Andrew's, and it was getting louder. Brock's lips kissing her neck were replaced by Andrew's.

Her eyes flew open.

Andrew was leaning over her, his hand resting on her shoulder as he tried to rouse her from her nap. "Wow, you are hard to wake up! I didn't want you to get a sunburn." He was dripping wet, toweling himself off after a swim.

A pool of saliva had formed at the corner of her mouth, and it took her a moment to regain her bearings. Then she hastily snatched up her cover-up and turned her back to him to dress. "Thanks for waking me up. I should go shower and change." She stood up and hurried inside, eager to put distance between them. For the second time that day, she asked herself what in the world was going on. Why was she thinking about Andrew this way? She had feelings for Brock. Didn't she?

Suddenly Megan was as vulnerable as a forest in drought. A tiny spark might turn into a blaze, consuming her. Better to snuff out this tiny flicker now, before she did something foolish.

Chapter Twenty Two

---⭐---

THE UNTHINKABLE

"Stop, Megs. Everything's going to be perfect." It was Saturday — wedding day — and Gabe was holding Megan by both shoulders, reminder her to breathe, as though they'd switched places and she was the bride while he was the maid of honor.

She had been running around all morning — trying to help Gabe get ready, checking on the caterers, the flowers, the bakery. At last Gabe blocked her from going into the reception hall for one last look. "You're still wearing your sweatpants, for god's sake! The wedding starts in two hours. Go get dressed!"

"But this is your day," she protested, "and I want to do—"

"You've done plenty, Megan, more than I could ask for." He hugged her tightly to him and kissed her forehead.

"I just want to do for you what Mom would have done," she said sadly.

Gabe smiled and looked deep into her eyes. "You always do right by her. And by me. Everything is going to be great. Now go." He shoved her toward the elevator. "Have a glass of wine or something!"

Megan dressed in a long, ice-blue slip dress and pulled her blond hair back into a classic chignon. She had that glass of wine Gabe had suggested, and another to boot. Then she strode down toward the beach, where she would be giving her brother away.

Partially hidden behind a palm tree, Megan observed as the guests were seated on the sandy white beach facing the Gulf of Mexico. Only a handful were from the Thompson side of the family. Gabe had invited their most tolerant relatives—a total of six. The remaining chairs on his half of the aisle were filled with friends he and Darren shared. Megan spotted Andrew in his tan suit jacket among them and gave a half wave.

Gabe appeared by her side, wearing a tailored white linen suit. His blond hair was styled immaculately. She straightened his orange blossom boutonniere, taking a moment to breathe in the perfumed scent and smooth out an imaginary wrinkle in his collar, desperate to draw out this moment. How many times had she tied his ties and smoothed his collars over the years? Since their mother's death, the line between mother and sister had blurred. Where did one begin and the other end? Now the end was in sight. After today, she would revert forever to her role as big sister.

"You look gorgeous." She beamed with pride. "Ready?"

As they walked down the aisle, her arm linked through his, she forced back tears. A quick peck on the cheek, and then Megan took her seat next to Andrew, who patted her leg in a friendly, reassuring gesture.

The sky was a deep, uniform blue speckled with fluffy white clouds. Despite the heat, a nice constant breeze flowed cool off the water. Gabe and Darren stood under the pergola, hands entwined, looking handsome and happy. The wind picked up and swirled around them, pushing their hair every which way, and their suits flapped like sails. Seagulls circled overhead, their cries competing with the violinist. Yet from the private looks the couple exchanged, Megan saw that the world did not exist outside their private bubble of happiness. A swirl of emotions rose to the fore. Her little brother was getting married. She wished her mother was there. She wished she wasn't single.

That last one surprised her.

You have Brock, she reminded herself.

But something wasn't sitting right with her anymore. Yes, Brock was incredibly attractive. But she found herself questioning who he really was, and whether he was even attracted to her.

At first, as he dodged her advances, Megan thought he was trying to be respectful, and she found it charming if a bit antiquated. He seemed to be putting on a show of respecting her reputation. And after all, theirs was an arranged pairing of sorts.

Several times she had hinted at seeing his apartment, but he always rebuffed her, saying it was too messy (which she doubted, given his immaculate truck) and he was embarrassed by his makeshift bachelor pad, or claiming he wanted to take things slow. She even wondered if his behavior was simply in line with his evangelical upbringing. After several dates, she'd started to wonder if perhaps he wasn't attracted to her. Once, as they had kissed passionately in his truck, she had stolen a glance at his face. His eyes were shut so tight, she'd wondered briefly if he was in pain.

The alternative—that he was still a virgin—seemed so laughably implausible, she had no choice but to consider that he found her attractiveness lacking in some way. Maybe all he wanted was the power match and nothing more. Maybe he already had someone on the side. What then? When she returned from this weekend away, she was going to have to confront him.

Andrew pulled her from her thoughts as he whispered in her ear, "You looked like an elegant matriarch, giving your brother away."

"Thank you, I guess." She couldn't get over how different he looked with a clean-shaven face. "I can't tell if that's a compliment."

"I hold matriarchs in high esteem. So… yes."

After that, she kept throwing glances his way throughout the ceremony, and was mad at herself for getting distracted. Once the ceremony was over and all the pictures were taken, she rejoined him at the poolside reception, where a string quartet strummed merrily.

"Having a good time so far?" she asked eagerly. After all, he had sacrificed his weekend to be there.

Andrew grabbed two blue crab cakes off the tray of a passing waiter and handed her one. "I am. Thank you. These are delicious, by the way. You also have to try the blackened shrimp with the smoked cheddar grits. I'll grab you one the next time it comes around."

She nibbled her hors d'oeuvres to keep herself from scarfing it down, and realized she was starving. Aside from half a muffin at breakfast, the only other thing she'd consumed that day was two glasses of Champagne and a bucket load of coffee. Scanning the crowd for a waiter, she found none except the one carrying yet another tray of Champagne, and she somehow ended up with a glass in her hand.

Andrew was humming along to the quartet.

Megan laughed. "You know this song?"

"Yeah, of course I know this song. I bet you do too. Listen." He placed a hand on her shoulder and turned her toward the stringed instruments.

A young violinist dressed in an evening gown played a solo, her eyes closed as though she were in a faraway dream. The melody floated through Megan, together with the bubbles from the Champagne, creating a lightheadedness that seemed ready to carry her away. Only the weight of Andrew's hand kept her tethered to the earth. A smile of recognition appeared on her face.

Close to her ear, Andrew's mouth sang quietly. "Black hole sun, won't you come and wash away the rain…"

Megan chuckled. "Nice one, Gabe."

"Yeah, the whole set has been nineties alternative. Between the food, the music, the setting — and of course, the wonderful company — this is a great wedding."

"Did you check out the vodka station? It's an ice luge!"

He held a highball glass aloft, filled with clear liquid. "I've got my ice-cold liquid courage right here. I'm ready to meet your family."

"Good call. You'll probably need to visit that ice luge a few times before the night is over."

"Speaking of family, how much have you told them about me?"

"I told them you were a nice guy," she admitted, "who happens to be a Bernie fan."

"Really?" Andrew set his vodka on a high table and gaped at her. "Why?"

She had to smile at his reaction. "Well, there's no hiding you're a liberal, is there? Knowing you, that will come out at some point, I'm sure."

"Very funny."

"And it's much better to be a Bernie guy than a Hillary guy. He was the Left's version of populism. My dad will respect that."

Andrew nodded as if making a mental note of it.

Megan held up a finger in warning. "He hates the Clintons, though. Don't bring them up. At all. But more important, don't mention how incompetent the president is. Trust me, there is no winning that argument."

When the guests were asked to proceed into the small reception room with floor-to-ceiling windows and an unobstructed view of the Gulf, Andrew knew he was walking into the lions' den. He and Megan were seated at a round table alongside her father Paul, her aunt Nancy, and her uncle Rick. Noting the minimalist centerpiece—a solitary white orchid—the roommates shared a private grin, remembering their trip to the Botanic Garden. But one look at Megan was enough to register her surprise at being introduced to her father's date. The woman who introduced herself as Tammy wore a hairdo straight out of the nineties and seemed to be wearing a tablecloth. Definitely not Paul Thompson's type, Andrew concluded. At least, not according to his daughter.

No sooner had the round of introductions been made than their dining companions descended on Andrew like crows on roadkill.

"So, Andrew, what do you do in D.C.?" asked Uncle Rick.

"I'm an environmental lobbyist." He took a sip of his water, bracing himself for the inevitable. He knew all too well that whether you're telling a conservative you work as an environmentalist, or telling a liberal you work for a coal company, the reaction is the same: value judgments followed by swift, immediate disdain.

"Ha!" Paul looked him straight in the eye, baiting him. "I'm glad

President Trump pulled us out of the Paris deal. You still have a job?"

"Dad!" Megan shot him a look of reproach.

"I'm glad, too," Andrew replied with his most patient smile. "Now people are galvanized, and decisions will come down to the local level. Mayors, governors, and business leaders are all declaring their intention to stay in the climate accord." He was relieved when a waiter appeared carrying a large serving tray and deftly doled out the wild arugula and spiced watermelon salads.

Everyone tucked in except Paul, who gazed at his plate suspiciously and then pushed it to the side.

"You know what I can't understand? This whole bathroom thing!" declared Aunt Nancy waving her pierced watermelon in the air. "I don't want no pervert walking into the ladies' room! Megan, you tell those people in Congress. It's ridiculous!"

Megan rolled her eyes and took a bite of her buttered cornbread.

Andrew choked back a laugh, knowing all too well the joys of fielding preposterous requests from relatives.

Uncle Rick took a swig from his beer bottle. "So, Andrew, you're a liberal. Right?" He didn't wait for confirmation. "What is up with this whole Black Lives Matter thing? Don't all lives matter?"

"Of course all lives matter." Andrew struggled to keep his voice calm. "But I think the point is to end police violence against black people in particular—"

"Uncle Rick, this is a wedding," Megan interrupted. "Not really the place for this."

When the salad plates were cleared away and the main course was served, Paul tucked into his filet mignon, muttering, "Now this is something I recognize." He narrowed his eyes at Andrew. "You're not a bloody vegetarian, are you?"

Andrew sawed off a piece of rare steak and popped it in his mouth. The filet was perfectly seared on the outside and practically buttery on the inside. He closed his eyes and moaned as he chewed, not needing to exaggerate his satisfaction. Beef was bad for the environment, with every cow fart contributing to global warming, but every now and then he gave in to his primal craving. He'd had enough cashew cheese and soy patties to last a life time.

Paul gave a curt nod, as though Andrew had passed a test. But the test wasn't over yet.

"You know, I think it's great President Trump is bringing back all those coal jobs." Megan's father spoke with a quiet ferocity. "That's what I like about him. He really is keeping his campaign promises." The other heads at the table bobbled in agreement.

Megan looked at Andrew and raised an eyebrow as if to telegraph a message: *Don't respond to that one.*

But he couldn't help himself "Well, Paul, I hope you enjoy waterfront property, because that's what you'll be getting in the next ten years."

Luckily, their dining companions paused their attack during the speeches and the toasting. And with an extra round of drinks, Andrew noticed, they were even able to tolerate the growing demand for the wedding couple's repeated kisses.

Paul turned his attention to Megan. "Well, that's Gabe all hitched up. You're next, right, Meg?"

Megan's face froze. Andrew saw that her discomfort was evident to everyone except her father.

"Andrew, did Megan ever tell you about Jason?"

Andrew had never heard about Jason, and he was pretty sure Megan didn't want to hear about it right now. "Say, Paul," he said, diving on the grenade her father had launched, "I'd love to get your opinion of CNN News."

As Paul droned on about fake news and liberal mainstream media, Megan mouthed a *thank you* in Andrew's direction.

Interesting family, he thought.

The night before, he and Megan had met Gabe and Darren for drinks. Even though Gabe was a libertarian, he and Andrew had agreed on a lot of things when it came to the environment and civil liberties. There had been only one awkward moment. "You're the hot roommate Megan's been talking about," Gabe had said. After than

Megan didn't so much as look at Andrew for a good five minutes.

Paul, on the other hand, was the quintessential Trump guy. In his mind, the Tweeter-in-Chief could do no wrong. Andrew soon realized that if the president was the captain and America was the RMS *Titanic*, Paul was the loyal servant who would go down with the ship, swearing the captain knew best, the captain would save them. Yet Andrew found his anger toward Paul and people like him was giving way to pity. They wanted change, were desperate for change, and they had gotten it — only for many of them, it would be change for the worse. They stood to lose health care and Social Security, and the tax cuts promised to them would end up in the hands of the wealthiest Americans instead.

The music switched over from light dinnertime jazz to the customary wedding mix, skipping and bouncing between the decades to satisfy the different generations. One minute the band played "The Twist" by Chubby Checker, and the next they were covering Beyoncé. Aunt Nancy was among the first to get sweaty on the dance floor. She swayed back over to the table and drunkenly asked Andrew if he'd like to join her.

Andrew shot a nervous look at Uncle Rick, and another at Megan as if to say, *Help me out here.*

"I don't dance, boy. Have at her." Uncle Rick's wink was decidedly lewd.

Left with no choice, Andrew stood up from the table and extended his hand to Aunt Nancy. "May I have this dance, miss?" He bowed slightly.

She giggled. "You got yourself a real gentleman here, Megan."

Out on the dance floor, Andrew rested one hand respectably on Aunt Nancy's sizable waist while the other clasped her sweaty palm. She was much shorter than him, and not fat per se, but the years had filled in what once was probably an hourglass shape, leaving a line of flesh straight down from shoulders to waist to hips. The tight red dress was an unfortunate choice. *Like a tube of breakfast sausage,* Andrew thought, and tried put the image out of his mind.

"You know, Megan is a special girl," Aunt Nancy was saying. "She's going places."

"Yes, ma'am." Andrew did get the picture, but he had to turn away. Aunt Nancy reeked of cigarette smoke and drugstore perfume—a repulsive combination.

"She's known a lot of heartache. This girl is so used to taking care of other people and putting their happiness before her own. She deserves someone who'll take care of her, someone who'll put her happiness first. No matter what. Get my drift?" She fixed Andrew with a stern look.

Nancy's voice dripped with maternal protectiveness. He half expected her to pull a pocket knife from between the recesses of large bosom to emphasize her point. "It's not what you think. Megan and I—"

"She's going to run for office someday, you know."

He nodded. "Yes, ma'am, I know that."

"And she's going to get elected." Aunt Nancy stabbed his chest with a pudgy forefinger. "And you can't mess that up for her. No one will elect her if she's dating a goddamned Democrat, even if you are one of the nice ones."

Andrew tried to protest. "It's not like that at all. Megan and I are just friends."

She ignored him. "That might fly in some fancy blue state or some elite city. But not in Florida."

"I know that, too—"

"She's always wanted to work in government. It's all she's ever wanted, for as long as I can remember. I just wanted you to know. Because I see the way you look at her."

Andrew's head was spinning. Was it from the perfume-smoke cloud encircling him? Or the accusation that he had a crush on his roommate? Sure, she was an attractive woman, and their friendship had grown over the past few months, but she was off limits. She had a boyfriend, and she was still a Republican.

"Who knows?" Aunt Nancy was saying. "Maybe she'll even be

president someday." Her eyes shone at the thought of her niece, and then flashed daggers at Andrew.

"Can I cut in?" Megan smiled over her aunt's shoulder.

Grateful, Andrew stepped back and bowed to Aunt Nancy, who gave him a final menacing look before tottering toward the open bar. As his eyes swept over the length of Megan's body, he sucked in a breath and reminded himself, *She's off limits.*

★ ★ ★

M egan laughed. "She's not as fierce as she looks."

"Could've fooled me." Andrew reached out and took hold of her waist.

"You two seemed to be having quite a discussion," she said as he grasped her hand. "I figured I'd come over and save you."

"Thanks." He grinned, and suddenly she was dancing with her roommate.

In fact, she was growing tired of running interference, and wondered how Andrew seemed to handle the inquisition so calmly. She pitied his discomfort, but he had shown he could handle himself. And with all the attention on him, she hadn't been forced to make small talk with her father's date. She owed Andrew big-time.

They glided across the floor in pleasant silence for a while. He was a good dancer, just as she'd expected. What she wasn't expecting was how good it felt to be held by him. He smelled of pine and citrus, and she found herself leaning in, wanting to breathe him in. And as she breathed him in, she found herself wanting more, to close the gap between them.

When their eyes met again, they smiled and said at the same time, "You look really nice..."

His laugh was infectious.

"You know, I really like the new look," she declared. "I mean, you looked fine before. But you know, this is so much—"

"Just fine?" He raised an eyebrow and pretended to pout.

"You know what I mean."

"Well, I did it for you."

Megan looked up at him warily from under her knit brow. "Really?" Over the course of the song, their bodies had drifted closer and closer, like the tide pulled inevitably to the shore. "Why?"

He looked at her, his eyes not giving anything away. "I wanted your family to like me, I guess." Before Megan could respond, he added, "Can I tell you something?"

She paused, a little afraid of where this was going. "Sure."

"I know this is none of my business, and I risk coming off as an asshole, but…" Andrew nipped at his lower lip, still guiding her to the music. "Brock is wrong for you. You two couldn't be more different."

Megan stopped short and pulled away from him. Who did he think he was, giving her advice? "You're right," she snapped. "Who I date is none of your business. You're out of line. And Brock is a very nice man."

"Then why did he bail on you last minute?"

"He had something else he needed to do." The truth was, she didn't know why. But she knew she was going to defend him for it.

"Alright, alright." Andrew tried to reach for her again. "Does he make you happy, Megan?"

She scoffed and took another step back. "One should never depend on a man for happiness."

Andrew frowned. "That's very Zen of you. Or very cynical. Either way, it's not really an honest response, if you ask me."

"I didn't ask you, just so we're clear." She made sure her tone was bursting with contempt.

"I just don't want to see you get hurt," he pleaded. "I just want you to be happy."

"You don't know me, Andrew." She lifted her chin in defiance. "And maybe I don't deserve happiness."

"Megan, that is so ridiculous…"

She opened her mouth to respond, but Aunt Nancy had returned with her drink, sensing some sort of conflict. She narrowed her eyes at Andrew and whisked Megan away, leaving Andrew standing alone on the dance floor.

A faster-paced song came on, and Megan halfheartedly moved her hips from side to side. Watching Andrew retreat from the reception, Megan silently berated herself. After all he'd done for her, she shouldn't have lost her temper. It wasn't him she was mad at.

Aunt Nancy's sexy dance looked anything but sexy. "You alright there, hon?" she yelled over the music.

Megan could smell her aunt's sour alcohol breath from three feet away. "Yeah, I'm fine. Who doesn't like being surrounded by people happily in love?" She had tried to make it sound lighthearted, but it came out bitter.

Nancy stopped her bootie-shaking and turned Megan's chin to meet hers. "Sweets, Jason was an asshole, and I'm glad you didn't marry him. And I know you already know this, 'cause you're a smart cookie, but your date is no good for you either. He'll ruin your career. Plus, he probably thinks he's too good for all of us. You can do better than him. And I told him that, too."

"Aunt Nancy, you didn't!" Megan stopped dancing. "Andrew has been nothing but kind to me. Besides, I don't feel that way about him, and he doesn't either."

"Wake up, honey. He wants you." Aunt Nancy gave a seductive little shake.

Megan's heart started to race. Did Andrew want her? "Aunt Nancy, I have to go."

Her aunt opened her mouth to speak, but Megan was already gone.

Midnight had come and gone, and Andrew was still lying awake on his hotel bed. He kept replaying his conversation with Megan, and how her eyes glinted with anger and something else beneath. Why would she believe she didn't deserve happiness? And why did that bother him so much?

It was true that she had stopped being "Megan the Republican," and then "Megan the roommate." Now she was just Megan, his friend. Andrew knew all about his need to place people neatly into their right boxes. But something had been nagging him. He didn't want to admit it, but she didn't really fit in the "friend" box anymore either. He wanted something else, though he didn't know what, exactly.

A soft knock on the door interrupted his thoughts. Through the peephole, he saw Megan in her long, pale dress, fiddling with her purse. He opened the door wide.

She hesitated in the entryway and bit her lip. "Look, I'm sorry. I was a jerk out there. Especially after all you've done for me, coming to the wedding and putting up with my family…"

He waved it off, hoping to smooth away the troubled look on her face. "It was nothing. Don't worry about it. I'm sorry for bringing up Brock. It wasn't my place to say anything."

"I feel like I need to explain myself."

"No need." He stepped backward and was surprised when she followed him into the room. Something was definitely bothering her, and it wasn't just what he'd said on the dance floor.

"Last year I was engaged," she began, "and my fiancé cheated on me. With my best friend."

Andrew nodded. That must be the Jason her father had referred to at supper. He'd suspected Megan had been hurt, but he didn't know it was so recent.

"It hurt. Badly." She took a deep breath. "But then I realized it was my fault he cheated."

"Megan, that can't be —"

"It was," she insisted. "I was so dedicated to my job that I was neglecting him. I was never around, and he realized that it was always going to be that way. I'm always going to put my career first, because that's what public service requires."

"You can't seriously blame yourself?" Andrew folded his arms and leaned against the wall. "He cheated on you!"

"Don't get me wrong. He was an ass for cheating." She sounded so tired and forlorn, he almost reached for her. "I don't excuse it, but I take responsibility for my part of the blame."

Andrew wasn't sure what to say. "I'm sorry he hurt you. But that doesn't explain why you're with Brock."

A conflicted look crossed Megan's face. "It's complicated."

He observed her for a long moment, and she didn't look away. "Well, as a concerned friend, I advise you not to sell yourself short. The right guy will understand. There's someone out there who will love and value you. All of you."

Megan shook her head, and a few curls fell loose. "I don't want to fall in love. Love is bullshit. Love is people dying on you. Love is people cheating on you and hurting you." She took a step toward him, and then another, closing the distance between them. "I want something else."

She kissed him, slowly and softly at first.

He hesitated.

This is not a good idea...

No good will come of it...

But those thoughts vanished when she wrapped her arms around him, melting into him as she had when they were dancing. He kissed her more fervently, his desire growing by the second. Megan closed her eyes as he teased the thin strap of her dress over her shoulder, caressing her collarbone with damp kisses. She dropped her purse, and it landed on the rug with a soft, decisive *thump*.

The noise had the effect of a starter gun, and suddenly they were stripping the clothes from each other's bodies, racing to get closer still. Andrew was surprised to discover how much he wanted her, wanted to explore every inch of her. How long had he felt this way? It felt like always.

One hand pressed into the small of her back. The other cupped her velvety breast and traced the nipple. A moan, barely audible, escaped Megan's mouth.

They moved intuitively as one unit, their lips never parting for long, toward the bed. As she pushed him to the bed and straddled him, he pushed all doubt from his mind. Like driftwood at sea, they had traveled alone for a long time, and now they were inching closer, wave by wave, until at last they crashed into each other.

The world as they knew it ceased to exist.

Chapter Twenty Three

✪

PLAYING WITH FIRE

Megan's heart was thumping in her chest as she snatched her clothes from the floor and began pulling them on in the dark silence of Andrew's hotel room. When she slipped out the door and tiptoed into the hallway, he was still fast asleep in a tangle of sheets.

Shit. Shit. Shit.

How could she have done this to Brock? Granted, they weren't officially a couple. But it felt like cheating. What on earth had she been thinking? That was just it—she hadn't.

Maybe it was just pent-up sexual energy, her frustration at not moving forward on a physical level with Brock. Maybe she just needed a release, and it had nothing to do with Andrew. Megan groaned as she slid between the crisp sheets of her own bed. This was officially the second stupidest thing she'd ever done. Hadn't she learned her lesson after sending naked photos to her ex-fiance? Now she had let herself be vulnerable and exposed yet again. Instead of making love to the guy she was supposed to want, she had screwed her roommate. What a mess.

As she drifted into oblivion, a final thought trickled through the flood of regret.

But the sex was amazing...

When she awoke later that morning, she said a silent prayer.

Please don't let me run into Andrew. Not yet. She needed time to process everything and figure out how to do damage control.

But as her hotel room door clicked faintly behind her, she heard her name echo down the hallway. She ignored it and hurried toward the elevator.

"Megan!"

She spun around to see Andrew jogging toward her, bright-eyed and chipper. "You walk fast for someone in those heels." His face wore that signature amused grin—the same grin he used when he thought he'd gotten the upper hand.

"So I've been told." She continued sailing across the carpet, fixating on the bold geometric pattern, hoping he would just go away.

"Look, about last night—"

Megan's blush was immediate. "I'm just heading to breakfast, meeting an old friend..." She didn't look up to see his reaction, afraid that she'd remember everywhere he'd put those lips the night before.

"Oh. OK. I'll walk with you."

He didn't seem to be getting the hint. "What time's your flight?" Megan mumbled.

"One o'clock. I'm leaving for the airport after breakfast."

In the elevator, an elderly couple wearing matching track suits shuffled to make room for them.

"I had a lot of fun at the wedding. And... after." His tone was even, but she thought she heard mischief behind it.

Megan shoved down the thought of what they had done, how they'd explored each other, at first frenzied and then more leisurely by the moonlight... She gathered the courage to look into his blue eyes, searching his stubbly face for some sign of what he was thinking. Did he have any clue what they were supposed to do now?

"Yeah, me too." She looked straight ahead. "Food was fantastic."

When the elevator pinged, they waited for the couple to shamble off first. As the old man brushed past, Megan could have sworn he winked at her. She wanted to yell after him, *It's not what you think!*

Megan halted her march in front of the hotel restaurant, with

Andrew still trailing a step behind.

"Ah, the two lovebirds!"

Megan's friend Mike was early as usual. His hair was disheveled, his face unshaven, his dress shirt wrinkled and stained—also as usual. He might not look like much, but Megan knew his true worth, as did anyone aware of his long string of political success stories. A diamond in the rough, he would make a perfect campaign manager for her.

When he released Megan from a gregarious hug, she was more than a little ruffled. Was she wearing a sign on her forehead, I HAD SEX WITH MY ROOMMATE?

"Well, well. I finally get to meet Megan's man. You're handsome, I'll give you that! But different from what I expected." Mike cocked his head to the side, as though appraising a piece of furniture or art. "She told me Don Draper, but it's more like Bradley Cooper, if you ask me." He reached out a hand.

Andrew shook it, grinning. "Thanks. I'll take that as a compliment. But we're... uh... I'm not—"

Megan tried to intervene. "Mike—"

"Sure looks like you are!" Mike winked. "But hey, if you guys want to keep it secret for now..."

"Mike!" Megan elbowed him in the ribs. "This is Andrew. My roommate."

Mike turned to her, bewildered.

"Brock couldn't make it." The three of them stood there a moment, and Megan gnawed at her bottom lip. The awkwardness was unbearable. She had to put an end to it. "Well, thanks for your assistance, Andrew. Have a safe flight."

Thanks for your assistance? She wanted to run and hide. Was she handling a business transaction? She could have been saying, *Thanks for helping me select this washer and dryer.*

Andrew stared at her for a moment, his amused smile fading. "It was my pleasure assisting you. Well, I'll leave you two to catch up."

He reached for her then, and wrapped his arms around her in an awkward hug. Her body was stiff and resistant at first, until his softness overpowered her. He was like a roaring fire, and she was captivated. She wanted to get closer, to feel his heat, but she held herself back. Getting burned was not an option.

"See you when you get back home, Megan." Andrew stepped toward the hostess station.

Mike was staring at her now, his brow puckered quizzically.

"Table for one?" Megan heard the hostess ask cheerfully.

Mike lurched forward. "Table for three," he interjected, clapping Andrew on the back. "We're not going to make you eat alone, bro."

Breakfast was no better. Megan tried so hard to keep her emotions tamped down, she sounded robotic. *Andrew, can you please pass the cream? Andrew, did you know my friend Mike also works on campaigns? Yes, I did enjoy the food last night, thank you for inquiring.*

When Andrew finally stood up and said good-bye, he lingered a few seconds at the table.

Megan didn't get up. What was she supposed to say? *I'm sorry? Thank you for the amazing sex? This can never happen again?* As he left through the glass doors, she followed him with her eyes.

Mike's round face broke into a goofy grin. "You dawg! You slept with him, didn't you?" He held out his clenched fist. "C'mon, don't leave me hanging."

She tapped his fist tepidly with her own. "How did you guess? Am I that transparent?"

"You're wearing your caught-doing-something-naughty look. Plus, you two were hella awkward all through breakfast."

Megan rolled her eyes at his choice of words. "You've been hanging around young people too much."

Mike's grin only widened. "Are you gonna share the deets, or what?"

She sighed. Disgusted as she was by her behavior, she was dying to talk about it with someone. Maybe Mike could help her salvage the situation. "Fine. We slept together last night. Happy?"

"Nice!" He lifted up his hand for high five.

Megan shook her head. "No high five. I do not deserve one. I slept with my roommate."

Mike's puzzled look said, *And... ?*

"And I kinda have a boyfriend—"

"Whom you haven't slept with."

Megan sighed. "That's beside the point."

"Was it any good?" Mike's eyebrows inched toward his hairline.

The waitress pouring their coffee refills tried in vain to pretend she hadn't overheard the exchange. Megan waited for her to move on to the next table.

"Best I've ever had," she admitted at last, "but he's still a Democrat."

"I thought you drew the line at snowflakes."

"I thought so, too."

He frowned. "Was this a one-time, I-had-too-much-to-drink thing? You're still with the NRA guy?"

"That's the problem, Mike. I don't think I want the NRA guy." And he most certainly didn't seem to want her.

She had never been fully convinced that White's plan was a good one anyway. Seriously, it was 2017! Why the hell did she need a man to win an election? She wanted to win this election on her own merit.

After a long, uncertain pause, Megan decided to be honest with her best friend. "I think I want my roommate."

Home, sweet home.

On Tuesday evening, Megan arrived at the apartment to find seventies rock blasting on the turntable and Andrew in the kitchen sporting his signature look, a dish towel over his shoulder. The tantalizing smell of wine and seafood—a match made in heaven if ever there was one—wafted through the apartment. The bar was set with two place settings and a lone, lit candle between them.

"Hi." She dropped her suitcase and put her handbag on the coffee table.

"Hey! I'm making dinner. Pour yourself a glass of wine?" He turned back to the heavy skillet steaming on the stove, flipping his spatula back and forth as he spoke. "It's Rioja. Should pair nicely. You like shrimp, right?"

She poured herself a generous glass of the Spanish red and threw back a big gulp before sitting on the barstool and kicking off her heels. Her feet were throbbing. It had been a long morning after her flight from Sarasota was delayed, and an even longer afternoon at work. Jean White had been taken to the hospital unexpectedly, and the congressman had returned to Florida to be with her. The office was half paralyzed with worry for the boss's wife and half in a frenzy trying to cancel appointments.

At least Megan had two whole days to think over what she was going to do about Andrew. Her plan was simple: Act like nothing had happened, and pray things would go back to normal. Every alternative to this scenario gave her a panic attack: What if they started fighting again? What if they got together again? What if he kicked her out?

She tried to put all that aside as Andrew came toward her now, carrying two steaming bowls of paella around the bar and setting them side by side. "So I learned how to make this dish when I spent three weeks in Spain a few years back. Chicken, mussels, sausage, shrimp, and rice. OK?"

Megan released her breath. She hadn't even realized she'd been holding it. Andrew was acting like nothing had changed. Maybe they wouldn't have to talk about their night in his hotel room after all.

She took a bite. "Delicious as always," she confirmed.

They chewed in silence. *No time like the present,* Megan thought.

"Mrs. White had a stroke."

"No!" Andrew looked up in concern. "When? Is she alright?"

Megan nodded. "This morning. She was playing golf. So far she's stable, but they're still running tests to discover the extent of the damage." She lifted her spoon again, heaped with the saffron-colored rice and its hidden treasures. "The congressman will be out of the office for a while."

Andrew reached toward her. "I'm sorry to hear that, Megan. How are you holding up?"

She shook her head and pulled back slightly. "I'm alright. It's just…
They're like family to me. I mean, you've met my family."

He chuckled, not unkindly.

"I'm not really close with many people. In all honesty, there aren't
that many people I like." She smiled, hoping it erased some of the
pitifulness. "I'm not the most… likable person."

"I like you." Andrew said softly.

He didn't even have to touch her. Those three simple words set her
skin tingling. Suddenly the apartment seemed muggy, even stifling,
and the spicy paella and zesty wine weren't helping things. The tiny
A/C, a window unit in the living room, struggled in vain to keep the
entire apartment at 74 degrees Fahrenheit. It was no match for the
95-degree humidity outdoors.

"About the other night… ," she started, putting down her
wineglass.

"Look, Megan, you don't have to say anything. It was…"

"I was drunk and confused."

"Yeah, me too. But I—"

"It was my brother's wedding—"

"I know. And I'm not that guy who sleeps with other people's
girlfriends—"

Megan let her hand rest on his forearm. Her desire for him was
building. It took all her willpower to suppress the feeling.

Mike had laid it out for her, plain and simple, after breakfast at
the Sarasota Hyatt Regency two days earlier. "Do you want my
professional judgment? Or my personal opinion?" he'd asked.

Megan had observed her unkempt companion, musing over how
unlikely a candidate he was for her friend yet alone her campaign
manager. But she liked him, she respected him, and his opinion carried
a lot of weight—not just with her, but with the whole Republican
party.

"Both."

"It wouldn't really matter in a reelection campaign. But this guy is
probably not great for your election chances."

She'd expected as much. "And your personal opinion?"

Mike had shrugged. "If he makes you happy, who fucking cares about the rest of it?"

"I care." Megan cupped her hands on the table and cradled her head between them.

Mike chuckled. "Sweetheart, how many guys have made you feel this way?

"This is a big risk, Mike. I can't throw my whole career away for a guy!"

Mike lifted her head gently off the table. "There's another option, you know. One that lets you keep the job *and* the guy."

She held her breath, waiting for his words of wisdom like a parishioner waiting for salvation.

"Casual sex. And keep it a secret."

Megan had moaned and let her head fall back into her hands. That was it, his magic solution? Have an affair and keep it hush-hush? It wasn't exactly a winning formula for Gingrich or Clinton or Bob Barr.

Right then, she had made up her mind: What happened with Andrew could never happen again.

"It wasn't your fault," she said now, even as the heat rose from his taut forearm and spread through her fingertips. "It was mine. I came on to you."

"Well, I wasn't exactly —"

"Andrew, listen. I'm sorry. I'm not that type of person either. I was drunk." She paused, realizing she'd said that already. "And Brock and I... well, we haven't even... you know."

An eyebrow shot up. "Know what?"

She stifled the humiliation. "We haven't slept together yet."

Andrew's second eyebrow joined the first. "Is he waiting for marriage or something?" he asked facetiously.

"Honestly, I don't know." She shrugged. "We've never talked about it."

"So you were drunk, and you were feeling frisky. Got it."

Did he mean it as a joke, or an accusation? "Yes, you can say that," she ventured. "Whatever it was, I promise it won't happen again."

"Hmm." Andrew seemed to consider this information for a moment. "I feel better about this now. Thank you."

Megan nodded curtly. "Let's just be roommates, then. And friends."

The single candle burned between them, disintegrating as the flame burned on. Andrew had started playing with the wax that had dripped onto the countertop, rolling little balls and then squishing them between his fingers. "Fine with me," he murmured.

Roll, squish. Roll, squish.

"Can I ask you something?"

She waited.

Roll, squish. "Was it good for you?"

Megan was caught off guard, but she saw no reason to hide the truth now that they'd reached an agreement. "It was amazing," she whispered shyly. "You?"

"Mind-blowing."

Her steely resolve melted away. She wanted to feel his strong hands on her body again. "You know, we could do it one last time." She spoke quickly, before she could change her mind. "Just to see if it was a fluke."

Andrew met her gaze, and she put a hand on his thigh. Then he dropped the wax ball and leaned in to blow out the candle: the perfect position for a kiss.

What the hell.

She reached up and circled her hands behind his neck. He wrapped his arms around her, lifting her effortlessly from the barstool, and she wrapped her legs around his waist. Then he pulled her to him and kissed her deeply. Pleasure pulsed in her veins.

He carried her to his bedroom, where they parted only long enough to peel off each other's clothing. Once again she insisted on being on top, and as she rode him, her mind kept repeating, *It's just casual sex, it's just casual sex...*

As they lay in each other's arms afterward, Megan wondered, *Is it casual if you never want it to end?*

In the darkness, she whispered to Andrew, "I'm breaking up with Brock."

"When?"

"Tomorrow."

A ndrew woke up hungry a few hours later. He had been too... distracted to finish his supper. His breath caught as he watched Megan sleep peacefully, her head resting in the crook of his arm. She was gorgeous. He hated to leave.

Slipping out from under her, he stole into the kitchen. The stove clock said it was only 11 p.m. Emily would still be awake. He grabbed his cellphone off the counter and dialed her number.

Before she could ask about the wedding or anything else, Andrew blurted out, "I slept with Megan."

Nothing but silence greeted him. He imagined Emily on the other end of the line, furrowing her eyebrows like their father did when he was deep in thought. "Didn't see that coming," she replied at last. "Did she kidnap you or something?"

"No!"

"Maybe it's Stockholm syndrome?"

"Emily..." He opened the fridge.

"Guess my counseling worked a little better than we expected. Though I must emphasize, *that* was never the end goal. The goal, as you may remember, was for you to stop being an asshole. Are you planning on resuming your asshole behavior?"

"What? No!" He pulled out some carrots and ranch dressing, and then changed his mind and put them back. "She told me she was drunk and it was a mistake, and I agreed with her."

"Good. She was right."

"And then we accidentally slept together again."

"What?"

"I think I'm falling for my roommate. She's perfect for me, except for the whole, you know, Republican part"

Emily gave an exasperated sigh. "What you have, Andrew, is a crush. Once you stopped being so judgmental and got to know her, you let down your guard. Realized she's a person, with feelings. Who also happens to be very attractive."

"We do have chemistry," he said wistfully, thinking all the while, *Chips. I want a big bowl of greasy potato chips.*

He searched through Megan's pantry. If there was a bag of chips anywhere, it would be there. "Even if she did like me, it could never work, right? I don't think I could marry a Republican." He paused. "Imagine what Mom would say!"

"Marry?? And she'd be furious." Emily's laugh sounded nervous. "But seriously, who cares what other people think? I am beyond thrilled you two are getting along. If only the rest of the fucking country could."

Andrew was taken aback. Emily, swearing? Things must really be bad.

"Sorry. You have no idea how many couples are in therapy now because of this whole Trump thing. My clients are arguing more over politics now than money. Some of them are actually breaking up because of this election!"

"Ha! And I want to get into a relationship with one." He ripped open the BBQ chips and shoveled a handful into his mouth. "Talk about swimming against the tide."

"You're not going to get into a relationship with her." It came off as a command, but then she softened her tone. "Don't get attached, Andrew. Not this time. I want you to be happy and settle down, but I don't think she's the right one."

"Why? Just because she's a conservative?" Andrew licked the spicy salt from his lips. "Jeez, now you're sounding like me. The *former* me."

"Under normal circumstances—one partner liberal, the other conservative—I'd say maybe you guys had a shot if you had great communication skills. Which, I'm sorry to say, you don't. Both of you have lots of work to do in that department."

"You could help us," he wheedled. "I know how much you like to help." Interfere was more like it, but now was not the time for quibbling.

"It's more than that. Plenty of couples who marry have different political views. But Megan is not just a Republican. She's the establishment."

"Huh?" he said through another mouthful of chips.

"Andrew, she wants to be a Republican politician. Now, remind me. How do you feel about Republican politicians?"

He shoved a few more chips into his mouth. "Hay-de-mall." He gulped back some water and cleared his voice. "I hate them all."

"And how would you feel about Megan if she were one of them? How would you reconcile loving her and hating what she does?"

"Well, I hadn't really—"

"Will you be able to stop bashing the GOP?"

"I don't think I—"

"Think of this another way, then. Would you marry a BP oil executive?"

"Maybe she won't run for office." Even as he the words left his mouth, he knew it was wishful thinking.

Emily knew it, too, of course. "I like Megan. I really do. But I'm telling you right now, she wants to run, and she won't let anything get in her way. Or anyone."

The conversation with his sister should have worked like an ice-cold shower. He was expecting it to deflate his feelings, which threatened to balloon out of his control. But the strange thing was, he didn't care if Megan was the GOP politician or a BP executive. He'd never felt like this before. Never had this connection, despite searching for it all this time. He hung up the phone, knowing he wasn't just falling for his roommate.

JULY HEADLINES

Former Miami Dolphins cheerleader divorces her rich husband…
all because he doesn't love Trump
—*Daily Dems*

Anthony Scaramucci's uncensored rant: Foul words and
threats to have Priebus fired
—*New York Times*

Why a woman blames Trump selfies for her divorce
—*The Washington Post*

Chapter Twenty Four

———————— ✪ ————————

FEELING THE BURN

A searing pain jolted through Andrew's hand. He yanked it back, but not before a loud *Fuck!* rang through the apartment. He leaped to the sink and flicked on the faucet, letting ice-cold water numb the spot that had met the frying pan. He could still feel the burning of hot metal against the tender skin of his hand. What an amateur move! He had just taken the frittata out of the oven, and not a moment later he had grasped the handle with his bare hand. Cooking usually cleared his mind, but today he could think of one thing only: Megan. Whatever was going on between them, it had been going on for over two weeks now. And tonight, over a supper of irresistible comfort food, he was going to confess his feelings.

Andrew was sitting at the counter with his hand in a bowl of ice when Megan walked into the apartment. Her smile was so immense — not to mention infrequent — that Andrew couldn't help but smile back.

She floated into his arms and kissed him lightly on the cheek. Andrew took a moment to enjoy the feeling of her lips against his skin.

She looked down at his hand. "What happened to you?"

"I burned myself making supper." Andrew pouted slightly, like a toddler with a boo-boo.

"Let me have a look." Megan lifted his hand slowly from the ice. Screaming red intertwined with the raised white lines of the burn. "Poor thing. Why don't I finish making supper?"

Andrew watched her glide around the kitchen, picking up where he'd left off. She was humming a Beatles tune. "You're in a good mood," he chuckled.

She poured a glass of rosé and placed it in front of him. "Oh, I am! We're celebrating tonight." She raised her glass toward him.

His body started to respond. *Should be interesting,* he thought, *seeing as I'm down a hand.* The thought made him smile. She would have to do most of the work. Then again, she always did do the heavy lifting in bed. He wished she would let him take charge for once, let him take care of her, cherish her, ravage her...

Rather than panzanella—a Tuscan bread salad he'd planned to serve, which would've complemented the egg dish perfectly—he said nothing as she prepared only a simple side salad, making small talk all the while. He kept sneaking glances at her, until finally he inhaled deeply and opened his mouth to come clean.

Megan got there first. "I have something big to tell you."

"Oh. OK." Andrew studied her eyes. They were like the ocean, but instead of reflecting the sun, they reflected her mood. When she was mad or stewing over something, they were dark as a rainstorm. Today, they sparkled like sapphires.

The words tumbled from her mouth. "You know how Mrs. White had a stroke? The good news is, she's doing fine. But it'll be a long recovery."

"That's great news." Andrew cut a piece of frittata with his fork. He sensed there was more.

"Nope. The *great* news is, White's retiring."

Andrew frowned. "But you already knew that," he managed through a mouth full of frittata.

Megan's laugh tinkled and clinked like wind chimes—light, airy and childlike. "Not next year. *Now.* He's making the announcement tomorrow."

Andrew nodded slowly, still chewing.

"That means I'll be running for his seat in a special election. The primary's in August, and the general election in November. Andrew,

I'm going to announce my candidacy tomorrow, too."

"Wow. Now?" His response sounded pathetic, even to his own ears.

Emily had been right about Megan. There was no stopping her. She was actually going to run for office, and maybe join the Republican establishment that stood for everything he despised. And it was starting now.

He forced a smile and pushed out a feeble "Congrats!" But his stomach had turned.

Megan didn't seem to notice. "I'll be meeting with some people from the PAC when I head down to Magnolia Ridge tomorrow. They're going to endorse me. I'm lining up meetings with mayors, chambers of commerce... And remember my friend Mike? You met him at the hotel? He's going to be my campaign manager..."

As Megan rattled off the to-do list for her new life as a bona fide candidate, Andrew began to fade. "I'm feeling a little woozy. The burn, maybe. Think I'll go put something on it."

Concern flooded her face. "Oh. Of course. I'll get you some burn spray. You want aspirin, too?"

"No, I'm fine. Just need to lie down for a bit." He kissed her on the cheek and slumped down the hall toward his bedroom, feeling sorry for himself.

Burned twice in one night.

Megan sat on the couch watching TV with the volume turned down low so it wouldn't disturb Andrew. She should go check on him, see if he was feeling better — maybe not now, but definitely before turning in for the night. She needed a little more time on her own. So much had happened in the past few weeks! Sleeping with her roommate, breaking up with her pseudo boyfriend, Mrs. White's stroke, and now the sudden change in her campaign timeline...

Brock had taken the breakup well, almost as if he'd been expecting it. Or maybe it was just that she had never really gotten a read on him. Was it that he liked her, but was unwilling to show it? Or that he didn't want her, and was unwilling to admit it?

They had met for dinner at the Monocle, where she had dealt with the issue head on. She couldn't be in a relationship—much less a marriage—with someone who wasn't attracted to her. Strategic power couple or no, a lifetime partnership had to include some physical element. And now, after everything with Andrew, she found she wanted even more than that.

Brock had called her beautiful and said it wasn't her—it was him. He'd turned on the charm, tried to persuade her to give it another chance. "We would be so good together," he'd said, sounding confident as ever. "We could achieve great things, you know." He had reminded her that with him as a husband, she would have the NRA's blessing for sure. He'd even suggested they could live separately if that was what she wanted.

Brock wasn't a man who begged. He was used to talking people into doing what he wanted. Yet Megan got the sense that beneath his cool demeanor was a desperate man. Whatever his reasons for wanting to make this match, she was sorry for him, but it wasn't her problem. As they'd parted ways outside the Monocle, he had kissed her cheek and whispered, "If you ever change your mind about us, call me."

Megan felt good about cutting Brock loose, but Congressman White hadn't taken the news very well. Tuning out Tucker Carlson, she replayed instead her phone conversation with White earlier in the day. He had broken the news as she touched up her mascara in front of the ladies' room mirror at work, her cellphone in the crook of her neck.

"I wanted to let you know first," came his distant voice through the phone. "Megan, I'm retiring."

Megan had almost dropped her phone into the bathroom sink. "You're *what*?" she had yelled, watching her eyes widen and her tongue stick out. Fellow staffers, streaming in and out of the bathroom, had given her weird looks.

"I need to take care of my wife," White had explained. "She's been there for me all these years, and now it's my turn."

"Of course, sir," Megan had replied when she found her voice.

She'd exited the bathroom in search of a quiet nook to continue her conversation, away from the eavesdroppers and gossipers. "I completely understand. I'm so relieved she's doing better. Your family is in my thoughts and prayers."

There—the janitor's closet, silent witness to decades of trysts and secretive conversations. She had quickly closed the door behind her.

"Thank you, honey. Now, assemble your team as quickly as you can. You need to work out a strategy."

"Yes, sir. Thank you, sir. For everything."

"Oh, and one last thing. Where do we stand with that NRA fella?" He sounded eager, even a little giddy. Had White fallen for Brock's charms, too?

Megan paused. "Um, we broke up, sir. I'm running single."

"What a shame." His voice had deflated. "I thought you two would be perfect together."

Through the phone, Megan heard a PA kick on in the background: *Paging Dr. Patel to the OR. Dr. Patel to OR.*

"Sorry about that. Hospitals are the worst place to do business. So, what happened with the Tolbert fella?"

"Sir, I just can't marry someone I don't love," she whispered into the phone. "I can't marry for political convenience," she said, hoping that would put an end to the conversation.

Silence.

"Megan, listen to an old man. This may be your best chance at getting elected. I wish I could say being a level-headed, moderate conservative would be enough, but I wouldn't bet the horse."

Megan recognized this tone. It said, *I've been around the block a few times, so I know best.* She knew he was right—and he hadn't even mentioned the cards stacked against her for being a woman.

"This guy is handsome, charming. A man's man. And very connected," Congressman White continued. "This is what we wanted all along. If you like him, then love can come later. Lots of people marry for less and still enjoy a long, happy relationship."

"Sir, with all due respect, you married Jean for love. You've enjoyed a long, happy relationship *and* a long, successful career in politics. I want that, too. And I won't settle for less."

Megan's declaration was met with silence on the other end of the phone line, but no one was more surprised than her. Until now, she'd been so intent on putting her career in one box and her romantic life in another, absolutely convinced the two couldn't mix.

Where did that come from?

She had been wrestling with her feelings for Andrew, searching for some perspective. At first, it had just been the excitement of doing something naughty and fun, something completely out of character. She hadn't really been with many guys, and this was the first time she'd ever had a friend with benefits. They hadn't really talked about it, but surely she and Andrew were on the same page. He knew it had to be casual. She couldn't be in a relationship — not with a Democrat, at least. Being elected a congresswoman was her destiny, and she wasn't going to throw that away for anyone.

Part of her was worried about getting caught. The other part was worried she was falling for him. What had happened to her better-safe-than-sorry outlook on love?

"Megan, I really think you should reconsider. You need the NRA in your corner."

Megan thought for a moment and then said confidently, "I'm sure Brock and the NRA will still support me." Why wouldn't they? Brock knew her, knew her position on the issues. Plus, the NRA had enjoyed a long, close relationship with Congressman White.

White sighed. "Well, I — " he began. Then another voice interrupted him. "Yes? OK, thanks. Megan, I have to go. More paperwork to fill out here than in the damned government. I'll see you soon."

"Yes, sir."

"And, Megan? You know I think of you as family. I just want you to win."

She turned off Fox News now and crept down the hall toward

Andrew's room. She was about to push open the door when a thought stopped her in her tracks: She was running for office. It was actually happening. She was vying for a spot in U.S. Congress, asking the people of Florida to name her to the House of Representatives. *Representative Megan Thompson...*

Where did Andrew fit into her grand plans? She had been able to push this question from her mind when the election was a full year away. Now it would take place in just a few months, and she couldn't put off the issue much longer.

Yes, she had a crush on her roommate, but only recently. But she wasn't convinced it was love. Even if it was, would she trade her lifelong dream away for him? She'd been waiting for this opportunity forever, since she was a little girl. Megan backed away from his door and toward her own room. If she were being honest with herself, he didn't fit into her plans. He didn't fit at all.

The next morning, Megan could tell Andrew knew something was up. Or maybe he just had something else on his mind. Whatever it was, his normal witty banter over breakfast had dried up. Every word seemed measured, like he was following a recipe but had lost his place.

Megan wasn't exactly in a conversational mood either. She was in a hurry to leave for the airport. There was so much to do if she was going to get her campaign started on the right track! But she also wanted to get this over with. If she didn't want to hurt Andrew—or end up being hurt by him—they needed to sit down and have a real conversation.

"Andrew, we need to talk."

"Hmm?" he said, looking up with a vacant expression.

"About us." Her voice sounded firm. *Good.*

He must have heard it, too, because he sat straighter on the stool and took a prolonged sip of coffee from Megan's Reagan mug. "Sure," he said, but it was a little too nonchalant.

She couldn't help but smile at the sight of him. God, he was adorable! This wasn't going to be easy. "I've been giving this some thought." She rested one hand gingerly atop his burnt one. "I'm leaving for Florida in an hour. This thing is heading into full-blown election mode. I'm going to have to keep things about us... under wraps for now." She held her breath, hoping he could understand the position she was in.

Andrew peered at her over the Reagan mug.

"It has to be casual, it has to be discreet, Andrew. Or nothing at all."

He slid his hand away and stood up. "I understand. That's fine. Have a good trip. See you in a week?" He gave her a weak hug and then headed to his bedroom.

Megan spent the whole plane ride to Orlando thinking about him. Did he mean it was fine to keep their relationship casual? Or fine to have nothing at all?

The memory of their conversation that morning was still bringing her down when Congressman White's car arrived at her hotel that evening. With the retirement announcement only an hour away, he asked her to take a ride with him. She had to put Andrew out of her head. *Now.*

Sliding into the back of his black escalade, Megan quickly appraised her boss. He looked older than the last time she'd seen him, before Mrs. White's stroke. His hair was sticking out like little wisps of white cotton candy that refused to be combed. The bags under his eyes were puffy half-moons. It was as though he, too, had fallen ill. She wanted to hug him, but it would have been awkward, the vehicle notwithstanding.

"How have you been, sir?" Megan asked.

"Well, Jean's on the mend, but it's hard for her. Being in Washington, I'm used to things moving at a snail's pace. She's not." He gave a forced laugh. "She's having to relearn how to get dressed, eat, walk, everything. And it's hard for me to watch her suffer. I want to jump in and do everything for her."

Megan had always admired the Whites' love for each other, even envied it. It seemed rare, exotic, because it was genuine. "I've been praying every night for her, sir."

The driver pulled the Escalade out into traffic. Megan knew it would take twenty minutes to go only a block or two. That was Florida—perpetually under construction.

Congressman White cleared his throat. "Well, Miss Thompson, you're about to jump feet first into this race. Are you nervous?"

She tucked an imaginary strand of hair behind her ear, a tic that needed to be dead and buried, as Mike had told her repeatedly. "Just a touch."

"Good. If you weren't nervous, I'd say you didn't care enough." He ran a hand through his cotton-candy hair. "I feel I haven't properly prepared you for what you're up against."

"It's OK, sir. I've seen it all before." Megan interlaced her hands and rested them on her lap. "I'm sure I'll hear a lot of unflattering things about me in the papers and on TV."

The driver slammed on the brakes as a shirtless, sunburnt man on a bicycle weaved in between the cars.

"It's not just that," said the congressman, shaking his head. "You know what to expect in a campaign, but what about once you're elected? Are you ready to hold town hall meetings even when your constituents are downright hostile? When they boo you or call you a liar to your face? I'm not saying this to scare you, Megan, but to prepare you."

Megan didn't respond. Clayton White had served his state and his country for many years, and he deserved to have his say.

"Are you ready to toe the party line, even when it goes against your principles? Are you ready for your every act to be picked apart? For the bill you worked so hard on to get tossed aside, or become unrecognizable thanks to a million amendments? And what about when things move along at a snail's pace? Can you handle that kind of discouragement? That kind of conflict and uncertainty?"

Megan didn't hesitate. What had he thrown her way so far that she hadn't handled? "I'm ready, sir."

"Good. Because public service is exactly what it says it is: public service. There's far less glory attached to it now than when I first ran, but if your heart is in the right place, it's still a noble cause. A calling, really. And the little wins — and sometimes even big ones — make it all worthwhile."

"Sir, I am ready." Her voice was firm, her chin lifted, and her conviction cemented. "I want this."

Congressman Clayton White stood before the packed ballroom of the Hilton Hotel in Magnolia Ridge, eight months after the final victory speech of his career, once again addressing his colleagues, supporters, reporters, and friends. After a minute-long standing ovation, the crowd settled down and he took to the mike.

"Some of you may know that my wife, Jean, had a stroke several weeks ago. She's in recovery, praise the Lord, but she's going to require a lot of help. I want to be there for her, just as she's always been there for me." At these last words, the congressman choked up a little.

Megan looked on from the side of the stage with the rest of his staff, willing the congressman not to cry.

White cleared his throat. "And so it is with a heavy heart that I stand here today and inform you of my resignation, effective immediately. As of today, I am entering into retirement after a forty-five-year career in the United States House of Representatives."

Groans and cries echoed throughout the audience.

"I heard congratulations are in order." Carmela had elbowed her way through the interns to Megan's side. "Well played. Enjoy your five minutes of fame," she snarled, flashing her pointy white teeth. "A little birdie told me who your opponents will be in the Florida primary. Chris Walsh, the attorney from Ocala. And Boyd Smith."

Megan knew who Boyd Smith was. Everyone did. Once the beloved football coach at Swampton University, he had retired now and become even more beloved as a bible-thumping proselytizer. But she wasn't rattled, even as Carmela hovered too close throughout the entire speech. The woman was just looking to get beneath Megan's skin. Well, let her try.

Megan smiled inwardly. Maybe she should offer Carmela a job, as a legislative director. It would be killing two birds with one stone — hiring a capable staff member and delivering a heartfelt insult. *Not very kind to kick someone when they're down,* she chastised herself.

Megan couldn't help but sympathize with Carmela's frustration. As the chosen one, she could graciously forgive Carmela now for having assigned her the most thankless tasks in the office and treating her like gum stuck to the sole of her expensive high heel. There was so little room at the top, it brought out the worst in the most ambitious people.

"I stand before you grateful for the time you've allowed me to serve you, my state, and my country," White continued. "But I feel it is also my duty to issue this warning: The conservative party is heading down the wrong path, and we're not walking, folks. We're running.

"The time of vigorous debates and intellectual conversations has passed. Conservatives have become mean and cynical and laser-focused on one thing and one thing only: getting re-elected. But when that happens, we've become nothing more than a government machine — the very thing that we're supposed to be against."

Congressman White took a sip of water, and Megan noticed his hand trembling. His jaw tensed as his voice grew louder and his tone more passionate.

"Representing the people and serving the people used to be a job to be proud of. But guess what? Our children and our grandchildren renounce politics and disavow public service. They've grown up watching and reading about politicians who are corrupt, power-hungry, dishonest, and ineffective. Many have decided that politics is not the means to achieve good in this world. It's ugly, and it seems self-serving. And now we've scared entire generations away from running for office."

He looked over a Megan and nodded.

Megan was already slipping into her campaign plans. She wouldn't set up her headquarters in Magnolia Ridge, the 100,000-strong, middle-class retirement community where White had hunkered down. Instead she would set it up in the next town over, Gatorville, signaling a shift in her demographics pool. Megan wanted to expand the tent to include both White's most dedicated volunteers, the retirees with lots of time on their hands, and the younger generation of college students.

"My hope is that this current administration serves — in one way or another — as an inspiration to young people, to rise up everywhere and heed the call. In fact, that's partly why we are here tonight."

This is it, thought Megan.

"I would like to introduce you to someone whom I've had the pleasure to get to know over the past two years. She is the next generation. She is the American dream. She came from nothing and has worked incredibly hard to get where she is today, with no handouts. She has studied politics all her life, not just in school but in the trenches, where it really counts: serving on the zoning board, managing political campaigns, working as a legislative aide, shepherding her family's small business. She is smart, she is principled, and she holds dear the conservative values that are sorely lacking in today's political arena."

He gestured to Megan, waiting in the wings. When she walked onto the stage and stood beside Congressman White, he placed a hand on her shoulder.

"I may be resigning today, but it is my great pleasure to pass the torch along to the next generation willing to fight for the American dream. I wholeheartedly endorse Megan Thompson to run for my congressional seat in this year's special election."

The hesitation was brief, but Megan noticed. Then the crowd gave three timid, obligatory claps followed by a polite smattering of applause, like a school recital audience after someone's kid has bombed.

Megan's heart skipped a beat, then another. She waited for her moist eyes to dry and her constricted throat to release her next breath. Then she stepped up to the podium.

"Thank you, sir," she began, clearing her throat. "No one could have asked for a better mentor than Congressman Clayton White. I thank him for his many years of dedicated service and for showing me what real leadership looks like. Many of you have received a card from Congressman White, whether to recognize your birthday, your engagement or marriage, a new baby in the family, or a loss in the family."

Many in the crowd nodded their head or raised their hand. And suddenly Megan's jitters faded, replaced by a rush like she'd never felt before.

"Well, then you know he signs every single one of those cards. And his wife hand-knits all the baby blankets." She paused for effect. "To Congressman White, representing you in Washington, D.C., wasn't just a job. It wasn't a stepping stone to better pay or greater esteem or a higher-level job. This was a labor of love. He has been a great role model in government, not to mention a wonderful person and mentor."

From the back of the room came a holler. "We love you, White!" The crowd responded with laughter and cheering.

"Congressman White is correct when he says there is widespread disgust among the younger generation. When I tell young people I want to work in government, they automatically think I want to enrich myself—or worse, help tear the government down. When I say I want to work in government to make a difference, they laugh. They think I'm naïve and insist that our government has failed them. And I can't tell them they're wrong. Because politicians today *have* failed us. They've failed us big-time. But the time for our elected figures coming to Washington either to shut it down and make it ineffective, or to line their own pockets, is over!"

Megan paused to access the crowd's reaction. They were paying attention now, a sea of gray, white, and bald heads, all nodding. "I stand here today as one of the *next* generation of conservatives, and I'm here to tell you: I've had enough. I've had enough bickering, bigotry, and burn-it-down politics. And I know you've had enough, too."

The audience started to clap louder and longer now.

"As I look to the future, I want to bring back from the past the things that worked for our party. I want to bring back fiscal responsibility.

We need to create a realistic budget, and we need to balance that budget! I want to bring back the fight for freedom. And you can't have freedom without jobs, educational opportunities, and lower taxes on small businesses. I implore the younger generations to look at the legacy we have been left with! Are you satisfied?"

Megan knew there were too few young people in the audience, but the audience didn't seem to notice. Her staff would put this up on YouTube right away, as she intended to do with all of her speeches.

"I didn't think so. If you're not satisfied, I encourage you to get informed. I encourage you to get out there and vote. And I ask you to consider running for office. Just not against me."

Megan held her breath, but her timing had been perfect. Laughter rippled through the audience.

"It's time for new leadership, old values. And in return for your vote, I will work as hard as it takes, with honesty and integrity, to make the government work for you."

As Megan walked off the stage, the thundering applause echoed through her body. She shook with adrenaline and purpose. She felt the urge to break a bottle of Champagne over the podium to christen her maiden voyage, her ceremonial campaign launch into the electoral seas.

There was only one thing missing, and she'd searched the crowd throughout the entire speech, even though she knew he wasn't there.

Leaning against his pillows in his bedroom and staring at the ceiling, Andrew wondered how Megan was getting on in Florida. Had she made her speech yet? He was almost tempted to fly down and watch. But he didn't belong there.

If she hadn't broken up with Brock last month, he could've forgotten the whole thing and moved on. But she *had* broken it off, and the first thing out of her mouth when she got home that same night was to tell him it was done. She was single. And the second thing she'd said was, "Let's order takeout and eat it naked in bed."

Wearing nothing but his T-shirt, she had sat cross-legged just there, on his bed. He could almost feel her there now. That night, they had been wrapped in each other's arms one moment and gorging themselves on Chinese food the next. He had watched her open a fortune cookie and unravel its hidden message.

"You make the world better just by being in it." Her voice had been serious, but her smirk betrayed her. "Too corny."

Andrew had cracked his cookie open next and read it silently. *Always tell someone how you feel. You'll feel much better when they know.*

She had tried to read it over his shoulder. "What's it say?"

He had crumpled it before she had a chance to see. "It says, 'Help, I'm imprisoned in a Chinese fortune cookie factory.'"

But images of that night—their bellies full, their bodies satisfied, Megan's head resting on his chest—kept appearing in his head, and the words hidden in that fortune cookie kept replaying. He knew it was random. He knew it meant nothing.

He knew it was right. But what could he do?

AUGUST HEADLINES

Trump threatens "Fire and fury" against North Korea
if it endangers U.S.
—New York Times

White nationalist rally in Virginia sparks violent clashes, turns deadly
—ABC News

Trump presidency is destroying marriages across the country
—New York Daily News

Bernie Sanders voters helped Trump win, and here's proof
—Newsweek

Chapter Twenty Five

---★---

FOCUS GROUP

"Ms. Thompson, what are your top three priorities should you be elected to the House of Representatives?"

Megan stood at the podium, perfectly poised. "I promise, if elected, I will tackle the budget deficit…"

Pause. Make eye contact.

"… preserve and protect Medicare and Social Security…"

Use hands to emphasize each point. Speak slowly and confidently.

"… and fight for jobs and grow our economy, by focusing on tax cuts for small businesses."

"Tax relief, not tax cuts!" shouted a campaign volunteer.

"Pizza fund!" insisted another.

Megan stepped out from behind her cardboard podium, took out two singles from her pocketbook, and put them in a coffee can labeled PIZZA FUND. Every time she used the wrong language, she had to contribute to the fund.

She stifled a yawn and glanced at the always-on coffee pot in the corner. *Time for another hit of caffeine?* she wondered.

"OK, great work, everyone. Let's call it night." As usual, Mike was looking out for her best interests. That man had eyes like a hawk and the instincts of a tiger. "You have exactly one hour to get shitfaced, and then you hit the hay. See you back here at six a.m. sharp!" he called out to the half-dozen staff and volunteers chatting among themselves as they moved toward the door.

"Or what?" retorted one man, his round young face red and sweaty from the underwhelming air conditioning.

"Or I will personally come and wake you up." Mike paused before allowing his goofy grin to make an appearance. "And trust me, you don't want me waking you up."

There was nervous laughter, even as people high-fived Mike on the way out. Her campaign manager was both class clown and hard-ass—and you never knew when he was about to make the switch.

The boy in the yellow oxford asked Mike to join them at the bar. "Not tonight, man," Mike replied, shuffling through some papers. "Big day tomorrow. Need my beauty sleep."

Megan took a sip of her coffee and looked around the makeshift headquarters. She'd found this space in a Gatorville strip mall, squished right between a vape store and an insurance agency. It was all her modest war chest could afford. Tony's Pizzeria, two storefronts down, was making a killing off her campaign.

Thompson campaign HQ, formerly known as Dollar General, was nothing special to look at. Sheer curtains hung in the window, revealing the large ELECT MEGAN THOMPSON: NEW LEADERSHIP, OLD VALUES sign inside. Gray plastic folding tables were set up in rows of three, and the only decorations—aside from her many political signs—were a giant whiteboard, a cheap floor-length mirror, and a dead palm plant in the corner. She had bought an old pinball machine (for the staff) and a treadmill (for herself) off Craigslist. To Megan, it was the most beautiful place in the world.

Every morning she greeted a rotating roster of staff and volunteers who wore her name plastered on their shirts. Gleaned from GOP mailing lists, previous campaigns, and her growing group of YouTube followers, they made thousands of phone calls, stuffed countless mailings, and wrote press releases in exchange for free coffee and donuts or a pittance of a salary. Her greatest feat had been gathering staff from across the age spectrum. Three generations sat side by side, from elderly, natural blue-haired volunteers to young, dyed blue-haired volunteers. Their belief in her was what buoyed her throughout the endless tide of calls, meetings, knocking on doors, and fundraising efforts. And their moral support would help get her through tomorrow night's Republican primary debate.

She and Mike had decided two things early on. First, she wanted to raise money from a lot of small donations rather than be beholden to the mega-wealthy donors. That way, she would be the one calling the shots. And second, she wanted to be inclusive, so she'd worked hard to get young conservatives involved and reach out to voters too often neglected by her party.

Finishing off her coffee, Megan noticed the room had cleared out remarkably fast. God bless the young ones. Their stamina and enthusiasm were remarkable.

It was nearly midnight, and just she and Mike were left now. She still couldn't believe he was running her campaign, any more than she could believe she was running for election. Everything had happened so fast, it all seemed like a dream. Standing beneath a fluorescent bulb that buzzed constantly and dimmed periodically, she breathed in the smell of musty carpet and burnt coffee. It was real. It was happening. And she couldn't be happier.

Well, almost.

Mike hoisted himself up to sit on a nearby table, waving the paper in his hand. "I know you're ready to hit the hay, Meg, but I've got some good news to tell you first."

Megan allowed herself a tired smile.

"Walsh is out."

Her face lit up. Of the two candidates running against her in the primary, Chris Walsh—a young, connected wealthy attorney—was the more serious threat. "That's great news! Why is he out?"

Mike hopped off the table. "A bunch of the signatures on his petition were thrown out. He's off the ballot." He crumpled the paper and took aim at the wastebasket, but he missed by a long shot.

"Was that meant to be part of the pep talk, like 'Tomorrow's a slam dunk'?" she mocked. "If so, I think it's a bad omen."

"Ha!" Mike grinned. "You know I'm more of a behind-the-scenes guy than a feet-on-the-floor man."

Megan glanced pointedly at Mike's protruding belly and the distorted image of Newt Gingrich's face on his T-shirt. "Never would have guessed."

His expression turned serious. "The thing to remember is, don't get cocky. It may be just you and Boyd left in this race, but tomorrow's not a sure thing. Even though *we* know this guy's a joke." He motioned his hand between the two of them.

It was hard to see Boyd Smith as anything but a joke, always carrying around his giant Jesus-on-a-cross and his gold-covered bible, spreading his hateful gospel everywhere he went. But he was quasi-famous and well-funded, and he had the public endorsement of the NRA (*Thanks a lot, Brock*) and even the President, for all that was worth right now.

"We can't underestimate him," Mike continued, flicking off light switches as he headed for the front door. "Tomorrow's debate needs to go well."

Megan followed him, in a bit of daze. She still couldn't believe they were just two weeks away from the primaries.

"Oh, and make sure to wear the red blazer with your black dress." Mike motioned to the clothes rack, where Megan kept half her closet now. Mike was constantly reminding her to change her outfit. She found it both endearing and annoying. But people were so much harsher on women politicians, and wearing the same jacket twice in a row was a serious no-no. She only had to make the mistake once, and the Twitter rant would go on for days.

When they reached the door, Megan slung her arm around Mike's neck. "I seriously couldn't do this without you."

"Yeah, I know." Mike grinned and patted her hand "You're gonna kill it tomorrow."

She locked up and they walked through the parking lot, dodging broken beer bottles and abandoned shopping carts. The pavement was wet from a recent thunderstorm, and humidity hung in the air like a wet blanket.

"I just hope I can fall asleep tonight." The news about Walsh had her feeling both energized and nervous about tomorrow. It would be her first televised debate.

"My advice? Find your, ahem, 'neck massager'—"

She scrunched up her face. "Gross."

"—and dream about Andrew. That should do the trick."

Andrew.

She had pushed him to the corners of her mind again and again the past few days while she focused on the impending debate. The question of what to do about Andrew had become a never-ending tennis match: *I want him. But he's bad for my career. But I want him.* The thoughts flew back and forth, making her dizzy with indecisiveness— one of the traits she despised most.

"Mike, I had a thought," she said on impulse, unlocking her car door. "After the debate, can we run a focus group?"

"Sure. What on?"

"I want to know what voters think of me running single…"

Mike shot her a look of warning. "I'm not sure I like where this is going—"

"… versus running dating a Democrat."

Andrew gently traced circles on Megan's back. She stirred a little and inched her body closer to his. He draped an arm over her and started kissing her neck. The midmorning summer sun streamed through the venetian blinds, and her hair glowed like wheat in September, smelling pleasantly like Herbal Essence.

Funny how she'll drop two hundred dollars on shoes but only four bucks on shampoo, he mused. She had once justified her clothing and shoes expenditures as a cost of doing business, saying that people were more likely to give you money if they thought you didn't need it. He'd laughed, but now he thought she might be onto something.

Megan turned over to face him, a slow grin spreading. "What's so funny?"

"Nothing." He leaned down and kissed her, desire flooding him. Just lying next to her reduced him to a horny sixteen-year-old all over again. He knew they were supposed to be keeping it casual, but as time went on, it felt like anything but.

After the debate, she had returned to D.C. and they'd fallen straight into bed. But it didn't feel like meaningless sex. It felt like much more than that. And despite all the stories he'd heard about couples breaking up and divorcing over the 2016 elections, he was unwilling to give up hope.

It was time to tell her how he felt. They would just need to keep this secret until after her election, and then they could be together.

On the bedside table, the phone vibrated. Andrew glanced at the name flashing on the screen. It matched the three most recent missed calls: his mother.

He answered on the second ring. "Hi, Mom. Everything OK?"

"Why don't you ever answer your phone?"

Andrew was too content to be bothered by her annoyed tone. "I was... sleeping. What's going on? I see you called three times, but you didn't leave a message."

"Why bother leaving a message? It's not like you'll listen." Jacqueline's retort was quick as a whip.

"Is there a reason you called, Mother? I'm... kind of in the middle of something." He gave Megan's nipple a playful pinch.

"Well! I'm sorry to be such a burden."

"You're not a burden, Mother." *Inhale, exhale.* "You know I love you. Now, please tell me what's going on."

"I want to take you to lunch."

"When?"

"In two hours. I made reservations."

Andrew's fingers stopped exploring Megan's body. "You're in D.C. right now? Why didn't you tell me?"

"The EMILY's List Gala is tonight. I wasn't certain I'd be going, so I never mentioned it. But here I am. And I would love to see you, sweetie. It's been forever."

Andrew hesitated. With only a few days to go before the Florida primary, he had so little time here with Megan already. Did he really want to share her? And was he ready for his mother to find out about was going on between him and Megan—whatever that was?

His mother's dramatic sigh interrupted his thoughts. "Andrew, sweetie, I don't have all day."

"Fine. I'm bringing Megan with me. We already had plans."

Now it was Jacqueline Croswell's turn to hesitate. "Wonderful," came her voice at last. "I'll just call and update our reservation at Le Blanc."

Andrew knew by her tone that his mother did not think it was wonderful. *Well, tough.* Maybe he still hadn't talked with Megan about what exactly was going on, but Andrew knew: He was in love.

As he laid the phone down, Megan raised her eyebrows. "Lunch with your mom? I'm not so—"

He rolled her onto her back, feeling her body both soft and firm beneath him. "We'll build up an appetite first."

★ ★ ★

Megan held Andrew's hand as they walked the streets of D.C., feeling as though she were living a double life: one as a political candidate in Florida, the other as the girlfriend of a very handsome man, roaming the great metropolis and heading to lunch with his mother. For a moment, everything around her came into sharp focus; the blue sky and puffy cumulus clouds, the strong warm wind, the immaculately cared for flowers surrounding the trees that lined the sidewalks, and one crystal clear thought, I am happy, truly happy.

As they walked, Megan noticed how much quieter the streets were. D.C. had practically cleared out for the congressional break. She filled Andrew in on the debate with Boyd Smith. He had quoted from the bible five times, made four misogynistic comments, used three anti-Muslim slurs, and disparaged immigrants at least twice, and he had stated not a single policy priority. Megan had won the debate, hands down. And the campaign had made sure to declare her victory to all the blogs and news outlets.

Now Megan had another opponent to face off with, a much more formidable one, with wit, sharp tongue and a deep hatred of Republicans. At least Andrew had given her a fair warning of what to expect. Apple and the tree, indeed.

Megan had never been to Le Blanc, a stuffy restaurant favored by the upper crust. The restaurant looked almost plain, with its understated palette and lack of ornamentation, but on closer inspection—as with a tasteful wealthy person, someone from old money—everything lay in the details. The silverware had heft and was thoroughly polished. The glassware was expensive and boasted no spots. The table linens were bright white. And the waiters were impeccably groomed. Yes, this place would suit Jacqueline Croswell like a fine wrap.

Andrew let Megan's hand go the moment he located his mother, sitting at a round table in the midst of the restaurant's calm bustle. She wore a tailored silk white suit jacket, and with her back to a white wall, you couldn't tell where the restaurant ended and Jacqueline began.

When Andrew leaned down, she offered her cheek for him to kiss and then motioned to the seat next to her, where a place setting was laid out next to hers in perfect proportions. Across from Jacqueline—Megan's seat, presumably—was the only other setting. Its partner had been cleared in advance. Megan hesitated, watching Andrew for a cue. When he sat down next to her at the table's only blank spot, Jacqueline's face was immobile except for a minor twitch near her right eye.

A waiter appeared, quietly and unobtrusively placing three martinis on the table, and then returned carrying a silver basket filled with an assortment of fresh-baked bread.

"Since you were late, I ordered us a round of drinks and Caesar salads," declared Andrew's mother, lightly drumming her fingers on the table. "I don't have much time to eat before I get my hair done."

"Mom, we're only five minutes late. But thank you, salads are fine for now." He reached for a roll and passed the basket to Megan before lifting his martini.

Megan took a swig of her own martini. Her eyes watered.

"I'm so glad you could join us, dear," murmured Jacqueline after swallowing her own generous mouthful. To Megan, she sounded anything but glad. "Andrew mentioned you two had plans today. I hope I'm not interrupting anything?"

Megan smoothed her napkin across her lap. "Not at all," she demurred.

The waiter prepared their salad table-side using silver tongs, and then portioned it out, head bent, intent on his task. Megan's plate was piled high with greens glistening in creamy dressing under hunks of crusty croutons and fresh parmesan curls. But Megan had barely taken a bite when Jacqueline started in on her true line of questioning. "So, Megan, what's it like working for the morally bankrupt party?"

Andrew shot his mother a look of warning.

Megan reached for her martini, then coughed a little as she tried to choke it down.

"A little strong for you, dear?"

Megan dabbed her eyes with her starched napkin. Andrew had tipped her off about his mother's skill at sniffing out her foe's weak spot and pressing on it to see what kind of reaction she could get. "It's fine, thank you. Although martinis are not usually my drink of choice."

"Ah. A beer drinker, then?" Jacqueline's tone was smooth and cold as ice. "Shall I get you a Budweiser?" She raised a delicate hand in the air, signaling for a waiter.

"No, thank you," Megan replied quickly. "I usually prefer wine. But that's very kind of you to offer. I think it will grow on me. Kind of like your son."

Andrew kept his face impassive while he reached one hand under the table and gave Megan's thigh a playful squeeze. She got the message loud and clear: *We're on the same team.*

Jacqueline ignored the comment. "Now then, Megan, how do you enjoy helping Congressman White kick DREAMers out of the country? Restrict immigration from Muslim countries? Take health insurance away from millions of Americans? Criminalize abortion and end insurance coverage for birth control? Start a war with North Korea? Oh yes, and cut taxes for the billionaires?"

Megan sat frozen in her chair. But she had just been through a harrowing political debate with a far-right Florida fanatic. If Andrew's mother thought she was going to back down, she had another think coming.

"What's wrong, dear? Am I missing anything?"

"Mrs. Croswell," she replied with a glint in her eye, "I'm afraid you are confusing Congressman White's work with the president's agenda."

Andrew's mother waved her hand once. "One and the same. You do his bidding, don't you? You're all too spineless to stand up to that man."

"Actually, on several occasions, my boss has spoken out —"

"I don't know how any of you sleep at night." Jacqueline shook her head sadly.

"Mother," Andrew cut in, "Megan is not responsible for any of it. She works as a legislative aide. In fact, she's helping me gain support for the carbon pricing legislation."

"Do you know how many times Congress has voted against carbon pricing, sweetie?"

"Twenty-seven," he replied.

"That's right! And carbon pricing is a *conservative* answer to climate change. It's the same shitty game you Republicans have been playing forever!" She pointed her manicured index finger at Megan. "Democrats take your idea and try to get some movement, and you all shoot it down because the Democrats suggested it. You think we wanted Obamacare? You gutted our health care proposals. Obamacare *was* the Republican plan!"

Megan sat forward. "Well, Mrs. Croswell, I don't always agree with what my party does. Just as I'm sure you don't always agree with what your party does. That's why I'm running for office." She raised her chin defiantly. Mike had trained her well. She was rock solid under pressure.

Now it was Jacqueline's turn to choke on her martini. "You're running for office?"

"If there's one thing I've learned from living with your son, it's that we all—the whole country—need to do a lot of better job of listening to the other side. Too often we pretend to listen, but the whole time we're just preparing our counterargument, and letting our emotions run wild."

Megan paused to allow that point to sink in.

"We need to start trying to understand where other people are coming from, and I—"

Megan's phone began to ring, and she glanced at it. "I'm sorry, but I have to take this. It's my campaign manager."

She stood up, eager to get away from this interrogation. Jacqueline Croswell was even more full of blind rage than her son had been. Although Megan had voted for The President, that didn't mean she supported him in everything. But she didn't think that distinction mattered much to Andrew's mother.

The apple and the tree, indeed.

Andrew watched Megan walk to the front of the restaurant, impressed with how she was handling herself. He had never seen her so serious and confident. Even though he was reluctant to face his mother when she was in this sort of mood, with Megan by his side, he felt evenly matched against her.

"So, Mom, how are things with you and Dad?"

"Don't change the subject," snapped Jacqueline. "What's going on between you two?"

"I asked you first."

She sighed dramatically and pursed her lips. "Your father's back home. I've forgiven him."

Andrew tried to suppress a grin. "He repented for his sins?"

"The most important thing is, he regrets voting for Trump. I couldn't possibly stay with him if he continued to support that man."

She lifted a tiny bit of salad with her fork, and Andrew recognized it as her way of putting an end to the conversation.

He couldn't imagine his parents getting divorced, having to split the holidays and all that nonsense. He was a grown man, but still he felt relieved.

His mother patted the corner of her mouth, placed her napkin back in her lap, and waited in uncomfortable silence for Andrew to confess.

Here goes nothing.

He shifted nervously. "Megan and I are... seeing each other."

"That explains why you shaved off that bird's nest you called a beard. Well, thank god for that, at least."

Andrew's shoulders relaxed a little. Maybe this won't be so bad after all.

"I knew it the moment you walked in the door. Sneaking glances at each other, finishing each other's sentences." For a moment, his mother seemed giddy. Was she actually happy about this?

"You're making a terrible mistake."

No, she wasn't happy. She was preparing to crush him.

"What happened to you? You used to be angry! You used to have a conscience." Her voice got lower and lower, until it was the opposite of yelling. "The Andrew I know—my son Andrew—hates Republican politicians. Now you want to date one?"

"Mother, first of all, its's exhausting being angry all the time. I can't keep it up," he pleaded. "I just can't. I was getting depressed, and drinking too much—"

Jacqueline held up her hand and shook her head, a quick reprimand. "She's changed you," she hissed.

Andrew caught his mother's gaze. "I'm still me."

"You deserve better than her."

Andrew knew what his mother was saying. That was Jacqueline Croswell code for *She's nothing but white trash.*

"No, Mom. She's incredibly smart and talented. I'd be lucky to have her—"

Jaqueline placed both hands on the table and leaned in. "And what are you going to do if she wins? Assuming she doesn't dump you before then!"

Andrew rolled his eyes. "Mom, with any luck, all the Republicans will lose. Their days are numbered," he joked. "I'm pretty confident the Democrats will take back the House in 2018. And then it won't even be an issue."

"You haven't thought this through, Andrew. If she wins, she'll be just another Trump lackey."

Andrew hung his head. "I haven't thought this through. That's true." A minute passed before he spoke again, looking up into his mother's steely blue eyes. "I don't want to think. I don't want to be logical. Because I love her."

There. He'd said it. There was no going back now.

The waiter arrived to clear away Andrew's and Jacqueline's salad plates, leaving Megan's plate half eaten and Andrew with a puzzled look on his face. How long had she been gone? He craned his neck, searching the dining room, but there was no sign of her. Was she still in the restroom?

He grabbed his phone, preparing to text her, but she had already sent him a message:

Had to run. Needed back in Florida.

"She's gone." His voice was flat. Moments before he had been a boy jumping in a bouncy castle. Now he was back on solid ground with the walls deflating around him.

Outside Le Blanc, Megan hailed a cab with one hand as she wiped tears away with the other. She needed to put as much distance between her and Andrew as possible. A plane ride should do it.

Of course, she hadn't really expected Jacqueline Croswell to welcome her with open arms. But nor had she expected Andrew to go behind her back and disparage her to his mother. He didn't defend her, didn't stand up for her. But it was what he had said that hurt the most: *With any luck, all the Republicans will lose.* It was the brutal truth that she hadn't wanted to hear. He didn't believe in her, the divide between them was too great, and he clearly didn't care about her.

A familiar piercing sensation bloomed in her chest, a tingling that spread to her extremities. She felt short of breath and imagined for a moment it was a heart attack. But no, she recognized this feeling: betrayal. It wasn't a heart attack. It was a broken heart.

Her phone conversation with Mike had been brief. Did he get the results back from the focus group? Would she do better running single or running while dating a Democrat? The answer was exactly as she thought it would be.

She was better off single.

Chapter Twenty Six

———— ✪ ————

THE HAIL MARRY

"This *should* be great news." Megan paced the floor of her Gatorville campaign HQ, her black Tom Fords wearing down a path in the already worn-down carpet.

"One would think." Leaning against an old filing cabinet, Mike held a newspaper before his eyes, reading aloud the headlines and allegations:

> BOYD SMITH ACCUSED OF SEXUAL CONTACT WITH THREE GIRLS, AGED 13-16
>
> REFUSING TO DROP OUT, SMITH DENIES SEXUAL IMPROPRIETY
>
> SMITH AND THOMPSON STILL NECK-AND-NECK DESPITE SEX CRIME ALLEGATIONS

"So why the fuck are people supporting him?" Megan threw her hands up in the air, even angrier now that she had let herself curse. Swearing was a class indicator she had worked hard to shake off. Her father had always cursed enough for them both.

Mike folded the newspaper. "Well, some of his supporters say they'll stay with him as long as President Trump does. Others still believe he's for Christian values, and you haven't taken a strong enough stance on abortion."

He paused, pushing himself off the filing cabinet.

"The most depressing response is, they simply don't believe the news media."

Megan stopped in her tracks, still twirling the strand of pearls encircling her neck. "They don't believe the allegations?"

Mike shook his head, dropping the newspaper on the nearest table. She spun around to face him. "So, where are we in the polls?"

"Too close to call."

"This is bullshit." Megan resumed pacing. "What more do I need to do? I have Congressman White's endorsement, for Christ's sake! Don't they believe in him anymore?"

Mike shook his head. "I think some of White's supporters are going to Smith. People love him. He was a football coach at the university for 25 years. He's more religious than you are —"

"I believe in God!" she insisted. "I just don't preach hellfire and brimstone, or go around with a bloody cross, clubbing people on the head and demanding repentance!"

"—and much more vocal on his opposition to gun control," finished Mike.

Megan cursed again. She shouldn't have taken for granted that the NRA would back her. Maybe it was time to reach out to Brock. The whiteboard didn't lie—someone erased and retallied the countdown each morning, and the primary was only seven days away now.

Seven.

Days.

"We need a game plan."

"I'm working on one as we speak." Mike placed a hand on her shoulder.

One of his contacts had dug up a bit of gossip, and Mike was debating whether to leak it to the press. If indeed there was proof Boyd Smith had paid hush money to the sixteen-year-old daughter of a local pastor, it might confirm the accusations against him.

"It could help us in the polls," Mike pointed out.

Megan knew Mike was the expert. But in this upside-down political era, wasn't it just as likely that tracing the leak back to her could taint the Thompson campaign instead?

"You don't have to decide right now, sweetheart," Mike reassured her. "It's not over yet."

Megan wasn't so sure. Her watch read 9 a.m., and she'd been at the office for three hours already, trying somehow to capitalize on what should've been a devastating blow to the Smith campaign. Was there any point to it all? She had no way of knowing—at least not for another week.

"I'm off to airport now," she sighed. "I'll be back late this evening." She took one last look in the full-length mirror, assessing her light gray form-fitting dress with its quarter-length sleeves and asymmetrical neckline. When she'd pulled this outfit on, it had seemed good enough for her luncheon fundraiser at the Republican Women's Club in D.C. Now, she wasn't so sure.

"Time's running out, Mike. We may need to do something drastic." Her voice was sharp with authority, but beneath the surface an immense fear gripped her. She had given everything in exchange for this dream. Her time and energy, her home, her personal life, even her chances at love had all spiraled beyond her reach. And now the dream, too, was being taken away from her, before she even had a chance to possess it.

Fear was dangerous—the fear of losing control, even more so. It made people desperate, as Megan knew well after the naked pictures fiasco. It was the slippery slope that led away from the moral high ground. But Mike himself had said she was the most honest candidate he knew. Maybe it was time to step down off her high horse.

I need to win this, she thought. But somehow it was about more than just the campaign. She needed a win, period.

S everal hours later, Megan plastered a bigsmile on her face and stepped up to the podium at the Republican Women's Club, where she would spend the next several hours talking to and with respected conservative women about babies, guns, and border walls. The room, with its dark wood wainscoting, bronze sconces, and crystal chandeliers, had borne witness to many such political speeches over the years. The thought comforted Megan.

Congressman White had been right: Glad handing was a skill that could be learned. She was getting better and better at it. After all, she was talking about something she was passionate about—doing good for the people. Her enthusiasm broke through her tightly contained self-image.

She supposed being an actor was pretty similar to being a politician. It was all a matter of slipping into character. She wasn't the candidate losing in the polls to a sexual predator, or the woman thwarted by love a second time. She was Candidate Thompson, and she was going to win this election.

Looking out into the audience of mostly middle-aged women in monochrome skirt suits and practical pumps, nibbling at their pavlova, Megan searched for a familiar face to whom she could deliver her speech—another tactic learned from her mentor. When her eyes landed on Brock Tolbert, she did a double take.

What on earth was *he* doing there? And what was the governor of Alaska, with her signature red skirt suit and puffy hair, whispering into his ear? Megan let go of these thoughts and made eye contact with the chair of the Republican Women's Club instead. Now was certainly not the time to get flustered over an old non-flame.

She began her talk with her intentions to fight for equal pay for women and bring new ideas to Washington. She would work on reducing onerous tax and regulatory burdens on small businesses. She would dedicate her office to creating jobs and economic opportunities for hard-working families. As she spoke, Megan drew strength from the backdrop of quiet noise: the clinking sound of silverware hitting plates, the murmurs of servers offering coffee and tea. This steady hum gave her the confidence to raise her voice, to be heard above the din.

When she'd finished, the crowd of posh women placed their dessert forks on the table before them and clapped politely. She only hoped their approval would translate to some much-needed funds in her campaign coffers.

Stepping down from the podium, she made her way past several tables toward Brock, stopping to accept another glass of wine from a server and chat with some potential donors. He closed the last few steps between them, smiling his heart-stopping smile and embracing her. "How're you holding up?" he said in a low voice that tickled her ear.

"Just peachy." Usually she could go hours at these types of events before she had to dig deep and find the effort to run the last few miles of that marathon. But today she seemed to be running on empty. She was tired of smiling and pretending. How many of these women were politely clapping and smiling to her face while still planning to vote for a sexual predator?

Brock guided her by the elbow to a quiet corner of the room. "You're in the middle of one tough race." His face wore a mask of sincerity. "And you haven't even made it to the Blue Tsunami round yet."

"I may not even *make* it to the general election," she replied grimly. Tears were building up behind her eyes, threatening to let loose. A tray floated by at eye level, and she lifted another glass, number three or four—she couldn't remember.

"Do you have a plan?" Brock whispered, nodding and offering a friendly grin to the hawk-eyed women milling about the room.

"Working on it." She gulped her wine.

"The offer's still on the table," he purred.

Megan looked at him quizzically. "What offer?"

"Marry me."

Megan snorted. "What? Why would I?" She realized that wasn't the only question on her mind. "And why would you?"

Brock locked her elbow in his gentle grip. "It'll be good for both of us. Trust me. I can get you the NRA support you need."

"Where were you two weeks ago?" Megan scoffed. "You chose Smith, remember? A pedophile!"

"*I* didn't choose Smith. The local chapter did."

"What difference would it make, then? If I got engaged to you, why would the local chapter shift its allegiance?"

Brock looked at her as though she were naïve as a child. "It's the difference between dating a B-list actor and an A-list Hollywood star. Together, we'd be a force to be reckoned with." He took her hand in his and gently pressed a kiss to it. "You want to win, right?"

His voice teased her, disarming the mechanism that normally prevented her from making impulsive decisions. Of course she wanted to win. Her answer was a knee-jerk reaction.

"Yes."

And then Brock was removing a platinum ring from his pinky and calling out, "Can I have everyone's attention, please?" His booming voice cut the volume in the room as though someone had unplugged the sound system. The crowd of women receded, and all eyes were on Megan and Brock as he bent down on one knee. Between the forefingers of his right hand, the solitaire diamond sparkled beneath the chandelier lights.

"Megan Thompson," he said, grasping her left hand, "will you do me the honor of becoming my wife?"

Shit.

Was he really doing this? Right now? In front of all these women — these politicians and bigwigs?

And reporters, she thought glumly. *Don't forget the reporters.*

Megan watched as the crowd watched her, expecting an answer. She had only seconds to think. And the only thought that pushed to the surface was, *Think of your career, Megan.*

A ndrew stepped off the elevator and onto the Metro platform, opening his free newspaper — the afternoon edition — and casually perusing the pages, waiting for his train to arrive. He was barely reading, thinking instead of Megan and wondering when he would see her again.

He hadn't talked to her in over a week, since she'd left lunch abruptly without saying good-bye. He understood, of course, how necessary it was to continue campaigning in Florida. He knew how much this election meant to her. What he did not understand was why she had left Le Blanc so suddenly. Had he done something to upset her? Had she just decided his mother was too much to deal with? Or had she simply changed her mind about him — about them?

And now she seemed to be avoiding him. She wasn't answering his texts. Whenever he called, it always went straight to voicemail.

An approaching train rumbled in the distance, and Andrew was about to put the newspaper away when something caught his eye in the Hill Gossip section.

It was a photograph of Megan, standing beneath a chandelier and surrounded by about ten women wearing skirt suits. Megan was smiling what he had come to think of as her politician's smile. And at her side, holding her elbow, was... Brock?

Stunned, Andrew scanned the headline:

CONGRESSIONAL CANDIDATE MEGAN THOMPSON GETS ENGAGED AT FUNDRAISER TO NRA SPOKESMAN BROCK TOLBERT

The train shuddered to a stop, and a sea of passengers swapped places, like a wave rolling into the shore and then out again. Moments later, Andrew was left alone in the station, staring at the newspaper, which had gone limp in his hand. Anguish ripped through him, and he stumbled backward and sat on a bench. A slow, steady trickle of people stepped off the escalator, flowing past him, until the platform was filled again. Andrew was going to miss his meeting, but he didn't care.

Sure, things had been a little confusing between him and Megan over the past two months — maybe even since they'd first met — but even more so in the past few days. At first he'd thought she was just busy with the campaign, but after a week went by, he realized what was going on: She was brushing him off. To a woman campaigning for the opposition, he was unwanted political baggage. She was dumping him, leaving him behind, just as his sister had warned. Megan had a choice to make, and she chose politics over him.

With shaky hands, he dialed her number one last time. It went immediately to voicemail.

"It's Andrew," he said in a monotone. "Congratulations on your engagement. Please get all your stuff out of the apartment."

He hung up, waiting for the familiar fury to build, but it didn't come. This feeling was much, much worse. It was the feeling of emptiness.

When Megan walked through the doors of HQ in Gatorville the next day, everyone stood and clapped. Word of her engagement had spread fast. Volunteers and staff members were hugging her and offering congratulations, commenting on the latest websites to share the happy news of Washington's newest power couple. When they asked to see the ring, Megan mumbled something about it needing to be resized. She had no intention of revealing that Brock had asked for it back right after the photo op. "I'll get you a ring worthy of a congresswoman," he'd promised, before dashing out the door to his next fundraiser.

Megan murmured her thanks to the staffers and immediately sought out Mike.

She had sobered up on the plane ride, replaying the scenario with Brock again and again. He had blindsided her, and she had a feeling it was intentional. Had he shown up at the fundraiser to ambush her, knowing she was low in the polls and desperate? And if so, why? The whole desperate deception had been dreamed up by Congressman White to help her chances of getting elected. If Brock was so eager to make this sham engagement a reality, then he had to be desperate, too.

Not that she could blame it all on him. She'd had too much to drink. She had been pissed off, hurting over the direction of the Florida campaign and her personal life in D.C. She had been vulnerable. And she had agreed to a very public engagement to a man she didn't want to marry.

Andrew must have flipped when he found out.

The thought filled Megan with sadness. She had ignored Andrew's texts and calls all week, and now he'd left a voicemail that she was too afraid to hear. She could have gone to the apartment yesterday and told him what happened, but she didn't. She could have called him from the airport or anytime in the hours since she'd landed. But whenever she picked up the phone to call him, as she'd meant to do so many times since that day at Le Blanc, she couldn't bring herself to press dial. She was a coward.

No. She shook that thought from her head. She was doing what had to be done. Andrew had made it very clear how he felt about her. He hoped she would lose the election. He didn't care about her after all.

She nodded at Mike, talking to the communications director, and they both made a beeline for her office, formerly a storage area little larger than a closet. Megan flopped into the office's lone chair.

Mike shut the door behind him. "Meg, you sly dog! Why didn't you tell me you were planning to go through with it?"

"Mike—"

"So this was what you meant by 'drastic'!" He plopped down on the edge of the desk. "Who needs insider information about your opponent when you've got a strategic engagement up your sleeve?"

He wasn't listening. Megan tried again. "Mike, this is all a huge mistake. I didn't—"

"A mistake? You've just joined forces with a super-hot male incarnation of the Second Amendment! I knew you were smart, but this is pure political genius."

The irony made it even more unbearable. This was what she had agreed to, wasn't it? She and Congressman White had been planning a politically expedient marriage all along.

The memory of Brock on his knee mocked her yet again. *Yes, I'll marry you,* she had mumbled. When he'd slid the ring on her finger, it had threatened to slide right off again. He had pulled her into an embrace and kissed her passionately, but the chorus of *aww*s and friendly applause at the Republican Women's Club had barely registered. All she could think was, *I just made a terrible mistake.*

She sighed and slumped forward until her head touched the desk. "I didn't plan it, Mike. It just kind of... happened."

Mike lowered his voice to an uncharacteristic whisper. "Sweetheart, this is the Hail Mary we've been waiting for."

"What do you mean?"

Mike's grin was goofier than ever. "You're up."

Megan lifted her head off the desk. "Up?"

It was like scoring the first touchdown after losing in the first three quarters of the game. She had started to lose faith—only now did she realize how much. But maybe all was not lost.

"Yes! Like, way up. And people vote in two days. You could really win this thing."

She was finally up in the polls. So *this* was what it took to win. "That's great." She didn't have the energy to hide her lack of enthusiasm.

Mike's grin faded to bewilderment. "I thought you'd be happy, Meg. Don't you *want* to win?"

A cynical snort escaped her. "What am I supposed to do after the primary? I can't keep up this charade."

"And why not?" Mike jumped off the desk. "You've pulled it off, Megan, just like you wanted. This is golden! The voters are going to love you."

"What about Andrew?" Her voice sounded tiny and confused.

"What about him? I thought that was over."

Megan almost laughed out loud. Mike was right. She was being ridiculous. Whether or not she was ready to admit it, her second chance on love was over. Andrew didn't love her. He had never been right for her anyway. But she could probably still salvage something from this whole escapade if she wanted to.

Time was running out, and Megan was tired of being the nice girl. She was tired of the qualified, upright candidate losing to the dishonest asshole. And she was tired of being burned by love. Winning was all she'd ever wanted, and now it was all she had left.

Once you set your sights on something, you don't back down.

"I suppose you're right." There was nothing to do now but keep up the façade. Just a few more days—a few weeks at most, if she made it past the primary—and then she would find some way out of it. Lots of people broke off their engagement. She didn't actually have to marry him in the end.

"Atta girl!" said Mike, clapping her on the back.

SEPTEMBER HEADLINES

How America went haywire
— *The Atlantic*

Anti-Trump Republicans need to unite or accept
inevitable defeat in 2020
— *National Review*

"Trump betrays everyone": The president has a long history
as an unpredictable ally
— *The Washington Post*

Chapter Twenty Seven

———————— ✪ ————————

BAD PRESS

Slumped on the couch, where he'd been spending most of his free time recently, Andrew lifted a sparerib from the box of takeout resting precariously on his belly. A clump of meat in an unnatural shade of red clung to his chopsticks. For a moment, his mind couldn't register what was between the chopsticks: a hunk of pork or a candy apple? It didn't matter. It tasted like a fatty sugar bomb, and that was just what he needed right now. Something to awaken his senses, to replace the numbness inside him.

The past few weeks had been a blur of fast food and corrosive television, punctuated by minor events at work and one bittersweet victory:

Thompson wins primary, rebukes president

GATORVILLE, Fla.—Newcomer Megan Thompson narrowly beat Boyd Smith in today's Florida primary vote, setting her up as District 11's Republican candidate for the U.S. House of Representatives in the upcoming special election.

Thompson was relatively unknown in political circles until just a few months ago, when her mentor Congressman Clayton White retired due to his wife's illness, putting Thompson in a unique position and offering her a competitive edge. While White's surprise announcement had other candidates from both sides of the aisle scrambling to get into action a full year ahead of the 2018 election, Thompson — who worked as White's legislative aide and, prior to that, ran his 2016 election campaign — was able to hit the ground running. This put her in good stead to pull out a close victory over Smith, who was plagued in recent weeks with accusations of past inappropriate sexual advances toward at least three teenage girls. The two candidates were neck and neck along much of the short campaign trail, until Thompson pulled ahead shortly after a sudden engagement to NRA spokesman Brock Tolbert.

In her late-night victory speech at the Marriott in her hometown of Swamptown, Thompson addressed limits on government spending, reducing taxes and strengthening the military, but also spoke about looking to the future of Florida and the nation as a whole, including her intentions to promote green energy technologies that would create jobs, reduce air pollution and potentially save Florida taxpayers money. But the most notable part of Thompson's speech was not its campaign promises, but the final minute of scathing remarks reserved for President Donald Trump.

Thompson boldly denounced the president's remarks in his Tuesday news conference, in which he defended white supremacists and blamed 'both sides" for the recent violence in Charlottesville, Virginia. "President Trump's statement suggesting moral equivalency between white supremacists, neo-Nazis and KKK members, and the Americans who were at the Charlottesville rally to stand against racism and bigotry, is unacceptable," said Thompson. "If I am elected in November, as congresswoman I will fight for the freedom of all Americans: the freedom from fear, hate and bigotry, and the freedom to prosper." Thompson reiterated her support of freedom of speech, but denied that the so-called alt-right are supporters of American ideals and freedoms, quoting the Declaration of Independence and stating that "there are no such things as good neo-Nazis" and that "we have a moral responsibility to stand against them."

It remains to be seen whether Megan Thompson can carry her victory into the general election and secure a seat that has been in Republican control for the past 45 years...

The toxic crimson lump teetered at the end of Andrew's chopsticks, threatening to add its stain to the collateral damage already smearing his favorite T-shirt. Had he just heard the doorbell? Hard to tell over the blare of warnings coming from Fox News. Andrew shoved the unidentified meat in his mouth and yelled, "I'th opnnn!"

Emily placed her Henri Bendel handbag on the countertop, between two piles of greasy takeout containers. "I could have been a robber or a murderer, and you just invited me in." Her sweeping gaze was already passing judgment.

She was just like their mother, but kinder about it. Andrew swallowed the lump of meat and shrugged. "If you wanted to rob and kill me, you have would have gotten in anyway. Our lock sucks."

Emily yanked the blinds open, and last of the Thursday evening sun flooded the apartment. She waded toward the couch through newspapers and dirty clothes, picking up takeout containers one by one with her thumb and index finger and dropping them into a discarded plastic bag.

"Wow. I can see things haven't gotten much better. Still drowning your sorrows in fast food."

"Better than drowning them in beer."

"True. But for Andrew, the king of clean eating, to be shoving factory-farmed, antibiotic-laden pork into his mouth, and clearly not for the first time this week... I'd say you're near rock bottom." She quickly appraised him, intuiting his internal world by the looks of his exterior, before sitting next to him on the couch. "And you look like shit."

Andrew rubbed a hand over the lengthy stubble shadowing his cheeks. He supposed they had been looking at him a little strangely at work. And last weekend he hadn't moved from the couch except to use the bathroom or answer the door for takeout.

"Want to talk about it"

"No," he grunted.

"You did call *me*, remember?" Emily said gently.

"I was trying to call Pollo Loco. Hit your number by mistake."

"OK, Andrew. If you've got a crappy fast food number in your phonebook now, we really need to talk." Emily switched off the television. "And for god's sake, why are you watching Fox News?"

Easy answer. He was waiting to catch a glimpse of Megan.

There had been a brief segment yesterday on the upcoming Florida special election, with a video clip of Megan, frowning and holding a gun at a shooting range. The headline banner — REPUBLICAN CONGRESSIONAL CANDIDATE TO WED NRA SPOKESMAN — had seared itself on his brain, alongside that first newspaper photo he'd seen of her and Brock, and every other article about her since then.

She wasn't who he'd thought she was after all.

"She's engaged," he groaned.

Emily rubbed his shoulder. "I know."

"It doesn't make any sense. They weren't even together anymore. She hadn't seen him in weeks." He stared at the dark TV screen. "Unless she was lying to me the whole time, and she never broke up with him."

Emily cocked her head. "Is that what you think?"

292

"What else? I'm such an idiot. What did I expect? Honesty and integrity from a fucking Republican? It's not in their DNA." His jaw muscle twitched, and he felt a flicker of the old flame come to life.

Andrew stood up, ignoring his cramped calves and aching back, and switched on the TV again. This time, though, he turned to channel to MSNBC, where Rachel Maddow was saying, *If you needed any further evidence that the government is in bed with the NRA…*

Sitting across from Rachel was an attractive, middle-aged Latina with a stern look on her face. The woman sat perfectly upright, her coiffed hair as flawless as her gleaming white teeth…. *will do whatever it takes to win,* she was saying confidently, followed by something about a publicity stunt. Andrew didn't know what the segment was supposed to be on, but the banner claimed the woman was a Republican congressional staffer. She reminded him of Megan.

Andrew sank back onto the couch, feeling the old fire fade already. "It's Naomi all over again. Why can't I just find an honest woman?"

Emily was doing her best to disguise her *I-told-you-so* look. "You know what I think? I think essentially Megan is a good person, an honest person. But it's not easy to get to where she's going without hurting people along the way."

Andrew gave a long sigh. "Well, go ahead and say it. You warned me about her."

"I didn't mean—"

"She even warned me about herself!" He had been over this a million times in his head. "The night of her brother's wedding, she said love was bullshit. Love was people dying and cheating on you. Pretty cynical, if you ask me."

"It sounds very much like Megan was trying to protect herself. Maybe she just wasn't ready to have a serious relationship. Maybe work is just the excuse."

Andrew thought about that for a moment, but it didn't help. He still couldn't believe that what they had—whatever it was—was over. He collapsed back into the cushions. "Then why is she ready for Brock?"

★ ★ ★

At Thompson campaign headquarters in Gatorville, the carefree jubilation over winning the Republican primary hadn't lasted long. Megan had more volunteers now, and the office was cramped and busy almost around the clock. But with less than two months before Election Day, she had less and less time to pound the pavement and drum up votes. She was also less and less enthusiastic about lying to her potential constituents.

Amid the constant campaigning and the planning for Central Florida's social event of the year—her engagement party tomorrow night—the mood at HQ had still been optimistic, cheerful, and filled with laughter. Until a few moments ago.

Megan huddled behind her desk, an array of disastrous scenarios running through her head. What had brought on the suddenly somber mood in the office? It was as though someone had cut the lights and music, trying to shut down a boisterous frat party. Whatever was going on out there, she didn't want to deal with it. If the news was really bad, it would find her.

A tentative knock came at the door.

"Um, Megan? You need to see this." A nervous intern stepped up to Megan's desk and handed her two sheets of paper. "Social media is blowing up... and cable news... MSNBC, Fox..."

Megan pushed her laptop to the side, took the papers, and leaned back in her chair. There was a breaking story about Megan Thompson, and it wasn't congratulating her on her engagement:

Republican candidate's naked ambition: Marrying for politics... and money?

WASHINGTON, D.C.—Republican candidate Megan Thompson went on a number of blind dates this year, and rumors are swirling. There's nothing wrong with a single woman dating — but when an attractive, young legislative aide lines up successive dates with a 78-year-old retired congressman, a billionaire businessman's son, the dark political operative Ted Eagle and her current fiancé Brock Tolbert, spokesman for the NRA, the question is obvious: What sort of mate was Thompson looking for? And who set her up with such connected bedfellows?

The rumors about Thompson looking for a rich, connected Republican husband have been confirmed by an anonymous staff member, who claims Thompson is willing to do anything to get elected — even marry a man she doesn't love. According to the source, Thompson just wanted to "get access to [Tolbert's] checkbook and deceive voters into believing she's a nice, wholesome housewife. The world needs to know who Megan really is: a ruthless, manipulative gold digger."

Now Thompson has bagged herself a handsome fiancé, the son of wealthy evangelical William Tolbert, pastor of a South Carolina megachurch. It remains to be seen how Brock reacts when Thompson's true character is revealed.

The color drained from Megan's face, and the office walls seemed to close in on her. How had this happened? Who would write such mean-spirited filth? And then she realized: Most of it was true.

How had she gotten here? Was this what she wanted? The whole past year, she thought she was moving forward toward something important. She had set out with lofty ideals and political goals. Now she was lying to everyone in order to achieve them. She had lost sight of herself and betrayed the people of Florida, all in the name of politics. And she realized now, after a chance encounter with her ex-fiancé a few days earlier, that she had sabotaged yet another relationship.

While canvassing in an upper-middle-class gated community, she had rung the bell of the eighth house of the day—or was it the ninth? They all looked the same. A very pregnant woman had answered the door with a bright "Hello!" Megan had barely looked up from her clipboard, where she was searching for the names of these homeowners, readying herself to make friendly comments about the weather and to remind them to vote.

"Good evening, Mrs. Bates," Megan had said pleasantly. When she looked up, she almost dropped her clipboard. "Connie?"

"Megan." The woman's voice had wobbled. She refused to meet Megan's gaze. "What are you doing here?"

Megan, her mouth agape, didn't answer.

The woman had placed a protective hand over her swollen belly, revealing a simple platinum wedding band encrusted with tiny diamonds. "Jason?" she called out uncertainly. "Can you come to the door, please?"

The door opened wider as Jason came up behind Connie. "What is it, dear?" His voice became gruff, suspicious. "Megan? What are you doing here?"

She held up her stacks of campaign fliers and Get Out the Vote cards. "Running for office. You might have seen me on TV?" She had to keep the mood light, stop her anger from taking over. But how could she play the politician right now? She was still the spurned lover.

Regaining her composure, Megan had managed a weak smile. "So, when did you move?"

Connie had shifted from one foot to the other.

"It's OK," Jason said under his breath, and his wife kissed his cheek before retreating from the doorway. He'd stepped onto the front stoop and closed the door behind him. "I'm sorry you had to find out like this."

"So, you're married. You're having a baby. And you moved into a bigger house." Megan's voice was cold, but she didn't care. "That was fast. And if I might add, exactly what I said you'd do."

Jason's smile was tight. "You called it, Megan. You're always right."

Megan had turned her back on him. She wanted to leave before the tears building up in the corners of her eyes could spill over.

"You know, when you found me and Connie together, you didn't even ask me why."

Megan stopped on the bottom step.

"Most women would want to know why," he'd continued, his voice sad. "You just grabbed your stuff and left, and never looked back."

"Are you some sort of expert on how women react to cheating?" Megan's eyes flashed with anger.

"No. And I am sorry. I really am." He tried to place a hand on her shoulder, but she shrugged it away. When he spoke again, it came out very softly. "I think deep down inside, you always thought I would cheat on you. You were holding your breath, waiting for me to screw up."

"That's ridiculous," Megan snapped, but even to her, it didn't sound convincing.

"You never really let me in. I loved you more than you loved me."

"That's not true," she insisted. "I loved you!"

"But something was lacking, wasn't it?" he asked. "Intimacy, I guess."

"I sent you those pictures, didn't I?"

Jason shook his head. "That's not the same thing. You never let your guard down around me. You kept a wall between us. How many conversations did we have before you finally told me you weren't sure about having kids?"

"I wasn't sure how I felt," she protested. "I didn't want to lie to you. I didn't want to commit to anything. And you always knew my career was my priority."

"Maybe you never lied to me, but you never shared yourself with me either."

Megan shifted her gaze from his feet to his face. "OK, then. I'm asking now. Why did you do it? Why did you cheat?" The word caught in her throat.

"You and I were never going to work. You know that. I felt you pulling away from me for a long time. You said it was because of work, but I don't know. I think the more I loved you, the more you backed away." He paused as if to gauge her reaction. "That night last year, when White won the primary, Connie and I danced to a few songs. We talked about things. She was so open and honest with me right away—"

"Such a contrast to me," Megan said bitterly.

Jason shrugged. "We clicked. We connected. I didn't mean to—"

"You humiliated me, Jason. Our invitations had already been sent. I had to call everyone and listen to their sympathy, their pity."

"I know. I never meant to hurt you. Please believe me."

Megan had straightened her shoulders "Well, now I know. Thank you for telling me." She turned to go.

"Wait!" he called out. "Don't you want to leave a postcard for us? I promise I'll vote for you." He gave her a smile, seeking one in return.

When she'd reached out with a flier in her hand, he had held it for a moment.

"I know you've had a lot of sadness in your life, Megan, and I'm sorry if I added to it. You're a good person. You deserve happiness, and you deserve love. I hope you find someone to love—as much as he loves you."

"Thank you, Jason." Megan had swallowed a lump in her throat. "And congratulations to you and Connie." She had taken a deep breath then and managed to continue canvassing the neighbors. In the back of her mind, though, she replayed his words. Jason had been right. She was afraid of getting hurt.

And now she had pushed Andrew away, too. But he deserved it. If you really care about someone, you didn't hope their dreams got ripped away from them.

"How many hits is this getting?"

The intern jammed her hands into the pockets of her jeans, keeping her gaze fixed on the floor. "Thousands. And more articles are coming out. By the minute."

"Any word from the Jackson campaign?" Megan rubbed her temples.

The intern darted a quick glance at Megan. "They're saying your engagement to Brock is nothing more than a last-ditch effort to save your failing campaign. And you should be ashamed of yourself for trying to deceive the voters."

Megan dismissed the girl with a quick nod of her head.

Fuck.

After a moment, she got up from her chair and yanked the door open. A group of volunteers were clustered around a television, whispering. Mike, who was talking quietly with a staffer, stood up at the sight of Megan. The whispers stopped as Megan trudged toward the television. She froze when she saw a familiar face on a *Fox and Friends* segment.

Carmela was smiling like a she-wolf, staring shamelessly into the camera.

So, came the interviewer's voice, *are you saying the Thompson-Tolbert engagement is nothing but… a publicity stunt?*

Absolutely. The camera closed in on Carmela's smug, beautiful face, her sharp teeth flashing white for all the country to see.

Megan balled her fists so tight, her knuckles began to ache.

Then Mike was by her side, draping an arm around her shoulder and guiding her away from the TV. "Let's get some air." As they stepped through the door, he yelled over his shoulder. "Don't lose hope! It ain't over till the fat lady sings, and I haven't sung yet!"

They walked toward Tony's Pizzeria, passing by an empty storefront, a liquor store, a check cashing store, and two sleeping homeless men. "I wish I smoked," Megan growled. "I'd smoke a pack right now."

Mike placed a hand on her arm. "Come on, Meg. It's not over. Not yet." He turned her to face him and wrapped her in a bear hug.

She had been told to prepare herself for ugliness during the campaign, and she was well aware that it came with the territory. But she hadn't been quite prepared for this. As far as the media were concerned, she was a self-serving, politically ambitious bitch looking for a trophy husband. It was hard to hear the truth.

Megan choked back a sob. "Everything they're saying is true. I'm the worst."

"No, you're not." Mike chuckled. "Boyd Smith was the worst. You're just human."

They continued walking along the sidewalk as cars whizzed through the busy intersection, like the constant hum of a mosquito near her ear.

"Dammmmmmn." Mike shook his head. "You did say Carmela had it out for you."

When they reached the end of the strip mall, Megan looked at her reflection in the pizzeria window. On the outside, she appeared calm. How was that possible? Underneath, her anger and frustration simmered.

Mike stood behind her. "Are you saying you want to throw in the towel, Meg? Do you want to tell the truth, and break off the engagement?" He looked deep into her eyes. "Are you ready to give up?" He knew how to ignite her fire. He was the coach toweling off her sweaty bloody face and telling her to get back in the ring.

Once you set your sights on something, you don't back down.

"No. I refuse to give up. I refuse to lose to that traitor Carmela. She didn't just screw me over, she screwed over the party." She was speaking to both reflections, hers and Mike's. She had won the primary—against the odds. She could win the general election, too. This was a red district. No way in hell was she going to let it go blue.

If she could just get through the election, she would figure this whole thing out.

Turning to her friend and campaign manager, she straightened her back and lifted her chin. "Mike, we have an engagement party to prepare for."

Andrew drummed his fingers on his knees, thinking about what Emily had said. Is it possible there was more to Megan ignoring him than just worrying about her career? He hadn't considered that there might be an alternative explanation.

"Have you talked with her?" Emily asked now.

"That's your solution to everything," he joked.

"Yes, and that's why I get paid the big bucks. Because people don't talk until it's too late."

Andrew shrugged. "I've left voicemails. She hasn't called me back." He looked over at his sister as a realization hit. "You know, everything was going great until we went to lunch with Mom. Then Megan just took off without saying good-bye, and we haven't talked since." He started to feel restless, distracted. Rachel Maddow's voice was droning on:... *government and a special interest group literally in bed together...*

Andrew got off the couch and walked to the kitchen. "I'm gonna make some tea. Want some?"

"Sure." Emily took a seat at the counter as Andrew filled the kettle and put it on to boil. "Was Mom nice to her?"

Andrew snorted and raised an eyebrow. "She's our mother. Megan's a Republican. What do *you* think?" He grabbed a mug from the cupboard "She basically insulted Megan right to her face. And then she said I deserved better, and asked me what I would do if Megan won."

Emily jolted, and her eyes grew wide. "When Megan was sitting right there?"

"No! Of course not. Megan had left the table to take..." He slammed the mug on the counter. Megan had excused herself to take a call, and when she had returned... The image of a half-eaten salad flashed before his eyes. Megan hadn't returned to the table.

Or had she?

The thought hit him like a punch to the gut. "Oh shit."

The whistle of the kettle blew angrily on the stove. Andrew moved it off the burner, still unraveling the chain of events that day at Le Blanc. Megan must have overheard the conversation with his mother. She must have heard him say the Democrats might win. She must have heard him joke that he was hoping for a clean sweep.

She must think I want her to lose.

"Uh, Andrew?"

"Emily! I know what happened. Megan must be upset because—"

"Andrew? I think you need to look at this."

Emily was staring at the television, where the interviewer was saying,... *but one thing's for sure: The NRA has given a lot of cash to the Thompson campaign. And you better believe Tolbert is not just looking to screw Thompson, but also the American people.*

Was this segment about Megan? He ran to the TV and upped the volume.

I'm Jane Williams, and my guest today is Carmela Sanchez, former chief of staff for Congressman White. Ms. Sanchez has the scoop on the Thompson scandal. Now, is it true your former boss set up all these dates so Megan could marry for money and political connections?

The gorgeous Latina woman was still smiling into the camera. *Yes, Jane, I can confirm the rumors that White was playing matchmaker for Megan Thompson. I can also confirm that she is marrying Brock Tolbert for his money and his connections. And I know for a fact that Megan is so desperate to win this election, she would do anything to win. Including make up a fake engagement.*

"It's my fault." Andrew grabbed his cell phone off the counter.

Emily's eyes followed him, puzzled.

"Yes, hello? I'd like one ticket to Orlando. I need to leave immediately." He looked up at his sister. "I need to make things right."

Chapter Twenty Eight

---❖---

PARTY CRASHING

Megan awoke the next day even earlier than usual, covered in sweat and trying to untangle her strange dreams from reality. In her dream, she had been driving in a torrential rainstorm, never able to see more than a few feet ahead, always hurtling toward danger with no place to pull over. All she knew was, she couldn't stop now. She had to keep going and trust she'd end up safe and sound and where she needed to be.

How had she let Brock talk her into an engagement party? She had gained a lot of practice in facing the public over the past few months, but tonight she would need to put on an Oscar-winning performance. At the party, she would be lying to everyone she loved—and thousands, maybe millions of people she didn't even know.

She knew Brock was right about getting the conservative base excited and rallying behind her as Election Day neared. She needed to put to bed the gossip stoked up by Carmela Sanchez's TV appearances. What better way than to throw a party for the GOP's hottest young couple? Brock was a brilliant political tactician who had thought of every last thing, from the boutique hotel venue and curated food and wine choices to the jazz band and the select invite list. She would be facing a mix of prospective donors, politicians, even some B-list celebrities Brock knew. And both of their families, of course. She found herself simply being dragged along with the details.

She was still shaken by her narrow primary win, and the general election was shaping up to be just as challenging. Now that she was the Republican candidate, all eyes were on her. And the Democrats were hungry and looking for anything to take her down. It was time to squash those rumors about her engagement being a marriage of convenience.

Megan lay in bed for a while before she was able to convince her bone-tired body to get up and put on a jogging outfit. But even as she ran through the early morning dew, her legs heavy like she was running through water, she couldn't shake the dream—or the eerie feeling that it was in fact a premonition. She couldn't go on like this. Something bad was going to happen.

When Andrew arrived in Gatorville on Friday morning, he didn't realize he would be crashing Megan's engagement party. At the Thompson election headquarters, the staffers sweetly demanded a $10,000 donation to the campaign in exchange for Megan's whereabouts—and a ticket to the event. If there was one time he'd ever been happy about his family's wealth, this was it. He only hoped Democratic campaigns across the country had that kind of chutzpah.

At the newly opened boutique hotel in Magnolia Ridge, trays of champagne floated through about a hundred guests milling about the ballroom, as mini quiches, flank steak with chimichurri sauce, ricotta toasts with fig jam, and cherry tomatoes skewered with bacon and basil were passed around. Andrew, searching the crowd and still clinging to the hope that this was nothing more than a perfectly executed PR stunt, hardly ate a bite.

When he saw Megan, his breath hitched.

She looked gorgeous. He hadn't lain eyes on her in weeks, and seeing her now in a royal blue cocktail dress that set off her eyes and décolletage… One could easily mistake her role as the eye candy—instead of the other way around.

Attached to her arm was Brock, wearing a fitted suit and smiling like a movie star. He had a way of commanding the room as the couple greeted and chatted with their guests. They were the sun in this temporary solar system of people spinning around them, attracted by their radiating energy and power, basking in their beauty and brilliance.

Andrew sipped his Champagne. It was buttery, toasty, and dry — the good stuff. What the hell was he doing here? This was a celebration of two people in love! Megan was engaged to be married. He didn't belong here. What if she saw him? He didn't want to upset her life any more than he already had.

He turned to go.

Behind him, a man muttered, "What the hell is this? I thought they said there'd be food here, and booze. All they got is tomatoes on a stick and sissy drinks."

Andrew thought he would recognize that smoker's voice anywhere.

He turned and saw Megan's father reaching into his unintentionally vintage suit jacket, and pulling out a bottle of Budweiser. Paul Thompson expertly twisted off the cap and flicked it with his thumb. It landed on a passing waiter's tray, a piece of junk among the tall, elegant bubbling flutes.

"Hello, Paul," said Andrew. "Good timing."

Paul chuckled and took a swig of his beer. "I was aimin' for the glass, actually."

"Speaking of a glass, can I get you one?"

"Nope, I'm good. Only brought the one." He took a swig of his beer and patted his belly. "Watchin' my waistline."

"Hi there, Andy. Nice to see you again!" shouted the woman standing by Paul's side.

Andrew recognized her from Gabe's wedding and remembered that she had just one volume setting: very loud. "Yes, a pleasure to see you again, Tammy."

They made quite the pair: Paul in his old suit, gray hair buzzed in the military style, oversized mechanic's hands permanently stained with grease and nicotine. Tammy in her dusty pink dress from the 1980s, as round as she was tall, her hair hanging limp past her shoulders like it had given up trying.

"Can't believe my little girl's gettin' married. Didn't even know it was serious." Paul lowered his voice and leaned in with a sly smile. "You don't think she's knocked up, do ya?"

Andrew couldn't hide his horror. "God, no!"

He had to get out of there.

Megan found Gabe at the bar ordering a scotch, wearing the half-pissed, half-pensive expression she knew so well. She pulled him into an embrace, but he barely returned the hug. "OK, what's the deal with Dad?" she asked.

Gabe's eyebrows shot up. "Can we talk about you first? What's the deal with you and Brock?"

Megan sighed, sliding her empty glass across the bar. He was hurt, of course, that she'd left out a few important details about her engagement.

"Megs, is this whole thing bogus like the papers say it is?"

"Yes."

"What th—?"

"Gabe, I want to know what's going on with Dad and Tammy. Are they… an item?"

Gabe nodded. "Ever since my wedding. I guess we Thompsons have a bad habit of keeping our love lives secret."

"You kept Darren from Dad forever."

"But not from you."

Megan's smile was tight, she hated keeping secrets from him. "I'm sorry. I'll explain everything soon. I promise."

"You shouldn't be so upset about Dad. They're a good match. Really. He's slowed down on the drinking. And he's happy…"

As Gabe rambled on, Megan thought for a moment. She had noticed her father's color looked better, and he seemed more like the Dad she remembered—for better or for worse. He had cornered Brock a few minutes earlier, his grip firm and vigorous as always, unconsciously puffing out his chest and sucking in his gut.

"Were you in the military, son?" Paul had asked, looking small and frail next to Brock.

"Yes, sir. Eighty-first Cavalry. Out of Fort Lewis."

Paul had finally released Brock's hand. "You deploy?"

Brock's movie star grin had disappeared instantly, replaced by a mask of stern devotion. "Thirteen months in Kandahar. Served under the Twenty-first Infantry. What about you, sir?"

Paul had given a rough chuckle. "Vietnam. And for too fuckin' long."

They had shared a laugh before Paul wrapped an arm around his daughter and yanked her toward him. Megan had tottered on her heels before leaning in to kiss his weathered cheek.

"Meg hasn't told me much about you. Usually I get to meet her boyfriends before she decides to marry them," Paul guffawed. "All I know is, you work for the NRA."

"Yes, sir."

"Love that ad you guys came up with. What was it? Saving our country from the lies… With the fist of truth… You're damn right!"

"Yeah." Brock grinned again. "it got us a lot of attention."

Paul shook his head and whistled as though impressed. "You must have a pretty sweet gun collection."

"I do, sir, I do. It's back in South Carolina. At my parents' place."

"Well, son, we'll hit the shooting range sometime. Say, are your folks here tonight?"

"Should be here any minute." Brock's smile had tightened. "They wouldn't miss this for the world."

Megan couldn't wait to meet Brock's parents either. He had been even more tight-lipped about them than about everything else in his life. It concerned her.

A man who won't talk much about his family, she thought, *is a man hiding something…*

Gabe interrupted her thoughts as though they were in the middle of an argument. "Dad deserves happiness, Megs. It's been almost twenty-five years since he lost his wife."

"I know that!" she snapped, before catching herself. Her short fuse was getting shorter, and she didn't want to say something she would regret. "Gabe, it's not..."

Before she could finish her sentence, Gabe shot a hand out. Darren was rushing across the ballroom, looking like James Bond in his black tux, weaving in and out of the crowd as though on a mission. Not for the first time, Megan admired how dapper her brother and his husband looked in their matching tuxes. But when Darren squeezed in between her and Gabe, forming a tight-knit circle, his eyes betrayed a sense of urgency. "Sweetie, I think you should know something."

"Is everything OK?" Megan asked, picking up a fresh glass of Champagne from the bar.

Darren took a deep breath, cleared his throat, and delivered the news with his best actor portraying a surgeon's face. "Your soon-to-be-husband is gay."

Suddenly everything made perfect sense. Why Brock had never properly kissed her, never tried to take her to bed. Why he never seemed jealous of her roommate. And, most important, why he wanted to marry her in the first place. Brock Tolbert was hiding.

Megan swallowed the knowledge like cough syrup. She was being played. He had been lying to her, using her. Just as she had been using him. And lying to everyone around her.

She set her glass back down. "How... how do you know?"

Darren lowered his voice. "He introduced himself to me in the bathroom. I thought he knew I was Gabe's husband, but he didn't have a clue who I was! Just wanted to know what I do for a living."

That didn't surprise Megan. Brock never had taken much of an interest in her personal life.

"When I told him I'm an interior designer, he asked for my business card. He said he was looking for someone to redo his apartment in Miami, but I—"

"He has a place in Miami?"

"That's not all! He said he'd be there tomorrow night if I wanted to come to take a look. And then"—Darren's voice dropped to a whisper—"he *winked* at me."

Megan was speechless. Was this actually happening?

"Straight guys don't wink at other men, Megan."

"Honey," Gabe muttered, "I don't think she needs help drawing that conclusion."

Megan couldn't look at her brother. She didn't want to see the disappointment on his face.

Gabe reached out and took a hold of her tanned, slender arm. "Sis, you need to tell me what's going on."

She slid from his grasp like a silk scarf falling to the floor. "Yes. You're right. I need to explain what's going on. Everything." Even as she spoke, she was moving away from him, letting the crowd envelop her. She needed to find Brock. *Now.*

Moments before, Megan had felt like a bird in a cage, terrified of making a move, trapped between two options: Keep up the lie and betray her integrity, or tell the truth and risk the wrath of the voters? But the revelation that Brock was gay changed everything. A door was open, and now she could taste freedom on the breeze. She needed to fly from that cage, no matter how scary the consequences.

When she slid up next to Brock, he was chatting with a Florida state senator who had enthusiastically backed Boyd Smith in the primary and was now battling accusations of sexual harassment from his own staff. She put on her game face and made polite chitchat, silently gloating at the reversal of fortune. Now this misogynist would have to vote for her. She would have loved to rub it in his face, but she needed to get Brock alone. She entwined her fingers with his and squeezed with all her might. "We need to have a quick chat."

Pulling him into the quiet shadows far from the crowd, Megan took a deep breath. She needed some answers.

"Brock, I want you to be honest with me right now. Why do you want to marry me?"

The smooth, tanned skin of Brock's brow wrinkled. "What's the problem, Megan?" he asked, sounding mildly puzzled. "I'm doing you a favor. You won the primaries, didn't you?"

"Cut the shit!" she hissed. "You put me on the spot at that luncheon. On purpose. Why the engagement, Brock? Why the party?"

"I'm doing this for you, Megan." His charming smile seemed pasted on, and his baritone voice tried to break her resolve. "Anyway, I've been a bachelor for too long."

She scoffed. "Brock, you're only looking out for *you*."

Brock's surprise seemed genuine. "What do you — ?"

Seething with anger, Megan straightened her spine. "I know what you're hiding."

"I don't —"

"Oh, yes, you do." Her eyes flashed her challenge. "That man you just hit on in the bathroom? He's my brother's husband."

Brock's face was still and pale as a tombstone. Then he began to clap quietly. "Bravo, Megan. You've finally arrived in politics. I suppose now you can't wait to tell everyone." His voice was drained of its usual pandering charm. To Megan, he looked lost.

She shook her head sadly. "I was always honest with you, Brock. But you lied to me."

"I didn't think I had a choice. My father caught me with another man. He was going to disown me." Brock's square jaw flexed. It was his own bitter pill to swallow. "When you're in his line of work, preaching fire and brimstone for sexual deviants, having a gay son is bad for business."

"Why did you lie to me this whole time?" Megan asked softly. "You knew about my brother. I'm no stranger to the gay-son-hiding-from-his-father story."

"I couldn't chance it. I can't have anyone compromising me." His laugh was dark and mocking. "Gay NRA spokesman. Do you think

I'd still have a job?"

"Well, Brock, while I sympathize with your plight, this is the end of the line. I'm not continuing with this charade anymore." She turned to leave.

Brock grabbed her wrist and spun her around. "Megan, wait! Think about what you're doing. You can't come clean about me. You'll lose your NRA endorsement. You'll lose voters. It's an off-year election—only the most dedicated voters will come to the polls, and you'll have pissed them all off."

She knew he was desperate, but she had no intention of turning back now. "I won't tell them you're gay. I'll just say irreconcilable differences."

"Megan, think carefully. Both of our careers are at stake here. And no one is going to buy that for a minute. They'll say you are exactly what the newspapers say, a self-serving trophy hunter."

She wrenched her wrist from his grasp, feeling sorrier for him by the minute. He was grasping at straws now.

"I get it. You don't want to lie," he changed tactics. "Let's just get through this engagement party, and we'll figure it out. Don't do anything rash."

Her anger had subsided, and her eyes changed from metallic gray back to pale blue. "Brock, you don't get it," she replied softly, backing away from Brock. "This whole thing is a lie. And lies always find a way of catching up to you."

She had already made up her mind the moment she heard Darren's story. Yes, she wanted to be a politician, but not if it meant compromising everything she believed in, everything she was. It was time to come clean.

At the front of the room, Megan had a word with the band leader, who handed her the microphone. Then she lifted a glass from a nearby table and tapped it with a tomato skewer. The crowd quieted, and a room full of people faced her with polite, expectant smiles. "May I have your attention, please?" She smiled back, searching the crowd for Gabe. Her eyes landed on someone else, someone unexpected.

Andrew? What is he doing here?

Megan's scruffy, blue-eyed liberal stood next to her father, wearing a fitted black suit and tie, smiling his Boy Scout smile. When he winked, it made her heart stop. Everything seemed suddenly clear.

If she removed the obstacles—her running for office, their opposing political affiliations—would she have allowed herself to fall in love again? She didn't know how to answer that question. Yet the not entirely unpleasant nausea racing through her stomach, like a hamster dancing on its wheel, answered for her. Her heart, without her permission, had already made that decision.

Megan started to speak. "Thank you all for coming tonight. I have a brief announcement to make." She held Andrew's gaze. "Brock and I won't be getting married after all. We have… irreconcilable differences."

The crowd gasped and stared at her blankly as the information sunk in. A few photographers took pictures and reporters rapidly wrote in their notepads with *I just got lucky* grins on their faces.

"Brock and I were dating, but we're not in love. He asked me to marry him, and on impulse I said yes. Although I immediately regretted it, then the story blew up and I was winning in the polls and… I didn't do any of this to deceive you. I just wanted to win this election so badly, and I thought I wasn't enough on my own. And the voters proved me right. One minute I was losing to an accused sexual predator with no government experience. The next minute I was winning—when I got engaged to the NRA."

She paused and caught her breath.

"Twenty-five years ago, when my mother was dying from cancer, she told me she knew I would do great things in life. She said I could be anything when I grew up, but no matter what I did, I should use my talents for good. 'Who knows,' she said, 'maybe you'll be the first female president!'"

Megan's eyes grew moist.

"God knows, this country needs leaders who are good, kind-hearted, and strong. We need people who will do the right thing. But over these past few months, I let my mother down. I let myself down, too, and you—the voters. And there is one other person I let down."

Megan recalled Jason's comment a few days earlier: *Do you remember when you finally admitted why you were so scared to commit, so scared to have kids? You were afraid of getting cancer and abandoning your family the way your mother abandoned you.* Megan had spent the past twenty-five years protecting herself, never letting anyone get too close, always preparing for their inevitable departure. But Gabe had moved on. Even her father was moving on. And now it was her time.

"That person is here tonight, and he's the one I truly love. I've been afraid to admit it, even to myself. Because, as I'm sure tomorrow's headlines will read, I've been sleeping with the enemy. The man I'm in love with is a Democrat."

★ ★ ★

A ndrew broke into a grin.

Megan's eyes never left his face. "I thought you, the voters, wouldn't want me to love a Democrat. That's how divided we are right now in America. That's how messed up things are, not just in Washington but in our communities, our families, our homes! We have a president who thrives on dividing this country, not uniting it. And it's working. Well, I'm not going to let it work!"

Andrew clapped loudly and enthusiastically, drawing stares and glares from the people around him.

"I went into politics to make a difference," Megan continued, "to be the change I wished to see. But then I saw how quickly my values started to be ignored, so I focused only on one thing: getting elected. I told myself that it would all work out fine, that the ends justified the means. Well, I'm here now to say: *no more.* I can't do that. You deserve better than politicians lying, being slick, getting the win by any means necessary. You deserve to know the truth. You deserve to know who you're really voting for."

Someone hollered from the back of the room. "I knew it! I knew it!"

The crowd parted, and an elderly man emerged, leaning heavily on his cane with one hand and shaking his other fist. "You and my coward son tried to pull a fast one, but I wasn't buying it. Not for a moment!" he croaked. "It's all a scam, nothing more than a publicity stunt. You two should be ashamed of yourselves."

Andrew looked around the room, but Brock was nowhere to be seen. Where was that snake, when his father was standing here calling Megan names?

The elder Tolbert pointed a vehement finger and spat, "I knew you were a lying whore."

Andrew moved toward him without thinking, ready to take the walking stick away and beat the old man with it. But Paul Thompson had already pushed through the crowd and was standing next to his daughter.

"Now, just hold on a minute! All due respect, pastor, but no man calls my daughter a whore. Not without a bloody nose! Now, if you —"

Andrew saw Megan place a gentle hand on her father's arm. "Dad. It's partly true. I thought I wanted a husband who could help me win the election."

From all around Andrew came the sound of people mumbling: *I knew it along... self-serving... a gold digger... dragging that poor man into this mess...*

"Now hold on a second." Megan's father grabbed the microphone from her hand and tapped it a few times. An ear-splitting squeak cut the whispers as everyone cried out, putting their hands over their ears.

Andrew stood frozen in place, not sure what to expect from Paul.

"Listen up, folks," he began, clearing his throat. "I hate politics and politicians as much as y'all do." Paul looked around the room and saw that no one clapped or smiled. "OK, well, maybe not you people. You're probably all here to line your pockets. But first, let me just state: y'all are hypocrites." He pointed a menacing finger at the men in the audience "I am willing to bet the horse that if she was a wrinkly old man marrying a hot young thing, and there was a pretty good chance it had nothing to do with love, y'all wouldn't say boo. In fact, you'd clap her on the back."

Paul had raised his hoarse voice and was swaying slightly as he spoke. Shocked, Andrew realized it was a result of too much emotion rather than too much beer.

"When my late wife was dyin' from cancer," Paul continued, "my Megan set up a lemonade stand to raise money for her treatment. She sat out front on the lawn with her lemonade stand dang near every afternoon, and all day on the weekends. For two weeks straight." He shook his head sadly. "I kept tryin' to tell her that time was better spent with her mother. But Megan had an idea in her head. She was determined to *save* her mother."

A hush took over the crowd, drowning out the muttered abuse.

"I think she raised maybe thirty bucks. Finally, I put my foot down. I wouldn't buy her anymore lemons. I made her to go to the hospital. Her mother passed away two days later."

Andrew saw his eyes mist over as he reached for his daughter's hand.

"Megan's heart was in the right place, you see? She just wanted to save her mother. But she can get so focused that she ignores her own sufferin', or even can't see that she might be hurtin' others, all because she wants so badly to do the right thing."

Paul paused to wipe his forehead with the back of his large hand.

"That's the way I see this mistake she's made, tryin' to marry a guy she didn't love so she could get elected. She wasn't thinking about her happiness! She wasn't thinking about how that might betray people's trust! She was focused on gettin' elected so she could do right by you, by the people where we live. And as for her falling in love with a Democrat—well, she always had a soft spot for strays."

He laughed as his own joke, and more than a few people joined in.

"You know, she might even convert this guy to our side. To be honest, Andrew is the first liberal I've actually talked to. And he's not half-bad." Paul handed the microphone back to Megan, and then leaned in for a final comment. "We're all Americans, for Christ's sake!"

Megan hugged her father fiercely, and Andrew wanted to run up to her right then, but he waited for her to meet his eye again. At last she looked up, and her eyes sparked to life when they connected with his.

She loves me. He couldn't stop repeating the words, afraid he was imagining the whole thing.

Then the reporters descended on her like buzzards on roadkill.

"Megan, is it true you got engaged just for the NRA endorsement?"

"Are you and your Democrat the modern-day version of James Carville and Mary Matalin?"

"Why did you lie to the voters of Florida, Ms. Thompson?"

"Megan, are you still running for Congress?"

Suddenly, Megan looked like a deer caught in headlights. "No comment, no comment," she repeated, holding up her hands and stumbling backward.

Andrew wanted to wrap his arms around her and protect her from this, from everything. But the next thing he knew, he was watching her disappear into the ladies' room, the door slamming behind her.

L ocking herself in the bathroom, Megan let loose a torrent of sobs. Her career was over. Where was the relief she had expected when she came clean with the public? Tomorrow — or sooner — she would become the laughingstock of the political world. And now she had to face Andrew. He would think she was the worst human on earth. How could she even talk to him now?

Her excuses for breaking it off with Andrew had been as flimsy and transparent as plastic wrap, yet Megan still hadn't seen through them. She wasn't just afraid of losing the election. She was afraid of getting hurt again. Andrew was like an undertow, drawing her away from the shore to which she clung, pulling her out to sea. She was afraid to fall in love.

Megan dried her tears with the rough, brown paper towels. Then she heard a soft knock at the bathroom door.

"Megan, it's me," Andrew called through the door.

She had no idea what she was going to say, but she owed him an explanation. She opened the door and let him slip through. His smile was more shy than usual, raising thousands of goosebumps on her flesh.

"You're shivering. Here, take this," he said, shrugging off his suit jacket and wrapping it around her shoulders.

"I think it's the air conditioning, not the fact that my life is falling apart," she joked weakly. "Andrew, I owe you an explanation. I'm sorry I walked out on you at lunch. I overheard you and your mom talking—"

"I know that now, and I am so sorry. I didn't mean—"

"I should've asked you about it. Instead, I just assumed the worst. I was looking for an excuse to break it off. I realize that now." She pulled his jacket tighter around her. "As for all the rumors about White playing matchmaker—"

He nodded. "I saw it on TV."

She signed. "Well, it's true. It started out as White trying to find me a partner who would soften my image, make me more appealing to voters and help me attract donors. I thought, why not? If I can find a partner who understands that work comes first and helps me achieve my goal, then what's the harm in that?" She took a breath. "Then you and I... happened. And I didn't want to be with Brock. The whole publicity stunt thing? He just caught me at a bad time. I was angry at you, and I was losing, and he put me on the spot in front of all these donors. I said yes, in a panic, and it was a stupid decision."

Andrew closed the divide between them until he was so close, he could almost kiss her.

"I know you're wrong for me on paper," she whispered, "but you're so right for me in real life."

He chuckled.

"And I'm sorry I hurt you. I never meant to lie, and I hope you can find it in your heart to forgive me."

"If you forgive me, too," he replied, searching her eyes.

"There's nothing to forgive." She took his hands. "Andrew, I love you. And it is scary as all hell to say that out loud. It's scary because I don't want to get hurt again. But I'm miserable without you. I need you in my life. We can figure out the rest."

"I love you, too. I want you to be happy. And I want you to win."

She let out a little laugh, happiness and sadness rolled into one. "My campaign is dead in the water."

Andrew's look was stern but playful. "The Megan Thompson I know, once she sets her sights on something, she never gives up. You have nine weeks to change the voters' minds. And I'll be right there by your side."

Megan grinned. "I think Emily would be really proud of us."

"Yes, she would be." Andrew brushed the pad of his thumb over her dried tears.

She pulled him to her, and when their lips touched, it was like the dried earth receiving rain, soaking up every last drop. They kissed and kissed and were still thirsty for more.

Epilogue

⭐

RED AND BLUE MAKE PURPLE

*C*BS *Morning Show* host Bianca Bates faces the camera and smiles. "My guest this morning is Republican Megan Thompson and her husband, Andrew Croswell, a registered Democrat. Megan just won the congressional seat in District 19 in New York."

Bianca turns to Megan, sitting next to her in a purple shift dress. "Ms. Thompson, you first ran for Congress unsuccessfully ten years ago, in Florida. How does it feel to finally get a win?"

Megan smiles. "Bianca, it feels great, as you can imagine. I am really excited to get to work. I've definitely learned a lot in the ten years since I first ran for Congress."

"Back in 2017, the political landscape looked a lot different from how it looks today. Do you think you lost that election because you and Andrew were openly dating despite being from opposite sides of the aisle?"

Megan pauses to think for a moment, recalling that part of her life. "Well, I don't think we can say that for a fact, Bianca. The race was tight, and most of the voters said it didn't change their mind about me."

Nine weeks after the sham engagement party in Magnolia Ridge, Megan had returned to the Hilton Hotel, preparing to make her concession speech. She had waited for Mike's cue to go on stage. The polls had long been closed, and the election was ready to be called.

319

Andrew had given her a few moments alone. The past two months had felt like a never-ending boxing match. She had been the underdog in the ring, the one people were rooting against. But every time she was knocked down, she got right back up and kept on fighting.

Megan had taken the stage with Andrew, Mike, her father, and Gabe and Darren, silhouetted by a giant American flag as her mentor always had been. "One year ago," she had said, "I stood next to Congressman White on Election Night, knowing one day it would be my turn to heed the call. I had no idea the opportunity would happen so soon. I am grateful for all the love and support you have given me throughout the campaign."

The crowd had been somber, but responded with insistent applause.

"We fought hard, and it has been a great privilege to work with all my wonderful, dedicated volunteers. It has been an honor to get to know the voters, who opened their doors to me, poured me a cup of coffee, and told me about their successes, their sorrows, and their struggles. I am changed because of all of you, and I carry your stories with me wherever I go."

A respectful hush had fallen over the room.

"When I look around this room, I see people united in their love for God and country, united by their fight for a better America. And that can never be taken away from you!"

The crowd had started to clap and cheer again.

"We lost today," Megan had concluded, "but this won't be the last time you see me. Change is coming!"

And indeed, she thinks now, change *has* come.

"What's it like being married to a Democrat?" Bianca continues.

Megan's smile grows wider. "Well, you can say I've been practicing the art of compromise and bipartisanship for eight years now."

The audience laughs, at Andrew's wink as much as Megan's words.

Bianca's next question is one Megan has heard countless times. "Were you worried voters would be turned off by your marriage to a self-avowed progressive?"

Megan leans back in the comfortable chair. "I think I've proved myself to voters. They know I'm not easily influenced by others. I don't take campaign contributions from organizations I don't believe in. My values are not open for negotiation. I am, however, willing to sit down and have a conversation in order to understand someone else's point of view."

"That's wonderful." Bianca's voice becomes hushed, almost wistful, before bouncing back to morning-show bubbly. "After your first failed campaign, you took a bit of a break from politics, is that correct?

"Yes." Megan turns her smile on Andrew. "We moved to a farm in upstate New York, where we live off-grid with our sheep, pigs, and chickens. Andrew opened up a farm-to-table restaurant, *The Snout*. So I've been busy taking care of our two girls and our little homestead, and speaking to conservatives about climate change."

Bianca chuckles. "You definitely have been busy! And for the viewers at home, if you haven't gone already, I highly recommend eating at The Snout!"

"Just make a reservation first." Andrew grins, lifting and straightening his purple tie. "We only have eight tables."

Bianca chuckle again, and then turns back to Megan. "So, why did you decide to come back to politics now?"

Megan straightens in her chair. "We had a family discussion, and we all agreed it was time for me to run again. I am ready to get to work for America. I never stopped believing in the power of public service. You know, it's kind of calling. At least, for me it is."

"Last question, Ms. Thompson. Viewers at home want to know how you, as a Republican, can be so happily married to a Democrat. What's your secret?"

Andrew and Megan exchange a glance, and he reaches out to squeeze her hand. "We know that love really can conquer all," he says.

Megan squeezes his hand back and looks into the camera. "That, and we agreed never to talk politics at home."

ACKNOWLEDGEMENTS

Love, Across the Divide was born out of a question: Could a Republican and Democrat fall in love in today's era of contentious politics? My gut reaction was to say, "No, not possible." I set out to prove that wrong, and my first book was born.

This book most certainly wouldn't have been possible without the patient, loving support of my husband, Darien Ford, and my friend and editor, Amy Dorta McIlwaine, the "midwife" who helped me bring my "baby" into this world. Thank you!

Thank you also to the hardworking volunteers at Citizens' Climate Lobby, on which the fictional EnviroLutions is loosely based. Through this organization, I gained insight into the importance of everyday people speaking with our congresspersons (also known as lobbying!) to get our voices heard about carbon pricing, and to tackle the very real and serious problem of climate change.

Gratitude is due as well to my friends who were willing to have frank political conversations with me and help me understand the other side, especially Kim Conner, for connecting me with people who worked on campaigns and in congressional offices; Nancy Montgomery, for sharing what it's like to be a woman in politics; and Jen and Morgan Stebbins and Christine Schaetzl, for giving me a greater understanding of therapy sessions.

Thank you to my early readers who had to endure the painful first and second drafts — not only my husband but also Carol Ford and Jacqueline Berenson — and to my brother-in-law Justin Ford, who let me bounce ideas off of him and help sharpen the novel's focus (even though it meant throwing out my first 10,000 words and starting again).

My appreciation extends also to chiropractor Casey Swann, for fixing my gimpy hand after all the mad typing and for allowing me to talk about my book while she adjusted me nice and good, and to the Desmond-Fish Library and its hardworking staff. I borrowed a lot of political books and talked their ears off. Support your local libraries! And of course, thank you to my parents for raising me to be the strong, independent woman I am today. For better or for worse, I've inherited my father's hunger for knowledge, entrepreneurial spirit, and ability to juggle a thousand projects at a time.

Lastly, this book was a work of love, sweat, and tears. If you enjoyed it, please review it.

ABOUT THE AUTHOR

Originally from Montreal, Krystal Ford has fallen in love with the Hudson Valley, New York, where she calls home with her husband and two children. She has a Master of Arts from New York University and, when she's not writing, works as a community organizer around environmental issues. Her favorite pastimes are reading books and gardening.

www.krystalfordauthor.com
www.facebook.com/krystalfordauthor
Twitter: @kfordauthor
Instagram @krystalfordauthor